I0772405

Secrets of the Flamingo Café

An Old Florida Mystery

Secrets of the Flamingo Café

Joy Wallace Dickinson

First hardcover edition November 2024
Florida Folio, Orlando

Jacket design by Rick Kilby, Kilby Creative
Book design by Joy Wallace Dickinson
Jacket photo: Judith Starnes

ISBN 979-8-218-50919-4 (hardcover)
ISBN 979-8-218-19885-5 (ebook)

www.FindingJoyinFlorida.com

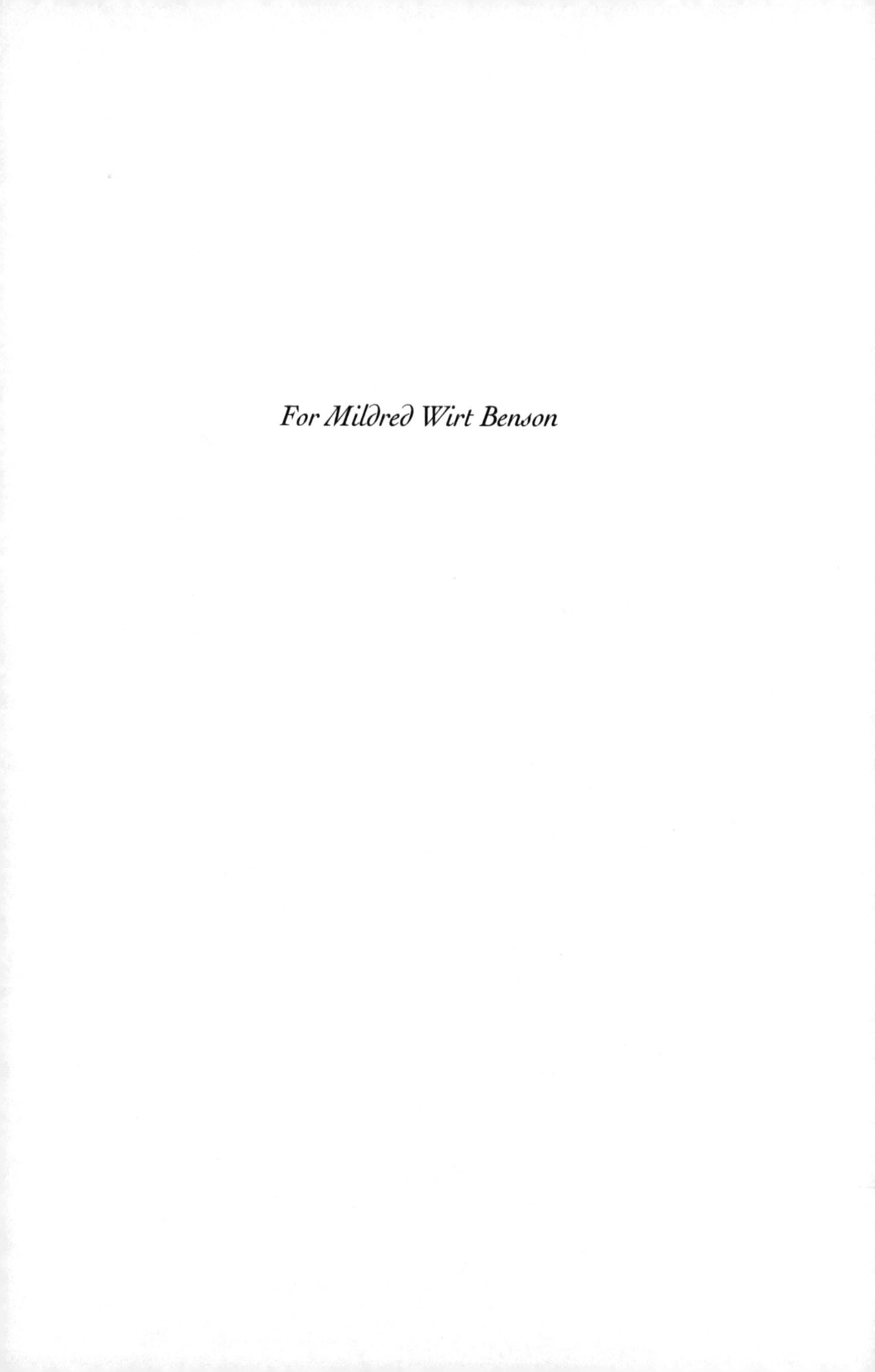

For Mildred Wirt Benson

Chapters

So we drove on toward death through the cooling twilight.

F. Scott Fitzgerald
THE GREAT GATSBY

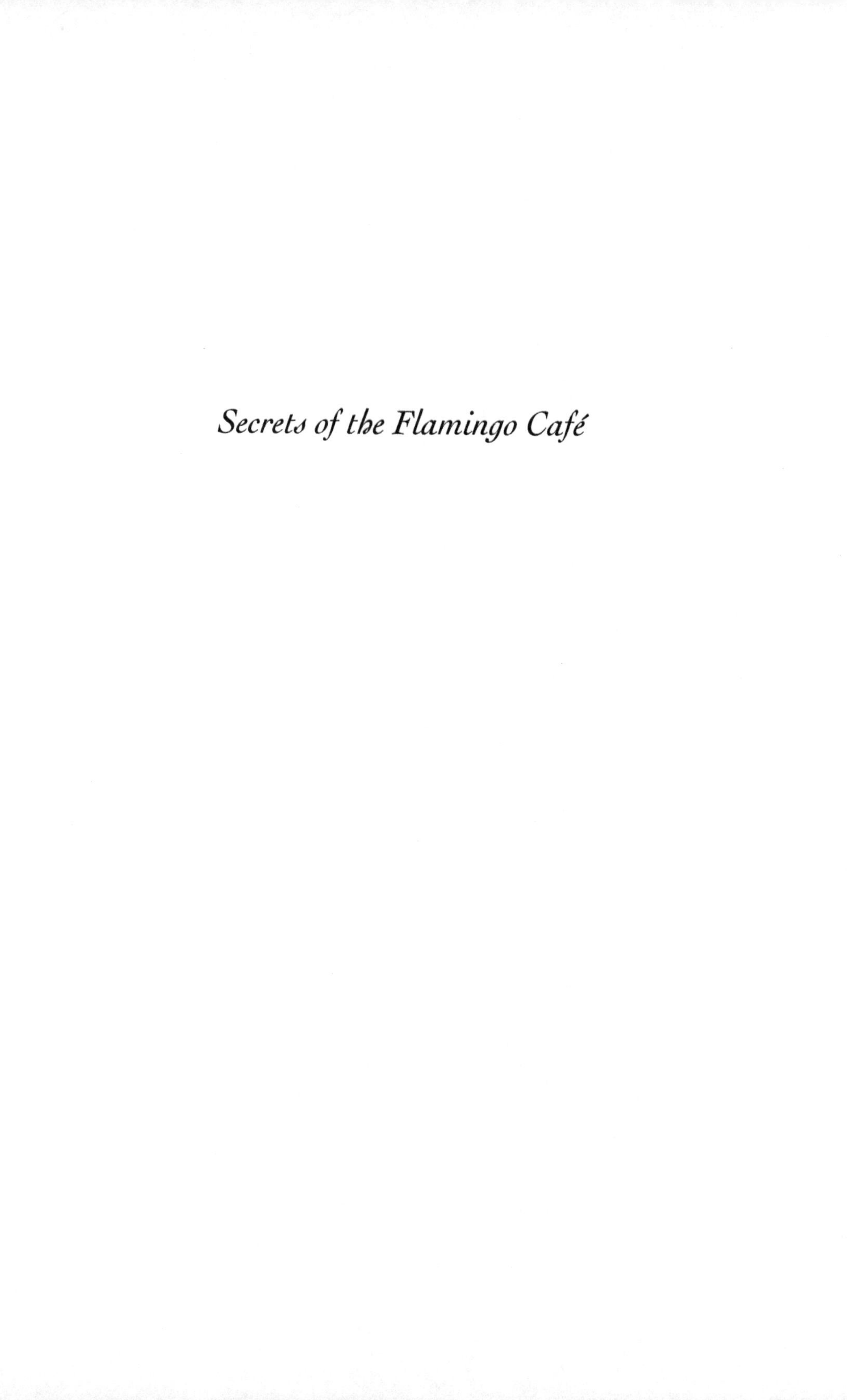

Secrets of the Flamingo Café

Chapter 1

A Reunion in Hades, 1948

EMILY PEERED OUT from the door of the dark, cool Pullman car, blinded by a blast of light and heat. For the hundredth time, she wondered why she'd even come. Grasping the large leather bag that held her paints and brushes, she reached for the conductor's brown hand, feeling a little woozy after her nap on the train.

"Yes ma'am, step carefully now," he said as he helped her scramble down the steps onto the hot, white sand. Steam hissed around the train's steel wheels, and she knew without question that coming to Florida was a big mistake. Good lord, it was hot as Hades. How had her aunt stood it? She should take the next train back to New York, back to good old steady Lewis and his proposal, and the safety of her art.

But as she walked toward the Orlando station and her eyes adjusted to the blinding light, radiant colors emerged around her. Columns of storybook clouds reached up into a cornflower-blue sky, and near the station door improbably large red flowers seemed to have sprung from a Gauguin painting. She had forgotten the beauty. Gauguin could have Tahiti. Aunt Liz had loved that Florida sky, loved that blue, that light. Now Emily's resolve vacillated, as she decided once again that, yes, she needed to be here—if for nothing else than to honor Elizabeth Washington—the woman who was the kind of painter Emily hoped to become, the woman who had been an anchor in Emily's life until her too-early and shocking death.

The baggage handlers had worked quickly. Emily saw that her luggage had been pulled from the depths of the train and now rested on a large wooden cart near the taxi area. She ran a hand through her dark curls and surveyed the taxis. One stood out: a black Cadillac Fleetwood from well before the war that exuded a faded elegance. It was nothing like the busy-bee yellow cabs she hailed in Manhattan. If the other taxis were tugboats, this would be the Queen Mary. "Armistead's Taxi," read the script on the door—"The City Beautiful's Finest." When the driver got out, Emily found herself staring.

Oh, goodness, it was really him.

The serious dark face behind the wire-rimmed glasses broke into a broad grin.

"Lord have mercy, I'd know you anywhere, Miss Emily," said Milton Armistead, as he deftly grabbed the paint box that was about to tumble from Emily's leather bag. How old was he now, she wondered. Her aunt's age at least—but he sure moved fast to catch her paints.

"Still traveling light, I see," he said with a smile. "Your aunt's lawyer told me what train you'd be on. I thought I'd surprise you."

"And you did, Mr. Armistead—the best possible kind of surprise. I'd know you anywhere—you haven't changed a bit."

She wanted to hug him, but that wasn't the way things were done, he would say. Although she hadn't seen him for years, Milton Armistead indeed seemed scarcely changed. As a girl, Emily had pondered what oil colors she would mix to get the deep tone of his skin down on canvas. Burnt umber? Raw umber? But she would never have dreamed of asking him to model. He was a formidable figure. Her Aunt Liz had called him "General Armistead" back when he had worked for her, managing her orange groves. After her aunt sold off most of that land, Milton had opened his own taxi company, perhaps with her aunt's help—it was the kind of thing her aunt did for friends.

General Armistead. The two of them, Milton and her aunt, could probably have defeated the Nazis all by themselves.

"And yes, still traveling light," she said, shaking her head. "Heaven knows why I brought so much because I expect I won't be here long. It's crazy, I know, but I can't stand to be without my paints. I figured I could use Aunt Liz's easel."

Milton nodded, looking down. "She'd like that, Miss Emily."

"Yes," she said, shocked that she felt tears coming. It had been weeks, and she hadn't been able to cry about her aunt's death. Struggling to recapture her poise, she pointed to her suitcases piled on the luggage cart.

"You see that small mountain over there? I'm afraid it's all mine."

"I can assure you, Miss Emily, the bags won't be a problem." Milton gave a slight nod, and an army of young boys, mostly Negro but some white, seemed to appear out of nowhere and began piling her motley collection of bags into the old Cadillac's cavernous trunk.

"Now, let's get you to where you're going," said Milton. "Eola Lodge, I assume?"

Emily nodded as he opened the Cadillac's back door for her and she slid into the cavernous back seat, her legs sticking to the worn leather upholstery. She felt like a roast in the oven. She watched Milton give each boy a coin before he started up the car. He spoke to one of the boys—a slender towhead who looked to be about nine or ten years old—and ushered the child into the front seat of the taxi.

"Miss Washington, this is one of your new neighbors. Likes to make himself useful. Introduce yourself, son," Milton said.

The words tumbled out. "Hello, ma'am. My name's Billy. I live real close to Eola Lodge. My pa says we don't need any more Yankees in Florida, but your aunt was a real nice lady—and I reckon you are, too."

Emily glanced up and saw Milton send an amused look her way in the rearview mirror, over his clip-on sunglasses.

"Billy, it's good to meet you," she said. "I sure try to be nice," Well, most of the time, she thought.

The child turned and, through the central opening in the front seat, handed her a cardboard fan emblazoned with a picture of Jesus and an ad for a local funeral home.

"This'll help a little, Miss Emily," he said. "This fan, and the breeze through the window when we get going. Mr. Milton drives fast. Your face is awful red."

"Thank you, Billy." Here was a real truth-teller. She bet her aunt had adored him.

She looked back at Milton Armistead in the rearview mirror. "Is it always this hot here, Mr. Armistead? I had forgotten. It's almost October."

"You know, Miss Emily, you can call me Milton. But I appreciate the courtesy. Hot? This is nothing. You want hot, keep riding that train all the way to Miami. They could fry up breakfast there across the hood of a car on a day like this."

"Well, this is hot enough for me."

"It should get a little cooler soon. Heck, it's almost time for the Flamingo to open for the winter season. That's a different kind of hot, though."

"That's a creepy place," said Billy.

Emily was about to ask why, but Milton's voice turned serious. "I know you're not here for the weather, Miss Emily, or the winter season. Your aunt was a great lady. She didn't deserve to die like that." His voice was almost a whisper, his face an enigma behind his sunglasses.

"It seems like a nightmare," said Emily. "I keep hoping I'll wake up."

"Isn't that the truth." She looked up again at him and then at Billy, who sat silently in the big front seat, looking up at Milton and waving his own paper Jesus fan with determination.

"I was traveling when she died," said Emily, "and I didn't learn about it for days. I couldn't get back from Egypt in time for the funeral." He nodded. "I wish I had written you—I hoped you knew that's why I wasn't there," she said.

"I understand, Miss Emily," said Milton. "Judge Stimpson did tell me he had cabled you, just like he told me what train you'd be on today. He gave me some keys for you, too—he had the locks changed." He reached back and handed her a set of keys on a ring.

"Your aunt picked an excellent lawyer there, Miss Emily," Milton said. "The Judge understood her."

"That's good to hear, Mr. Armistead."

"Yep, and he made sure she had a nice sendoff. That big funeral home downtown was packed—they've even got a balcony for us colored folks."

Emily frowned. It was coming back to her now. The water fountains labeled "white" and "colored." All the rules about race—all the lines that could not be crossed. Like the way she couldn't hug Milton, when she'd arrived, even though for her it would have been the most natural thing in the world. And it wasn't just about black people. There were no Jewish people at the Country Club. All that craziness.

They rode in silence as the big Fleetwood sailed along brick streets beneath oaks heavy with Spanish moss. The breeze from the open window did bring some relief from the heat, as Billy had promised. Looking out the car windows, Emily felt better about her surroundings—about the landscape her aunt had loved. On the train, she had overheard a woman complaining that Florida's moss-strewn trees looked as though they needed a proper scrubbing. But to Emily, the touches of gray-green softened the scenery, adding atmosphere that would be fun to capture on canvas.

And then, suddenly, the house Aunt Liz had christened Eola Lodge loomed out of the trees, with its gables, big coquina-rock chimney, and welcoming porches. The Prairie Style à la Florida, Liz had called it. Emily looked out at it and then glanced in the visor mirror. The silver strands that laced her dark curls seemed to be multiplying, she thought. As Milton opened the car door for her, she extracted herself stiffly from the depths of the old Cadillac's red leather seat, realizing for the first time how tired she was. She pulled out her big paint bag and leaned it against the side of the car.

Milton had already opened the trunk, and as she reached for the handle of one of her suitcases, he stopped her with a look that would freeze water.

"No, ma'am, that's no job for a lady. Billy can help, too. You just go on up the front steps and unlock the door to the house with those keys I gave you."

Emily felt her face flush and started to blurt out that she didn't need to be coddled, thank-you-very-much, but in truth the few yards she had to walk to the front door seemed like the end of a marathon race, and what energy she could summon was focused on getting herself inside the house.

But the part of her that was always watching and taking mental notes on everything around her couldn't help noticing the black Ford parked across the street, or the man behind the wheel, wearing a fedora. For Emily, noticing things was part of being an artist, an important part.

She started to ask Milton about the Ford, but he was focused on extracting bags from the trunk. He handed one to Billy, who scrambled past her and up the front steps, banging the bag against his small body while Emily hurried after him. What the child lacked in size, he certainly made up for in energy. While she rummaged in her purse for the keys, the boy deposited the bag by the front door and went back to the taxi for another, passing Milton on the front stairs.

"We'd best hurry, Miss Emily," he said, turning to get another bag. "Our afternoon thunderstorm is coming in. Feel the wind picking up?" He nodded toward clouds that seemed to have turned dark in an instant.

"Got it," Emily called after him, fumbling with the key in the lock. Finally it gave way, and she edged the door open a few inches, but it refused to swing further. As she peered through a crack into the dark house, she felt the hair stand up on the back of her neck—an almost rhythmic noise seemed to be coming from the back of the house.

"The door's stuck, I'm afraid," she said to Milton, "and do you hear that noise?" He was behind her now, followed by Billy, lugging another bag and looking quite red in the face himself.

"Is something wrong?" Billy asked.

"Everything's fine, son," said Milton, stepping past Emily. "Let me go first, please. Billy, just keep putting the bags on the front porch for now."

As Milton put his shoulder against the dark-red door, it finally edged open on creaking hinges. Emily and Billy followed him inside, where she shrank from odd shapes that loomed in the dim light—her aunt's furniture. The air was strangely still at first, and then, in a flash, the shock from the loudest thunderclap she'd ever heard shot down her spine.

Milton continued down the hall toward the noise. "You got to give Florida lightning very serious respect, Miss Emily. It isn't anything to fool around with. It can come right into a house and grab you."

Emily tried to grasp the idea of killer bolts from the sky blasting down the chimney, but the sound was louder now—a banging noise that seemed to come from the back of the house.

"There—Do you hear that?" she whispered.

She pushed past Milton, who followed right behind her, and raced toward what she remembered was the kitchen, with Milton and Billy behind her.

Another flash and a crack of thunder rattled the windows. The back door stood wide open, and the screen door banged back and forth in the rising wind, making the loud rhythmic thwacks Emily had heard from the front entrance. Through the screen, pellets of rain began to pummel the black-and-white linoleum floor her aunt had put in the kitchen years ago.

When Emily rushed forward to grab the screen door and pull it shut, her feet almost slid out from under her, and Milton moved again fast to steady her.

"Careful, Miss Emily. This floor can be slippery."

Catching her balance, Emily looked down and let out a yell. Lying on the floor on its back, smack in the middle of a muddy footprint, was a two-inch-long loathsome creature, its legs twitching.

"I'll sweep up that thing. It's just a palmetto bug. Don't hold it against Mattie Sayles—Liz's house cleaner—she got this place ready for you. No matter how clean you keep your house in Florida, those big flying roaches have a way of getting inside and prowling around at night."

Emily shuddered as she imagined armies of giant insects that clashed by night, marching across the linoleum squares.

"I remember them now," she said, as Milton swept up the giant bug in a dustpan and tossed it out the back door, which he then shut, turning the key in the lock.

"Those bugs don't bite or anything," said Billy. "The skeeters are a lot worse."

"Now, there's a comfort," said Emily. "Billy, would you get my train case and carry it upstairs?"

As he nodded and scampered away, she looked at Milton. "That bug startled me, Mr. Armistead, but the open door bothers me even more—and look at this." She pointed to what appeared to be more muddy footprints in a couple of the white squares. "I didn't want to say anything in front of Billy."

"Don't worry about that, Miss Emily. Takes a lot more than mud to scare that boy. You got me a touch worried, though—I thought you might faint."

Emily wasn't sure if it was her exhaustion or the shock of the thunder and a stranger's footprints in her aunt's kitchen, but it was true that suddenly she felt a bit lightheaded, and Milton sat her down in one of her aunt's yellow kitchen chairs and fanned her with his snap-brim straw hat.

"Mr. Armistead, I'm fine," she said. "Don't make a fuss. I'm just tired. It's a long train ride from New York." The last thing she wanted was to act like some kind of shrinking, fainting violet.

"Maybe some neighborhood kids were snooping around," she added, nodding at the muddy floor, though the instant she said it, she knew the footprints were too big to be any kid's. "You know, the lure of an empty house. Ghost stories, maybe?"

"Uh-huh," Milton said. "Not many kids around here, Miss Emily, except Billy, and sneaking around—that's not his style at all." He nodded toward the sound of thudding footsteps and grinned as the boy burst back into the kitchen.

"Billy, open that cupboard and fetch her a glass of water," Milton told the boy, back from his errand.

"I tell you what, Billy," he went on, "just to make sure, absolutely sure, some scalawag isn't lurking about, let's you and me haul the rest of the baggage upstairs and then check all the closets in this big ol' house."

The boy nodded and was on his way, when Emily stood up and motioned to Milton.

"Did you see that black Ford outside?" she whispered. "Would you call that 'lurking' around?" Milton just frowned, and shook his head.

"We're real near the park, Miss Emily," he said. "Lots of folks park on the street. Right now, I'm locking the doors. You just sit here and get calm. I'll be right back."

Emily nodded and sat back down at the yellow Formica table. She was glad Milton and Billy were with her, especially Milton. It would have been strange to be in Eola Lodge again under any circumstances, even if the back door hadn't been open. It was apparently her house now, according to her aunt's attorney, Judge Stimpson. She was still trying to absorb what had happened, why she was here. In the weeks since she learned of her aunt's death, it had all seemed strangely remote, like something she was reading about in a novel. But being here, in Aunt Liz's kitchen with Milton and this boy, Billy, the loss seemed all too real. They were with her, but Liz was not and would never be again. Emily felt her absence deeply.

It was Judge Stimpson who had pressed her to come to Florida to look after her aunt's estate — matters that were too important to deal with long distance, he said. And so she had come, against the advice of her father, for one, who had perceived his bohemian sister — Aunt Liz — as the most inky of black sheep. Still, he had seemed sad to hear of her death. It was hard to tell with him. His true feelings were elusive.

Lewis, Emily's quasi-fiancé, certainly hadn't wanted her to come. She would miss important social commitments, he claimed — important to him, at least. That simpering Patsy van Rensselaer was probably already angling to fill in for her at some big event, Emily thought, stifling a crazy impulse to giggle. Oh dear, she was tired.

Emily took another sip of water. Aunt Liz—that's what she wanted to focus on right now, not some muddy footprint or what Lewis had wanted. Aunt Liz had wanted her to take care of something—had said so in her will, according to Judge Stimpson—that was important. And in truth, despite her misgivings about coming, she noticed a sense of relief at being away from New York, mixed with her grief and her worries about disappointing Lewis. He was a dear, but she didn't really long for a husband, no matter how determined Lewis was to convince her otherwise. She valued her independence.

She was vaguely conscious of Milton and Billy banging through the house, slamming doors and calling out "all clear" to each other, but it still startled her when they appeared back in the kitchen, announcing they had found the house not only free of gremlins but clean and tidy.

"Billy, you've been a big help," Milton said to the boy. "I can bet you Miss Emily's going to rely on your help just like her auntie did." He turned to Emily.

"Billy and his papa live just a stone's throw from you," he said, going to the back door. "And now, it's time to skedaddle home, young man. The rain has let up a bit, and your papa will be expecting you."

He unlocked the back door and ushered the boy out, making sure to give Billy his tip money and handing him an umbrella he must have found on their sweep through the house. For a brief moment Emily worried over Billy's safety—if there really had been someone in the house, might the intruder still be skulking about? And what about the lightning?

"Bye Miss Emily," she heard the boy's high voice and waved at him.

"He's a good kid," Milton said, latching the screen door behind Billy. "His papa . . . well, that's another story for another time."

The storm had subsided by now, and Milton left the back door open with just the screen door latched. Emily felt a blessedly cool breeze sweep into the kitchen.

"You mind if I sit down, since it's just the two of us?" he asked. "I know you are dead on your feet—but I'd like to talk for just a minute."

"Of course I don't mind! Please forgive me—I'm not myself." She hated that Milton felt he had to ask to sit down, that she had forgotten—again—the world he lived in, the world of this town with all its nonsense rules. In his case, not obeying them could get you killed.

Milton looked in one of the cupboards, took down two empty jelly glasses and an unlabeled bottle, and poured a bit of a caramel-colored liquid into each glass.

"You know your way around this kitchen," Emily said, and smiled.

"I do." He smiled back. "And I wouldn't be so bold, but this business"—he pointed to the muddy spots—"has given my nerves a little shaking too, I'll confess."

"Maybe Mrs. Sayles left the footprints over there," said Emily, trying to keep the mood light, so she didn't tip over into real fear as well as the grief she'd been holding at bay.

"I don't think so," said Milton. "It's probably nothing more than a kid looking for stuff to steal. Here, drink that down."

Emily took a sip, hoping the drink would warm the cold feeling in the pit of her stomach. "Okay, General Armistead, I don't mind if I do," she said. "You know my aunt always used to call you that, don't you?"

"Of course, and I called her Queen Elizabeth. Bet you didn't know that, did you?" He smiled and took a drink.

"But when you checked the house, you didn't find anything stolen, right?" she asked him.

"No, nothing stolen or disturbed, that I could see. Lordy, I almost forgot," he continued, patting his lightweight jacket. "I was also supposed to give you this from Judge Stimpson, along with the keys."

He handed Emily an envelope from his inside jacket pocket with the attorney's now-familiar engraved insignia, addressed to her in neat fountain-pen script—the same handwriting she'd seen on the thick, starchy letter, made even thicker with elaborate condolences, that Stimpson had sent her in New York, telling her about the will making Emily her aunt's main heir and executor. Its terms were rather unusual, Judge Stimpson had explained. She was to see him as soon as possible after she arrived.

Despite the trappings, the note Milton handed her now was much less formal.

"We're so sorry we can't welcome you in person," it began. "We're going over to our cottage at New Smyrna Beach for the weekend. Please enjoy the supper in the icebox. We know Mr. Armistead and Mrs. Sayles will take good care of you.

Looking forward to seeing you soon.

Cordially, Mr. and Mrs. George Stimpson."

"Ah, the fabled Southern hospitality," said Emily with a smile. "No state secrets here, General Armistead"—she waved the note— "but good news—there's food in the fridge. Let's see what we've got. It's been a long time since my dining-car lunch."

They both got up to peer inside the old Frigidaire and found potato salad, fried chicken, a lattice-topped apple pie, and a bottle of milk.

"You'll have some with me, won't you?" Emily asked.

"Just try and stop me. Mattie Sayles is some kind of good cook, for one thing."

He rinsed off flatware along with two yellow Fiestaware plates he retrieved from the kitchen cupboards and set two places while Emily arranged the food on the table. It tasted as good as it looked, and they ate for a few minutes in silence that was broken by another loud rumble. Emily heard hard rain again pelting the roof like bullets.

"The storm let up, but now it's here for real," said Milton, just as Emily glimpsed a bright flash through the kitchen window, followed by another window-rattling rumble.

"I had forgotten the thunderstorms," she said. "Just the gods bowling, my parents used to tell me when I was little and would get scared. Right now, I'm more scared by the thought that someone was here in the house—maybe even someone who has a key."

"I can understand that." Milton finished off his drink.

"Really, it isn't possible that Mrs. Sayles simply left the door unlocked?" said Emily. "I'd never hold it against her, please understand, but—"

Milton studied her quietly.

"Doesn't seem likely. Mattie is known for many things, but the size of her feet isn't one. Look here, Miss Emily, I was going to wait for a day or so to talk with you about this, but sooner is probably better than later. What did Stimpson tell you about your aunt's death?"

Emily sighed. "He said it was a terrible accident," she began. "That she was at her fish camp—out there by herself. Some fishermen saw the flames from their boat on the river. I'm sure I'm not telling you anything you don't already know, Mr. Armistead."

"I hate thinking about it," Milton said. "But your aunt would want us to. Hell, in my mind, she talks to me all the time, Miss Emily. She's not gonna let me rest until I find out what really happened to her."

"But what are you saying?" She looked up at Milton, her eyes wide. "What do you mean, 'what really happened'?"

"I don't think it was an accident, Miss Emily. It just doesn't make sense. Your aunt was not a careless woman. I think someone killed her. There, I've said it out loud."

She put her head in her hands and then straightened and held his gaze. "I have to admit, Mr. Armistead, it all sounded strange to me, but I told myself I was overthinking things."

"I know the feeling. But this house being broken into—if that's what it is—it fits right in with my worries, as much as I'd like to think it's just some silly kid stuff."

"Now you've really got me worried," she said, aware that she was shivering. "Sorry. Rabbits running over my grave, I guess."

"Now, I've never heard that one," Milton said, rising to his feet, "but I know what you mean. I've said enough for tonight, Miss Emily, but before I go, I'd like to call a friend on the city police. Okay if I use the phone? The Judge said it should be working."

"Of course, Mr. Armistead."

                    Joy Wallace Dickinson

She watched as he went to the front of the house, listening for his voice, but in a moment, he was back in the kitchen.

"No answer," he said.

"No answer at the police?"

"I called his house. I'd rather not call the police switchboard about finding the house open, Miss Emily. No one will take it that seriously."

"Why not, for goodness sake? Isn't that what they're supposed to do—help people?"

"I'd say that depends on the color of your skin, for one thing. But it's true, too, that your Aunt Liz—well, she and some of our law-enforcement folks didn't get on so well. To tell you the truth, I don't trust a lot of them, Miss Emily—not the county squad, at least."

"Oh dear." She rolled her glass back and forth in her hands.

"Plenty of them are in the Klan, and proud of it," said Milton. "But I do trust Joe Maxwell—that's the fella I called. Detective with the city. I'd like you to go with me to meet him in the morning. I have a pretty good idea where he'll be."

"If you think it's important, of course I'll go," she said.

"Good. Now I'm going to let you get some rest. Try not to worry."

"Easier said than done," she said.

"Yep, but for what it's worth, no one has a key except you, Mattie, and me."

"It's probably nothing," she said, not feeling nearly as confident as she tried to sound.

"Tell you what," said Milton. "You might sleep better tonight in a hotel. I can take you down to the San Juan, easy as pie."

"Absolutely not," she said. "It's been a long time, but this house feels like home to me, in a strange way. I'm holding down the fort, Mr. Armistead. That's what Aunt Liz would do."

Milton gave her a long look. "Okay," he said. "Tell you what. I planned to work late tonight anyway. I'll cruise around and pass by the house a few times tonight."

She tried to object, but he interrupted.

"And you call me anytime, Miss Emily. I'm doing so well, I gotta fancy answering service."

He extracted a business card from his back pocket and pushed it across the table to her.

Emily nodded.

"Now, how about I pick you up bright and early tomorrow, say at 8 o'clock, and we'll see Detective Maxwell before you see the Judge. You'll like him."

"Which one?"

"Both of them, I'd guess. But I was thinking of the detective. He's a handsome fellow."

"Mr. Armistead!"

"Well, he is. I'd forgotten how much you are, indeed, like your aunt. Now, lock this door behind me, Miss Emily. No one's gonna bother you. Get some sleep."

She nodded again as she closed the back door behind him.

Alone in the house, Emily cleared the table, washed the few dishes she and Milton had used, and then, because she couldn't stand the sight of them any longer, mopped up the muddy footprints. Finally she grabbed her train case from the hall where Billy had left it and found her way upstairs. She had planned to stay in the guest room where she'd stayed as a girl when she visited her aunt, but when she looked in on her aunt's room, Emily saw that it had been made up for her with clean linens—the bed was even turned down. Her luggage sat stacked at the foot of it. It didn't feel right to stay there, but she was exhausted.

She felt like collapsing in a heap on the bedspread but threw open the window to air out the room. If her aunt's death had seemed remote back in New York City, back on the train before she'd arrived, now the reality of Emily's loss came crashing down on her. Was her aunt's spirit still here, as Milton had almost suggested? And if he was right that the fatal fire had not been a straightforward accident, surely it was Emily's duty to find out the truth. She owed her aunt a great deal. Aunt Liz had been an island of comfort for her in a lonely childhood—the person who encour-aged her to be an artist, to follow her dreams. For Emily, she had seemed invincible. Could someone have wished her harm? Would they wish harm on Emily, too?

The rain seemed to leave as fast as it had come. Outside, audi-ble through the open window, the spiky arms of the palmetto trees brushed against the house in the evening breeze. In the distance, a train whistle howled. Emily padded to the bathroom, toothbrush in hand.

The bathroom was dark—the light had burned out—and as she brushed her teeth, she looked out the window that overlooked the driveway by the side of the house. To her left, a streetlight cast an eerie spell on the brick-paved street. Under its violet glow, the black Ford that had been parked across the street scurried away like a giant beetle into the shadows under the old oaks.

Chapter 2

Coffee and Cinnamon Toast

EMILY SLEPT FITFULLY, tossing and turning through dreams that rumbled with thunder. In one scene, she was a little girl, holding her aunt's hand in a surreal version of the Metropolitan Museum of Art on Fifth Avenue. As they wandered through the Egyptian galleries, a large scarab beetle rose up in front of them, its front legs twitching. Her aunt looked right at her. Don't worry, darling—you'll do fine in Florida, the older woman said. My scarab will protect you.

What on God's green earth did that mean, Emily wondered, still groggy with sleep. Her aunt's signature piece of jewelry had been a bracelet of carved scarabs set in silver—maybe that was it. Seeing Aunt Liz again, even in a nightmare, had been strangely comforting, but as Emily began to wake up, the realization that she would never see her aunt again, except in dreams, hit her anew. Milton had said Liz wouldn't let him rest until he tracked down the truth about her death. Was her aunt's spirit reaching out to her, too?

One thing was certain—it wasn't a spirit who had left the back door to the house open the day before.

She lay in bed, watching patches of sunlight play on the walls as the old metal fan stirred the curtains. It was early, and already she was damp with perspiration. The clothes she had packed were probably all wrong—too heavy. In this heat, even wearing nothing probably felt too heavy. It was odd, her mind rambled: she had never seen Lewis wearing absolutely nothing. They had slept together, of course, but in some ways, he seemed so Victorian, in his pressed pajamas. Not so with John, whose sheer physical presence was still so real to her—even though the months since his death had turned to years.

Suddenly her grief for that loss felt fresh again, like her grief for her aunt. Emily's time with John might not have been so full of passion if she'd been his wife instead of his lover. Did his wife still feel the loss as deeply as she did? If Emily couldn't muster much excitement for the prospect of marrying Lewis, maybe she just wasn't over John yet—if she ever would be. Good old Lewis. She should call him to report her safe arrival—but a phone call was so expensive. Maybe a cable would do.

Stumbling out of bed, Emily smoothed the sheets and the chenille spread and threw on a light robe, remembering she had seen a tin of coffee and a percolator in the kitchen. She padded down the hall toward the stairs, yawning, when she stopped cold. From the kitchen below, which should have been quiet as a tomb, she heard noises. Drawers opening and closing. Oh god, the intruder had returned.

Emily felt like she was still staggering through her beetle dream. Heart pounding, she grabbed an ancient umbrella from a stand in the hall and crept down the stairs and up to the swinging kitchen door, which hung closed, for the moment anyway. Slowly she inched the door open with one hand, holding the closed umbrella like a spear behind her head with the other.

To her shock, the door was pulled away from her and into the kitchen, revealing a tall Black woman holding an iron frying pan. Both of them let out a yell.

"Child, what are you doing creeping about? You 'bout to scare me to death." Then the tall woman collapsed with laughter as she put the pan down on the counter. "Miss Emily, you sure favor your auntie."

"Who are you?" Emily clutched the front of her robe. "And why are you here?" It was early, for god's sake. This was ridiculous—couldn't a woman have a little peace to get her bearings?

"I'm Mattie Sayles, Miss Emily. I made you supper and left it for you yesterday."

"Of course," said Emily, her cheeks going hot. "And it was wonderful. I'm so sorry, Mrs. Sayles. Apparently, my body has arrived, but my mind and my manners haven't caught up. How did you get in?"

"Judge Stimpson gave me the new keys. He hired me to help you settle in—I used to work for your aunt. Didn't he tell you?"

"Mr. Armistead told me—he picked me up at the train station. Oh dear, I think I'm still half asleep." She felt confused. At first glance, she liked Mattie—the woman had a sense of humor and was obviously a fine cook—but Emily hadn't really expected a housekeeper. The one who had worked for her family when Emily was a child had been rather scary, actually, and Aunt Liz had no housekeeper years ago when Emily had visited her. She longed for the solitude of the train. And this tall, animated woman didn't seem like someone one could easily ignore.

"You just need some coffee, Miss Emily, that's all," Mattie said. "Now sit yourself down and I'll get you some. You drink coffee, don't you?"

Emily hesitated but then nodded as she plopped down in the same kitchen chair Milton had sat her in the night before. It felt strange to have somebody wait on her. If this keeps up, she thought, I'm going to spend this whole stay in Florida sitting here, cowering.

She looked up at Mattie Sayles, now facing the stove, her shoulders shaking again with laughter. "I know it's not funny, Miss Emily, especially since you're grieving and all—but the two of us, Lord have mercy—we could have knocked each other silly."

Emily started to laugh, too. It felt good. She hadn't realized how wound up she was. And she hadn't thought of herself as truly grieving. Maybe that's what this feeling was—like she was moving, slowly, through cotton wool. Everything seemed fuzzy.

"Miss Elizabeth liked her coffee strong," Mattie said as she put a cup in front of Emily, along with a plate of buttered cinnamon toast. "Like a lot of things. I sure am sorry for your loss, Miss Emily—she was a great lady. I miss her, I can tell you."

"Thank you, Mrs. Sayles. And thank you again for a wonderful supper."

"You call me Mattie, now—it's fine—that's the way it's done.

We get along fine." She looked at Emily. "My my, you sure do favor her."

"Really? I never thought I did. She had such presence—those great cheekbones—and I've always tended to be a little round . . ." She paused, feeling like she was babbling a bit. "Anyway, thank you. Is that why you thought I'd like the cinnamon toast—because she did?"

"Honey, I never met nobody who didn't like cinnamon toast. Here, have some more coffee." She added some to Emily's cup and quickly moved to the stove, where the frying pan was now filled with thick slices of bacon.

"I don't know if I'll need more than toast, Mrs. Sayles—Mattie." Emily nodded to the bacon, which Mattie continued to cook, unfazed. Emily stared into space for a minute, and then, her mind clearing as the caffeine kicked in, picked up her train of thought from the night before, about how the house could have been left open.

"I asked about how you got in," she went on, "because when we got the house yesterday—Mr. Armistead and me and a neighbor boy—Billy, his name was—"

"You met Billy already?"

"Yes, he was very helpful," Emily rushed on, "but the thing is, the back door was wide open—and the rain was coming in. I wondered if maybe you were in a rush and forgot to lock the doors?"

Mattie frowned. "Oh no, ma'am. I would never do that. When I left, the house was all locked up."

"You're sure, Mrs. Sayles?" The bacon popped and sizzled in the pan, producing an aroma that made Emily much less sure that she didn't need any.

"Miss Emily," said Mattie, straightening her back and rising to her full and considerable height. "Milton Armistead will tell you—if there's one thing I am, besides being a damn good cook— excuse me ma'am—it is dependable. No way I'd leave this house unlocked."

"Oh yes, Mr. Armistead did tell me exactly that—and how

lucky I was to have your help. There must be some other explanation."

"There has to be," said Mattie, hands on hips.

"Of course I trust you," Emily said, trying to smooth any ruffled feelings. "And you won't really have to put up with me for very long—I'm just staying long enough to see Mr. Stimpson about my aunt's estate and to visit her grave. I'm hoping he can act as executor for me. I don't know if I can take this heat." Emily picked up one of the Jesus funeral-parlor fans that was still on the kitchen table and began fanning her flushed face.

"Miss Emily," said Mattie, her expression softening, "you know, this is your house now, even if you just visit in winter. I know your auntie's death has hit you hard. I'm here to help you, not to have a hissy fit. I loved her, too—hope that's not speaking out of turn."

Emily looked up and reached for Mattie's hand, giving it a squeeze. She found she was fighting tears but wasn't sure why.

"Yes, ma'am," said Mattie, patting Emily's shoulder. "You know, if we can get that big attic fan working, it'll cool down this house a whole lot, Miss Emily."

"Really?"

"Without a doubt. And Judge Stimpson's paying me good to take care of you for at least a month, so you just let me earn my pay. Why don't I unpack your pretty things this morning and, later, maybe we can talk about what to do with Miss Elizabeth's clothes, for one thing. Makes me feel bad to see them hanging in the closet."

Emily realized she hadn't thought about that—about all the practical things that might need to be done—why she was here. She had agreed to come to Florida, after all, because her aunt's lawyer, Judge Stimpson, had assured her it was essential. But until she had actually boarded the train, Lewis's constant proposals—his obsession with a Christmas wedding—had soaked up her attention and diminished her focus on how she could best honor her aunt.

Judge Stimpson had told her the estate was somewhat complex. She would have to stay for a few days, anyway. She owed it to Aunt Liz—who had given her so much, who had helped shape who Emily was, really. As for whoever had been snooping in the house—if someone had been—she didn't want to give them the satisfaction of seeing her leave almost as soon as she had arrived. Maybe that's even what the prowler wanted—to get rid of her.

What a silly thought, though. She was letting her imagination get away from her. Too many crime novels—that's what Lewis always said whenever her thoughts went too dark. She was about to ask Mattie about the scarab bracelet—if Mattie knew where Liz had kept it—when her gaze fell on the kitchen clock. Oh dear, Milton would be there soon to pick her up, and she hadn't even begun to get dressed, much less unpack.

"Mrs. Sayles—Mattie," Emily blurted out, "speaking of unpacking, I haven't even begun. I just realized the time. Mr. Armistead will be here soon, and I don't want to keep him waiting."

"He is something, isn't he," said Mattie, shaking her head. "Can I help?"

"Just stall him until I'm ready."

Dashing upstairs, Emily dug into her smallest suitcase and threw on her most tropical outfit—cotton top, broomstick-pleated skirt, huarache shoes, and her favorite Mexican silver earrings—while the smell of more bacon frying wafted up the stairs, along with the sounds of Mattie talking with someone, but it didn't sound like Milton.

What now, Emily thought. Hurrying back downstairs, she paused to listen through the closed kitchen door.

"Just because Miss Elizabeth let you be coming around for breakfast on your way to school, that don't mean Miss Emily will feel the same way," Mattie was saying. "She's from New York City, after all. It's a different world up there."

"I know," came the response, "but Miss Lizzie was from there, too. I can do chores for my breakfast, just like I did for her. Golly, Mattie, did Miss Emily tell you about the rain coming into the house when we got here? It was spooky—this big empty house, and the thunder and the storm coming, and wondering if someone was going to grab us."

"Ask me, you listen to too many of those scary radio shows," said Mattie—just the kind of thing Lewis would say—as Emily swung open the door to see none other than young Billy Mizell, consuming a small mountain of eggs and toast.

"Morning, Miss Emily," he said, kicking his feet against the chair legs.

"Boy, sit still," said Mattie. "That racket like to wake the dead. And yes, Miss Emily and I talked about all that."

"Good morning, Billy," Emily answered the boy. "So you often had breakfast here, with my aunt—is that right?"

"Yes ma'am," said Mattie before Billy could answer, "and every other meal he can manage. Boy got a hollow leg. I was gonna tell you earlier, but we got talking about other things."

Her tone was stern, but the look she gave the boy spoke only kindness.

"Pa's out at the ranch a lot," Billy said.

"I see," said Emily. "Well, it sounds like breakfast here is a tradition. And traditions are important." It also sounded like the boy's father wasn't doing his job. And where was the mother?

"I will say, Miss Emily," said Mattie, "Billy is a hard worker."

"I appreciate both your help," said Emily, finally feeling awake after the adrenaline rush to get dressed. "I'm sure we'll sort it all out."

The doorbell rang. It was time to take care of business.

"I hope it's a good day at school, Billy," Emily said and then turned to Mattie as she moved toward the front door. "Mrs. Sayles, would you mind very much starting on that unpacking we talked about? That would be helpful."

"I sure will," said Mattie, motioning at Emily to keep moving toward the door.

Maybe having some help wasn't so bad after all, Emily thought. Soon she would see her aunt's lawyer and find out why she was really here. And, because Milton seemed to want it, to meet this supposedly handsome detective.

Chapter 3
The Way Things Work Around Here

SLIPPING BEHIND the wheel, Milton turned and fixed Emily with a stern look as he started up the taxi. His clip-on sunglasses were flipped up so he could see better—a habit of his that she recalled from years ago. He had just ushered her into the back seat of the old Cadillac.

"Miss Emily, we need to talk," he began. "I'm afraid you've forgotten how things work around here, or maybe you were too young to get the picture when you used to visit your aunt, but I want you to get the lay of the land, especially before we talk to Detective Maxwell."

"What do you mean?" Emily bristled. General Armistead, indeed. Right now, he was speaking with all the authority of Eisenhower at D-Day.

"I mean, that before I got the car's back door open for you, you reached for the front door like you were going to sit in the passenger seat. I mean, that white ladies don't ride in the front seat with a colored man, even if he's being paid to drive them. Even if he's like part of the family."

Emily's cheeks turned hot. She looked down and sat in silence as Milton guided the old Cadillac out of the driveway, surprised by how much the rebuke had stung. Then she caught his eyes in the center rearview mirror.

"I was young, but I do remember things, Mr. Armistead. For one, I used to sit next to you—you even showed me how to drive, remember?"

"Yes, I do—but that was in your aunt's old truck, out at the fish camp or the grove—just you and me and Elizabeth, on her private property. And you were a girl then—a child, really." He looked back at her in the visor mirror, and his expression softened.

"Now that you're back, Miss Emily, if you don't want a whole mess of trouble for me — and you too, most certainly — you'll pay attention to the rules about what Black folks do not do in the South."

Emily's face was still flushed, and she was grateful for the breeze through the open window as they drove along under the moss-strewn oaks, and she remembered another time with Milton and her aunt at the fish camp, years ago, when she was afraid they'd all be killed. Gazing out at the sun-dappled brick streets, she realized Milton was talking again.

"Now, it's true that I have more freedom than a lot of Negroes in this area," he was saying, "because my daddy and mama had a certain standing in the community, and because I've had business dealings with so many of the white gentlemen in town . . . but no matter who I am, this county has some crazy old white men just itchin' to find fault with any Negro man they think is acting uppity, especially where a white lady is concerned. Worse, they're more than ready to dole out their own kind of justice. And a few of them have it in for me, especially." Milton's grip on the steering wheel tightened.

"Why is that — why for you?"

"That's a big subject, for another time. Let's just say that I've lived long enough to make some enemies. And please understand, what I'm talking about is behavior for public consumption only. Say, we visit in your kitchen like we did last night — we sit around the table and play cards, have a bite to eat. I sat there with your aunt many, many times. But in public, you generally act like you pretty close to ownin' me, and we put on a fine appearance."

"I never want to act like that, Mr. Armistead."

"I know, Miss Emily." He flipped his dark glasses down into place.

Emily fumbled in her purse for her own sunglasses. Soon she would be back on the train, returning to Lewis and her life in New York — a world she understood, or thought she did. She edged forward on the back seat so Milton could hear her better.

"But I understand what you're saying," she said. "Please believe that. The last thing I'd want is to cause you any problems. Now, tell me. What's he like—the detective?"

"He's different from a lot of cops here. He's honest for one thing. Some of them are up to their elbows in payoffs. And he's a northern boy—came down from Chicago for a job with the city police force—not the county."

"Wasn't it a county officer who notified me about my aunt's death?"

"The very same," said Milton. "Her fish camp, where she died—that's in the county. More than a few county deputies are in the Klan, Miss Emily. But Maxwell—he's no friend of the Klan, and he didn't grow up with old Jim Crow. He seems comfortable with colored folks. We're gonna meet him at Wilson's Diner, in fact. That's an institution in the dark part of town—he gets a lot of meals there."

Emily picked up the funeral-parlor fan she had used the day before from the back seat beside her and studied it.

"Okay, Mr. Armistead, since we've been talking about race, here's a question: why are all the bible people on the fans white?"

"Now, you're getting it," said Milton. "Because the white funeral home has the money to buy the fans. Because white people control a whole lot of things, including how Jesus looks in pictures."

"Maybe I should paint him as a Black man," said Emily. "I wonder what the rule-makers would think about that."

In the mirror's reflection, she could see Milton smile. She surely did want to be his friend, no matter how tricky that was. She had made a joke, but she had also heard the seriousness behind Milton's comments about the Klan. And she had her own scary memories.

They had been driving west on one of the town's main avenues, and the landscape had changed after they crossed the railroad tracks. Two-story homes surrounded by greenery gave way to smaller wooden houses, many with well-tended gardens. Milton turned onto a busy business street with a movie theater: The Carver. All the people they passed on the street now were Negroes, and some of them waved at the taxi as it drove past. It was a vibrant street, alive.

"We got a nice little business district, Miss Emily. White folks call it 'colored town'—you'll be hearing that."

"What do you call it?"

"I reckon I just call it home."

"One more question," said Emily. "About Maxwell—if there are so many rules about how white people and Black people behave, how is he allowed to eat here—this white policeman?"

"Because it's us who are supposed to stay in our place, not white people. But, like a lot of things—it's complicated. Maxwell's made friends among colored folks here. He treats folks right. You'll see. And, don't worry—you'll be welcome at Wilson's, too, Miss Emily."

"I'm not worried," she said. "But I'm not sure I understand why we're meeting Maxwell. I know you think Aunt Liz's death wasn't an accident, but why talk to him if she didn't die in his jurisdiction? It can't be just because of the muddy footprints—I'm sure the detective has bigger fish to fry."

"He does indeed," Milton said. "Just humor me."

She smiled. She might be ready to head back to New York, but it sure was good to be back in General Armistead's company.

Milton stopped the taxi in front of a rambling white-frame building, where he expertly guided it into a parking place. "Wilson's Diner: Best Food in Dixie since 1926," a sign read. Instinctively, Emily reached for the car's door handle.

"Now, just hold on," Milton muttered as he unwound his long legs, got out, and rather elaborately opened the back-seat door for her.

"After you, Miss Emily," he said, and she could have sworn he winked at her behind his clip-on sunglasses.

As they entered Wilson's, a pretty Negro woman wearing an apron over her print dress approached Milton and Emily, holding a stack of menus.

"Mr. Milton, I haven't seen you in too long," the hostess said. She smiled at Emily. "Welcome to Wilson's, ma'am. Best food in town, on either side of the tracks."

The greeting seemed genuinely warm, and the tenseness in Emily's shoulders relaxed a little. She had just told Milton she was perfectly worry-free, but in truth she was wound up like a spring. Maybe she hadn't been so sure she'd be accepted at Wilson's. Maybe it was Milton's almost palpable concern about the house being open yesterday evening. Nothing seemed to be missing or out of place, but was Milton right that it was connected to Aunt Liz's death?

"Hello, Earlene," answered Milton. "Always a pleasure. This is Miss Emily Washington. Just arrived in town. She's staying at her aunt's place, Eola Lodge. I think you knew that good lady."

"Yes," said Earlene, her face softening with sympathy. "I am so sorry for your loss, ma'am. Miss Elizabeth sure was special. Nothing like family, is there?"

"How kind of you," Emily said, her throat suddenly tight.

So Earlene had known her aunt. Everyone in town seemed to have known Liz. Family? Emily was the woman's flesh and blood—surely she could have taken more time to know her aunt better. Whatever else she had been doing—traveling, painting, meeting John and then Lewis—had always seemed so much more important. Maybe, without even realizing it, she had let her father's judgments about his free-spirited sister influence her. It hurt to think that might have been true.

Earlene was motioning for them to follow her.

"I expect you all are looking for Mr. Maxwell," the hostess said. "He told me to keep an eye out for you. Just come this way."

She led Emily and Milton past tables topped with red-checked oilcloth to a sunny back room where a man sat hunched over a newspaper, smoking, the remains of his breakfast in front of him. His wavy brown hair hadn't seen a comb in a while, and his tie hung loose around the collar of a rumpled white shirt that he wore with the sleeves rolled up to his elbows, revealing tanned forearms. It was hard to tell his age, but when he saw Emily and Milton approach, his whole face wrinkled up into a grin and he looked almost boyish. Standing up quickly, he tossed the paper aside, stabbed out his cigarette, and shook hands with Milton.

"Milton—it's good to see you, man." Then, as Milton introduced him to her, Maxwell turned to Emily with a gaze so direct she found it almost startling and extended his hand, which was strong and warm to the touch. She sensed the color rising slightly in her cheeks as she sat down and found herself strangely relieved that Lewis wasn't there to see it.

"Y'all want some coffee?" Maxwell waved to Earlene as he raised his mug and pointed to it as Milton nodded yes. He may be from Chicago, but he's been in Florida long enough to adopt the ubiquitous "y'all," Emily thought.

"I'd love some," she said.

"Good. It's on the way."

Emily found herself bristling a little. Very take-charge, wasn't he? She wasn't sure if she was charmed or irritated by him. And handsome? That was a stretch.

"So, Milton told me you had a strange reception, Miss Washington," Maxwell began. "The back door wide open?"

Emily waited to answer while a waitress produced a tray bearing sturdy mugs of coffee and placed one in front of each of them.

"Yes, that's right," she said, "but I'm sure you have many more important things to deal with. There must be some simple explanation."

"Like what, would you say?" Maxwell held his eyes on hers as he vigorously stirred sugar into his coffee.

"I don't know," said Emily. "My aunt's lawyer might have asked a workman to come by. Or, Mrs. Sayles—the housekeeper—may have forgotten to lock up—although she swears that's impossible."

"If she did forget, it would be a first," Milton interjected.

Maxwell kept stirring his coffee, now slowly. "It's true"—he paused, seeming to weigh his words—"it's true there's not much crime over your way, Miss Washington. Nice neighborhood. About the only criminal activity over there involves buying bolita tickets."

"What kind of tickets?" She swore both men suppressed a smile.

"Betting on numbers every week in an underground lottery," said Milton. "It's our state vice, Miss Emily. Everybody does it."

"Everybody?"

"Yes ma'am," added Maxwell. "Hell—excuse me, ma'am— even nice little old ladies buy tickets from the numbers runners. That's what we call the folks who sell them."

Had Maxwell thought of her Aunt Liz as a nice little old lady, Emily wondered. If he had, he hadn't known her, surely.

"The Mizell boy lives right near you, doesn't he?" Maxwell asked.

"Billy?" Emily looked up from her steaming coffee.

"That's the one. You'll have your chance soon enough. He sells bolita tickets, and that kid could sell ice to Eskimos."

"You said 'underground.' Do you mean Billy works for gangsters?" asked Emily.

"That makes it sound a lot worse than it is," said Milton. "The boy's probably doing some good. Some of the ladies he visits to sell tickets appreciate his checking in on them. And people love their bets."

"This is a lot to take in," Emily said, shaking her head. She turned to Milton.

"By the way, Mr. Armistead, I just saw Billy at breakfast this morning."

"He didn't wait even a day, huh?" said Milton.

"You didn't tell me he was such a favorite of my aunt's," said Emily, as she took a sip of coffee, now cool enough for her to drink.

"I figured it wouldn't take long for you to find out. She had a way of gravitating toward people who needed her." Milton's voice was quiet.

"Maybe that's why she helped me so much," said Emily, absently, into an awkward silence.

Milton looked at her, and then shifted his attention to Maxwell.

"Speaking of Miss Emily's aunt," he said, "I'll confess, Detective—she's the main reason I wanted Miss Emily to meet you so soon. I was concerned when the house was open, but there's more to it."

"You sure you want to go there, man?" Maxwell shook his head.

Milton took a breath as if to steel himself and plunged ahead.

"Here's the thing, Detective. I just cannot believe the fire that killed Miss Emily's aunt was an accident. Elizabeth Washington was not a careless woman."

"Let me get this straight, though," said Maxwell. "You're not saying she set the fire on purpose—that she wanted to kill herself?"

"Decidedly not," Milton continued, as Emily's chest tightened and the warmth drained from her face. She hadn't really let herself think much about the circumstances of her aunt's death. With difficulty, she pulled her attention back to what Milton was saying.

"Detective, you know she had a habit of getting under the skin of some of our noble defenders of the Lost Cause," he said. "I'm talking about the Klan again, Miss Emily. The true believers of white supremacy—they're a special subject of the detective's study, by the way."

"It's tough, Milton," the detective began. "The sheriff's report was clear about calling it an accident." He looked at Emily and added, "I didn't go to the scene—it was a county investigation."

Emily nodded, as Milton leaned forward, his voice rising slightly. "But you heard the talk, Detective."

"Yes, I heard talk about someone seeing a kerosene can inside the cabin, and when I asked about it, I was told to shut up and mind my own business. No less than the chief himself told me to keep my nose out of the Washington case—that it was Mizell's business—our illustrious sheriff."

"That's just the problem," said Milton.

"Mizell?" Emily interrupted, but Milton had anticipated her question.

"He's talking about Carter Mizell," he said. "He and Billy's father, Jeff, are half-brothers—same daddy, different mothers, and like night and day. Jeff's had his troubles but even on his worst day, he's worth ten of Carter." He turned to Maxwell.

"Look, Detective," Milton said. "First Miss Emily's aunt dies, and now, before Miss Emily — her heir — even gets into Eola Lodge, someone's snooping around there. They were brazen enough — or rushed enough — to leave muddy footprints. Either way, I don't like it."

Maxwell straightened, as if suddenly eager. "Did you leave the footprints alone?"

Emily sagged inwardly. It was clear she'd made a mistake. "No, I'm afraid they're gone. I mopped them up last night."

The detective sat for a minute in silence before looking again at Emily, with that gaze that was so direct she felt her cheeks turn pink again.

"How long are you here, Miss Washington?" he asked, as he looked at his watch and rose to his feet. "I want to hear more about what happened at Eola Lodge, but now I need to get going."

"I'm not sure," said Emily. "Probably not long. I'm on my way to meet my aunt's attorney about her will, to learn what she wanted me to do as her executor. Mr. Armistead and I are going there next."

"The attorney — it's George Stimpson," said Milton, and Emily thought she saw the detective raise an eyebrow slightly.

"Your aunt picked a good lawyer, Miss Washington. You can trust him, which might not always be the case with our so-called pillars of the community," Maxwell said as he gathered a hat and wrinkled suit jacket from the back of a chair. "I'll check back with you in a day or so. In the meantime, keep your doors locked and your eyes open."

"I'll do that, of course," said Emily.

"And if anything should happen before I get back to you, Miss Washington — anything that worries you — I would like you to call me any time, day or night. I mean it."

Maxwell paused, reached in a pocket, and handed her a rather rumpled business card.

Then he turned to Milton. "I understand your concern, Milton. Don't hesitate to call me, too. You know all the places to find me, that's for sure. I'm at the Coffee Club a lot after hours."

Milton nodded as he rose to shake the detective's hand, and

then Maxwell was gone. As Emily and Milton followed him out of Wilson's, Emily watched as Milton tipped his hat to Earlene and spoke briefly to a couple of men at the counter. He seemed to know everyone, just as he had at the train station. What kind of a place have I come back to, Emily thought — a place where a man who seems so respected, even beloved, tells me to treat him like a servant. A place where old ladies gamble and children help them, and some law officers may be anything but lawful.

It was also a place where an accident seemed an awful lot like murder, at least to Milton Armistead. Maybe he was just letting his understandable distrust of white men like Sheriff Mizell get the better of him.

Back at Milton's old Cadillac, Emily spotted a sign across the street as she slid into the back seat.

"The place Maxwell just mentioned, Mr. Armistead — the Coffee Club — is that it over there, next to the Carver?" She pointed to the unlit neon sign, which featured jaunty coffee cups and martini glasses. "It certainly doesn't look like any coffee shop I've ever been to."

"More jazz and beer than coffee," said Milton. "The detective practices on the piano there after hours."

"A man of many talents." She wanted to know more, but something else grabbed her attention. As the taxi pulled away from the curb, Emily could swear the same black Ford she'd noticed the night before at Eola Lodge was parked across from Wilson's. When the Cadillac pulled away from the curb, the Ford came to life, turning into a driveway. It backed out and pulled into traffic a couple of cars behind the taxi.

Emily reached forward and lightly touched Milton's shoulder.

"Mr. Armistead, I know this probably sounds silly," she said, "but that black Ford I noticed last night outside my aunt's house — my house — I think it's following us. Can you see it?"

Milton studied the rearview mirror and made a sudden right turn. "Yes ma'am, I do see that Ford. And if you don't mind me asking, Miss Emily, why in hell — excuse me — didn't you tell me about it last night?"

"I did tell you, and you said something about lots of people parking on the street near Eola Lodge. And it didn't seem important," she shrugged. "I mostly noticed because the man behind the wheel was wearing a hat, and I was so hot — I wondered how he could stand it."

She tried to sound nonchalant, but inside she was berating herself — just another example of how inept she could be sometimes. Like the way she'd mopped up those footprints. Last night she'd been sure she was making too much of all of it.

"And you think it's the same car?" Milton asked. "I'm gonna slow down and maybe we can take a look."

"I'm pretty sure it is. It's got the same dent in the right front fender."

"You don't miss much, Miss Emily — you see things, like your aunt did. Just do me a favor: Next time let me in on what you don't miss."

"I'll do that," Emily said, feeling a hint of irritation in the wave of anxiety that was overtaking her. She wanted to say something like, "You know, Mr. Armistead, sometimes when men are concerned, it's not easy for a woman to get a word in edgewise." But all she managed was, "And, by the way, please don't apologize to me for swearing."

"All right, Miss Emily," said Milton. "I'll let her rip: Damn that Ford! I don't like this one bit."

She turned to look out the taxi's rear window. That Ford was still behind them. When Milton slowed, it slowed, too, always staying a couple of cars behind the Cadillac cab. Milton drove faster and faster still, and neat bungalows sped past Emily's window as they hurried toward Judge Stimpson's office. Watching Milton accelerate and take more corners, Emily held on to the front seat and had a strange thought: She was scared silly, but she felt more alive than she had in weeks.

Chapter 4

A Letter from the Dead

"WELL, THAT WAS SOME kind of craziness," said Milton, his eyes inscrutable behind his sunglasses. "I'm not sure if we lost him, or he just took off. You doing okay, Miss Emily?"

"Just peachy—or I will be after a couple deep breaths." Maybe in a minute, what felt like steel bands around her chest would go away.

If Emily had felt exhilarated riding at high speeds on brick streets, she also felt terrified. As much as she'd loved Aunt Liz, it was true that if you wanted a smooth and comfortable course in life—as Emily had increasingly pursued, especially with Lewis—Elizabeth Washington was the wrong person to emulate. What had her aunt gotten her into?

With any luck, Emily would find out in the next hour. She would learn from this lawyer why her aunt, reaching out from death, had wanted her to return here. Then she could head back to her life in New York, where no mysterious black-beetle Fords had ever followed her.

"We're a little early," said Milton, "thanks to the efficiency of our arrival."

Emily looked out of the taxi's windows at the imposing Mediterranean-style building that housed the offices of George S. Stimpson, Attorney at Law, as a sign by the entrance proclaimed.

"Why does everyone call him Judge Stimpson?" she said. "What kind of judge was he—or is he?"

"I honestly couldn't tell you, Miss Emily. Seems like half the old white men in town call one another either Judge or Colonel. Whatever kind of judge he was, it's been a good while since he was on the bench."

"I appreciate all your background information," she said. "And I appreciate your bringing me here, despite the risk and having plenty else to do—important clients who depend on you?"

"As it turns out, Miss Emily, I had to come here today anyway. I got a call early this morning from the Judge himself. Said he wanted me at this meeting this morning with you. Stubborn old cuss would not say why."

"I'm glad you'll be there." How interesting, though. Milton had said she needed to act like "she was close to owning him"—yet it seemed here that he was being included as her virtual equal, a participant in her appointment about her aunt's will.

"It's downright strange, if you ask me," he said. "And when it comes to important clients, nobody ranks higher than your aunt. By helping you, I'm helping her, too." He paused. "Now, you go on in and get settled, Miss Emily. I'll park in the shade and meet you in there in a few minutes. I'll be expected to use the back entrance."

"Which is just crazy," said Emily.

"Can't say that I disagree."

Milton got out, helped Emily excavate herself from the old leather back seat, and held the door open for her to enter Stimpson's offices, which were housed in a former home near the county courthouse. Inside, mahogany-paneled walls and elegant wing chairs lined the waiting area where a black metal fan stirred the air in front of a formidable-looking woman seated behind a large desk.

"Miss Washington, welcome," she said, as she rose and came around the desk, extending a hand to Emily. "I'm Margaret Rankin, Mr. Stimpson's secretary. I'll be handling a lot of your paperwork. He's grateful to you for making the journey south this time of year—braving this heat!"

The secretary wore an immaculate seersucker shirtwaist dress, pearls, spectator heels, and stockings. Her blonde hair was set in fashionable waves. To Emily, who was feeling decidedly damp and underdressed in her peasant skirt, Margaret Rankin looked as though she had the power somehow to repel perspiration, no matter what the temperature. What had Aunt Liz thought of her?

"Thank you so much for all you've done," said Emily, shaking the secretary's hand.

"Your aunt had been a client of Judge Stimpson's for many years. We were only too happy to help. I'll tell him you're here. He's expecting you, of course."

Just then a back door to the waiting area opened, and Milton approached the women, holding his Panama straw hat.

"Mr. Armistead, how good of you to come," said the secretary, without extending her hand to Milton.

"Miss Rankin," said Milton, nodding a greeting.

Margaret Rankin turned to Emily. "Judge Stimpson said you knew Mr. Armistead, Miss Washington. If you have no objection, he'd like to see both of you together."

"Of course," said Emily, although she continued to find it a bit odd, based on Milton's recent lecture to her on strict social hierarchy. She and Milton followed the spectator pumps as they glided across a long oriental carpet toward an office at the end of a dark corridor, where they found Judge Stimpson behind a large antique desk surrounded by floor-to-ceiling bookcases. Framed maps and photographs filled the wall behind him, and Emily thought she spotted the current governor of Florida in one photo and, in another, the golfer Ben Hogan. The wall across from the Judge's desk contained a fireplace. Would it ever be cool enough here to use one, Emily wondered.

Stimpson rose, walked around the desk to greet them, and extended a hand first to her and then to Milton. He reminded her a little of the humorist Will Rogers — a thatch of iron-gray hair and laugh lines around blue eyes that looked as though they didn't miss much. He gestured to a couple of chairs in front of his desk.

"Well, Miss Washington," he said. "I'm happy to meet you in person at last. Thank you for making that long journey. And it's always good to see you, Milton. Thank you for coming on short notice. It seemed the most efficient thing to do — to talk with you both at the same time. Your aunt was not a conventional woman, Miss Washington, and she did not leave a conventional will."

He was about to continue when a soft knock came at the door, and Margaret Rankin quietly entered, carrying a tray that held a silver pitcher and a leather folder. Three glasses full of ice sat on an antique sideboard near Stimpson's desk.

"I asked Miss Rankin to make us some iced tea," Stimpson said, as he picked up the folder and opened it. Milton had risen at the secretary's entrance, moving toward her to take the tray, when Stimpson's voice stopped him. "There's no need for that, Milton," he said. "You are the client here today, too."

Emily and Milton muttered thanks as Margaret Rankin handed them each a crystal tumbler of ice-cold liquid before quietly disappearing again. Stimpson looked in the leather folder and extracted what looked like a telegram.

"Before we begin, this is for you, Miss Washington," he said, handing her the envelope. "I gather it came just before you arrived. Please, we can wait while you open it."

Puzzled, Emily tore into the envelope, her stomach tightening. Was anything wrong at home? As she read, though, her worry turned to irritation.

"Darling, great news," the message began. Lewis. It was from Lewis. Of course, Emily remembered—she had given him Stimpson's address as well as hers at Eola Lodge. But why on earth had he used it for what was surely personal business? Sometimes he could be so infuriating.

"Miss you bunches!" the telegram began. "Father says marriage = full partnership for me. Let's set date. Come home soon! Yours, Lewis."

Emily put the telegram in her purse, realizing her face was flushed again. Lewis had dropped hints that his father would be especially pleased when they married, perhaps in hopes the union would soon produce a grandson and future heir to the family's prestigious law firm. But she hadn't had any proof of that deal until now.

Presumably female children would be tolerated, Emily thought, taking a sip of cold tea. Just minutes ago, she had been eager to get back to Lewis, but she had to admit the last thing she wanted right now was to start a family. Truth be told, she was satisfied with things as they were between Lewis and her. He wasn't John, but no one could be. He was good company. But if she didn't feel a great passion for him, she also found herself a little insulted that it wasn't passion for her but the promise of a partnership that seemed to be spurring him on.

"So sorry for the delay," she said, placing the glass of iced tea on the coaster Miss Rankin had left on the side table between her chair and Milton's. "It's nothing urgent."

Stimpson nodded, and Emily felt Milton's gaze, those dark eyes studying her.

"Glad it's not bad news," Stimpson said. "You've had enough of that, Miss Washington. Before we begin, let me ask, how are you settling in? I do think we've seen the last of the hurricanes for this year and can expect cooler temperatures soon. And, of course, in winter, Florida weather sure beats shoveling snow, I can tell you."

Emily's eyes widened. Settling in? With the giant bugs and the heat? She had planned to take care of business and leave as soon as possible—at least she had before Milton had revealed his worries about her aunt's death and they had played hide and seek with a black Ford. Realizing she was on the verge of being rude, she rallied. Aunt Liz might have been unconventional, but she was unfailingly gracious. Emily had her standards to uphold.

"You've been so thoughtful, Mr. Stimpson, arranging things with Mr. Armistead and Mrs. Sayles. Your welcoming gift of food was wonderful. Please thank Mrs. Stimpson, too."

She took another sip of tea and shifted in her seat.

"Happy to be of service," said Stimpson. "Now, we'd better get to the business at hand." Emily found herself fascinated by his manner of speech, somehow extracting the sound of more than one syllable from the word "hand." Southern accents in movies did not quite match it. Some New Yorkers, including Lewis, believed all Southerners were stupid because of the slow pace of their speech. And Southerners had their own ideas about New Yorkers, too—crass, fast, and smarty-pants.

Stimpson opened the file on his desk.

"I knew, of course, the contents of Elizabeth Washington's will because she confided in me while she was making it. But in truth, I thought it would be many more years before her passing, and I might never have to be speaking with you like this. I owe her a lot, you see," Stimpson went on. "No one knows this—well, perhaps you do, Milton—but she helped me out of a jam once, in a big way. Lent me a good deal of money, no questions asked. Now, I want to do right by her, too."

From the folder on his desk, he extracted a letter-sized envelope. "Before we go on to the legal papers, why don't you read this, Miss Washington?"

He handed her a cream envelope, addressed to her in her aunt's hand. She was aware again of Milton's quiet attention on her, surrounding her almost like some kind of protective cloak. She was surprised to feel tears stinging her eyes at the sight of her name in her aunt's handwriting. Slowly Emily opened the envelope. She didn't want to tear it. She quickly scanned the letter and, on impulse, began to read it out loud. These men had known her aunt and cared about her, and it seemed to include them too—especially Milton.

The letter was dated only a few months ago, in April.

"My dear girl," it began. "I'll always think of you as the girl who visited me in Florida, even though I know you've grown into a fine and wise woman. Don't let anyone let you think otherwise, despite the things my poor short-sighted brother—your father—used to tell you.

"I hope you won't be opening this letter for a while, because when you do, it means my life as we know it will be over. But, Emily dear, please know that I am not afraid of death. In fact, I am eager to find out what lies beyond the limit of our seeing and of our hearing and do not think the Over There will be any the less interesting than the Right Here, since the universe seems to be of one piece, offering boundless possibilities of growth."

Emily realized that Milton was handing her a crisp white handkerchief. She nodded thanks, touched it to the corner of her eyes, and continued.

"But even if I'm not afraid of death, I'm stubborn enough to want to see the legacy I've built continue. I've been fortunate in Florida, and I've always wanted what I achieved here to live on through you, Emily. I've always hoped for you the kind of life you deserve—not a life in the service of any man. If you do find a great love, Emily, let it be one in which you coexist as equals.

"Mr. Stimpson will tell you the terms of my estate. I am leaving Milton Armistead a bequest, too, and also something for the father and son who rent a cottage next to Eola Lodge—Jefferson Mizell and his son, Billy. I have grown quite fond of the boy, and of his father, too, in spite of everything. But I am leaving you most of my legacy, Emily, including Eola Lodge. I trust you will enjoy it as much as I have, and the beautiful park nearby. It's a bright spot, but dark currents also run through this city."

Emily was reaching the end of the letter. Her heartbeat felt so loud, she wondered if Milton could hear it.

"At the risk of sounding melodramatic," her aunt's clear, black script continued, "if something should happen to me before my natural time, I am asking that you look into it, with Milton's help. You know you can trust him. I don't have a great deal of trust in some of our so-called law officers.

"I ask your help in one other thing, Emily, should my life end before this autumn. (Perhaps I'm becoming neurotic in my worries. What would Freud say?) I have been working on a women's art show to present before the end of the year. It's very important to me.

"I fear these requests seem like conditions on my gifts to you, and perhaps they are. But I ask them in love and the bonds of family and friendship. Hopefully, you will have to do neither, and we will have many more years in which to visit.

"But if you do open this in the same year I write, 1948, take care of yourself, my dear, and please do look out for the child, Billy, and don't hesitate to turn to Milton Armistead. He has been more important in my life than he could possibly know.

With all my love,

Your Aunt Elizabeth"

Emily looked up to meet the Judge's gaze. Beside her, Milton was looking down at his hat in his hands. She couldn't see his face. They sat in silence for a moment.

"She certainly had a way with words," said Stimpson. "I knew the details of the will, Miss Washington, but not that letter."

"I'm still taking it all in," said Emily. "It does sound as though she thought her life was in danger. My father always accused her of being too dramatic . . ." Her voice trailed off, as she thought not only about the black Ford but the rain-splashed floor, the muddy prints, and the sounds of the unlocked back door slamming open and shut in the wind yesterday at Eola Lodge. And now Liz was asking her—no, telling her—that it was her duty to get to the bottom of whatever had happened at the fish camp.

"One thing is clear," she heard Stimpson saying. "Your aunt's estate is considerable. She bought grove land that she later sold at a great profit—and she invested her profits wisely. You should be able to live quite comfortably. And, Milton, there's quite a generous bequest for you in the formal documents she signed."

"May I have this letter?" Emily asked. She didn't care about the money—she was already fortunate in that regard—it was everything else that was overwhelming her. She looked over at Milton to see how he was taking all of this, and saw he was still looking down.

"Of course," said Stimpson. "And I have carbon copies of the whole file for you." He handed her a large envelope. "And this is for you," he added, handing an envelope, too, to Milton, who now looked up and returned the Judge's gaze. "If you invest that, you'll never have to drive a taxi again, I believe."

Milton nodded but said nothing. Was this a total surprise to him? Somehow it didn't seem like it was. Pulling herself together, Emily remembered another thing in the letter that had struck her as odd.

"By the way," Emily began, "when she mentioned Billy Mizell, what did she mean by 'in spite of everything'?"

"The boy's father, Jefferson, has had his troubles, I'm afraid," said Stimpson. "I don't like repeating gossip, but since his wife died, he's been fighting a losing battle with the bottle — or at least that's the talk. Some folks think he and the boy don't belong in that part of town, Miss Washington. In fact, your aunt kept getting offers for that parcel of land they live on — it's next to the house — from folks who'd like to get the Mizells out of there."

Emily nodded and made a mental note to ask Milton about this, too. He had risen from his chair and was now standing silently at her side, as if he was ready to leave.

"And do you have any idea what she's talking about — her fears about her life being in danger?" Emily asked.

"No, this is all news to me," said Stimpson. "As I said, I knew the terms of her will, but that letter was addressed to you privately. In the last part of it, Miss Washington, I noted a kind of apology for appearing to make your inheritance conditional on completing her requests . . . But, that's what she did, basically."

"I'm not sure I understand," Emily said. Did this mean, in fact, she was expected to stay here more than a few days?

"You'll see in that envelope some papers to sign that basically ask for reports and assurances about proceeding with the art show — and, well, I suppose we'll draw up some additional ones about an investigation into her death," Stimpson said. "It's highly unusual, I know. And Milton, there are no such stipulations linked to your bequest."

Emily felt almost angry that her aunt had seemed not to trust her in putting conditions on the will. Had her father been right about his sister when he complained that she was quixotic, egotistical?

"But her death was ruled an accident," said Emily, looking up at both men, both of whom were now standing.

"As I understand it," said Stimpson, "that's for you to decide, as she expresses it in her bequest. So long as you look into it and document your findings about the cause of her death, the estate is yours. She's just asking you to look into it."

She looked up at Milton, who said nothing but gave her a meaningful look.

"Well, there's certainly a lot to think about," Emily said, feeling hot, confused, and exhausted. "I'll read through these things and call you, Mr. Stimpson—I'm sure I'll have questions. Thank you for all you've done."

"Of course," he said. "I look forward to helping in any way I can."

She reached out and shook his hand, as did Milton, and as he opened the office door for them to leave, Emily nearly ran right into Margaret Rankin, hovering outside the door. Had the secretary been listening? And as Emily slid into the old Cadillac, feeling the warm breeze through the open window as she waited for Milton to get in, she wondered if this Judge was someone who could really be trusted. It seemed almost as if her aunt had set Stimpson up to act as a judge, indeed, of whether Emily should even receive her aunt's bequest. On the other hand, if Elizabeth had really faced danger—as Milton feared—and crossed someone who took her life, then she deserved justice. But would looking into it put Emily in danger too?

Chapter 5

When All That Craziness Really Began

EMILY AND MILTON drove in silence along the oak-lined streets, as Emily pored over her aunt's letter, her mind racing. The morning air had been cooler when they were on their way to Wilson's, but now the heat of the day was at full power, and Emily rolled down the car window more as she tightly grasped the funeral-home fan in one hand and her aunt's letter in the other. For now, she swept all thoughts of the black-beetle Ford aside.

Her aunt's death had left her a bequest of mystery and questions as well as property. Elizabeth had obviously cared enough for Billy Mizell—and his father—that she had also left them something, in addition to Milton. She looked up at the rearview mirror to gauge Milton's expression, but his eyes were hidden behind his sunglasses. As if sensing her watching him, he turned to look in the mirror and flipped up the clip-on glasses so she could see his eyes.

"I'm afraid I'm a bit overwhelmed, Mr. Armistead," she began, but he spoke at almost the same time.

"Miss Emily, I have to tell you I was shocked," he said. "When the Judge called, I thought she had left me something in the way of remembrance—maybe a painting, you know. But that money should be yours."

Instinctively, she leaned reached forward and touched his shoulder.

"Oh my goodness, Mr. Armistead, that was the last thing on my mind. I'm happy about that."

"You ever gonna be able to manage calling me Milton?" In the mirror, he shot her one of his patented no-fooling-around, X-ray looks—serious but laced with good humor.

She smiled, shaking her head and shrugging her shoulders. "Old habits die hard," she said.

"Speaking of which, I'm taking a long way back to Eola Lodge, if that's okay, Miss Emily. I could use a few minutes to clear my head myself, and driving does that—one of my old habits."

"Sounds good to me." The breeze from the open window felt good as they passed through tall trees that cast dappled shadows on the brick streets.

"About the will, Mr. Armistead. I'm happy about you and about Billy, too. I'm fortunate, I guess, that money seems to be the least of my worries." She stared down at her aunt's letter.

"So what does have you worried?" Milton said. "What she wrote about 'dark currents' around Eola Lodge?"

"Yes, and her concerns that something might happen to her—plus that damn black Ford."

Milton shot her another look in the mirror, and then grinned.

"You can see there's no need to apologize for certain language around me," said Emily, hunching over her aunt's letter. "And even though I keep calling you 'Mr. Armistead,' I hope you know you're like family to me—more than some of my so-called real family."

"The feeling certainly is mutual, Miss Emily, but you know there are plenty of folks around here who wouldn't see it that way, like I was telling you. In that regard, I'm wondering how much I should keep this inheritance business under my hat, so to speak."

Was it that bad? Emily wondered. She hated that he might feel the need to keep an employer's generosity hidden. Was there something more to it?

"But you're right," Milton continued, "the worrisome stuff in that letter isn't about the bequests—it's about her concerns and fears. She was not, as you know, a fearful woman. And she never said a word to me about anything that was scaring her."

"My father always said Aunt Liz didn't have the sense to be afraid. Sometimes I guess I was concerned he might be at least a little right—that there were times she might have been more cautious—I don't know. He wouldn't let it go, over all these years."

"She referred to him in the letter," said Milton.

"Yes." Emily looked down at the heavy cream-colored paper, now wilted in the heat and her hands. "She tells me not to pay attention to what her 'poor short-sighted brother'—my father—has told me."

"You know when that all really began, don't you?" Milton said. "All that craziness between Elizabeth and your daddy?"

Emily gazed out the window. The car and the road and the trees seemed to fade as she went back in memory to another road, another Florida day when the sunlight danced through the oak leaves, flashing bright among the shadows.

"It was that day with Sam, wasn't it? I was thinking about it earlier today. I had almost forgotten."

"Maybe that's good," said Milton. "Sometimes remembering is hard."

But once the memories started, they rushed back to that day when she was fifteen, when things, like Milton said, had really gone wrong between her father and her aunt.

She had been visiting her aunt between school terms in February, an especially pretty time in central Florida, well before the heat really took hold. She had come down on the train by herself and had stayed for more than a week. Her parents planned to motor down and drive her back with them.

On the last weekend of her stay, Aunt Elizabeth had planned a special expedition. That was the word she always used for such adventures—an "expedition," as if they were explorers heading into the great unknown, to the deserts of Egypt or the slopes of Kilimanjaro. They might go only a few miles, to a lakeshore or the coast, but from the time Emily was a young child, Aunt Elizabeth had managed to invest such experiences with a spirit of adventure and fun. Typically, both art and some kind of exploration of nature were on the day's agenda.

Emily treasured moments from these outings: Aunt Elizabeth, her skirts billowing in the ocean breezes, pointing out special shells in the hard, wet sand; Milton showing Emily how to cast a fishing line. Those were the days when Milton had worked for her aunt, and he was often their guide and companion. The summer Emily was eight, both of them had come running when a small but determined crab had latched onto the back of her ankle, sending her shrieking from the surf. She still got nervous sloshing into the small waves at the ocean's edge, no matter how much she loved the water.

On that visit when she was fifteen — her last, as it turned out, to stay with Elizabeth in Florida — the plan had been to venture out to the St. Johns River for a day of fishing. She and her aunt also hoped to do charcoal sketches of birds and other wildlife. Milton's nephew Sam, who was a little older than Emily, was visiting Milton, and Aunt Liz had invited him to come along.

Milton had driven them all to the campsite, where her aunt eventually built the cabin where she died, Emily thought with a shudder.

At first she hadn't been so sure about Sam, Milton's nephew, who would soon start college at Howard University. She had known Milton for a long time, but she hadn't really talked much with boys her own age — she had gone to a private girls' school. She certainly had never talked to a Negro boy or girl close to her own age and had been nervous and shy. Sam was almost a college man, who might find her childish.

As it turned out, she and Sam had hit it off right away. He'd slid into the car holding a battered copy of *The Maltese Falcon* and, when she told him she had read her father's copy in secret — and that she had a passion for crime novels — she discovered Sam loved books, too. They talked a great deal about their favorite authors. That summer, his was Langston Hughes, she remembered.

Emily guessed that Sam probably hadn't been so crazy about the prospect of spending the day with her, but he had been easy to talk with and kind — he had a wonderful smile — and in the end Emily had peppered him with questions — about his life, about his plans for college. After his studies at Howard, he hoped to study law.

When Aunt Liz was making supper, she had asked Milton to

go down to the river to look for bait, but Emily—if she remembered right—had suggested that she and Sam would be glad to get the bait and Milton could keep on tending to the fire. Milton had not thought this was a great idea, but he had not said why, and all these years later, Emily wondered if she had possibly been angling to be alone with Sam, or if it looked that way. She mostly remembered acting on impulse—and regretting it later.

"Come on, Uncle, I'm not a kid anymore," Sam had said, with that smile of his. "You know I'm good at gathering up bait fish—we'll bring you back some minnows that'll have the bass come running." So off they had gone, immersed in their enthusiasm for books. They had talked especially about Mark Twain, she recalled.

Deep in discussion, Sam and Emily took a break from scooping up minnows in a net to sit for a minute on a log. It had been a magical evening up to that point in Emily's memory, with a twilight sky laced with coral from the setting sun. Sam had told her how he hoped to return to Florida and work hard to better the lives of Negroes. She resolved that she, too, would go to college and would also devote herself to working for a better world. So many of her friends at home only looked forward to their next party. Sitting there under the night's first stars with the smells of supper floating from the campfire, the world seemed a wonderful place, and any-thing—even this unlikely friendship with Sam—seemed not just possible, but real.

Then, in an instant, noise and outrage surrounded them. Even after so many years, Emily felt almost sick as she remembered it. Seemingly out of nowhere, several men came crashing through the bushes.

"Boy, what the hell you think you're doing with this white girl?" one of them hollered, his face twisted in anger as he waved a shotgun. Emily wanted to scream but found herself frozen. She had wanted an adventure, but nothing like this.

The men, all white, enclosed them in a half-circle as they stood several yards away, nearly all of them armed in some way.

Neither Sam nor Emily spoke. She had never been so afraid.

"Answer me, boy," the man with the gun yelled again. "It's probably the last thing you ever get to say." Sam sat frozen, not moving.

In spite of her terror, Emily heard herself saying something like "Sir, it's all right, he's my friend, and we're with my aunt, Elizabeth Washington . . ."

But the man said, "Shut up, little girl, don't you have no better sense? Maybe we need to teach you a good lesson, too."

Just then someone else spoke, a teenager with a red face and thick neck. "Hell, did she say Washington? Ain't that the Yankee lady who owns the grove up off the Trail—?"

But before he could finish the thought, Aunt Liz and Mr. Armistead burst into the clearing, both holding rifles and looking ready to shoot.

"Gentlemen, I believe you are trespassing on my land," said Aunt Liz, standing very straight. "Please leave now."

She stared at them with a look so hard it could break glass. Emily had never seen her aunt look so fierce.

And then, things got even worse. Unbeknownst to Emily, her aunt had invited her father and mother to come to the campsite and join them for a catfish supper. It was supposed to be a surprise. As it turned out, her mother didn't feel well and had stayed at the hotel, but Emily's father arrived just in time to see the hullabaloo. The awful men did leave, but the camping expedition was ruined. The adults all agreed that they would go back to town. Emily thought she heard her aunt say something about the KKK.

Emily's father insisted she ride back to town in his car while Sam rode in Aunt Liz's car with Milton and her aunt. On the way, he spoke quietly but with great intensity and anger. He should have known better than to trust Emily with his free-thinking sister, he said. And she herself had been crazy, too, to go off into the woods alone like that with Sam, a Negro boy, her father had said, without even a care in the world about the KKK.

Didn't she realize that white girls did not talk to Negro boys, especially in the South? It was almost the same kind of speech Milton had given her earlier that day, Emily realized. Her father had more to say, too: If anything bad had happened to Sam, it would have been all her fault. Emily remembered being especially mortified at that thought. Her father had never said more about what could have happened to Sam, but later, in college, Emily had seen some photos taken at lynchings, and the images still terrified her.

It was the responsibility of good white people to take care of Negroes, her father had said. They were not like us — they were like children. She remembered, in spite of her shame and fear, being incredulous about his words, when Milton especially had always seemed to her the epitome of responsibility and good sense — as he seemed right now, driving her home from Judge Stimpson's in the cavernous silence of the big Cadillac, taking a little longer on the way so he too could absorb the news they had learned, the questions to be answered.

But after that day, her father forbade her to visit his sister. No more Florida expeditions. She never saw Sam again, although from time to time she thought about him and wondered what path his life had taken. She did see her aunt over the years on carefully planned rendezvous during Elizabeth's visits to New York and during Emily's college years and after, but those visits had grown more rare, especially during the war, when both Emily and her aunt had thrown themselves into volunteer work and travel was more difficult.

Now, she would never see her aunt again. And her dear mother had been gone for a decade, a victim of cancer. Her poor father — with his silly ideas about "childlike" Negroes — had never really gotten over her mother's death. Perhaps, she too was in danger of never getting over John's death — never moving on. Looking back, she feared her father had been right about at least one thing that day long ago: her bad judgment had almost gotten Sam killed. After that day, Emily realized, she had begun increasingly to doubt her own decisions and instincts, to not trust herself.

But a new worry came crashing over her: had her rash decision to go off with Sam alone in some way led to problems for her aunt, then or later?

Perhaps Milton could help her sort out some things at least. Thank goodness he was in her life again. Emily certainly didn't feel like someone who was up to the tasks laid before her. From beyond the grave, her aunt had asked for her help and for Milton's, too—had told them, in essence, that she was depending on them. Emily expected she could handle the art show—although God knows what she was really getting into. But the whole thing about danger and her aunt's death—what could she possibly do that the police couldn't? She tried to push away Milton's concerns—and Maxwell's hints, too—that the investigation into Liz's death was not what it should have been. And what on earth was she going to tell Lewis about all this?

Almost as if Milton had heard her thoughts, he broke her reverie.

"You doin' okay, Miss Emily? You sure been quiet for a long time."

She looked up from the letter, where her eyes had been fixed, and realized Milton's old Cadillac was almost at Eola Lodge.

"Lost in the past, I guess. I was thinking about that day out at the river when all that craziness began—that's how you described it, I think, Mr. Armistead. It's been coming back to me. Do you hear from Sam, by the way?"

"Not as much as I'd like," said Milton, steering the car into the driveway of the house. "He's done real well, though—works for the NAACP. Lives in New York City, just like you."

"I liked him," she began, but the rest of her words died in her throat when she saw the black-beetle Ford, parked on the other side of the road in the next block.

Chapter 6

The Terrible Terraplane Lives

"THAT DAMNABLE black Ford left us again, as I was parking the Cadillac," said Milton as he came into the kitchen. "I aim to find out just who that is, Miss Emily, and what kind of game he's playing at."

"How will you do that?" Emily gathered up the papers Judge Stimpson had given her, along with the telegram from Lewis that she'd dropped on the table.

"Oh, I've got my sources," said Milton. "I've even thought about becoming a private eye. Always been a nosy son of a gun. Speaking of which, Miss Emily—that telegram the Judge gave you—I hope it wasn't bad news. Seems like they often are."

"Oh, that! No. Supposedly good news," said Emily, laughing. "Would you believe, Mr. Armistead, there's a man back in New York who is desperate to marry me?"

"I most definitely would believe it. And after he hears about that will and how rich you'll be, I bet he'll be even more desperate." Milton shot her a grin and Emily laughed in spite of herself.

"I'm glad you can make jokes, but I want to talk about the will and what we should do next," she said, as Milton slid into a seat, before plates of chicken salad and sliced tomatoes, with more tall glasses of iced tea. It seemed to be the fuel that kept Florida going. And all of it was thanks to Mattie, who had vanished to the other room with the Hoover vacuum. "And I want to ask you about my aunt's car—the Terraplane."

"That one's easy," he said. "It's in the garage out back."

The kitchen was quiet except for the whir of the ceiling fan overhead and the dull roar of the Hoover rumbling from the living room.

Emily took a long sip of cold tea and looked at Milton. "Well,

Mr. Armistead, what comes next? It looks as though you and I are in this together, thanks to my aunt—if we do think there's evidence that her death was suspicious."

Milton leaned forward, his dark eyes fixed on her as she continued.

"You said something yesterday about how you felt Aunt Liz was speaking to you from beyond the grave, asking for your help. It turns out you were right. She really has asked us to find out what happened. And it sounds like Detective Maxwell did have questions about the fire—whether it was an accident," Emily added.

She was surprised to feel tears welling up, but she went on, fighting them back.

"Aunt Liz asked me to help her. She felt she could depend on me, but I really haven't been someone she could depend on."

"Now, Miss Emily," Milton began. From his pants pocket, he produced yet another pressed handkerchief. "Here, this is clean—I swear."

Emily blew into the handkerchief, thinking it smelled like Milton. Old Spice?

"Thank you," she said. "Always prepared." Her shoulders shook with laughter along with the tears that were really coming now.

"After that day at the river—maybe you already know?—but after that, my father forbade me to come here to visit my aunt, and I guess I just blindly followed his wishes—his 'ban' on visits to Aunt Liz. I saw her in New York, but not often enough."

"She understood, Miss Emily," Milton said in a low voice. "She never blamed you."

"But it made no sense. Why didn't I question it? Why didn't I argue with him? And if Liz was in danger, why didn't any of us know about it?"

Milton's gaze was intense, but his eyes were kind.

"She knew you had a busy life, Miss Emily. She wanted you to have a busy life. Hell—excuse me, ma'am, I was right here in town, and if something was bothering her, she sure didn't tell me about it. And that hurts plenty, I can tell you."

"Yes, I can understand that," said Emily. "I didn't mean to hog all the guilty feelings for myself." She gave him a rueful smile. "She did always arrange to see me, at least once a year, sometimes twice."

"That's right," said Milton. "She would take the train to New York, wouldn't she? I used to drive her to the station."

"Yes, or we would meet someplace else—that wasn't so easy during the war. She was such a wonderful traveling companion that, in retrospect, I probably didn't want to trade any of those adventures for a trip here."

"Sure, that makes sense," said Milton.

"And the truth is—I think I just realized this today—after that day out on the river when those awful men showed up—well, maybe deep down I was scared to come back."

They sat for what seemed a long time, with the hum of Mattie's vacuuming in background, until Emily broke the silence.

"About Sam—I wanted to say before that he seemed like such a fine person, and so smart."

"Oh, he's that," said Milton. "Smart and determined. Wants to change the world. His mother—my sister—worries about his NAACP work, and so do I. It takes him to some dangerous places."

"It's wonderful he's been able to follow his goals."

"That's true. I'll tell him you asked about him, Miss Emily. You didn't do anything wrong that day, you know. Only people in the wrong were those Kluxers."

He got up and started to clear the table, turning to look at her over his shoulder.

"But to get back to your first question, Miss Emily," he said, "how do we begin?"

"Maybe we should begin at the beginning—go out to the fish camp where she died," Emily said, her brows knitted into a frown. "Detective Maxwell said he was told not to go there, but who could stop us? I must own that land now, or will when Judge Stimpson completes the necessary papers."

"It will be sad to see it again," said Milton, rinsing their plates, "and I'm not sure what we'll learn—but it's as good a place to start as any. Sunday might be a good time."

"Good, let's plan on it," Emily nodded.

"Anything else I should know about your telegram man?"

"For now, let's just say I like being single, I guess."

"An independent lady like your auntie." Milton smiled and opened the kitchen cupboard nearest the back door, where neatly labeled keys hung on a rack.

"You asked about your aunt's car—the Terraplane," he said. "You got some good wings to fly there. It is indeed in the garage, and the key's right here."

"It's a newer model than she had back when you visited her, Miss Emily, but still a Terraplane. You know who's its biggest fan? Young Billy. I wouldn't be surprised if you'll see him after school, by the way."

"He's something," said Emily. "It seems he's part of my aunt's rich legacy to me."

"Better believe it, Miss Emily." Suddenly, his voice sounded much louder, because the roar in the living room had stopped.

"Praise be, that hellacious old Hoover is finally quiet," said Milton. "I'd better get going. Time for me to give Mrs. Sayles a ride home and hit the train station for the afternoon rush. Mrs. Sayles, you ready?" he called into the living room, and Mattie appeared, an envelope in hand.

"I almost forgot, Miss Emily," she said as she gathered up her purse. "An invitation came for you. Hand delivered by that Spanish fellow who works for Mr. Sloane. Very elegant."

"The man or the invitation?"

"Both, I'd say," said Mattie. She handed a cream-colored envelope to Emily.

"I expect that's Juan, Sloane's assistant," said Milton. "I'll be interested to hear what's in that envelope," he added as he and Maddie made their exit with his parting words: "Don't forget to lock the back door."

She waved them goodbye and plopped down on her aunt's old sofa in front of the living-room fan to open the elegant invitation, written in a distinctive, left-slanting hand. Mr. Julian Sloane requested the pleasure of her company for cocktails on the following evening at his studio, it said, and included a phone number for regrets only.

A note had been added at the bottom: "Miss Washington — Emily — I join you in grief at the loss of dear Elizabeth," it read. "I so look forward to seeing you again. It's been a very long time. J.S."

She searched her memories for when she could possibly have met Julian Sloane. She had heard her aunt mention him, of course. He was a painter and sculptor who had founded a winter artists' colony of sorts on the shores of a large lake near the city. As Emily remembered it, he had come to Florida because of her aunt, who had known him for many years, since they were young art students. It seemed odd such a close friend hadn't garnered a mention in her will, but he probably already had plenty of money, Emily guessed. Perhaps he could shed some light on her aunt's death and any fears her aunt might have expressed in the weeks before.

She put the invitation down on the coffee table, now gleaming with lemony polish after Mattie's ministrations. She resolved to ask Milton to drive her to this party at Julian Sloane's, but it was indeed time to investigate her aunt's car. She couldn't keep always depending on Milton to get around, and, besides, she liked to drive and had a license, although she was a little out of practice. She would think twice about taking the wheel on a Manhattan street.

She went to the fridge to get some more iced tea, and inside it found what appeared to be a peanut butter and jelly sandwich and a glass of milk, with a note neatly laid on top with pencil letters reading "For Billy" — clearly, Mattie's doing. And sure enough, just then she heard a knock at the back door and a high voice calling out "Yoo-hoo, Miss Emily, it's Billy Mizell. Do you need me to get any groceries for you? I used to do that for Miss Lizzie."

Looking at the clock, she noted that it was indeed time for school to be over. She wondered where the school was. Hearing the boy's voice, she was surprised at her reaction. She had been looking forward to a nap, and she wasn't someone who warmed to children much — in fact, she found some of her New York friends' youngsters a bit of a trial, full of precocious self-absorption. But she was glad to see Billy again. He was different from the children she had known at home. He seemed so direct and tough — not an ounce of guile in him.

"Mr. Mizell," she said with pretend seriousness, as she opened the back door. "I believe there's a sandwich here, with your name on it — literally. Come on in, and we'll talk about this grocery business."

"Thanks, Miss Emily. Miss Mattie is the best," the boy said as he sat down and tucked into the sandwich. "She puts a whole lotta jelly on the sandwich. There's probably some cookies, too," he added, pointing to a large pottery cookie jar on the counter.

Emily shook her head as she looked inside the cookie jar, smelled fresh-baked oatmeal cookies, and handed Billy two of them, helping herself to a third. She sat down facing him.

"Just where would you get these groceries?" she asked. "If I'm going to send you to a store for orders billed to an account, maybe I'd better go to the grocer's and introduce myself."

"Aw, old man DiMartini will believe me," Billy said. Seeing Emily's frown, he added, "I mean Mr. DiMartini. The store's just up the street. He's real nice, actually. But, sure, I can take you there. Miss Elizabeth got her groceries from him for a long time."

Emily thought a moment. "Let me ask you about something else, Mr. In-the-Know," she said. "Mr. Armistead tells me my aunt's car is in the garage, and you are quite the expert on it. I'd like to give it a spin, for practice. I don't want to keep depending on him for transportation."

At that, Emily thought Billy looked almost as though she had said that Santa Claus and President Truman would be landing together in the backyard in a helicopter any minute.

"The terrible, terrific Terraplane," he yelled. "Oh Miss Emily, she's a beauty. Can I ride with you? Aw please."

In a rush of words, Emily learned that her aunt's green Hudson Terraplane was as much a local institution as her aunt had been. It was a 1938 model, the last year the Terraplane had been made—a sporty convertible that exuded style and speed. Her aunt had bought it in part because Amelia Earhart, whom her aunt adored, had once helped advertise the Terraplane, Emily remembered. The family who owned the gas station just a block away, near DiMartini's store, had babied it and kept it in good shape, Billy said. He had even memorized one of the more memorable advertising slogans for the cars, which he exuberantly repeated for her: "On the sea that's aquaplaning, in the air that's aeroplaning, but on the land, in the traffic, on the hills, hot diggity dog, that's terraplaning!"

Lewis would love that zany slogan and love the car, she thought, remembering that she had intended to call him. But just now, he and New York seemed far away, and the Terrible Terraplane was calling.

With Billy almost dancing behind her, Emily crossed the backyard to the garage, where they found a large shape swathed in a tarpaulin. When they yanked it off, they found the green convertible gleaming, just as Billy had promised. The tires looked solid and the gas tank full, and after a couple of tries, the car started right up. When Emily gingerly backed it out of the garage, its chrome trim sparkled in the sun. The Hudson was not the kind of car one expected a woman of a certain age to drive, Emily thought as she and Billy worked to get the top down, but her aunt had never conformed to expectations. Neither did she, Emily hoped.

Billy climbed in beside her, and they headed down the driveway. Emily squinted in the late afternoon light—she didn't care for dark glasses, but she would have to get some now that she was in Florida, she thought—the Sunshine State, and with a vengeance. But the glasses would be a small price to pay for driving this car.

All of a sudden, Emily felt much more at home. The sensations of the late-afternoon breeze in her hair and the sun on her shoulders were simply grand. She snapped on the radio and found an oldies station with the Tommy Dorsey Band playing "Song of India" from before the war. At the wheel of the Terraplane, Emily did feel almost as if she were flying along the ground, the pilot of her own ship, captain of her own destiny. She found herself laughing out loud—something she had not done in a very long time.

Joining Emily's exhilaration, Billy waved his arms in the air. "Yahoo, the terrible Terraplane lives," he called over the music, as they zipped out onto the now-empty street in front of Eola Lodge. For this moment, at least, her worries about her aunt's death, about Lewis and his proposal, and about that damnable beetle-black Ford, all vanished in the warm breeze—especially when a quick check confirmed that ominous vehicle was nowhere in sight.

Chapter 7

In the Cemetery

THE RUSH OF PLEASURE Emily felt behind the wheel of her aunt's old Terraplane might have carried them all the way to Miami, but suddenly an idea came to her about a closer destination that didn't exactly fit with a joy-riding spirit or the swinging music on the radio.

"I'll tell you where I'd like to go, Billy," Emily said. "I'd like to visit my aunt's grave at the city cemetery. Do you know the way?"

"Sure, Miss Emily." Billy turned to look at her, his blue eyes now serious. "It's not far at all. I take a shortcut on my bike through there all the time."

Following his directions, Emily drove through the tiny business district that lay just east of Eola Lodge. They passed a service station and what looked like a neighborhood bar and grill. She recognized DiMartini's grocery, where Billy had picked up orders for her aunt. Under the cheery striped awning that shaded the entrance, a man wearing a white butcher's apron waved to Billy as they passed. Emily joined in waving back.

"That's Mr. DiMartini," Billy hollered over the wind, as she nodded. "He's from New York City, just like you," the boy went on. "He sells stuff you can't get in the Publix or the Piggly Wiggly, Mr. Milton says. Cold cuts and stuff. He saves grape sodas for me. Once he even let me have a taste of wine he had. But don't tell my daddy—or Mr. Milton."

"You don't say," said Emily, suppressing a smile.

"I thought it was crummy—grape soda's much better—but I didn't tell Mr. DiMartini that. I didn't want to hurt his feelings."

"I like the way you think, Billy."

Emily was still buoyed by the fun of driving again and listening to Billy's chatter, but her mood darkened and her heart skipped when she looked in the rearview mirror and saw the black Ford about a block behind her, with no other cars between them. Despite the warmth, she felt a chill race up her spine. She looked over at her young companion.

"Billy, I'm guessing you don't miss much about what goes on in this neighborhood," she said. "Don't turn around, but if you can, look in the mirror on your side of the car at the black car that's behind us. Have you ever seen it before?"

"Wow, Miss Emily, do you think it's following us? This could be like a movie, you know, about somebody like Al Capone."

"Trust me—it's not Scarface. I just thought it might be a friend of my aunt's," she lied, feeling a bit guilty at her deception.

Billy was well into his G-man fantasy. He slid down in his seat and peered into the Hudson's big right-hand rearview mirror.

"I can tell you one thing for sure," he said. "That car's from Tampa."

"How do you know?"

"Easy! You can tell by the number 3 on the license plate. Plates from around here begin with a 7—like that, see?" He pointed to a car parked on the street.

She looked in the mirror again and saw the Ford still at least a block behind her. Her heart was racing. An independent spirit was all very well, but she would have felt better if Milton were with them.

"Now that you mention it, Miss Emily," he said in a low voice. "I think I did see a car like that parked on your street earlier today. And I don't think he's any friend of Miss Elizabeth's."

She turned to look at the boy, who had grown quiet.

"Well, let's see if our mystery Ford back there wants to come along to visit a graveyard," she said, trying for an expression she hoped looked brave and adventurous. But Billy's spirit of adventure seemed to have evaporated, too.

"I hope you don't mind going to the cemetery," she said to him. "I didn't even really ask you."

"Oh no," he said. "I don't mind. I go there a lot. My mama's buried there. Sometimes my daddy goes, too, but I don't think he likes to."

Emily felt a pang at the thought of the boy sitting by his mother's grave, alone. She tried to recall what Milton had said—he had mentioned a father who sounded a little sketchy but nothing about a lost mother. No wonder Aunt Liz had taken the boy in.

"Billy, I'm so sorry about your mother." She was both chagrined at herself that she hadn't thought to ask more about his family and nervous as she looked back at the Ford in the rearview mirror. She had taken a right turn and followed Billy's direction, and the Ford had turned too. The fear she felt was now giving way to anger.

Damnation, Emily thought. What could this guy possibly want? You'd have to be pretty dim to not realize he was there, after all, following her. Maybe that was the point—to spook her. She'd much rather be giving Billy her full attention.

"It's okay, Miss Emily—about my mama. She's been gone a long time," he said, in an even quieter voice. "She got sick, real sick. I was just little. I have a picture of her in my mind, though, and I have a photo, too. I copied it to draw a picture of her."

"So you are an artist, too," said Emily, distracted by her rising anger at the driver of the black Ford and his intrusion into this quiet world of memory and grief. The boy only nodded.

Both Emily and Bill were silent for a moment as she drove on, under a canopy of trees with their ever-present drapery of Spanish moss, thinking about how long it had been since she'd visited her own mother's grave, and how estranged she'd become from her father. Looking in the mirror, she saw no sign of the Ford.

Billy pointed to a sign for the cemetery on the left, and she turned and guided the car through open gates into a green expanse broken only by more large oaks and by monuments of various sizes and by gravestones. The cemetery was called Greenwood, a sign said.

She stopped the Terraplane and left the engine running quietly but turned the car radio off, so it would be easier to hear the low rumble of another car if its driver had decided to follow them. The hush of the cemetery enveloped them. The green garden of the dead, she thought. Billy deserved her attention, and she pushed away her fears about the Ford. Surely, she was letting her imagination run away with her.

"My mother has been gone a long time, too—she died when I was in college. She got sick, too."

"So you know sort of what it's like," he said. "Where's your mama buried?"

"Up in New York, on Long Island." She pictured the family plot where generations of her family were expected to end their life journeys.

"It's surprising, really, that Aunt Liz isn't buried there," she continued, more to herself than to Billy. "Surely there was a space reserved for her."

Her voice had trailed away, as she wondered if the feud between her father and Aunt Liz had extended even into death.

"It's just a little way ahead to where Miss Elizabeth is buried," Billy said. "There's no gravestone yet. It's a real pretty spot."

Just then, Emily looked in the rearview mirror to see the beetle Ford entering the cemetery gates, creeping slowly. She turned around a sharp curve in the paved road that wound through the thick lawn of the cemetery and stopped the car. Suddenly, the anger that had been fighting with her fear had won. She had had enough of this—of this guy following them and harassing them, clearly worrying Billy as well as her.

The narrow one-way road had room for only one lane. The driver of the Ford wouldn't be able to see the Hudson until he was right behind her, she thought as she threw the car in neutral, yanked up the parking brake, and got out of the car.

Billy looked at her, his eyes wide. "Miss Emily, what are you doing?"

"I'm not really sure, Billy," she said, "but I'm tired of not doing very much."

"Don't—" he started, but she was marching away and didn't hear whether he finished whatever he was going to say.

Sure enough, in a few seconds, the Ford appeared right behind her, the driver's way blocked by the Hudson on the narrow road. The windows were rolled down in the heat, and she saw the driver pretty clearly now, although his face was shaded by his fedora.

Emily had the strange feeling that she was watching someone else move toward the driver's door, but hers was indeed the voice who called out to him, "Excuse me, but do I know you? You seem to be following me."

The man made no answer but shot her a look she wouldn't forget. Then he put the car in reverse and skillfully backed around the curve until she couldn't see the Ford. She did hear its tires squeal, and as she walked, she looked around the curve and saw it turn around on a grassy spot near the entrance and speed out of the cemetery gates.

As she got back behind the wheel of the Hudson, Emily realized she was shaking. After a minute sitting in silence, she heard Billy's voice.

"Holy cow, Miss Emily, that was scary," he said.

They sat in silence in the Hudson for a minute. A late afternoon breeze stirred the trees nearby but had little effect on the heat. A bead of sweat ran down her nose. She wiped it away and looked at Billy. She felt numb, but also strangely exhilarated.

"He's gone," she said. "Nothing to be scared of."

But the color had drained from his face, and his thin shoulders were tense.

"I should have told you, Miss Emily. I think I do know who that man is. I think his name is Marvin. And if what I heard on my bolita route is right, his job is killing people."

"What?" This had to be a dream, a bad one.

"That may not be right, Miss Emily. That man may be somebody else," Billy went on. "And even if he's who they say, there's no reason he'd kill us."

Oh my god, Emily thought, Billy's words echoing in her mind—his job is killing people. Milton had suggested that someone had killed her aunt, and she herself had her own suspicions. What had she been thinking in challenging her creepy shadow in the Ford, especially after Detective Maxwell had told her to be careful? Had she turned into some kind of stereotypical, privileged New Yorker, thinking she knew better than the locals? And she had a child with her. She was responsible for more than herself. She felt chilled to the bone, in spite of the heat.

Billy looked up at her.

"Don't worry, Miss Emily. He really is gone. And we're almost to Miss Elizabeth's grave," he said. "We can't go home now. It's over that little hill there. We can walk from here."

She pulled the car off the road onto a patch of grass under a tree, and they both got out of the Hudson, closing the doors quietly. Billy took her hand and led her across the grass, between headstones, some very old. They passed a stone angel, its hands poised in prayer, and markers for sections where veterans of both the Union and Confederate armies rested.

The reality of her aunt's death descended on Emily, like a heaviness that joined the cold fear she already felt wrapped around her heart. But what was the truth behind it? How and why had Elizabeth Washington met death, and what, if anything, did the man in the Ford—the man Billy said killed people—have to do with it? Why was he following her?

"It's just over there," Billy pointed as they neared the top of the small grassy hill. "There's a bench we can sit on right by it."

But as they approached, Emily felt a jolt of adrenaline again when someone was already there—she'd seen no other cars—and was occupying the graceful wrought iron bench facing the obviously fairly new grave, topped with a mound of sandy earth where grass was just starting to grow. On the grave lay a single red rose. And on the bench, Emily recognized now as they approached, sat Milton Armistead, his head bowed and his eyes closed. His snap-brim straw hat rested on his lap. Perhaps sensing their presence, he opened his eyes.

"Well my goodness, what a surprise," Milton said as he smiled, his voice low. "Your aunt would be so happy you're here, Miss Emily. You, too, young Mr. Mizell."

He stood by and nodded at the bench.

"Here, y'all have a seat—there's plenty of room," Milton said. "I need to stretch anyhow."

Emily realized she was still holding Billy's hand and released it as they sat down.

"We'll need to get a headstone for her," Emily said, swallowing hard and feeling tears ready to come, whatever residual anger she felt over having been followed washing away as new emotions flooded her. "Coming here, it's all suddenly so real to me."

"I know," said Milton. "Believe me, I know."

He knelt down next to Emily, letting silence surround the three of them for a moment. Then Emily began to talk, her voice still almost a whisper, telling Milton how she had gotten the Hudson on the road and had wanted to visit her aunt's grave. She wasn't going to mention the Ford—what would Milton think about her rash behavior?—but Billy was already diving into those murky waters.

"We were followed, Mr. Milton," he forged ahead while Emily looked at her feet. "It was that black Ford with the Tampa license plate we talked about."

Shocked, Emily turned to look at him.

"Then you knew more about that car than you let on, Billy," Emily said.

"Not much, Miss Emily, honest. I didn't want to worry you. But Mr. Milton, I saw the driver this time, and I think it's someone I heard Uncle Carter talking about—and he's a really, really bad man."

"Well, we are three really, really good folks," said Milton, "and whatever's going on, I'll bet you got more smarts in your little finger, Billy, than one of these mob jerks. They're worried about bigger money than we got, even Miss Emily Moneybags here."

Emily managed a smile. But she remembered the driver of the

Ford, looking at her with dead, expressionless eyes. Fish eyes. She felt a shiver, and it had nothing to do with being in a graveyard or with the dark clouds she noticed were gathering.

"Here comes another one of our late-afternoon thunderstorms," Milton said. "Remember I told you yesterday to give our Florida lightning some respect? Part of that is knowing not to be under a big ol' tree when you hear thunder coming your way."

Emily looked up at the slate-colored sky and heard the rumblings moving closer. Perhaps Milton's warning applied to more than electric danger from the sky. If a killer was following her, that put lightning in perspective, as frightening as it was.

Emily hated to leave so quickly, but the prospect of a storm didn't give them much choice. Milton stood up and offered his hand to Emily, and they followed Billy toward Emily's car. Milton said he'd left his taxi at the cemetery office and had walked over to the grave, so Emily dropped him off on the way out.

As Milton said goodbye, they agreed he would drive Emily to Julian Sloane's party the next day. She found it hard to think ahead, surrounded by the green finality of the cemetery, but clearly, there was work to be done. The confrontation with the man in the beetle Ford had convinced her of that. She had to call Lewis as soon as she got back to the house, for one thing. A quick return to New York was out of the question, no matter how disappointed he might be.

The charge her aunt had set before her might be tinged with danger, if her own experience today and the hints in her aunt's letter were to be believed, or even her dream from the night before, of the scarab bracelet and its protection. But she would not shrink from her duty, just as she had not backed down from the Ford's driver. It was the least she could do for her aunt and, besides, she was no longer a girl. She had known other deep losses and had seen her countrymen and women defeat a force of unspeakable evil in the Nazis. Despite her fear, whatever was needed to take on her aunt's quest, Emily felt ready. It was time to begin.

Chapter 8

A Call About a Killer

BACK AT EOLA LODGE, Emily waved Billy off toward home, where he said his father would be waiting. The boy disappeared into the silvery palmettos that lined the path through the trees, and she felt a sense of unease wash over her as she looked up at the big, empty house, silhouetted against darkening skies. The storm that had driven them from the cemetery was taking its time arriving, producing only distant rumbles. Soon, though, it would be time for the bolts of lightning that could strike you dead, even inside your house, to hear Milton tell it. The sunny brochures about Florida sure kept the dark parts of this paradise under wraps. What other secrets lay in wait?

She grappled with the key and rushed upstairs to check the windows and make sure everything was secure. Moving from room to room, she peeked inside the closets, her heart pounding. Just what did she expect to find? Fish-eyed Marvin lurking in the linens? Steady, old girl, she told herself as she went back downstairs, looking for anything that might seem out of place. Her eyes fell on one of her aunt's paintings, above the mantelpiece, that didn't seem quite straight. Chiding herself for being neurotic, she reached up and adjusted it, increasingly aware of her aunt's large, black telephone perched on a small table next to a wicker chair. She could almost hear it talking to her. Avoiding me, Emily? Yes, guilty as charged.

It was partly that she didn't really love telephone chats, period. She liked to see a person's reactions during a conversation, especially an important one. But she already knew how Lewis would react to her news—that she would not be bouncing right back to New York, as he had assumed. He would not be happy, and Emily liked to make people happy. But surely Lewis would understand her duties to her aunt. He was big on duty, too. And Milton's fears that her aunt had been murdered? She wouldn't be getting into that.

So she reached for the phone, but when her eyes fell on the business card she had tucked next to it — Detective Joe Maxwell's card — she found herself dialing his number first. She wasn't just procrastinating about Lewis, she told herself. After all, if you're being followed and you learn — even if it's from a ten-year-old boy — that your pursuer is a paid killer, you don't have to be Einstein to figure out it's a good idea to tell the police. She should definitely tell Maxwell about the black Ford and her confrontation with this Marvin, its supposedly evil driver.

Emily dialed the number carefully and then stopped. Maxwell would almost certainly be off duty by now. But she pressed ahead, remembering his words — "call me any time, day or night" — and redialed, this time using the at-home number he had written on the back of the card. To her surprise, he answered after just one ring.

"Oh, Detective Maxwell," she began with some hesitation. "It's Emily Washington. We talked this morning? I apologize for calling you at home."

"No need to apologize, ma'am. I told you to do just that. Any more open doors?"

"No, thank goodness," she said. "It's just this: There's been a black Ford parked near the house. It followed Mr. Armistead and me this morning, and this afternoon it followed me to the cemetery."

"To the cemetery?"

"Yes. I wanted to visit my aunt's grave. Billy Mizell helped me get her old Hudson started up and rode along with me to show me the way. And Billy said he thought he knew who the driver might be." Even to her own ears, she sounded like a babbling idiot.

"Go on," said Maxwell, "what did the boy say?"

"He said the car's from Tampa. The driver — well, someone told Billy the driver was a paid killer. Mr. Armistead seemed to take it all seriously."

There was a pause. Her heart thudded hard against her chest, and a knot twisted in her stomach. She was torn between thinking he couldn't possibly take her seriously, on the one hand, and grasping that she had just said "paid killer" on the other. What had she been thinking in challenging that man?

"I'm feeling a little sheepish," she said, breaking the silence. "Maybe I've watched too many Humphrey Bogart movies."

"Don't sell yourself short, Miss Washington. Did you happen to catch the license plate number?"

Oh, goodness. He was actually taking her seriously. Emily's art training had made her a keen observer, and she had in fact memorized the number and written it down when she got home. Now, she recited it for Maxwell, beginning with the 3 for Hillsborough County, home of Tampa.

"Good girl!" said Maxwell, and Emily was surprised to find her face flushing. She was pleased at the detective's praise, even if he had called her a "girl"—something she had always found irritating.

"I got a look at him, too," she finally said into the awkward silence. "I spoke to him, actually—but he didn't reply. He just turned the Ford around and headed out of the cemetery . . ."

"I'll bet he did. Any sign of him now?"

"No." Emily rose from her chair and peered out the window near the telephone table. She saw no cars parked on the street.

"Good," said the detective. "Anything else you remember from this adventure?"

"Billy said he thought his name was Marvin. No last name. Not exactly a Humphrey Bogart kind of name."

"Names can be deceptive." Something in Maxwell's voice sent an icy feeling up her spine. Did he know something about this Marvin? Was Marvin someone who might sneak into the house and murder her in her bed? But the detective's next words sounded calm and reassuring.

"If you see a police car around later, don't worry. I'm going to call the station and have one of our patrol teams give your place a little extra attention tonight."

"Thank you, Detective. I appreciate that."

She had felt a bit foolish, but she was glad she had called him. Whatever was going on, at least she had a competent police officer on her side. And Maxwell had not chided her for any of her actions, either, or told her to leave it all to him, the way her father or Lewis probably would.

"Do you have anything planned for tomorrow?"

"Mostly just unpacking," said Emily. "In the late afternoon, I'm going to a party at Julian Sloane's—an old friend of my aunt's. Mr. Armistead's going to be my chauffeur and unofficial bodyguard, I guess."

"Good," came the response again. Another pause. Emily found herself having to stifle a sudden, absurd impulse to ask him if he wanted to come along to the party.

"It looks like I'll be here a few months," she said instead, returning to the present moment. "There's a lot to take care of with my aunt's estate."

"I expect there is," he said.

She didn't say any more about what the "caretaking" would involve, such as snooping around to find out if her aunt had been killed. Emily liked Maxwell, but she was sure he wouldn't be keen on her playing detective on her own—even if he hadn't reprimanded her this time.

"I think you'll find it's a nice town," he said. "Good people—like Milton. And young Billy, too. Your aunt's friend Sloane is quite a big fish, by the way. Should be an interesting crowd at your party."

He had mentioned Billy, she noted, but not Billy's father—a man she realized she was picturing as a version of Huck Finn's Pap, an abusive town drunk, maybe with a scruffy beard and bad teeth. From what Billy had said, though, his father had gone along to visit Billy's mother's grave. If he were as bad as Huck's Pap, how could he even have attracted a wife? Another mystery, she thought, as Maxwell's voice came through the line, closing the conversation.

"I'm glad you called, Miss Washington," he said. "Do make

sure you lock the doors and try not to worry. And if you see that Ford, or anything else that makes you uneasy, call me as soon as you can."

Emily assured him that she would, looked at the clock, and got ready to face the music with Lewis. She got up, stretched, and padded in her slippers to both the front and back doors, making sure again that they were indeed locked. Checking the street through a crack between curtains, she saw the streetlight's violet glow, but no beetle Ford in sight. A few raindrops had come down, but the storm still seemed to be at a distance. You're perfectly safe, old girl, she told herself. Soon, she would probably spy one of the patrol cars Maxwell was sending to keep an eye on the place. All was well—so why did she feel so queasy?

Maybe she was just hungry. After all, it wouldn't be a bad idea to get a bite before she called Lewis. In the kitchen, Emily turned on the radio for company, made herself a sandwich, and poured a glass of milk before sitting down at the yellow table. She browsed through the newspaper while she ate. Turning to the women's pages, she noticed local ads featuring the same "New Look" styles she'd seen advertised in New York, with the longer, fuller skirts that had been impossible during the war and its fabric shortages. Christian Dior, wasn't it? Lewis would know, she bet.

On the same page, she was surprised to see a familiar face next to the byline of an "about town" column—goings and comings of the local worthies. It had to be the same Maureen—a friend during Emily's girlhood visits. Despite the years, she looked much the same in the small black-and-white photo, although in real life, her lovely long hair was auburn red. So, she had at least one more old friend here. It would be fun to reconnect with Maureen.

She rinsed her dishes and headed back to the telephone, heaving a sigh as she plopped down again in the big wicker chair and moved the heavy phone to her lap once more to finally call Lewis—the man who claimed he wanted desperately to marry her. Then why wasn't she eager to talk with him? She held her breath as the long-distance operator connected her.

"Are you all right, Darling?" Lewis exclaimed, and her dread gave way to a smile as he launched breathlessly into a humorous account of his boredom in her absence.

Emily had known that voice now for such a long time, since their college days, and Lewis had always been able to make her laugh better than anyone. She remembered the droll look he'd shot her once in art history class when a particularly pompous lecturer referred to Albert Bierstadt's Yosemite paintings as depicting "Yosa-might." Lately, though, he seemed to have lost some of his old sense of fun — but who hadn't since the war? He fretted a great deal and constantly questioned her behavior. So, even as she warmed to his opening ramble, she bristled at his next question.

"Why didn't you call yesterday? I've been worried."

"Good grief," said Emily. "Don't be silly." As if she were not a grown woman who could take care of herself. But if he only knew. What would he think about Marvin in the fedora and the black-beetle Ford? Truth be told, she did have plenty to worry about, actually.

"Come on, Pooh," said Lewis, using the ancient nickname that for some reason they both called each other, although neither could remember why. "Of course I worried. There are alligators in Florida, for god's sake, and snakes. One of Father's friends has a hunting lodge there, and he says it's a wilderness where wild hogs run loose."

"Silly Old Bear," said Emily. "I miss you, by the way."

"And you know I miss you," he said. But his "wilderness" comment had struck a nerve.

"Lewis, I'd say the real hogs in Florida are the folks — like some of your father's hunting buddies — who keep rooting around here for more money from their real estate deals, no matter how much they already have."

"Ouch. Calm down, Mrs. Roosevelt," Lewis laughed. "I didn't mean to rouse your sense of social justice. Let's start over. Have I told you lately that I love you madly — and that you're a paragon of beauty and talent?"

"You shameless flatterer," she said, smiling in spite of herself. "You're impossible—and I truly have missed you."

She felt a little guilty about her pleasure in talking with Maxwell earlier, and now she reminded herself about the many things she liked about Lewis. He was a fabulous companion at parties, and on their travels, he was ready to try any museum, any new restaurant—well, almost any. She enjoyed shopping with him, too, even for clothes. He could spot a rare find or good fit for her that she might ordinarily overlook.

On those travels, more than anything, they enjoyed the easy familiarity of people who had known each other in their youth, and who had been through some bumpy times together—including the death of Emily's mother. It was on a trip, to Europe, that Emily had begun to take his proposals more seriously. But when Lewis was home in New York, it seemed to Emily that he became a different person—much less carefree and always under his father's fat thumb. That was the Lewis she had dreaded calling. That was the Lewis she wasn't keen to tell that she was possibly being followed by a hit man and that she'd decided to investigate her aunt's death.

"Truly, no need to worry, Pooh," she said, aiming to keep the tone light and chatty. "And you'll be happy to hear that it's quite civilized here. The newspaper is full of ads for the latest styles, a la Dior. I'll admit, though, that the roaches are gargantuan, and the lightning storms are apocalyptic."

"My god, it sounds dramatic," Lewis said. "But seriously, love of my life—and speaking of fashion, have you given any thought to your wedding gown? I'm picturing you in ivory silk with a train a mile long. You'll look divine."

Emily was glad he couldn't see her rolling her eyes.

"Dear Lewis." She slowed down her words for emphasis. "I'm not a dewy debutante. I hadn't even thought about that kind of wedding dress."

Virginal white—that was pretty rich—and Lewis knew it. More to the point, she had not ever actually said, "Yes, yes, I'll marry you." Sure, they had long ago made a humorous pact that if both of them hadn't found another partner by the time they were thirty, they'd tie the knot. They had killed a bottle of champagne with their toasts.

But in her heart of hearts, Emily had never taken their pact that seriously. Now, as she listened to Lewis elaborate more about what she might wear on the big day, it was clear that Lewis did. And whenever he brought up a wedding date, which he did with increasing frequency, she never really told him to get lost, had never wanted to end it. He was eminently eligible—just the kind of husband her family had wished for her. If she couldn't muster much excitement for the prospect, she assumed mostly that she just wasn't over John yet, if she ever would be. What did she really want, deep down?

"All right, enough about wedding dresses," Lewis said, and she yanked her mind back to the conversation. "How are you, really, Emily?"

"To tell you the truth, I'm fine—really—but I'm tired, and a little overwhelmed. It's been a long day. I saw my aunt's attorney, and it was a very interesting and surprising meeting."

"I'm all ears," said Lewis, and Emily believed him. He could be a good listener—at least about certain kinds of things. Money, for instance. Gossip, for another.

"Well, it looks like I'm inheriting quite a large estate," said Emily. "Judge Stimpson—he's the attorney—didn't give me exact figures yet, but it sounds as though I'll be able to engage in some serious philanthropy—do some real good, I hope. Maybe I'll set up a studio large enough to have students come to me—and I can paint whatever I please."

"Darling, after we're married, you'll never have to even think about working," he said, almost as if he hadn't heard a word.

Emily was glad that her aunt had installed a long cord on the telephone, because by now, she was on her feet, carrying the heavy phone and pacing back and forth like a speed walker.

"Lewis, we've talked about this so many times," she said, her voice rising. "Married or not, I'll still want to paint and show my work and teach, because I enjoy it. It's what I live for."

"And I want to use these new resources—what Aunt Liz has left me—to help other people, especially children," she went on, as Billy's face popped into view on her internal movie screen— "and I want to do that in ways other than arranging flowers for charity teas."

There was a long pause.

"Come on, Pooh." Lewis used his most reasonable voice. "That's a bit of a low blow about the charity teas. You know Poppy works hard for good causes."

He was talking about his mother, Pauline, whom everyone called Poppy, including Lewis. Emily's own family had never been one for nicknames. Thank goodness, she thought—she could have been Binky. She paced faster, almost snapping the phone cord and tried to calm down.

"I stand corrected," she said. "And I know you love Poppy very much."

"She is a sweetheart," Lewis went on, "and Lord knows, those teas give her something to do besides sneak sips from the sherry bottle. She gets very bored, I'm afraid." Then his voice took a more serious turn.

"I don't want you to be bored, Emily, when we're married. And you know I kid you out of love when I call you Mrs. Roosevelt, but your heroes don't have a monopoly on good works."

She sighed to herself about Lewis's views on politics, his parents' friends, and his lamentable Eleanor jokes. This probably wasn't the best time to take him to task on that score, though. Nor was it the best time to tell him that his mother's life was exactly the kind of life Emily did not want. Hell could freeze over first. Thank goodness, Lewis changed the subject.

"You just mentioned your aunt's lawyer," he said. "Did he give you my telegram?"

"Yes, he did," said Emily. "Why did you send it there, by the way?"

"You had given me that attorney's name, and I thought he could be trusted to get it to you." Was she imagining it, or was he really talking to her now like she was ten years old? She felt a knot growing tighter in her stomach. It was time to tell him she was staying for a while.

"Well, the attorney—Judge Stimpson—did get it to me, Lewis. That's why I called you. And I need to tell you the important thing I learned from him."

"I'm all ears."

"Good. Here it is," said Emily. "In order for me to inherit my aunt's estate and fulfill the wishes of her bequest, I'll have to stay here for a few months—I'll need to put together an art show, for one thing. So a fall wedding just isn't possible, Lewis—not if you want to marry a rich woman. And that could help both of us, I assume."

There was silence, for what seemed like a long time. Emily imagined how she might feel if Lewis were to say, "This is the last straw, Emily. I'm tired of waiting. I've been seeing Patsy van Rensselaer, by the way, and she's absolutely crazy about me."

Or was that Emily's real wish, she wondered—that Lewis would just go away. Good old Patsy, always fawning over him, would be a champ at charity teas. The truth was, Emily had been quite satisfied not to be married, satisfied with the arrangement she and Lewis had enjoyed.

She might torture herself with visions of Patsy replacing her, but she didn't like the idea of a wedding, either. But instead of reports about Patsy, Lewis steamrolled right over her, as usual.

"Are you really sure that's the case, Emily?" he said. "I'll bet that if I talked to this lawyer, we could straighten it all out. Surely someone else could do this art show."

"Judge Stimpson was perfectly clear: it has to be me who spearheads the art show."

"Emily, listen, it's just that a couple things have changed for me, too." Lewis's voice was suddenly solemn. No teasing, no cajoling.

"What's changed? You sound quite serious."

"I am, I'm afraid-. My father's come up with a kind of ultimatum—that we get married by the end of the year—or I can expect no partnership in the firm."

"What?"

"Yes, and he's not kidding, Pooh. Says I've played the 'bon vivant playboy' too long, as he describes it. Time to settle down and start a family. Otherwise, he and Poppy won't live to see their grandchildren, and on and on. Frankly, it all sounds a little grim, but with you it wouldn't be. We have fun together."

"But I don't understand why it can't wait a little longer," said Emily. "I'm sure if you just tell your father the details of my situation, he'll be even happier when he hears about my inheritance. You'll be marrying a regular Miss Moneybags."

But she knew that neither Lewis nor his papa would be happy to hear she also wanted to stay in Florida to find out whether her aunt had been murdered. Mum's the word on that, she thought.

"I'll admit I do like the sound of Miss Emily W. Moneybags," said Lewis. The lightness had returned to his voice.

"And Emily," he went on, "you don't have to understand Father's crazy reasoning—you just have to say 'Yes, I'll marry you,' and we'll get that Florida lawyer to find some wiggle room in your aunt's bequest, with the proper incentives. Father will help. He excels at that kind of thing."

I'll just bet he does, thought Emily.

"Now, get on the first train you can," Lewis rolled on, "and we can deal with this long distance from New York. We can be dining at Delmonico's before you know it. All those snakes and alligators and wild hogs will just be a bad memory."

And that was how it always went—with her never really challenging Lewis's pursuit of marriage. She was just so tired of always finding new ways of saying "not yet," and his never hearing it.

Emily had stopped pacing and had taken refuge again in the big wicker chair. She was getting nowhere with Lewis, and it was exhausting. Hearing the rain return and begin to pound the roof, she realized she was being rescued by the weather, at least for the moment. The thunderstorm had finally arrived.

"Actually, it's not the snakes and alligators—right now it's the lightning I need to worry about," she said.

"Lightning?"

"Yes, really, Lewis. It's starting to storm, and I need to get off the telephone. There's a great deal of lightning in this area, and it can even come through the phone wires, I'm told."

As if on cue, a thunderclap rumbled from the darkening sky.

"My god, I heard that," said Lewis. "That does sound serious. I hope that lightning can't travel all the way to New York."

"Yes, I do need to get off the phone. And, I'll confess, I'm pretty tired. I went to Aunt Liz's grave today, and it really sunk in that she's gone."

She went on before he could say anything.

"Believe me, I would love to see you, Lewis, and it won't be all that long. Perhaps when I get settled in, you can come down to visit." Was she just saying that to be agreeable, she wondered, to say what a good girl would say? Or would it truly be nice to have him there? Yes, she thought, it would—if he could be his old self.

There was an even louder roll of thunder, followed by a crackle on the phone line.

"Lewis, I absolutely must go—please try to understand," she said. "We'll talk again soon. Give my best to your parents."

"Will do—and Emily? Try to relax."

She said a final goodbye and hung up, but she didn't relax. She heard a sound coming from the kitchen and, once again, a chill moved up her spine. Getting up and moving fast to investigate, Emily discovered that it was only the screen door, slapping against the door frame in the breeze. She had locked the interior door but hadn't latched the screen door properly. As she secured it, she breathed in the damp, fragrant night air and turned on the back-porch light. The air was lush. It almost had mass, texture, form. And the daily rains felt cleansing and renewing.

Lewis would just have to understand. It really could be fun if he were here. He'd probably charm the pants off everyone at Sloane's party. But, as she climbed the old creaking stairs, she was more relieved than anything else to be on her own. She hadn't felt that way in a long time. Not since before she met John—whom she still missed so much. She had never seen his grave in Arlington Cemetery. If she were to go to the vast, green expanse, would she place a single red rose on his grave?

From her small traveling bag—the bag she had carried on the train with her —she drew a small silver frame containing the picture of a handsome, smiling man dressed in a uniform. John, not Lewis. If she looked hard at herself, she thought, she had not been fair to Lewis. She had been selfish in welcoming his companionship to escape her grief about John.

Deep down, she knew that the only real problem with Lewis wasn't his mother or his father or his propensity to not take her seriously, really seriously —it was simply that Lewis wasn't John and would never be John. She had taken a risk in loving John, and the hurt and grief were so great that she couldn't take that risk again.

She put the picture of John on her aunt's dressing table, amid several small framed photos her aunt had placed there. One was a picture of Emily as a girl. John's picture fit right in with the group. Anyone who saw it would think it was a photograph of her aunt's. Even after all this time, she felt that she had to keep her love affair with a married man secret. Silly goose, she thought.

Her eyes traveled to one of the larger pictures on the dressing table, showing a group of people somewhere on a beach, under a large umbrella. There was Aunt Liz, looking glamorous and impossibly young in a free-flowing kimono, worn over an old-fashioned bathing costume. She stood between two men, one of them posing humorously, flexing his muscles, body-builder style. The other man looked oddly familiar—piercing dark eyes.

She turned the frame over and saw a label, lettered in her aunt's distinctive hand: "On the beach in France with Julian, visiting P.P." So one of these men was Julian Sloane, Emily thought— her host tomorrow night. He and her aunt truly had been friends for a long time. And who was P.P., she wondered? She looked again, catching her breath. It couldn't be — but it did look like him. Pablo Picasso. My god, no wonder he looked familiar.

Her head spinning, Emily collapsed on the bed again. Had her aunt really known Picasso? Why didn't you tell me, Aunt Liz, and what else did you never tell me? She thought of all the things she wished she had said to her aunt, before the road of time they traveled together had abruptly ended, just as it had with John.

She had thought she knew her aunt so well, and yet here was something her aunt had never mentioned at all — that she had known perhaps the world's most famous artist. Come to think of it, her aunt had never really talked with her about Julian Sloane, either. Were there parts of her life she kept secret? And why? Emily recalled the strangest part of her aunt's letter to her — the part that said something like "if anything happens to me." Courageous, independent Elizabeth Washington had feared something — or someone — in this sunny Florida town. And Emily was determined to learn which of Aunt Liz's secrets had led her into danger.

Chapter 9

A Rustle in the Palmettos

THE NEXT DAY FLEW BY, as Emily escaped her fears in a quest to figure out what to wear to Sloane's party. The choices she dragged from her suitcases seemed pretty dreary, but Mattie came to the rescue with the suggestion that she dig into her aunt's closets.

"Lordy, Miss Emily—Miss Elizabeth would want you to wear her things," Mattie had said when Emily protested that it might seem disrespectful. In the end, Emily relented, and the result was an outfit built around black palazzo pants and an armful of the Mexican silver bracelets that both she and Aunt Liz collected.

Despite Emily's initial dread, she had loved looking through her aunt's jewelry and found the memories it inspired more comforting than anything. The only disappointment was that they didn't find the piece of jewelry she most associated with her aunt—the scarab bracelet Liz was almost never without—the one that had inspired her recent dream.

"It should be here, Miss Emily," Mattie had said. "I don't understand it."

"Don't worry—it'll turn up. She probably put it in a pocket or something," said Emily, finally dressed and ready just as she heard Milton ring the doorbell. She made a mental note to ask him about the bracelet as she rushed down the stairs to answer the door.

When he saw her, she thought she saw a hint of shock flicker across his face. Had she been all wrong to emulate her aunt, even a bit? But Milton's expression transformed into a broad smile as he exclaimed, "My my, Miss Emily, wouldn't your auntie be proud if she could see you."

"You really think I'll pass muster, Mr. Armistead?"

"Belle of the ball, Miss Emily," he said, as she slid into her seat in the big Cadillac. "You look mighty classy, just like your aunt."

They waved goodbye to Mattie and were on their way to Sloane's home and artists' compound, which Milton said was on the shore of a large lake a few miles outside town.

Milton had flipped up his sunglasses, and his eyes met hers in the rearview mirror.

"Miss Emily," he began, "did you see anything of that guy in the black Ford today?"

"No, thank goodness. I did call Detective Maxwell about him—about him following Billy and me."

"Did you tell Maxwell you'd challenged the guy?"

"Sort of," she fudged, looking down at her hands. "I did remember the license number—he seemed happy to have that. He said he'd have a patrol car come by the house last night."

"Good. Maybe the Ford guy got scared away."

"And maybe Maxwell will find out who he is."

"Maxwell's a good man," said Milton, letting the thought hang in the air.

By now both the commercial buildings and houses of the town had disappeared from Emily's view from the taxi window, and the landscape on either side of the road was dominated by orange trees. Milton had switched on the radio, filling the car with soft music, and the fading afternoon light cast long shadows across the road.

"Maxwell described Julian Sloane as a big fish," Emily said after a moment's pause. "And he said something about how it should be an interesting crowd."

"Uh-huh," Milton said, with emphasis. "You might see anybody at his place—big shots, odd balls, famous artists, even movie stars. In the winter season, they come to thaw out in a bunch of cottages behind the main building. He calls it his "Studio for the world," with a capital S, or some such BS—excuse me, Miss Emily."

"Like I keep saying, no need to apologize."

When Emily met his glance in the rearview mirror, he added, "Let's just say Sloane and I don't exactly go together like salt and pepper."

"You don't like him?"

"He sees me as on a par with hired help—probably the uppity hired help."

"I'm not feeling keen about him already. I was hoping he might be able to shed some light on Aunt Liz's death."

"How he feels about me has nothing to do with you, Miss Emily. You are the perfect person to ask him questions, to see if he has any insights."

Emily felt a queasy sensation, a little like an elevator dropping in her stomach. Was she up to the task? Then she remembered her question for Milton.

"Speaking of questions," she said, "remember the scarab bracelet Aunt Liz always wore? It hasn't turned up, and it's probably the thing of hers that I'd most like to have—it reminds me so much of her."

"I remember it. I don't think it was with her things, come to think of it, you know—when she was found. Did you ask Mattie?"

Emily shuddered. She had wondered whether Liz had been buried with the bracelet.

"Yes. She says she hasn't seen it."

"I'll bet it's tucked away somewhere in the house—it'll turn up," said Milton. "You might ask Sloane about that. Before you talk with him, though, I should give you a little fast inside dope about his place—the cast of characters."

"I'm all ears," she said, fussing in her purse to find a small notebook and pen.

"First, there's Juan Blanco—the one who delivered the invitation. He's kind of a general factotum. He acts as manager for the gallery, but he also dances around Sloane like a fussy nanny—takes care of him. Far too slick, if you ask me."

"Got it," said Emily. "What else?"

But Milton jammed on the brakes, and the car lurched to a stop in the middle of the road.

"Damnation, it's that old idiot," Milton muttered. "Miss Emily, you just stay in your seat, now. I'll handle this."

"What old idiot?"

She looked up to see an aged, bearded man wearing overalls standing in the middle of the dirt road under a canopy of moss-strewn oaks that made the already-dark skies even darker. He held up one hand in the gesture that commanded Milton to stop, and with the other hand grasped a rope that trailed off behind him.

"Hold on, you jus' stop now," the old man bellowed in their direction. "All these cars is messing up my road, and it's Bone's dinner time. He gotta get across the road." He nodded toward the rope.

Consumed by curiosity, Emily started to open her car door.

"Miss Emily, just sit tight, I'm begging you," Milton snapped, as if he'd read her mind.

"Who's Bone?" she said. "His dog?"

The old man had reached the car and spat on the ground as he leaned against the old taxi to peer in at Emily.

"Yes, ma'am, that's right," he said. "Whatever you do, do not get out of this automobile. Bone ain't had his dinner yet. And he's all riled up because of all these cars going to that Yankee's house, that Sloane. I ain't had a day's peace since he moved in there."

Emily's eyes were more adjusted to the shade, and she now saw the end of the long rope the man clutched like a dog's leash. Her eyes followed the rope to where it dropped to the sand and snaked across the road. Several feet from the man, it disappeared behind a thicket of palmettos.

It must be quite a big dog, she thought.

"Everyone who comes to visit that Yankee gotta learn to stay away from my place," the old man said to Emily. "I'll forgive you, though, cause you're mighty pretty."

A leering grin cracked his leathery face, and Emily felt a jolt of anger—so much anger that it never occurred to her to be frightened.

"Hold on, Mr. Mizell, we're leaving right now," said Milton. "I know who you are: Aaron Mizell, isn't it? Mr. Jeff and Carter's great uncle? I used to work for their daddy."

More Mizells, thought Emily. Good grief—they must be half the county's population. But her thought was interrupted by a rustle in the palmettos, and when she saw what was connected to the end of the old man's rope, her veins turned to ice.

She had seen such a creature only in newsreels and maybe once in a zoo. Its coloring blended into the gray sand and the silver-green palmettos, but she was quite sure about what it was—a crocodile or an alligator, at least 12 feet long. Its mouth was closed, but long teeth protruded.

"Come on, Bonebreaker, come on, ol' Bone," the old man cooed to the giant reptile. "This lady won't hurt you none," he said, ignoring Milton. "She's a pretty lady, ain't she?"

"So the old beast is still alive," Milton muttered. Emily wasn't quite sure if he was referring to the alligator or the old man.

"Oh, he's doing fine," the old man said, finally acknowledging Milton. "I raised him from an egg, you know. Thinks I'm his daddy. Trying to get him back in his pen."

"You do that, Mr. Mizell," said Milton. "We'll be leaving now." He eased past the old man and waited until they were out of hearing range before he broke out in the loudest laugh Emily thought she'd ever heard from him.

"Lordy, that old coot is half crazy. I thought he'd died. Lives on the property next to Mr. Sloane. You okay, Miss Emily? Had enough of our local color? And you thought he was gonna produce a nice doggie on that leash. If you could see your face . . ."

"All right, all right," said Emily, laughing in spite of herself. "I hope things are calm at the party. My nerves couldn't handle more surprises like that one."

"We're almost there," said Milton, his shoulders still shaking.

"Good. And I definitely want to know more about what just happened, but we'd better wait for that. Best to not be late. Tell me quickly—is there anything else I should know about Juan?"

"Just keep your eye on him. You should know, too, that Sloane walks only with great difficulty—some kind of war injury. He uses a wheelchair and sometimes leg and arm braces. He usually holds court in a big chair—so he won't get up to greet you."

"Interesting. Anything else?"

"There's a cook, too, but he's a good guy—Manuel, a buddy of mine. He moonlights a little for me driving a cab in his off hours."

Emily nodded, busy scribbling. More proof Milton Armistead seemed to know everyone in town, she thought.

"What I was thinking," Milton continued, "was that I'd pay a visit to Manuel during the party, if he's not too busy. I know his kids, too."

Emily stopped writing and looked up to catch his eye. Maybe he still thought of her as a kid herself. She was about to say something, but Milton forged ahead.

"When you're ready to go, just tell one of the folks serving drinks to look for me in the kitchen," Milton said. "Sloane's regulars are used to me hanging around, waiting for your aunt at his parties—even though she was going to them less and less."

"Understood," she said, wondering why Aunt Liz had cut back on going to Sloane's soirees.

"And if you need me for any reason, Miss Emily," he added, "you let somebody know."

She was grateful for Milton's presence. In spite of her earlier, fanciful thoughts imagining Lewis or even Maxwell at her side, it was Milton who made her feel safe, and it was ridiculous that he had to be in the kitchen rather than at the party. When she gave a party, she'd change that, she thought, as Milton guided the taxi under low-hanging moss toward a series of low buildings tucked by a lake. They pulled into a circular driveway, and Milton was on his feet, opening the door for her.

"I'll be interested to hear what you think of the place, Miss Emily," he said. "Some of it is pretty strange—I think Sloane brought in folks from Mexico to work on the carvings."

And as Emily got out of Milton's taxi and looked up at the entrance, she had to agree she had never beheld anything quite like Sloane's "Studio for the world." Its architectural style, a sort of Aztec Art Deco, seemed almost to come from another world— perhaps the world of the imagination. Around the entrance, bas-relief figures stared down at Emily from a frieze painted in yellow, orange, and aqua. She waved at Milton, who had gotten back in the cab and was piloting down a driveway that seemed to head toward the back of the main building.

"Spectacular, isn't it?"

Emily jumped. The question came from a young man standing in the doorway. "The architecture, I mean—it has received international acclaim. Señor Sloane designed it all himself, you know."

"Very impressive," said Emily, getting her bearings and looking up at a purposefully primitive carving of a rising sun above the main entrance.

"Allow me to welcome you for Señor Sloane." The young man offered her his arm. His dark hair was combed straight back from a handsome face. "I'm Juan, at your service. You must be Miss Washington."

"Guilty as charged," said Emily. "How did you guess?"

"If I may say so, you look very much like your aunt—except much younger, of course. Please accept my condolences about her passing."

"Thank you—that's very kind."

Following Juan Blanco's lead, Emily stepped into a large gallery where Sloane apparently also did his entertaining. The late-afternoon light poured through open French doors along one long wall that looked out onto a patio with a lake view. She was startled to see one of her own paintings hanging near the entrance. She couldn't even remember what dealer might have sold it. Could her aunt possibly have given it to Sloane?

She had hoped there would be only a few guests, so that she could have a private chat with Sloane and try to find out what he knew about her aunt's death, and about the bracelet. But the room was full of people, some standing and a few seated in groupings of wicker chairs. The murmur of their voices blended with the sounds of a lone guitarist at the far end of the room near a huge fireplace surrounded by more of Sloane's Aztec-influenced carvings.

Then she noticed the man who must be her host, Julian Sloane himself, seated in a large wicker chair in front of a window and deep in conversation with a woman about Emily's age. She looked like the same woman Emily had spotted in the newspaper, next to the "about town" column—her girlhood friend Maureen. Emily admired her simple slacks and shirt and the turquoise necklace that complemented her deep-red hair.

Sloane was dressed all in white—trousers and a tunic that looked vaguely Eastern Indian. Emily thought of the kimono her aunt had worn in the beach photo, as well as the saris and other Asian-influenced clothes in the closets at Eola Lodge, and thought she detected a resemblance between the elegant older man in front of her and the young one who had posed with Aunt Liz in the photo long ago.

As she and Juan Blanco approached them, Emily could hear Maureen speaking to Sloane with some urgency. "Julian, something's got to be done," the columnist said. "This kind of thing is just intolerable in a group that claims to represent the arts." She was about to say more, but just then looked up and saw Emily and Juan.

"Oh my, you're here," Maureen said, rising to her feet. "Emily, I hope you remember me—Maureen Eppes, but it's Maureen Davis now. Let me introduce our host: Emily Washington—Julian Sloane."

"I'm so sorry to break in like that, Juan," Maureen added, turning to the young man, whose handsome face bore a slightly veiled look of irritation. "I just was so excited to see her."

"Of course you were, my dear," said Sloane, smoothly. "We are all so excited and happy that Miss Washington is here. Thank you, Juan," he added, seemingly dismissing Blanco, who was already gliding away as Emily tried to add her thanks to him as well.

"My dear Emily—if I may call you Emily?" Sloane began, turning to his new guest.

"Of course," she said. "I'm so very happy to meet you. I know you were such an important friend to my aunt."

"Well, my dear," said Sloane, "I have to admit you gave an old man a start when I looked across the room and saw Juan escorting you this way." He reached out and took her right hand in both of his. His grip was firm and smooth.

"You looked so much like your aunt, my beloved Elizabeth," Sloane continued, "that for an instant I thought her spirit was paying me a visit."

"Gracious, what a lovely complement," Emily said.

"I do believe in the spirit world, you know," said Sloane. "I have ever since I spent time in India. Centuries of wisdom there. And of course we are lucky to get a taste of it at our own little town of Cassadaga, just across the river."

Emily remembered Milton's comment in the taxi about "BS" and wondered if Sloane really saw a resemblance to her aunt. She had always thought of herself as a bit of a brown wren, while her aunt was definitely more of a swan. But still, she was flattered, and Sloane seemed perfectly sincere as he beamed at her.

"Please—don't let me interrupt," Emily said to both Maureen and Julian. "It sounded as though you were discussing something important." She admitted to herself that she was just being plain nosy.

"Oh, I'm afraid politics has invaded our little artists' association," Maureen said, rolling her eyes. "It used to be quite a convivial group, but now a few loose cannons are starting to see Communist plots behind every palm tree."

"Lamentable," added Julian, shaking his head.

"The whole thing makes me furious," Maureen said. "But let's talk about something else." She turned to Emily and nodded to a large painting that hung on one of the room's whitewashed walls. "Let's talk about you, Emily. You've become such a fine painter! That still life over there? I love how you handled those vibrant colors. That blue almost seems to glow."

"Maureen, that means a lot to me," Emily said, turning to Julian. "I'll admit, Mr. Sloane, it was a big surprise to see that painting here."

"Please, my dear, call me Julian. Yes, your artistry has preceded you," he added, nodding toward the still life. "I treasure that painting especially because it was a gift from your aunt, you see." His voice started to break, and he looked down at the floor, leaving Maureen to pick up the thread of the conversation.

"Emily, we were all just devastated by her death," she said. "Especially Julian. We're terribly sorry for your loss." Now Maureen reached for her hand and gave it a squeeze.

Emily nodded, smiling at them both while blinking back tears herself.

"It helps to know that she had such good friends here," she said. "Thank you both so much. In fact, Julian, I was hoping I could talk to you about—well, about what happened to Liz." She was about to say more, about the scarab bracelet, but for a moment Julian looked almost stricken, and then Juan Blanco returned, bearing cups of sangria for her and Maureen. With him were some new arrivals, eager to speak with Sloane. One of them, a man, looked familiar to Emily but she couldn't place him.

Sloane drew Emily toward him, and whispered, "I apologize, my dear, but I need to give these people some special attention—patrons, you see—he's a well-known actor," he said. "But I'll look forward to speaking with you privately soon." But somehow, as the newcomers made a huge fuss over him and Emily got up and followed Maureen's lead toward the refreshment table, she felt as though she had lost an important chance.

Chapter 10

Gossip and Glitter

WITH MAUREEN at her elbow, it was easy enough for Emily to, if not forget, at least put aside her disappointment over Julian's dismissal. The party offered plenty of distractions. For one thing, she was fascinated by the variety of speech she heard around her. Blanco spoke with a trace of a Spanish accent, while Sloane displayed what she used to call "boarding-school lockjaw," the upper-class Northeastern accent that sounded almost as if someone were holding a pencil between their teeth while they talked. One of Emily's favorite actresses, Katherine Hepburn, talked like that.

In contrast, Maureen sounded definitely Southern, which Emily remembered from their girlhood—but Emily had no idea what area Maureen's accent represented. Except for her voice, the redhead's manner had little in common with the Southern belles of books and movies.

"Try one of these," Maureen said, as she piled a couple of small empanadas on a plate and handed it to Emily. "Julian has a Cuban cook. I can't pronounce half the things he makes, but I know what to call them—scrumptious."

Emily bit into the savory pastry Maureen had given her and nodded agreement. "Umm, delicious. Mr. Armistead mentioned the cook—Manuel, I think," she said. "You know, Milton Armistead, who used to work for my aunt? He drove me here tonight."

"Goodness, yes, everyone knows Milton," said Maureen.

"He didn't know exactly what had happened to Julian—how he got injured," Emily said. "Do you have any idea?"

"Just something during World War I," Maureen continued. "I think it still causes him a lot of pain—I mean physical pain. That's why Juan hovers over him so much, I expect."

"Oh yes, I see," said Emily, wondering what her aunt had thought of Blanco—what she would have thought of this party.

"Mind you, Emily, I probably should know more about Julian," Maureen continued, plopping plump boiled shrimp on her hors d'oeuvres plate. "Knowing things about people is sort of my business."

"That's intriguing," said Emily, but of course, she'd seen Maureen's byline in the newspaper.

"What I mean is, I write a column for the local paper," said Maureen. "It's not exactly a gossip column, but . . ."

"Maureen, that's wonderful! I saw your column in the paper, in fact. It reminded me that when we were girls, you wrote the best letters of anyone I knew."

"Did I really?" said the redhead, blushing a little. "I don't think anyone's ever told me that. I did major in journalism, but I don't think anyone at the paper is looking to me to land any Pulitzer Prizes. It's only the women's pages—but, you know, you'd be surprised at what you can do there, when you're not on the male editors' radar."

"I paint a little, too, Emily," Maureen went on, "The group I was talking about with Julian, the Artists' League, consists mostly of amateurs—many of them better than me—but none in your league."

Emily looked at her old friend, squeezing her hand. As sorry as she was to have had Julian whisked away from her, she was glad of Maureen's company. "It's so good to see you," Emily said. "I've got a lot to talk with you about. For one thing, in her will, Aunt Liz asked me to put on a women's art show—here. I really need your help."

"I remember her saying something about that," said Maureen. "I don't know about you, but my feet are killing me. These heels and I are not friends. How about we fill up our plates and sit down?"

As she joined Maureen in doing just that, Emily inwardly rejoiced that her old friend didn't engage in the routine she had observed among so many women at cocktail parties—the "oh, my, I mustn't, well maybe just one" ritual they seemed to feel was necessary before allowing themselves a bite, often followed by a refrain about how fat they would get if they even looked at food. Pretty tiresome, really.

Emily and Maureen armed themselves with more sangria and settled into two wicker chairs on the stone patio outside the French doors. A breeze from the lake and the large oak tree over their heads made the twilight air surprisingly cool.

Maureen spoke first, her voice now soft and serious. "I was telling you how Elizabeth's death affected so many people, Emily. Julian broke down at the service and had to leave. And your aunt meant a lot to me, too, you know."

"You knew her a long time, Maureen."

"Yes. When my husband was killed during the war, she was so kind to me—she even took me down to Key West for a little trip—something to keep my mind occupied."

"One of her expeditions," Emily said, her voice catching.

"Oh yes," Maureen said. "She wasn't one to make you tea and cluck over you. Get up, get out, and order a good Scotch was more like it . . . "

Emily nodded her head, laughing.

"But I was so down, and she got me going again," Maureen said.

"And I'm so sorry for your loss, Maureen."

"Thank you, sweetie. I still miss him every day—but I'm finding how to live on my own." She stopped and looked at Emily.

"But oh dear, I didn't mean to jump into such deep waters. You're looking a little pale, Emily—are you feeling okay? There's a private loo in Julian's apartment, if you need someplace to retreat."

"I'm fine," Emily lied. "Still tired from the trip, I think." In fact, Maureen's mention of her husband's death had stirred thoughts of John again. But unlike Maureen, she hadn't been the wife who received the telegram bearing official notification of his death. And she was horrified to realize, too, that the idea that her aunt had been so important to another younger confidante came as a slight shock, and she felt a pang of jealousy toward Maureen, whom she actually liked very much.

"You were telling me about your artists' group," Emily said.

"Yes, the Artists' League," Maureen said. "If you'd ever consider teaching a class, we'd be over the moon. Julian said he thought you'd done some teaching up North."

Emily nodded. "How about life drawing? That's such an important class."

"Naked models?" Maureen laughed. "Our little group may not be ready for that."

"That's the classic way to do it, but we could compromise, of course."

"Some of our ladies would probably only be comfortable if a model had on a winter coat, or a suit of armor," Maureen said, and Emily laughed out loud, prompting heads to turn in the group seated next to them.

"Julian's given us a real art gallery here, though, with paintings by real artists, like you —not just sweet little watercolors. Of course, I suppose some people would prefer that. See that nude over there?"

Maureen pointed to an impressionistic figure study. "A few of the ladies in the league were horrified." She popped an hors d'oeuvre into her mouth and was chasing it down with a healthy sip of sangria when Emily heard her mutter, "Well, I'll be."

"What is it? You look mesmerized." Maureen's gaze was riveted on something inside the French doors, and Emily leaned forward to catch a glimpse inside. Next to the bar, she could just barely see a good-looking man dressed in a white dinner jacket, smoking a cigarette. He handed a cocktail glass to an older woman next to him.

"It's Charlie Wynne," Maureen whispered. "With his mother—she's a friend of Julian's. Big as life, I'll bet she dragged him to this affair."

Emily realized that if she leaned any farther forward, she would topple over.

"The one with the dimples?" she asked.

"Oh yes indeedy," Maureen began. "Would you believe he graduated from Princeton, and now he's our own homegrown underworld boss, if the rumors are right. Doesn't look like the ones in movies, does he? Let's get some more sangria and then I'd like to go find out what he's doing here."

Emily was looking forward to talking with Maureen more about her aunt, but she could understand Maureen's curiosity, especially since her old friend was now in the business of having a nose for news. And she had to admit that she was interested in learning more about Wynne, and his dimples.

Both women rose from their chairs to go back into the party, but Maureen was accosted by a little sparrow of a woman, another member of the artists' group, Emily suspected. After lingering a bit, hoping to be included in the conversation, or perhaps learn something of the art show Aunt Liz's will had mentioned, Emily gave up and wandered off to try mingling. She was alone, just behind Wynne and his mother, when Juan Blanco approached them.

"Señor Wynne, if you'll come this way?" Emily overheard Blanco say. "A gentleman on the telephone in the hallway says he must speak with you."

"Oh really, Charlie! How infuriating," Mrs. Wynne's voice rose in irritation. Then, Emily almost jumped when she realized the older woman's next words were addressed to her.

"Excuse me, my dear—it's Emily, isn't it? Julian told me who you were. I'm Serena Wynne, and that scamp who was just here is my son, Charlie. He's eager to meet you, too."

Emily wondered if the shock showed on her face, but she managed to stammer some appropriate response. She found herself facing a rather glamorous blonde of uncertain age whose sapphire earrings certainly looked like the real thing.

"Aren't men infuriating," she asked Emily in a drawl not unlike Maureen's. "I finally got Charlie to spend an evening with me, and he's already taking business phone calls."

The business must have been brief, Emily thought, because

she looked up to see the errant son heading back down the hall toward his mother, and her. Something about him brought to mind a line of poetry: "He glittered when he walked." But that had been from "Richard Cory," a poem about a man who had killed himself, perhaps after a life of quiet desperation. Judging from what Maureen had said about him, as well as the charming smile he was beaming at her, Charlie Wynne didn't seem stifled by respectability, or inhibition. She couldn't help but think of Lewis, fretting about his father's wishes and what was expected of him. What would this smiling man before her do in a similar situation, she wondered?

"Mother of mine, I am so very sorry," he began, leaning over to give her a peck on the cheek. "Something urgent has come up, so I'm afraid Joseph will have to drive you on to the Country Club." He turned to Emily. "And I'm doubly sorry to leave without having a chance to greet this charming lady," he said, picking up Emily's hand and lightly kissing the back of it "Charles Wynne, at your service, Miss Washington."

Emily wondered if her mouth was open.

"I'll wait to give you the piece of my mind you so richly deserve rather than embarrassing Miss Washington," Mrs. Wynne said.

"Forgive me if this sounds impertinent, Miss Washington," Wynne said. "But I'd know you were related to Elizabeth even if no one had told me. Please accept my condolences. She was a remarkable woman. I'll look forward to talking with you soon, I hope."

Then, excusing himself, he was gone, leaving Emily a little breathless. A prosperous-looking older gentleman who had been hovering at Mrs. Wynne's elbow whisked her away to the drinks table, and Emily found herself on her own again. As she looked around, she caught sight of Juan Blanco wheeling Julian toward a darkened doorway at the other side of the room. She rushed to catch the two men.

"Mr. Sloane! Might I have just a moment?"

But it was Juan who turned to her, as Julian's head lolled forward.

"Miss Washington, I must offer Señor Sloane's apologies,"

Blanco said. "He's exhausted and must retire. He doesn't have the stamina he once did, I'm afraid. But he very much hopes you will come back for lunch soon."

"That would be wonderful. How about the day after . . . " But if Juan or Julian heard her, neither of them acknowledged it as they disappeared into the hallway.

Feeling a bit deflated, and with no prospect of talking more to Sloane, Emily was more than ready to go. She asked one of the waiters to please find Milton, and to tell him she was ready to leave whenever it suited him. Then she slipped out the front door and stood in the circular driveway under a lavender sky in which stars were beginning to appear.

Emily sighed. She had made no progress in talking with Sloane or in learning much about her aunt's world, beyond hearing that the artists' group was full of squabbling factions—and what was new about that, she thought. But the evening wasn't a complete bust. She had learned that, if rumors were true, the local crime boss looked more like Cary Grant than Edward G. Robinson, and you had to admit that was interesting. She wondered if Charlie Wynne was Billy's ultimate boss. And she had reconnected with Maureen Davis, who was approaching her now, cigarette in hand, just as Milton pulled the taxi into the driveway.

"Oh, Emily, there you are," the redhead said. "The people I came with want to go on to a nightclub down on the Trail, and I would much rather go home. I don't live too far from Eola Lodge. I apologize for asking at the last minute, but might I impose on you for a ride?"

"I'd love the company," Emily said, and soon the two women and Milton were sailing along in the old Cadillac on the road into town.

A full moon hung low in the sky over the highway. Both Emily and Maureen rolled down their windows, and the fragrant night air wrapped around them. At the same time, Emily quietly checked in the rearview mirror to see if any headlights were behind them. She hadn't forgotten about the black Ford. But she saw nothing.

Milton had turned on the radio to a program featuring the Jimmy Dorsey Orchestra, and now one of Emily's favorite songs floated back to her—"Tangerine," a war-time hit about a beauty with lips as bright as flame. Her mind traveled back to a long-ago dance floor, and to John. She leaned forward toward Milton.

"Mr. Armistead, can you please turn the radio up a little?"

She doubted that she would ever be able to call him "Milton," just as she had never been able to call some of her art professors by their first names for years after she had studied with them. Sometimes she was so stymied that she didn't greet them by name at all, but just made polite noises if she saw them at gallery openings: "Well, how are you? How's the family?"

And I believe I'm so unconventional, she thought. In reality, here was more proof of just how conventional she was.

Then Emily noticed a glare in one of the side mirrors, and her heart jumped a little. Was the Ford following them again? Was the man with the dead-fish eyes about to force them off the road? Bright headlights shone right behind them now, close to the Cadillac. And although Milton accelerated smoothly, so did the car behind, but with much more noise, muffler rumbling and horn blaring.

Emily turned to see a convertible roar past them, the top down and filled with what she judged to be high school kids, a couple of them laughing and waving—probably taking someone's papa's car out for a joyride under the stars. She breathed a sigh of relief and turned back to Maureen.

"Just stop me if I'm getting too nosy," Emily said, "but I was just thinking about that conversation you were having with Julian when I arrived at the party—the people with the Communist fixation. Did they have anything against my aunt, I wonder—see her as some kind of evil influence from New York?"

"Oh, I hardly think so," said Maureen. "Elizabeth had been here so long no one thought of her as an outsider. I was talking about Jim Fortescue and his wife, Lillian. He has political aspirations. She's on the art association board and has started to pick on one of the young men teaching children's classes — hinting he was 'Red' in college because of some rumor."

"Do you think anyone would have those kinds of ideas about me? I didn't mention it earlier, Maureen, but when I arrived at my aunt's, the door to the house was open, and someone had clearly been inside. And a car has been following me."

"Good grief," said Maureen. "I really can't imagine one of the Fortescues sneaking into your house. What do you think, Milton?"

"One of my nieces works for them." Milton raised his voice a bit to be heard. "He has a Klan hood in the closet and is all riled up about this Dixiecrat business, was complaining at the lunch table about how President Truman was gonna put colored men in with the whites in the U.S. Army. But you have a point there, Mrs. Davis. Men like him get other folks to do their dirty work."

They were almost back at Eola Lodge, driving along quiet residential streets. They passed the barbershop and DiMartini's grocery in the small business area down the street. On the corner, a small neon sign blinked in the window of the neighborhood bar and grill.

Suddenly, Milton spoke in a whisper: "What have we here?"

They were at the stop sign a block from Emily's house, and every ounce of Milton's considerable attention appeared riveted on something he'd spotted straight ahead.

Leaning forward, Emily saw the object of his interest, too: The black Ford with the Tampa license plate had not been behind them on the way home because it was smack dab in Emily's driveway. Its lights were on, casting sharp shadows through the palmetto fronds.

The Ford didn't move.

"Oh, Emily, do you have company? Hope I didn't hold you up!" Maureen burbled out the open car window.

In unison and without thinking, Emily and Milton both hissed, "Shhhhh."

"I hate to be melodramatic, Maureen," Emily whispered, "but that's the car that has been following me. I have no idea why. Or any idea why it's here right now."

Milton coasted up in front of the house and parked under the streetlight that cast a sort of violet glow. Emily couldn't see anyone sitting in the Ford, but the driver's side door was slightly open. Then she gasped.

What was that shadow, moving in the car?

An immense orange cat leapt from the Ford and raced across the street in front of them, its legs a blur.

"Well, some things don't change," Maureen whispered. "That would be Mrs. Jackson's cat, Jiggs, into everything. If you haven't had a chance to meet him, he's quite a presence."

Quiet returned, and more moments passed. No movement from the Ford.

Emily could feel Maureen start to fidget, and she knew that for her, too, the call of nature was getting about as insistent as her fears. She looked at the house, which was dark except for one light she had left on in the kitchen. Could someone be lying in wait for her inside?

"Well, we can't just sit here all night, can we?" asked Maureen. "Even if someone's inside the house, there are three of us, and I've got a gun in my bag. Daddy gave it to me."

"Lord preserve us," Milton whispered, and then added firmly, "You ladies stay here. I've just been waiting to see if someone was going to drive away. Under no circumstances should you get out . . ."

But Emily didn't hear a word he said. In a rush of adrenaline like she had felt at the cemetery, she launched herself out of the big back seat on the right, just as Maureen did the same on the left, both of them exiting the car before Milton could even finish his thought.

They crept behind Milton as he moved slowly toward the Ford. Between the moon and the violet-tinged streetlight, Emily could see quite well. Very faintly, she heard music. The Ford's radio was on, and now the Jimmy Dorsey band was swinging to "Green Eyes." The love song had never sounded ominous before.

Emily stopped cold behind Milton. Jiggs must have had company. The driver's door of the Ford, now almost closed again, lurched open as a second large cat scrambled from the back. Jiggs and Maggie like the cartoon? Emily wondered.

But that wasn't what actually had stopped her. In the violet light, a pale hand hung from the car, limp and lifeless, a trail of bright red trickling down the fingers. The next sound Emily heard was Maureen, beside her, screaming.

Chapter 11

Death in the Driveway

THE NEXT FEW MINUTES were a blur for Emily. Milton took charge and supervised the chaos, which was considerable. For one thing, Maureen's screams were enough to wake the dead, which the man in the Ford decidedly was—from a gunshot wound to the head, Milton whispered to Emily. He pulled a flashlight from the Cadillac's glove compartment and rushed to the Ford, motioning for Emily and Maureen to stay back.

"Get Mrs. Davis into the house, Miss Emily," Milton said, "and call Detective Maxwell. I think you have the number." Emily frowned, her arm around Maureen, now sobbing. She disliked being ordered away, although she wasn't about to abandon Maureen—and, in truth, she probably wasn't keen on seeing the rest of the man at the wheel. His blood-streaked hand had been enough.

"Go, now!" yelled Milton, and Emily did, guiding Maureen up the front steps and into the house but inwardly fretting. She didn't want to be shielded from something just because it was unpleasant, especially if she were involved. If that hand belonged to the man who had followed her—the man named Marvin, who Billy said killed people—she wanted to know. Now, it seemed that someone had killed him.

Emily settled a more subdued Maureen on the living room couch and brought her a shot of Scotch and a glass of water. Then she called Detective Maxwell, who listened intently, asked her if she was all right, and hung up briskly after assuring her he was on the way. She turned back to Maureen, whose color was much better and, in response to Emily's entreaties, protested that, really, she was fine. Sipping her Scotch, she asked Emily for another and for her purse, from which she extracted a small notebook and pen and started taking notes while Emily returned from the kitchen with a finger of Scotch for each of them.

"Good lord," said Emily, taking a sip. "You really are a reporter."

"Not a real one—not yet, but someday," Maureen said. "If I'm not, it won't be for lack of trying." She blotted her eyes. "And Emily . . ."

"What?"

"Thanks for helping me just now. I'm so sorry. I'm afraid I went all to pieces—somehow seeing his hand, and the blood . . . it reminded me of pictures from the war, nightmares."

"Yes—I saw it too. Pretty ghastly. You've got nothing to apologize for, believe me."

Just then, Emily heard the whine of police sirens and looked up through the still-open front door to see two patrol cars arriving. She realized she was holding her breath when she heard her heart pounding in her ears. You're not as calm as you'd like to think, old girl, she said to herself.

"Here's the police," she said to Maureen. "They'll want to talk with us. I'd better go outside."

"I'm not going anywhere," said Maureen, taking a mouthful of Scotch.

As Emily stepped out onto the front porch, Detective Joe Maxwell pulled up and parked in front of the house in a dark, unmarked sedan. The patrol cars sat in the middle of the street, their beacon lights flashing. Maxwell got out, issuing orders to the uniformed police, waved a hand in her direction, and approached the porch steps.

"Miss Washington, I'll want to talk with you in a little while," he said. "Just stay inside for now."

"I can come outside," she called, feeling her face flush. She wasn't sure which was worse—seeing something awful or being treated as though she had to be protected from it.

"Absolutely not."

With reluctance, Emily nodded and went inside to see Maureen, now on her feet, drink in hand and peering out the front windows.

"Emily," Maureen said. "I did get down a few notes, and I'm going to phone the newsroom if it's okay with you."

"Certainly," Emily said, pointing to the phone.

"And by the way, the man who was calling to you just now — quite the dreamboat."

"Detective Maxwell? You think so? Hadn't occurred to me."

Maureen raised an eyebrow. "I expect he'd appreciate some coffee," she went on. "How about I make myself useful and make some? I know my way around your aunt's kitchen — your kitchen — pretty well. I used to help Liz with Artists' League parties."

"Good idea," Emily said. "Make your call and I'll start getting out the fixings. It's so strange, Maureen. I actually met that detective yesterday, and he may want to talk with me first."

"You don't say?"

"I know," Emily said, with a weak smile. "I just arrived in town and I'm already on the radar of the law."

Moving into the kitchen, she heard Maureen dial the phone and then say, "Jinx, that you? Goodness, you're working late. Listen, something odd's happened over here at Elizabeth Washington's place . . . "

After closing the swinging door to the kitchen to give Maureen more privacy — even though she did want to hear the conversation — Emily found herself half expecting to see her aunt's tall figure at the stove, already starting the coffee.

"Elizabeth Washington's place," Maureen had said, understandably. Suddenly Emily felt alone and frightened. Perhaps taking the train back to Lewis wasn't such a bad idea. Then Maureen swung through the door into the kitchen, breaking her mood.

"Now, what's this about your meeting the detective outside — the one you called?"

"Maxwell. I was going to say more about it earlier, at the party. When I arrived, the house was open and it looked like someone had been snooping around. Milton Armistead wanted me to tell him."

"Really?"

"Yes, and the whole thing has gotten a lot more complicated,

Maureen—and, please, this is not for the newspaper. Promise?"

Wisps of Maureen's deep-red hair shook as she emphatically nodded yes—her neat pageboy now in disarray.

"You see, Mr. Armistead's convinced that my aunt's death wasn't an accident—that it was murder. At first I thought that was crazy, but not now. That fellow out there in the car—the dead one—he's been following me."

"Good grief, Emily! I feel like I need another drink— but it had better be strong coffee, I guess. We want to appear sensible for Detective Dreamboat." Emily couldn't help but laugh.

"If you say so," she said. "Mr. Armistead might want some, too."

"Here, I've got it under control," said Maureen, putting a percolator on the stove and looking in the fridge for the milk bottle. "Feeling quite recovered from my hysteria. Now, be stealthy and see if you can find out what's happening outside."

So Emily stepped quietly back out onto the front porch, where she could see that even the formidable Milton had his hands full. Police cars apparently weren't common in this tree-lined area of town, next to the city's central park. Several teenage boys stood across the street from Eola Lodge, craning their necks and smoking cigarettes with an air of feigned nonchalance while one of the officers gestured to them to keep their distance. Emily wondered if they had come from the corner bar near DiMartini's store. Then she saw Mr. DiMartini, too, his brows knit with concern. A woman she judged to be Mrs. DiMartini stood next to him, her eyes wide as she talked to him, clutching his arm. Perhaps they lived above the grocery.

Milton came up the porch steps to speak to Emily—no doubt to tell her to go inside—but his attention was diverted by an elderly woman hobbling across the brick street toward them with the aid of two canes. She was swathed in a pink chenille robe, with house slippers to match and her pin-curled hair covered by a scarf. Milton seemed to find her appearance on the scene almost as remarkable as finding a body in the driveway.

"Lordy," he murmured to Emily. "That's Mrs. Jackson from

across the street. She doesn't get up and out for nothing or nobody except her bridge games at the Magnolia Club. She can't see real well and hears even less. Coretha Jones works for her, but she must be off for the weekend. She'd never let the old lady get out of the house dressed like that."

Milton hastened to intercept Mrs. Jackson, with Emily following fast behind him. Once again, he seemed to know everyone in town. He introduced Emily to Mrs. Jackson, speaking more loudly than usual but with kindness in his voice.

"Mrs. Jackson, there really isn't anything to see," Milton said. "You take it easy now and go on back to bed. You'll help her, won't you, Miss Emily?"

Emily shot him a look as he hurried back across the street toward Detective Maxwell, who was talking with a uniformed officer in her driveway, near the Ford. Here she was being pushed to the sidelines again, she inwardly sighed, but she could hardly leave this unsteady old dear wandering in her bedroom slippers.

"I'm so happy to meet you," she said to Mrs. Jackson, who smiled at her and then bellowed, "Can't hear a thing, my dear. Forgot my hearing aids."

Emily smiled back as she guided the pink-swathed figure back across the street.

"You look like her tremendously, you know," Mrs. Jackson said. "Your aunt, I mean. We didn't always see eye to eye, but she was a good neighbor. I'm sorry for your loss."

Emily nodded, taking her hand as they made their way up the front steps of a Craftsman bungalow, conversation difficult. She was flattered, yet again, to be told she reminded people of her aunt, though she struggled with the feeling that she might always be a pale shadow of Elizabeth. The mind was indeed a wonderful servant but a terrible master, as she had once read. Best to not let its stray thoughts get the best of you.

But other thoughts came at her too, like snowflakes in a blizzard. It was just beginning to occur to her, for example, that if someone had killed fish-eyed Marvin, the killer might still be in the neighborhood, thirsty for more blood. Shuddering, she returned her attention to Mrs. Jackson, who had made her way to a well-cushioned chair on the porch, collapsed into the seat, and was smoothing the pink folds of her bathrobe.

"I can hear all right now that we're away from the fracas," she said, looking up at Emily, her eyes narrowed. "Thank you for helping me, dear. I just had to see—it's that man, isn't it? That awful man."

"What awful man? I'm afraid the man who was driving the Ford parked in my aunt's driveway is dead—is that who you mean?" Emily asked.

"Yes," Mrs. Jackson nodded. "Coretha wouldn't take me seriously when I told her he worried me. He'd sit out on the street in that black car, reading the newspaper for what seemed like hours—not just this week but before your aunt died, too."

It took Emily a minute to take in what Mrs. Jackson was saying.

"Are you certain? Before my aunt died?"

"Yes. I swear sometimes I'd see him looking over at your aunt's house with binoculars. One day when Coretha was off, he came to the door. Said he was a Fuller Brush man—can you believe it? He looked about as much like a Fuller Brush man as I do. He was asking questions about your aunt—if I thought she was home."

"That is odd," said Emily, noting that Mrs. Jackson's habit of watching from her window made her an excellent potential source of information.

"Mrs. Jackson," she continued, "you might be a lot of help to the police, with your knowledge of the neighborhood and all. Did you see that man tonight, or hear anything? Loud noises?" Emily asked.

"Dear, I was in the back of the house doing my hair up for the night," she said. "With my arthritis"—she held up gnarled hands—"it can take a long time. And, like I said, I had taken out my hearing aids. So, no—I heard no loud noises. It was the lights that finally got my attention."

Just then Emily heard a tap at Mrs. Jackson's front door and saw Billy Mizell, of all people, motioning to her.

"Hey Miss Emily, Mrs. Jackson," he fairly shouted.

The old lady's face lit up at the sight of him. "I've got some real good numbers ready this week, Billy," she said. "Don't you forget me."

"You did great last week, Mrs. Jackson," Billy exclaimed. "I'll be around tomorrow to collect your bet."

Of course, thought Emily. Detective Maxwell had told her that even the nice little old ladies gambled in the underground bolita lottery, and here was a bona fide example: her genteel, bridge-playing neighbor.

After Mrs. Jackson assured Emily she was fine and the women said good night, Billy began to pummel her with questions as he followed her back across the street to Eola Lodge.

"Do you know what happened, Miss Emily? Did you see much blood? Was it really, really awful?"

"Slow down, Billy," she said, giving him her attention but also pausing at the curb to see what was going on at her house, where a tow truck now sat in the street, with its driver leaning against it, waiting.

She managed to learn that Billy had heard the police sirens, had crept through the crowd, and had actually gotten a glimpse of the bloody hand before Milton spotted him and made it very clear that if he wanted any more taxi tip money, he needed to go to Mrs. Jackson's at once and ask Emily to take him back to Eola Lodge and feed him a sandwich.

"I'm not a baby," the boy rushed on. "But I don't want to go home. Pa isn't there, and I didn't want to be alone, I guess. That doesn't make me a baby, does it, Miss Emily?"

"Of course not, Billy," she said. "I think you're very brave."

"I did see some blood," he said.

"I'm afraid I did, too," Emily said. "Where is your father, if you don't mind me asking?"

"He had to go out to the ranch," he said "Some kind of emergency. He knows I can take care of myself." But he let her take his hand as they crossed the street. Emily blinked at a barrage of flashbulbs exploding by the Ford. Along with the tow truck, an ambulance had pulled up in the driveway behind the Ford, presumably to take the body away.

Walking up the path to the front steps, Emily looked for Maxwell and Milton, and finally saw them standing in front of the Ford, talking intently. As she and Billy headed inside, she longed to know what they were saying. Once again, she felt relegated to the sidelines, but took comfort in knowing that Milton would surely fill her in later.

In the kitchen, Maureen made Billy a peanut butter sandwich while Emily poured coffee for herself and Maureen and milk for Billy, along with two cookies and a slice of her welcome-to-Florida apple pie. It seemed like forever since she'd found the pie in her refrigerator soon after stepping off the train—and into what?

She had expected sadness, grief, even hard work to care for her aunt's belongings and property. She hadn't expected mayhem and murder at her doorstep. Asking questions about her aunt's death was one thing, but facing off with gangland killers was another, if that's what this was. But what on earth could someone like this creepy Marvin have had to do with her aunt? She looked up to see Billy attacking his sandwich with even more than his usual gusto.

"My goodness, Billy," said Maureen, "you're going through that food like Sherman through Georgia." The expression reminded Emily that although Florida might have palm trees and beaches and plenty of Yankees selling real estate, it was still a part of the old Confederacy, and in many ways, she was a stranger in a strange land.

Emily looked at Billy and realized that almost as soon as she had poured his milk, it had vanished. She refilled the glass, reminding herself to leave out a note asking her new milkman for an extra quart. She looked at Billy's sharp shoulder blades under his thin T-shirt and wondered what, if anything, he'd had for dinner.

"How about some more coffee," she asked Maureen, who sat in a yellow and chrome kitchen chair next to Billy. "I think sleep is probably a lost cause, and anyway, I seem to always be able to drink the stuff and then go to sleep—that is, if I haven't just found a dead body in my driveway."

"Holy cow!" Billy cried out between bites of pie. "I thought he was dead, but no one would really tell me. This is like something on the radio—that show 'The Shadow.' "

Maureen rolled her eyes and smiled at him. "You're too young to listen to that scary stuff, Billy. It'll give you nightmares."

"I do sometimes have nightmares," Billy said, suddenly quiet, "but it isn't about anything like that stuff—like what's on the radio."

Emily was about to ask the boy more about his nightmares when there was a knock at the back door. She opened it to find Milton and Detective Maxwell illuminated by the back-porch light. Maxwell spoke first.

"I know you're shaken up, Miss Washington, but I'd like to speak to you." He shot a glance at Billy. "Outside."

Well, thought Emily. I was miffed at being left out, on the sidelines. But am I ready for this? She paused for a minute, then nodded and followed Maxwell out the front door.

Chapter 12

Under a Florida Moon

It seemed Emily didn't feel much of anything—was just putting one foot in front of the other as she followed Maxwell—but once again her heart was pounding. The detective wanted her to make an identification, he'd said as they'd come outside.

The cloudy sky had cleared, and a full moon cast long shadows in her aunt's yard. If it weren't for the looming police ambulance and the task at hand, it would be a lovely night, fragrant and warm, full of promise. Emily felt strangely unafraid about seeing dead Marvin, as she found herself thinking of him. She recalled the cadaver she had studied in her college anatomy class. But that body had seemed abstract almost, something that would enhance her knowledge rather than a person she had seen in life—a person to whom she was connected in some unknown way.

And Emily was, indeed, connected to dead Marvin. He had been following her specifically, it seemed, in his black-beetle Ford. What were the unseen threads that linked them? Had she in some unknown way helped bring about his death? It seemed hardly plausible, but here he was, in her aunt's driveway—her driveway now. She felt oddly responsible for his violent end rather than relieved he would no longer be following her.

"You okay, Miss Washington?" She heard Maxwell's voice as if it came from a great distance as he lightly touched her shoulder. She was still dressed in the party clothes she had worn to Sloane's— the outfit that included a bare-shouldered halter top—and she was intensely aware of the warm sensation of his fingers on her bare skin, however fleeting. She nodded and followed Maxwell to the back of the police ambulance, where a sheet covered the shape of a body that rested on a wheeled stretcher. A couple of uniformed men she judged to be the ambulance attendants leaned against the side of the vehicle, smoking. The tips of their cigarettes glowed red in the night.

"It'll be over in an instant," Maxwell said, giving a signal to one of the men, who tossed down his cigarette, ground it out in the gravel with his shoe, and came toward them. He nodded to the detective, bent over the stretcher, and carefully folded back the top of the sheet, revealing most of a pale face. Marvin was indeed dead.

His dark hair, once combed smooth and slick, was now in disarray. The side of his head remained hidden by the sheet, no doubt to conceal the gunshot wound, Emily thought, and with the bloody signs of violence hidden, his face looked strangely peaceful. This was someone's son, Emily thought. Maybe he was also someone's husband or lover. Was there a woman somewhere, devastated to hear that she would never see him again, as Emily had been devastated about John? Although it was hard to imagine, he might even have been the father of a child—a child such as Billy. What had brought him to this cruel end?

"Miss Washington," Maxwell asked in a low voice, "do you think this is the same man you saw in the cemetery?" Suddenly, despite the warm night, Emily was shivering. She felt Maxwell place something—a suit coat?—around her shoulders.

"I think so," she said. "I really didn't see his face all that well, but I think so."

But she had seen this man well enough, she recalled. She remembered his face in life with those fish eyes, those dead eyes that had looked right through her. It seemed so odd that his face, with those eyes now closed, somehow looked more human in death than in life.

"That's enough, gentlemen," Maxwell said to the two ambulance attendants. "He's all yours. You can take him away."

One of the men stepped forward and replaced the sheet. As he did Emily looked down the driveway, toward the street, and saw that not only was the Ford gone but the police also seemed to have dispatched any onlookers. Two patrol cars still sat in the street in front of Eola Lodge, but otherwise things were quiet.

She started to turn toward the house when Maxwell spoke, this time to her.

"Miss Washington, before you go back inside—I need to interview you and Miss Davis about finding the body, but not at the same time. Is there some place we can talk that's out of the way, and the hearing of young Billy Mizell? I like that kid a lot, but if you want something broadcast to the whole town, he's a good place to start. Like a one-person radio station. I've already talked with Milton."

"The screened porch." She pointed toward the side of the house.

So it's finally my turn, she thought to herself. But her questions for Maxwell seemed to have evaporated. Just after the discovery of the body, she had wanted nothing more than to talk with him and be in the center of the action, but instead she had been shuffled away from the excitement and told, in essence, to take care of the "women's work." She had looked after Maureen, Mrs. Jackson, and Billy instead of being able to ask Maxwell what he knew about Marvin, how he had died, and what the detective really thought. But now that her initial rush of adrenaline was over, her mind was foggy, and she felt numb. Come on, old girl, she told herself. Gather your thoughts.

In a few minutes they were seated in two of her aunt's old wicker chairs on the big side porch of Eola Lodge. Maxwell's suit coat still rested around her shoulders.

Looking around the big porch, Emily could see why her aunt had loved this part of the house so much. It had been one of her favorite places, too, during her girlhood visits, and it seemed especially magical at night. Through the screen, the moonlight splashed a silvery river across the worn cypress floor. She and Maxwell sat in silence for a moment, except for a chorus of crickets.

"I meant to ask you, Miss Washington, how was the party out at Sloane's?" he began, as he got out his notebook. "You look very nice, by the way."

Emily realized she was blushing and wondered if it showed in the dark. That sure came out of nowhere, she thought.

He paused and then added, "I'm sorry. That wasn't the most appropriate thing for me to say under the circumstances." Maybe not to you, Emily thought, but the words had sounded good to her, perhaps because they were so surprising. But she wasn't supposed to thrill to compliments from a man who was not her maybe-fiancé, was she?

"You mean not appropriate to say to someone who has just found a dead man in her driveway?" she said with a smile. Good lord, she thought, her grandmother—and Lewis's mother, too—would no doubt have strong opinions on exactly what was the perfect thing to say, or not say, in any situation, including this. Certainly they would have opinions about exactly the correct thing to wear. Something like, "Wardrobe for identifying a body: A navy blue day dress with a string of pearls is always appropriate."

They would surely take a dim view of the bare-shouldered halter top and silver hoop earrings she was wearing with Aunt Liz's flowing palazzo pants. In their view, it was hardly appropriate dress for a party, let alone for identifying a body or being interviewed by a handsome detective.

She was getting sort of silly-tired, she thought, as she was aware of Maxwell's voice again.

"No, Miss Washington," he was saying, "I meant perhaps not appropriate considering my professional role here. I don't usually compliment witnesses on their attire. Now, tell me what happened when you arrived back at the house tonight. Milton said you're an artist—paint me a picture—in words, that is."

Emily described returning from the party, seeing the Ford in the driveway under the violet streetlight—radio on and door open. She finished with the dramatic appearance of the cats, Jiggs and Maggie, and ended with the lifeless hand dangling from the open car door.

"That's really all I saw," she concluded. "I had been concerned that the Ford might follow us on the way to the party, or on the way home, but we saw no sign of it. When we got to the house and saw the car—and the hand—well, Mrs. Davis was very upset, and I helped her inside and telephoned you."

"That was about 9 o'clock, right?" Maxwell said.

"Yes," Emily said. "It felt like forever, but it couldn't have been more than five minutes before I reached the telephone."

"And you saw no one else?"

"No," said Emily, "but I think you should talk with Mrs. Jackson across the street. She told me earlier that she hadn't seen or heard anything tonight, but she had quite a lot to say about the dead man. She said he'd been watching my aunt's house for quite a while, since well before her death."

Maxwell had been listening intently.

"You don't say."

"I do say," Emily replied, "and I further say that it seems to me that all these things have to be connected in some way." All of a sudden, the foggy feeling was gone, and her thoughts rushed in with clarity. She felt energy and rising excitement. Lewis would have told her she was getting "all wound up," she thought with a smile. That was not a good thing in his book, except when they were traveling, and then he found her excitement exhilarating. At home, he would usually tell her to calm down.

"I mean," Emily rushed on, "someone is watching my aunt, according to Mrs. Jackson, and my aunt dies, and then the watcher is watching me, and he dies two days after I arrive and find signs that someone has apparently broken into the house."

She looked at him hard, then said exactly what was on her mind. "Mr. Armistead says you're very sharp, as well as very fair. A straight arrow. Are you sure you don't know something more about what the connections between these things might be?"

"And if I do know something more, I need to tell you right away—is that what you're saying, Miss Washington? Are you accusing me of hiding things from you?"

"No—oh, I don't know," she said, feeling flustered and a bit defensive. "If you were hiding things from me, it wouldn't be a first, believe me," she added, struggling to stifle the memory of how even

John, her dear John, had kept secrets from her—had not revealed he was married until she'd fallen for him hard.

As for the man with her now, this disarming detective Maureen had called a dreamboat, Emily still half expected him to accuse her of imagining things, even though he had not dismissed her concerns the night before. Surely, he was ready to tell her to leave the hypothesizing to him. But he surprised her, and not for the first time.

"I'll tell you the truth, Miss Washington. I have a few ideas, but they're not cooked yet—not ready for me to talk about. I can tell you, though, that this fellow who was following you was bad trouble. Billy was right about him. His name is Marvin—Marvin Willetts. And from what you just said about Mrs. Jackson, he was nosing around your aunt, too. So I have to wonder—how could a nice lady like your aunt have ended up in the crosshairs of someone like him? Or how could you, for that matter?"

He waited in a rather uncomfortable silence, looking at Emily intently.

"I don't think I quite understand you," Emily said finally, her internal temperature rising. "Are you suggesting that my aunt did something wrong, to attract this guy, or that I did?" She heard a hint of anger in her voice.

"Not at all, Miss Washington," he answered quickly. "Not at all. But please understand, my perspective on this has to be different than yours. You want pieces of the puzzles to fit a certain way. I need to look at the whole picture and try to make all the pieces fit—and by the way, before tonight, it was a puzzle that I was directed explicitly to stay away from."

"And yet, you didn't," said Emily.

"No," said Maxwell. "I don't like leaving things to the sheriff's boys, for one thing. They're a sloppy bunch at best, and a crooked one, at worst. But don't quote me on that, ma'am. And this case tonight, this death, is squarely in my territory."

"And that includes why he died here, I gather."

"Yes, and any connection he might have had to your aunt, and by extension, to you. No offense meant—but you can see that line of inquiry has to be pursued."

Again, they sat in silence for a moment. "But you can't possibly think—" Emily began, but Maxwell spoke first.

"What I mostly think right at the moment—and I'll overstep professional decorum once more—is that, although you do look very nice, you also look exhausted. You've told me about finding the body. That's enough for tonight."

Emily started to protest. She had more to say, more to ask. But Maxwell cut her off again before she could speak.

"Look, Miss Washington, even if you're not exhausted, I've got a long night ahead of me, still, taking care of reports about this business. And it's been a long day. We'll talk again."

He did look tired, Emily thought.

"All right, I understand," she almost whispered.

"Do you think you'll be able to get some sleep?" he said, as she started to get up. "How about I assign an officer to stay outside tonight—keep an eye on the place? We can do that for a couple more nights, too."

Emily paused, her brows knit. She was still frustrated at being silenced for now, but all of a sudden, she did feel like her limbs were made of lead.

"Yes," she said. "I'll take you up on that, Detective. It would help me sleep to know that an officer was keeping watch. I'll see if Mrs. Davis can stay the night, too."

"That would be good," he said. "Now, send her out, if you don't mind, and after I speak with her, I'll be on my way. I do hope you both get some sleep."

He paused and looked at her.

"And Miss Washington, I am on your side, you know." She still bristled a bit from what she regarded as his suggestion that her aunt had somehow attracted Marvin's attention. But overall, she found herself believing that, yes, he was on her side.

"I'm glad to hear it," she said, handing back his suit coat. "Thank you for that. Good night."

Then she turned and headed to get Maureen, switching on the porch light just before she stepped inside. She looked over her shoulder one last time — both at Maxwell, sitting in her aunt's big wicker chair, and at the silver splash of moonlight on the floor. Good old moon, she again thought, as she had on her first night at Eola Lodge. At least that felt like home. And at least she would not worry tonight about the beetle Ford. Then it hit her. The absence of the Ford didn't mean she was safe at all. Dead Marvin's killer — whomever he or she might be — might very well be gunning for her, too.

Chapter 13

Secrets and Flowers

EMILY AWOKE EARLY to the smell of coffee and the sounds of clattering crockery. As she stumbled downstairs, she remembered that Mattie wasn't due to work again until Monday. She hadn't slept much, if at all. Every time she drifted off, she once again saw Marvin's pale, lifeless hand and heard Maureen screaming.

Now, as she nudged open the kitchen door, those screams seemed a lifetime ago. The Maureen who greeted her bore no resemblance to the sobbing figure she had helped into the house the night before. Wrapped in an old dressing gown of her aunt's and wielding a coffee pot in one hand and milk bottle in the other, her red-headed friend radiated energy, while Emily could only manage to plop down at the yellow table and rest her head on her arms. She looked up at Maureen with slits for eyes. "Good lord, woman. Aren't you tired?"

"I know—it's crazy," said Maureen. "I get up with the chickens. Under this thin veneer of sophistication beats the heart of a cracker farm girl. Have some of your good coffee." She sat a steaming mug on the table.

"Bless you," said Emily. "And I get the farm part but what in heck does cracker mean? Aunt Liz once told me she had turned into a tough old cracker, and I still have no idea."

"I know, it's an insult in some places, but in Florida, it sort of means the old pioneers—the hardy folk who settled the land, raised cattle. Our young friend Billy doesn't realize it, but his family is cracker royalty. Still, it's complicated."

"Right now, everything seems complicated—at least for me."

"You're not the only one," Maureen said, with a pat on Emily's shoulder. "I'm still trying to absorb last night."

Soon fortified by sips of cream-laced caffeine and bites of buttery toast, Emily felt more alert. Maureen joined her at the table, tugging to adjust Aunt Liz's robe as she sat down. The folds of its light cotton sleeves rippled in the breeze from the ceiling fan. It was actually an Egyptian caftan that Liz had found during her travels, and it seemed eerie but pleasantly comforting to see Maureen in it. Emily could remember her aunt wearing it years ago. It was so typical of Liz; she would never have worn a robe by Vanity Fair or some other lingerie brand.

"I hope you don't think I'm too nervy for wearing wear this," said Maureen, noticing Emily studying her. "Disrespectful or something."

"Of course not," said Emily. "I'm glad you're so comfortable here, truly. It helps me feel more at home. And I'm glad you stayed the night—and that there was a patrol car parked across the street before I went to sleep, and also this morning."

"This morning it's Officer Heyward," said Maureen. "I slipped out and took him a thermos of coffee a while ago. Seems like a nice young guy."

They sat in silence for a minute, sipping their coffee. Emily reached out to touch the embroidery on the sleeve of her aunt's caftan. "I'm really happy you wore this. It's so good to see it again," she said. "I can almost hear Aunt Liz saying how much it suits you."

"That means a lot to me," said Maureen. "I wish I had even a sliver of her style, or her strength. By the way, I'm so sorry I acted like a fool last night—all that hollering. You've got your aunt's kindness—the way you looked after me, the way you treat Billy."

"Oh, I don't know—sometimes I feel like I've turned into an old grouch."

"No, you definitely reminded me of Liz last night. When my husband was killed during the war, she was so good to me. My mother just wasn't helpful—she and my father hadn't really approved—"

"Why not—if I'm not being too nosy. Why didn't they approve?" Emily wondered if her own father would have approved of John—if John hadn't had a wife, of course.

"I'm actually relieved to talk about Robert," said Maureen. "I put on a brave face for so long. Maybe that's why I came so unglued last night. That blood dripping down Marvin's hand—it brought back the old nightmares."

Emily nodded. "For me too."

"But about my parents," Maureen continued. "When I told mother I was in love with Robert, she just moaned, 'But darling, we don't know his people,'" imitating her mother in an exaggerated drawl that brought a laugh from Emily.

"Oh dear! How did you meet him?" she asked.

"At a USO dance—he was stationed at the base here. To Mama, he was a dreaded Yankee."

"Like my aunt—and me," Emily said.

"It's funny—Mama accepted Liz, and she'll love you. Artists have a special rung on her social ladder, especially if they're important. She adores Julian."

"Believe me, I understand," said Emily. "You should meet my grandmother. She's hopelessly devoted to her notion of family position."

"Mama might even have taken to Robert if he hadn't wanted to marry me," Maureen said with a smile. "He was very good looking. But we got married in quite a rush because he was going overseas. No big church wedding, no country club reception—not at all what Mama had in mind for her only daughter."

"How much time did you have together?"

"A few months. I got to go along with him on his next assignment," said Maureen, blotting her eyes with a fold of the voluminous caftan.

Emily again reached out a hand and placed it on Maureen's arm.

"Those were the best months of my life, Emily—even with all the fear about the future. We had such good times with the other couples in our quarters—it was up in Cape Cod. They were from all over the country. It opened up the world to me."

"I am so very sorry," Emily said, at the same time struggling with pangs of envy. Even those few months Maureen mentioned had been so much greater than Emily's time with John. And that time had been sanctioned, blessed. Her eyes went to Maureen's wedding ring. She pictured herself and John on a beach in Cape Cod, maybe digging clams, laughing together. What would that have been like?

"Emily?" she heard Maureen say. "You okay?

"Oh, sorry—fine," she said. "I was just wondering whether to tell you how very much I do understand. I lost a love in the war, too—and now that I think of it, I've never told anyone, except Aunt Liz—and that was in a letter. We never had a chance to talk about it."

Maureen stopped blotting her eyes on her caftan sleeve and handed a napkin to Emily, who now found her own tears coming.

"Oh Emily, I am so sorry, too. Go ahead—have a good cry. You loved him very much?"

"Oh yes," said Emily, now dabbing at her own eyes. "The love of my life, I think. He died in France."

"We're some pair—I should let you cry into the other sleeve of this thing," Maureen said. "The war may be over, but the scars it left are far from healed for many of us, I'm afraid."

Emily nodded, blowing her nose into the napkin.

"Is he buried at Arlington?" Maureen asked, reaching for Emily's hand. "How did you manage at the funeral?"

"Yes," Emily began. She stopped to blow her nose again and looked up at Maureen. "But I couldn't have gone to the funeral in any case. Oh damn, I'd better tell you the rest of it."

Maureen didn't say anything but gave her hand a squeeze. "When you're ready," she said. "God knows, I am not going anywhere dressed like a soggy sheik."

Emily laughed in spite of herself and let out a large sigh.

"Maureen, I was the secret 'other woman.' He was married. In my family, what's left of them, they'd put a scarlet A on my chest in a minute if anyone knew—anyone but Liz. So I've just kept the whole thing as dead and buried as poor John."

Now Maureen got up and came around the table.

"You dear thing," she said as she put her arms around her old friend's shoulders.

"What would your Mama say, huh?" Emily said, her shoulders shaking in a mix of laughing and crying. "Befriending a scarlet woman—and one who's now mixed up in murder, to boot."

"We'll get Barbara Stanwyck to play you in the movie version," said Maureen, her shoulders now shaking, too. "Honey, I may have been married, but when it comes to sin in other aspects of my checkered life, I'll bet I've got you beat silly." Now both were trying to stop the giggles that had overtaken them.

"We've got to get a grip," said Emily. "Billy is apt to appear any minute. That seems to be as dependable as the sunrise."

"Yes, but before I forget," Maureen said, "when you told Liz about John—surely she understood."

Emily nodded. "I wrote her a long letter, and she wrote me a wonderful one back. I used to read it over and over. It was the only thing that helped."

"Liz was also my salvation after Robert's death—I think I told you about the Key West expedition? But she also took me under her wing. I like to take photographs as well as draw—and Liz did her best to boost my confidence. She even arranged a photo show for me, and she said she was keen on organizing a larger show here, for women artists and photographers."

"That must have been important to her," said Emily.

"Really?" said Maureen, with considerable surprise. "I honestly thought she only talked to me about it to keep me busy, keep the grief at bay."

"There's actually a lot about it in her will," said Emily. "She asked me to continue with the women's show if anything happened to her. You'll help, won't you? I wouldn't know where to begin."

"Of course," said Maureen. "But doesn't that seem strange to you—that she put it in her will? I mean, surely she expected to be around for a long time. She was in good health."

"And she was not a cautious person, God knows," said Emily.

"I agree—it does seem strange. It's almost as if she expected she might disappear." Now Emily was wide awake. She took a sip of lukewarm coffee and got up to get more from the electric percolator.

"What do you mean?" said Maureen.

"Oh dear, here we go," said Emily. "As if last night wasn't bad enough, Milton has me half-convinced that Aunt Liz's death wasn't an accident—more than half-convinced."

Maureen stared at her with saucer-wide eyes.

"I know," said Emily. "Crazy. But last night Mrs. Jackson across the street told me that Dead Marvin had been hanging out in the neighborhood before Liz's death."

"Who?" said Maureen.

"The man we found in the driveway," said Emily. "I know it's silly but that's the way I keep thinking of him. Dead Marvin. He actually seemed much more human dead than alive, poor man."

"How do you know his name?"

"Detective Maxwell told me," said Emily. "Marvin Willetts. Apparently, he was some kind of mob hit man. Reassuring, huh? Do you think Liz knew him?"

"I can't imagine how," said Maureen.

"I know," said Emily. "Can you think of any reason he would have been shadowing her—and then me? I've wondered if he was the reason the house was open when I arrived—if he'd been in the house."

"There's a cheery thought."

"It just seems like it has to all be connected in some way, but I have no idea how."

"Did Maxwell have any ideas when he talked with you last night?" Maureen asked.

"None he'd reveal. By the way, how did your interview with him go—didn't you call him Detective Dreamboat?"

Maureen blushed. "I did, didn't I? Lordy, I don't think I've said such a thing since Robert died. It was just peachy," she added. "In fact, except for the circumstances, it was almost pleasant. Don't you think he's rather handsome?"

Emily nodded and laughed, surprised to feel a twinge of something—jealousy?—about Maureen's admiration for Maxwell. She remembered the sensation of his fingers touching her bare shoulder, ever so quickly, under the moonlight. But how could she be jealous? She who had an almost-fiancé in New York? She liked Maureen and had felt compelled to tell her about John, but she wasn't about to confess her own moonlit thoughts about Maxwell, vague as they were.

"I know what you mean, I'll admit, but I nearly got into a spat with him," Emily said. "He didn't really say this directly, but I keep feeling like he's telling me to mind my own business while the big strong men take care of things. Which I am not about to do," she said.

"Well, honey, if he wants to take care of things for me," said Maureen, laughing, "I am not complaining."

"All righty," said Emily, laughing too. "Duly noted. But I do feel that it's important—and Milton Armistead does, too—for me to start asking questions on my own. Liz left a letter that basically asks us to do just that if her death was in any way suspicious."

"Good lord—you're serious about this," Maureen said as she got up and began to clear the table—"you really think she was murdered?"

"I'll admit I don't know what I think—and I'm telling you this in confidence, Maureen—none of this is for publication."

"My dear, I am not Hedda Hopper—some gossip monger who betrays confidences," she said, scooping crumbs off the table rather more energetically than necessary.

"Of course not, and I'm sorry if that's how it sounded—I'm really depending on you to help, too. You know how to ask questions, to find out information."

"What kind of information?"

"Well, just for example, you and Julian were talking last night about conflicts in your artists' group. Might someone have had it in for Liz—really held a grudge?"

"I can't think of anyone," said Maureen. "Like I said last

night, we have our political squabbles. And, mind you, some of the group are strange. One of the Murat sisters is practically nuts." She paused and broke into a grin. "And Simon Green in my sketching class does give me the creeps. He looks like that actor Peter Lorre, and has the manners of a clam. And he only draws ladies' feet—he's obsessed. Oh Lordy, I hope he wasn't creeping through the house before you arrived, sniffing around Liz's satin evening pumps."

That does it, thought Emily. After the morning's confessions and her lack of sleep, the image of a shoe-obsessed Peter Lorre lurching around Eola Lodge was enough for both women to dissolve into laughter until tears rolled down their cheeks.

"Oh dear, if I keep telling you about some of our local lovelies, I'll never get you to teach an art class for us," Maureen moaned through her laughter. "But now that I think about it, the Murat sisters? There are two, and the one who is decidedly not nutty was a friend of your aunt's—a pretty good friend. She might be a place to start."

"Yes!" said Emily. "I would love to start there. I don't want to just sit around and fidget—I want to ask questions, even if it ends up irritating Detective Maxwell."

"Okay, Miss Sam Spade—we'll pay a call on them," said Maureen. "I don't want you to have to face them alone. They're a little daunting."

"How so?"

"I think they are better experienced than described." Maureen arched an eyebrow in mock mischief.

"I can hardly wait," Emily said, still laughing. "I'm glad we can see some humor in all this—but Dead Marvin was no laughing matter. That's for sure."

She was about to say more when they heard a knock at the back door, which, just as Emily had predicted, was Billy Mizell. He'd brought with him a small, battered wooden wagon that sat on the brick path behind him and carried in his arms an immense bouquet of colorful gladiolas, wrapped in florists' paper.

"Hi Miss Emily, Miss Davis," the boy said through the screen, pronouncing each honorific as "Miz," which inspired Emily to wonder if all women were "Miss" in this world, whether married or not. She made a mental note to ask Maureen later.

"These are for you," Billy said as Emily opened the door for him and he thrust the gladiolas into her hands.

"Ooh la la," said Maureen, giving Emily a raised eyebrow. "The new lady in town has an admirer." Now it was Emily's turn to blush as she fumbled for the card.

"Someone all the way from New York City called in the order, long distance!" said Billy, and Emily recalled Maxwell's remark about the boy being like a one-person news network in town. How many people would already know she had received flowers from Up North?

"They were supposed to be roses, Miss Emily," Billy went on. "The folks at the florist shop said to tell you they don't have any right now and they hope you'll like these instead."

"I like them even better," Emily said, as she got out the bread for toast. Already she realized there was no point in asking him if he was hungry. In her short time in town, she knew the answer.

Billy explained that he'd stayed at Milton's after last night's big excitement. He had headed out early and stopped by the flower shop at one of the downtown hotels, where he apparently was doing a hopping underground business on Saturdays selling bolita tickets to the staff. When the shop's regular delivery boy hadn't come in, Billy volunteered.

"I figured you might need some help laying in some groceries, too, Miss Emily," said Billy. "That's why I brought the wagon. If I get them for you, you won't have to see those folks outside."

"Folks outside?" Emily and Maureen said, almost in unison.

"Didn't you all see them? Everybody's pretending to be walking to the park so they can see the scene of the crime—the murder! Someone was just out front taking pictures."

"Oh good lord!" said Maureen, who was washing up the dishes while Emily got out more food for Billy. "I'll bet it's someone from our weekly rag, Emily," said Maureen. "They call it *Society and*

Secrets—our own version of a Hollywood scandal sheet, can you believe it?"

"After the last couple of days, there's not much I wouldn't believe," Emily said with a smile, as she rummaged through cupboards for something to hold the flowers.

"Come on, Emily," said Maureen as she poured a large glass of milk and set it in front of Billy. "Spill the beans. Who sent the flowers."

"Do you have a boyfriend in New York, Miss Emily?" Billy chimed in. "Do you?"

Emily opened the card and confirmed the blooms were indeed from Lewis, who would no doubt be horrified that the roses he probably paid a fortune for had been replaced with more humble flowers. Emily truly did like the glads better, though—they were more real.

"Mind your beeswax, my young friend," she said to Billy with a grin, and then turned to Maureen.

"Here's an idea," Emily said to Maureen. "I really don't relish the idea of sitting here all day, wondering who's outside taking pictures and pointing at the house. Do you think we could call on the Murat sisters today?"

"I'll bet they would love it," said Maureen. "I need to talk with them about an Artists' League tea, too—that's a good excuse. I'll call them!"

"Wonderful," said Emily. "Then I'd at least feel like I was doing something to find out more about what Liz was dealing with—maybe they know something about her art-show plans, or maybe they'd have an inkling about why Dead Marvin was hanging around."

Chapter 14

Meeting Lex Luthor

"Yahoo, the terrible Terraplane lives," Billy yelled from the rumble seat, as they zipped out of Emily's driveway, just as he had done the first time he rode with her in the Hudson. Maureen, now clad in a skirt and shirt from Aunt Liz's closet, sat on the seat beside Emily. She laughed out loud and waved to Officer Heyward, parked across the street.

"Wait!" yelled a young man who stood by the driveway fumbling with a camera. "Are you the ones who found the body? Wait! You can be in *Society and Secrets*!"

"Now, honey," Maureen said as they rolled past him, the convertible top down. "Don't you wait for hell to freeze over."

The weather had cooled a little, and the dark scene in the driveway the night before receded a bit for Emily as she turned onto the road under the bright blue sky. At the wheel of the old Hudson, she took in a deep breath of the fresh breeze that ruffled her hair.

She adjusted the rearview mirror, tuned the car radio to a big-band station, and looked back at Billy in the rumble seat. She wished she could bottle his expression of pure delight.

"I'd forgotten how much fun this car is," Maureen said, strands of her blazing hair dancing in the wind. "It would be great to take this baby over to the beach. Wait until you see it, Emily. Nothing but sea and sand for miles, and the beaches are so hard and flat they race cars on them."

"I'd love that," said Emily. "I went to Daytona Beach with Aunt Liz—and Milton, too, I think—but it was a long time ago. The memory's a little hazy."

"Oh, can we go?" Billy shouted into the wind.

"Not today, Billy," said Maureen, "but here's an idea, Em — why don't we ride out to the city limits to shake the cobwebs off the good old Hudson? We can turn around at the Flamingo, and come back into town and go to the Murats' house. They really live close enough to you to walk."

"Oh yes, Miss Emily, please — with a cherry on top," came the voice from the back seat. "If we go right to Miss Odette's, we won't get much of a ride at all!"

So, nodding agreement, Emily focused her attention on Maureen's directions and found that, in a remarkably short time, the landscape changed from brick streets lined with houses to open pasture land as they took the road that Maureen said headed toward Florida's East Coast. They passed a dairy farm, where even the cows seemed to turn and admire the green Terraplane as it soared by, powered by Emily's foot resting a little heavier on the gas.

"This car is even more fun to drive when you can open it up like this," Emily found herself shouting to Maureen.

"It was kind of your aunt's trademark around town," Maureen yelled back. "And she wasn't known for being a cautious driver." All three of them laughed at their individual memories of Elizabeth Washington, moving through life with plenty of impact.

"And you say these sisters we're going to visit were friends of my aunt's?" Emily asked when they came to a stoplight and she could be heard without hollering. "What else should I know before I meet them?" She could hear Billy start to laugh from the backseat.

"Where to begin?" said Maureen, "For starters, they claim to be descended from Prince Murat, Napoleon's nephew who somehow ended up in Florida. They'll tell you all about it within the first five seconds of meeting you. He was a real person — I've looked him up — but it's hard to tell what's real about them — about Colette, anyway. Odette, I can handle, even admire. She's the one we want to talk with."

"Odette?" Emily had asked, raising an eyebrow. "As in the *Swan Lake* ballet?

"Yes indeedy, but our specimen is more like a Martha Graham dancer," said Maureen. "And you back there in the peanut gallery," she yelled to Billy, "be nice and stop laughing. They adore you."

"Yes ma'am," said Billy. "I like them, too, but Miss Colette is just funny."

"Her chocolate cake isn't funny," said Maureen.

"No ma'am. It's the best!"

Emily pulled herself back from a mental vision of licking thick, rich chocolate icing from a spoon and looked up to see they were passing a roadside marker for Orlando's city limits. Just beyond it on the right sat a sprawling Spanish-style building surrounded by a large, sandy parking lot. Only a couple of cars were parked there now, but the huge lot looked capable of holding at least a hundred. Large neon signs by the roadside and on the building, bedecked with pink birds and green palm trees, declared it the Flamingo Café.

"Boy, that went fast. That's the place where we can turn around," Maureen shouted into the wind, pointing at the building.

"All that neon out here on the open road?" asked Emily. "What is it?"

"Remember Mister Dimples at Julian's party—Charlie Wynne?"

Emily nodded.

"He owns it—the fabulous Flamingo. It's quite the hot spot," Maureen went on. "Great food—the chef is from Havana, and sometimes even the floorshows are, too."

"That's intriguing," said Emily. "It sounds almost like the Copa back home."

"Your aunt actually knew Wynne pretty well. Sort of surprising, when you think about it."

"How so?"

Maureen shot her a look, nodding her head toward the back seat and Billy, and mouthing the word "Later."

"Miss Maureen, I know all about that place," Billy hollered from behind them, with a shrug. "They've got gambling there, Miss Emily.

Everybody knows that. I've even worked there some, in the kitchen."

The boy stopped suddenly at the sound of a siren. Emily could see in her mirrors that a police car of some kind with a flashing light had appeared behind them. The driver motioned for her to turn into the Flamingo's lot.

"Holy crap," Billy muttered. "Just when things were going so good today. It's Lex Luthor."

"Billy, it appears to be your Uncle Carter—also known as the sheriff," said Maureen, as Emily guided the Terraplane into the parking lot and pulled to a stop.

"Surely, he's one of the good guys?" said Emily, but she heard both Milton's and Maxwell's voices in her head, reminding her of their none-too-flattering opinions of the sheriff and his men.

The boy was silent as a county sheriff's car pulled up next to them and parked, and a tall officer strode to Emily's side of the car. The cotton shirt of his uniform strained to cover his biceps. "Ladies," he said with a nod of his head. Emily couldn't see his eyes: Dark glasses covered them. "Billy, what in heck are you doing in this car?"

"It's Sheriff Mizell, isn't it?" said Maureen, looking up at him with a rather dazzling smile. What's she up to, Emily thought.

"I'm Maureen Davis," the redhead said. "I think we've met once or twice. I write a column for the daily paper. Dr. James Eppes is my father. And this is Billy's new neighbor, Emily Washington."

"I asked Billy to come along with us," Emily broke in. "I don't think I was exceeding the speed limit, was I, Sheriff?"

"No, ma'am." Mizell bared his teeth in a wide smile at Emily. "Welcome to our fine county, Miss Washington," he nodded again. "I saw this old Hudson go by—it's the only one I know of in these parts—and just wanted to make sure nobody had nabbed it."

As he spoke, Emily looked in the rearview mirror to see Billy sitting in silence, his thin shoulders hunched and his arms folded.

"How considerate of you," Emily said with no trace of a smile. "No, everything's in order. Would you like to see my license?"

She wasn't even sure she had her New York driver's license with her — the words had just popped out of her mouth. The sheriff's concern about the car rang as false as a wooden nickel.

"No, ma'am, that's not necessary," said Mizell. "By the way, I heard you had some excitement over there last night."

"Nothing wrong with your hearing," Maureen said, continuing to smile.

"Hope those pretty boys in the Orlando Police can handle something like a murder," Mizell said. His eyes were still hidden behind his sunglasses. The hair on the back of Emily's neck was beginning to stand up.

"Murder?" Emily and Maureen said almost in unison.

"What makes you say that?" Emily added. "The police have just started to investigate. The poor man might have shot himself."

"Oh, you'd be surprised, ladies. News travels fast, and there's not many law officers who'd be sorry to see that buzzard dead — or think he might have shot himself."

Emily squinted up at him in the bright sun.

"Since you're so knowledgeable, Sheriff Mizell, I wonder if you have any new information about my aunt's death — the fire out by the river. I think I heard somewhere that you investigated the scene."

"The sheriff's office did look into that fire, ma'am, but I didn't have much to do with the investigation. Sad accident, I heard. I'm sorry for your loss."

I'll just bet you are, Emily thought, recalling that Maxwell surely had said the sheriff himself was at the scene. Why would Mizell lie about that? He could say it was an accident with even more certainty if he had seen the evidence firsthand.

He touched his hand to the brim of his hat and nodded at them. "Since you and the car are all right, I'd better get about my business." He nodded at Billy. "I hope this little pest hasn't been causing you trouble."

"Not at all," said Emily. "Billy has been a big help to me."

"Glad to hear it," said Mizell. "You ladies take care." Then he spoke directly to Emily.

"Just one more thing. You might want to be extra careful, Miss Washington, after that shooting at your place last night—you being alone and all."

Emily felt a chill run down her spine as he turned and walked to his patrol car, got in, and drove off, leaving a dusty cloud behind. Then she looked after the departing car and turned to look at Billy, raising an eyebrow.

"So, Billy, he's your uncle?" she asked as she started the car again. If that were true, how could the sheriff be so solicitous about her aunt's car but show no interest in his nephew except to suggest the boy was a pest. She deeply disliked the way he had spoken to Billy.

"Yes'um," the boy said. "He's my pappy's half-brother. We don't see him very often." His elation at riding in the car had vanished, and he continued to stare into the distance in silence. It was the first time Emily had seen him in any other than an exuberant mood.

Emily and Maureen rode in silence too. Emily wondered how Mizell had known, not just about the discovery of Dead Marvin, but that she was alone at Eola Lodge. Maybe she was being silly. After all, news did get around in small towns, especially about newcomers.

But one thing was certain. In contrast to Detective Maxwell, this man had decidedly not made her feel reassured about any help she might expect from the sheriff's department—or at least from Mizell. His warning to be careful had sounded more like a threat than an expression of concern.

"Well, if that was supposed to make me feel better, it didn't work," she muttered to Maureen, who nodded agreement and looked over her shoulder at Billy.

"Billy, we'll be at Miss Odette and Miss Colette's soon," Maureen shouted over the wind that was again whipping curls of red hair into her eyes, as Emily drove the car back toward town. "There's bound to be something good to eat."

The boy was beginning to unwind a little, Emily noticed.

"I hope it's the chocolate cake," Billy yelled back, into the wind.

"The lemon tarts aren't too shabby either," said Maureen.

"Yep—Miss Colette can be a little daffy," the boy laughed, "but she sure can bake."

"Yes, well, enough said, Billy," Maureen said. Emily shot her friend a questioning look and only got a murmured "you'll see" for an answer.

And soon, Emily did see, after she turned off the highway and onto a brick street, following Maureen's directions, and parked in front of a large Victorian frame house that Maureen said was only a few blocks from Eola Lodge. As they approached the porch, she saw that a sign over the door proclaimed it "Chez Bonaparte" in fancy script letters. The tiny, round woman who answered their knock peered up at them while a second woman, tall and severe, loomed behind her in a dark hallway that seemed unchanged since the house was built—probably in the 1890s.

"Ladies, do come in. Enchanté," the small woman cooed, so that the word came out "enchan-tay-eh," as if the French chanteuse Edith Piaf had been playing Scarlett O'Hara. Her hair, an unnatural shade of black, was cut into a short bob with bangs. Wiping her hands on a disheveled apron she wore over a red dress, she extended a floury hand to Emily, who realized she was staring, and looked away. The petite woman rushed on.

"Welcome, mademoiselle," she said to Emily. "Welcome to Chez Bonaparte—our little bit of France here in La Floride. I am Colette Murat, and this is my dear sister, Odette." The tall woman nodded to Emily.

"Do come in and have a seat, ladies. And young Monsieur Guilliame, bonjour." Billy followed Emily and Maureen into the house, the picture of politeness.

"Bonjour, comment ça va?" he said to the tall woman. "I've been practicing my French, Miss Odette."

"C'est bon, Guilliame," she said, giving him a serious nod in return.

"We've been baking all day," the little woman rushed on, "getting a head start on the Artists' League tea, you know, Madame Maureen." Emily saw Maureen shoot her a quick glance.

"Wonderful," said Maureen. "We were just discussing your fabulous baking with Billy on the way here."

"How kind of you," said Odette. "We'd love to have your opinion of a few samples," she added to Billy, who looked more than ready to help out.

"Do have a seat," cooed Colette, gesturing toward a threadbare sofa and again wiping her hands on her apron. She must have first touched a hand to her rouged cheek, leaving behind a streak of something that looked like library paste. Emily looked from her to her sister, whose gray hair was swept back and up into an elegant twist. She could see little resemblance between the two women. Odette reached out to turn on a black metal fan that sat atop an upright piano near the sofa.

"Thank goodness it is a bit cooler this morning," said Colette. "Dear ladies and Guillaume, please do have some refreshment. Odette has been good enough to make us some lemonade." She indicated a pitcher and glasses on the coffee table in front of the couch, where Odette had also placed a display of baked goods that included slices of Billy's hoped-for chocolate cake.

"These glasses are precious to me," Colette continued as she began pouring into one. "Our dear ancestor, Prince Murat, brought them to La Floride. We're related to the Emperor Napoleon, you know, my dear," she said to Emily. Just as Maureen predicted, it had not taken long for the subject of the noble ancestor to be introduced. Emily avoided looking at Maureen for fear she might let out a giggle.

"Mademoiselle Washington, am I to understand that you too happen to be an artiste?" Colette said—all chirpy Parisian charm. Odette, the tall sister, who seemed to have no accent at all, was quietly preparing a plate of cake for Billy, whom she sat down beside.

"Yes, I'm a painter, and I can see I'm in the home of colleagues," Emily replied, with a nod at the drawing room walls, which were covered almost floor to ceiling with paintings in watercolor and oils. Some featured old-fashioned scenes of kittens, puppies, or bouquets of flowers, while others, in a very different style, captured Florida's natural beauty with accomplishment. Emily found her eyes drawn especially to a scene depicting tall sabal palms silhouetted against a sunset rendered in streaks of warm reds and yellows. Clearly a skilled hand at work. These must be Odette's paintings — the sister who had been a friend of her aunt's, according to Maureen.

"Ah, but of course, some of them are mine, and some are my sister's," said Colette, while Odette continued to slice cake and butter bread in silence and offer it to their guests. In contrast to her sister's disheveled state, her dark dress was immaculate, touched by nary a crumb.

"A wonderful variety of paintings," Emily answered, looking up at the art.

"I would like to experiment a bit more," Colette continued, "but I'm in such demand to paint the dear feline and canine members of our first families that I don't venture out in nature as much as Odette does. You are quite the adventuress, aren't you, dear Odette?"

She shot a sideways glance at her sister, and for just a moment, Emily thought she'd seen through a crack in Colette's sweet façade. Was she truly as dithery as she seemed or was she perhaps a woman who could be quite venomous?

Odette Murat looked back at her sister without a change in her expression and then turned her gaze toward Emily. "We have scenes of great unspoiled beauty here in Florida, Miss Washington," she said in a low voice. "Perhaps you'd care to join me one day on a trip out to the river. Your aunt did so on occasion. She taught one of our Artists' League classes, you know. Perhaps you could take her place."

As if anyone could take Aunt Liz's place, thought Emily.

"Sister dear, Miss Washington has just arrived," gushed the smaller woman, now sugary again. "We must give her time to unpack before we prevail upon her good nature."

"How nice of you to ask me," said Emily, not sure how else

to reply. "I'll certainly think about it. In her will, my aunt asked me to undertake a show of women artists, and I know I'd certainly appreciate your help."

She turned to Odette and added, "I was wondering, Miss Odette, did you ever go to my aunt's fish camp with her?"

Odette seemed not to hear, and as she buttered more home-made bread, an awkward silence followed, until Maureen came to the rescue and plunged into a discussion with the sisters about preparations for the upcoming Artists' League tea.

Emily found her gaze drifting back to Odette Murat's sunset scenes. They were very good indeed. A different style than her aunt's, but compatible. Then she heard Maureen's voice, smoothing the way for their exit.

"Ladies, thank you so much for your hospitality," her friend said, starting to rise from her seat. "We'd best be going. I just wanted to make sure Emily met you both, especially after what happened last night."

"But, Madame Maureen, of what do you speak? Last night?" asked Colette.

"Oh dear, I thought you might have heard on the radio," said Maureen, who was now standing and smoothing her skirt.

"There was a shooting in the driveway at Eola Lodge. The two of us and Milton Armistead—I expect you know him, don't you—well, the three of us discovered the victim. What a thing to greet Emily so soon after her arrival."

"Mon Dieu!" Colette exclaimed. Odette had risen too, but the little woman was still sitting, shaking her black bob.

"I know—it was very distressing," said Maureen. "Again, thank you so much. Lovely cake, Miss Colette."

The little woman nodded absently and didn't get up from the sofa. Goodness, what had just happened, Emily wondered. All of a sudden, it seemed as though their warm welcome had turned cold.

"The cake was good as ever," Billy chimed in, and Odette handed him a parcel wrapped in wax paper, along with a slip of paper that Emily saw bore a series of numbers, noted in an elegant hand.

"Wow, thanks," said the boy, in a whisper that could have been heard all the way to Georgia. "Don't worry, Miss Odette, I'll get your bets in."

"Thank you, Guillaume," Odette murmured. "Ladies, I'll walk with you to the door," she nodded to Emily and Maureen.

When they were in the dark hallway, she pressed an old-fashioned calling card into Emily's hand. "Here's our phone number, Miss Washington," she whispered. "I'm very glad you're here."

"Please do call me Emily."

"Indeed. Au revoir, Emily," Odette answered, and the hint of a smile broke the sternness of her face. "By the way, I did hear about the shooting, and I told Colette, but sometimes she simply doesn't take things in if she finds them unpleasant. She spends a great deal of time in a world of her own."

"I can understand that," said Emily. "Maybe it's part of being a painter. I often find myself in my own world when I'm working."

"That's very kind of you," said the older woman. "But I'm afraid Colette is a rather extreme case. And there's something I wanted to tell you privately, actually. You asked about Elizabeth's fish camp. Yes, I did accompany her there occasionally. I was honored that she asked. She considered it almost a sacred spot. I think the only other person she ever invited there, besides Mr. Armistead of course, was Mr. Sloane. They were very old friends, I believe."

"Yes, since their art school days," said Emily.

"It's a subject of great guilt to me, Miss Washington. I can't forgive myself," Odette Murat continued.

They heard Colette's voice, calling from the back of the house to her sister.

"Guilt? I'm sure you were a good friend to my aunt," said Emily. The older woman shook her head.

"I tried to be," said Odette. "But here's what I must tell you — my guilt."

Colette's voice came again: "Sister, ma chéri? Whatever is

keeping you?" Odette touched Emily's arm and looked at her intently.

"You see—the day your aunt died, I was supposed to—"

There was a cry from the other room, and then the crash of something breaking. "Sister! I need you!"

"I'm sorry, Emily. I really must—" Odette couldn't even finish her thought, for the sobbing that came from the other room. "I'm coming!" And with that, Odette Murat glided back into the dark hall, tall, elegant, and somber, leaving Emily stunned and confused.

Chapter 15

The Cabin in the Woods

ON THE DRIVE, first to Maureen's home, then to the grocer's, and finally home to Eola Lodge, Emily's thoughts were filled with Sheriff Mizell's lie and Odette's almost-revelation. She and Milton had talked about going out to visit the scene of Liz's death — the next day — and it seemed even more urgent after learning there were people hiding information about that day.

But as she and Billy put the car away, Saturday night loomed empty ahead of her, and she found she didn't want to be alone either, even with the city police car still parked outside her house — though she'd most certainly take a "pretty boy" city police officer over the bull-necked sheriff any day.

She wondered if Billy was on his own, as he seemed to be most of the time. Maybe she would offer him supper, but first, it might be a good idea to meet his dad, who might not approve of how much time the boy was spending at what was, after all, the scene of a crime.

After Billy helped her carry the groceries into the kitchen, she slipped the boy two quarters for the help.

"Golly, Miss Emily," he said, looking up at her, his eyes wide with surprise. "You're a peach."

"I'm grateful for your help, Billy, but I'd like to set some ground rules if you're going to be working for me. Since we're neighbors, too, I want to come over and meet your father, and make sure it's okay with him for you to help me out."

Emily also wanted to get a look at the place where Billy lived and see just what kind of father would let his child sell illegal gambling tickets, especially if his half-brother was the sheriff.

She also wondered why Billy's dad seemed never to have any

food in the house. He hadn't even appeared during all the fuss the night before—where was he?

"Naw, Miss Emily. That's not a good idea—you gotta believe me, it isn't," his face serious again, although not as much as it had been when confronted with his Uncle Carter. "It's all fine with my daddy. Honest Injun," the boy said, twisting the cap he held in his hands.

"But Billy—good grief, someone was killed here last night. Your father may not want you spending time here. And is it really okay with him that you help people break the law?"

He almost rolled his eyes, but not quite.

"And what about your Uncle Carter, Billy," Emily pressed on. "You said he's a big bully, but he is the sheriff. Is it fine with a law officer that you help people do illegal gambling?"

To her shock, Billy chortled.

"Oh, Miss, Emily, Uncle Carter is the last person who would care. He's pure hell on wheels—excuse me, ma'am."

"What do you mean, Billy?"

"Look, Miss Emily, I've gotta go." His smile faded. He squirmed and shifted his weight. "From what you said to Miss Maureen, you didn't think he was so hot, did you?"

Emily blushed, feeling the color rising in her cheeks.

"You told Miss Maureen he sure hadn't made you feel better," the boy continued, looking at her now, almost beseeching her. She hadn't intended for Billy to hear that.

"You're changing the subject," she said, her puzzlement beginning to turn to frustration. Why had the boy almost shut down at the sight of his uncle? And why did he seem to want so very much for her not to like the man?

"No ma'am." He shook his head. "It's the same subject. Just thinking of his ugly mug reminded me I really need to finish my bolita route. The drawing's late tonight, and I got regular customers depending on me."

As he spoke, Billy was moving toward the back door. His laughter had vanished.

"Gotta get my wagon, Miss Emily," he said, as he fairly sprinted out the back door. "Don't worry about my daddy."

Emily watched him head toward the path that led from her driveway into the dense woods that grew next to the grounds of Eola Lodge. All of a sudden, to her surprise, she found herself going after him, hurtling down the back stairs, across the driveway, and onto the path.

"Billy, wait! Please," she called after the boy. Good grief, what had gotten into her?

Low, silvery green palmetto trees lined the path as Emily scrambled along under gnarled oak limbs draped with the ever-present Spanish moss. These weren't Robert Frost's New England woods, but they were lovely, dark, and deep. Most of Emily's attention, though, was focused on Billy's feet running ahead of her, and on her own pounding heart.

She caught up with the boy, who had bent over to catch his breath, in front of the door to a rustic cabin. They hadn't gone far—the cabin was quite close to Eola Lodge.

Billy stood up and turned to face her, looking as though he was on the verge of tears.

"Okay, Miss Emily," he said, "you win. But the truth is, you can't talk with Pa. He's been gone for a couple of days."

"You mean, you were alone over here last night—after what happened?" She realized her voice was rising.

"I can be alone." The boy flung the words at her. "I'm not a baby." Then his voice was quieter. "But, no ma'am—Mr. Milton took me to his house. He brought me back real early so I could get my wagon—that's when I went downtown to the hotel and got those flowers I brought you."

Ah, yes, the flowers. Lewis. She wondered what he was doing back in New York. She would call him again tomorrow. Now she was in the shadowy Florida woods, a million miles away from Lewis's world. She heard a bird call out and wondered what it was.

She looked at Billy, who returned her gaze.

"Miss Emily, I wasn't fibbing. See, I can't let my regular ladies down—I need to get their bets, you know? They depend on me."

"I understand, Billy—I guess—as much as I can understand a boy your age being involved in a gambling ring."

"Gambling ring?" He laughed, somehow lifting her spirits. "Miss Emily, you make it sound like I'm some kinda criminal. Everybody bets on bolita. My ladies, especially, look forward to me coming by—and it's good to have pocket money."

He smiled at her. "Tell you what, Miss Emily—I do have to go—it's getting late—but since you're here—can you come inside for a minute?"

"Of course, Billy. I'd love to."

She wasn't exactly sure what she had expected to see when she followed the boy. Since she'd first laid eyes on him just a couple of days ago, she had been thinking of Billy as a kind of Florida Huck Finn and his unseen father as Huck's Pa—brutish and mean, someone who might live in a cave, or like a troll under a bridge. So this tidy rustic house came as a surprise. A large rocking chair sat by a stone fireplace, while an oak table bearing a polished brass oil lamp dominated one side of the main room. The cabin did have electricity, too. Billy moved to turn on a black metal fan that sat on the table near a window. The fan's warm breeze rustled several pencil sketches tacked to the cabin walls—scenes of a boat, a couple of deer, a picture of a house that might be Eola Lodge, even a still life of oranges.

"My goodness, Billy—these drawings are good," Emily said. "Who's the artist?"

"I like to draw, Miss Emily. Miss Elizabeth—she helped me a lot. She was a real good artist, wasn't she?"

"Oh yes," said Emily. And so much more, she thought—so much more than Emily had understood, it seemed. Then her eyes were drawn to the silver-framed photo on the mantelpiece and at the lovely dark-haired woman who gazed out at her from it, over a single, red flower that had been placed in front of the frame.

"That's my ma," said Billy. "Like I told you at the cemetery, she's been dead a long time. I can't hardly remember her."

"Can hardly," said Emily, and then immediately regretted her impulse to correct him. She made a mental note to ask him about his mother later, when they had more time—she hesitated to test the rapport that had returned between them after he had been so upset with her following him. Billy was eager to change the subject too, as he pointed out a large coil of braided leather rope that hung on a peg on one wall.

"Bet you never seen one of these, Miss Emily," he said.

"A cracker cow whip," she said. "That's a beauty." She moved closer to look at the caramel-colored coil.

"You know what it is?" the boy asked, his eyes widening. "You're pulling my leg, aren't you, Miss Emily? I'll bet they don't have those in New York City!"

"It's no joke, Billy. I had forgotten all about it, but Mr. Armistead had one, back when I was a girl and I used to visit my aunt. May I look at it?"

"Sure," he said, reaching for the braided leather and unfurling the whip as he handed her the wooden handle attached to one end. "Pa said Mr. Milton used to work for my granddaddy—a long time ago."

"That's right." Emily was beginning to feel transported back many years. She pictured Milton showing her the whip, smiling. She always felt so safe with him. Now she loosely held the whip's handle, which was more than a foot long, and began to move her arm slightly back and forth, dragging the whip on the floor of the cottage.

"He showed me how to use one—Mr. Milton, I mean," Emily said, her voice soft and a little dreamy. "I used to practice and practice out at my aunt's grove. The sound you could make fascinated me."

Billy ran a hand through his hair and shook his head.

"Come on, Miss Emily—you sure you're not putting me on? Cattle whips aren't for girls."

"They certainly were for this one—but I'll confess I didn't get to use it on herding cattle—only on the tin-can targets I'd set up on a fence."

"Let me see you crack it," Billy said, his eyes alight now. "I double-dog dare you."

"I can't do it here, inside your house — I'll break something," said Emily. Suddenly she felt like she was 12 years old again and sharing some deep, esoteric knowledge. And that was true, in a way. The "cracker" whips that Florida cowmen used to herd cattle could turn back a charging steer and not even touch the animal, she remembered Milton telling her. The whips could surely administer pain, he had said, but the cowmen didn't want to hurt their animals — only to control their movements. Milton had shown her how using one was a little like casting a fly-fishing rod, which she had seen her father do. Gradually she had gotten the hang of it — throwing the whip forward and then pulling it back fast, so that the end of it popped, creating an alarming, loud crack.

"Give it back to me, Miss Emily — we won't hurt anything — I'll show you how to make this baby really talk," Billy said.

Then a noise behind them made them both practically jump out of their skins.

"What the heck are you going on about?" said an intense voice behind them.

Heart pounding again, this time from fear, Emily turned to see a tall man coming through the front doorway. She almost screamed and then heard Billy's voice.

"Pa!" Billy hollered. "Holy cow, you scared me."

"Me, too," said Emily. She realized she was staring, and made sure her mouth was closed. The man in the doorway looked nothing like Huck Finn's Pa. True, he did look a bit disheveled and unshaven, with dark circles under startling blue eyes that were much like Billy's. And he did look like a fictional character, Emily thought — maybe from a Western movie. He wore Levis and cowboy boots, and his long, flaxen hair was tied with a cord at the nape of his neck. He had opened the cabin door with one hand and held a Stetson hat in the other.

"Oh, you're Billy's father," she said, gathering her wits. Now there would be a face to paint, she thought. She was building quite a collection of mental models.

"Yes ma'am. Jefferson Mizell."

"I'm so glad to meet you. I'm Emily Washington—your new neighbor, at Eola Lodge—my aunt's place?" She heard herself blurting out words—like she did when she was nervous. And this man definitely made her nervous. It was more than his unexpected entry. Maybe it was the shock of finding him somehow attractive— that was the last thing she had expected.

"Billy was helping me some today," she rushed on. "I hope that's all right with you. I came over, actually, in hopes that I'd meet you."

Jeff Mizell nodded at her. "I figured you didn't plan on herding cattle," he said, looking at the whip still in her hand, and Emily felt herself turning scarlet as she laid the whip handle down on the nearest chair.

Mizell turned to Billy without a trace of a smile.

"Boy, I hope you haven't been making a pest of yourself," he said. They were exactly the same words that Carter Mizell, this man's half-brother, had hurled at Billy earlier, she realized—but now they sounded very different. Gentle, not taunting.

"No sir, Pa," said Billy, shaking his head. "Miss Emily asked me to help. She's really nice, Pa—just like Miss Elizabeth."

"Well, that's high praise indeed," Jeff Mizell said, his arms crossed over his chest. Then he turned to her. "When did you arrive, ma'am?"

"It's hard to believe, but it's only been a couple of days," she said.

"We were real sorry about your aunt. Amazing woman."

"Pa, I gotta go," Billy blurted out. "I need to get to my regulars. I got a real serious schedule to keep to. Old Miss Carruthers will have a hissy if I don't come by and get her bet. And she ain't the only one."

"Isn't," said Jeff. "Not ain't."

"Oh, Pa."

"The big businessman," Jeff said, but with a faint smile this time. "Okay, Son, but you be careful," he said. "I heard what happened here last night."

Emily pictured the blood running down the lifeless hand of

Dead Marvin and shuddered. The nickname was irreverent, but murder was no joke. Why had Marvin Willetts been there? Why had he followed her?

"Maybe you heard about it from Sheriff Mizell?" Emily said on impulse and received a puzzled look in return. She went on in a nearly breathless rush. "We met him today. Billy came along with Maureen Davis and me to visit the Murat sisters, but we took a ride to the city limits first, and the sheriff stopped us—said he wanted to make sure no one had stolen my aunt's car."

"Did he now? Well, that's mighty interesting," Jeff said. "That reprobate was worried about Miss Washington's old Hudson? That's rich. No, I didn't hear it from him. Milton Armistead saw me going into the feed store, and tracked me down." He was silent for a moment and then turned back to Billy.

"Go on and get your bike, Son, and do what you have to do— take care of business. I have to go back to the ranch. I just drove in to get some supplies and check on you."

"Oh dang, Pa," the boy said. "Do you really have to go back? Can I go, too?"

"Not this time," his father said. "But I need you to do something for me. It's important."

"Sure thing, Pa. What?"

"I'd like you to check in with this good lady when you come back," he said, nodding at Emily. "If she'll be home and it's okay with her. I'll talk with her about that in a minute."

Well, that's a surprise, Emily thought. Her "Huck's Pa" vision of Billy's father would have spat on her, probably, and told her to leave his young'un alone.

They watched through the window as Billy got his bike and pedaled away from them down the dirt path, the silence between them stretching.

Finally Mizell broke it. "I'll walk you back to your house, if that's all right, ma'am. These woods and the path can be sort of forbidding." He held the door open and gestured Emily out of the cabin.

"I owed your aunt a great deal of thanks, and I expect I owe the same to you, if my boy's been up to his usual tricks," Mizell said, as he let the door bang closed.

"I can honestly say that I like him very much," said Emily. "In fact, I was going to ask him to have supper with me, if that seemed okay with you. That was why I followed him to your house—to meet you and ask. After last night, the house feels a little spooky on my own."

"I don't doubt it," he said. "That would sure help me out, too. That child has always been a live wire. He deserves better than the hand he's been dealt—deserves better than me."

Emily wanted to say something but couldn't think what. They walked on in silence in the fading late afternoon light. A breeze stirred through the palmettos that lined the sandy path. What kind of creatures might be nestled among the pale green leaves, she wondered. Lizards, snakes? Might other dangerous creatures—the most dangerous kind of all—have hidden themselves here to watch Eola Lodge? Jeff's voice broke the silence.

"I'd like to ask you about even more than giving my boy supper, Miss Washington—and I know I've got some nerve doing it."

"I'm happy to help, Mr. Mizell. Billy's good company, you know."

"He's a good boy, I know that. But Milton told me he's been over at your place plenty already, just like he did with Miss Elizabeth. So I know I'm asking a lot. I'm asking if he can bunk at your place tonight."

"Of course," said Emily, without even a second thought. "I've got plenty of room. I sure don't want him to be on his own."

By now, they had reached Emily's back door, and Mizell turned to go.

"He's still all broke up about Miss Elizabeth's death, you know," said Jeff Mizell. "Doesn't let on, but I can tell. I appreciated her kindness, and appreciate yours too."

Emily nodded, again not knowing quite what to say. She found him otherworldly somehow.

"Sometimes I feel like the boy is raising me instead of the

other way around," he said. "And he can handle being on his own. But there's something foul in the wind around here lately. Milton said that dead guy was some kind of mobster. And I have a feeling Carter wasn't just interested in the old Hudson. He's trouble, Miss Washington. I learned that the hard way. I want to keep Billy well out of his way."

That sounded ominous, Emily thought. What stood between these half-brothers, so very different from each other?

She started to say something, but it was too late. In what seemed like one lithe, graceful move, Jeff Mizell had tipped his hat and bade her good night, sprung down the back-porch stairs much like Billy had earlier, and started back toward the cabin, where he had parked an old flatbed truck. Perhaps it was the gray light or the paleness of his hair, but he looked insubstantial, like something that was not quite real—partly transparent.

When he got to where the path entered the woods, Emily saw Jefferson Mizell take a flask from his back pocket and raise it to his lips and take a long, hard drink. Then he was gone, swallowed by the silvery palmettos and the twilight.

Chapter 16

Odette's Confession

EMILY SLIPPED INSIDE the back door, making sure to lock it, and began going from room to room, checking in closets to reassure herself that the house was indeed empty and chiding herself with each step for being so edgy. She was peering into a linen closet that she hadn't realized even existed when she heard the telephone ring, raced to answer it, and grabbed the receiver, panting.

"Hi honey," announced Maureen's voice. "I just thought I'd check on you. Where were you—Timbuktu? I let it ring forever. You okay alone in that big old house?"

"I was upstairs. I'm fine, but I'll admit I was searching nooks and crannies. Spooked a bit, I guess."

"Is that young officer still out front?"

"Looks like someone is," said Emily, drawing aside a drape to peek out the window overlooking the street. As she caught her breath, she told her old friend about her encounter with Jeff Mizell.

"You actually talked with him?" said Maureen. "That's pretty remarkable."

"Why?"

"No one has seen him for so long, and—well, I hate to say it, but someone told me he had become a rather sad drunk. He was such a handsome boy, Emily—you'd never believe it."

Oh no, Emily thought as she pictured those azure eyes, I very much can believe it.

"Has he always worn his hair that way?" she asked.

"What way?" said Maureen.

"It's long; he looks a little like something out of *The Last of the Mohicans,* that's all," said Emily.

"Sometimes your literary allusions escape me, honey. I'm just happy he seemed okay, and you, too. Better run now — Mama and Daddy are coming for supper."

After she put down the phone, Emily switched on her aunt's big Philco radio and turned to a news broadcast to break the silence. The big empty house, with its creaks and sighs, was getting on her nerves, she had to admit. But it was ridiculous to be so jumpy when a young police officer was sitting just yards away. Deep breaths, she told herself.

She went back to the kitchen and was gazing at the contents of the cupboards, thinking about dinner and telling herself to calm down, when over the radio's crackle, she heard something else — was it a noise coming from the front of the house? Most of the house except for the kitchen was dark — she had turned on only one small light by the telephone when she talked to Maureen — and found herself sliding along a wall in the near dark and then peering at the front door from behind the corner of a bookcase. She felt ridiculous but couldn't stifle the images of Marvin's pale, dead face that crowded out her messages of reassurance. And she hadn't imagined it — through the sheer curtains that covered the window in the front door, a tall, shadowy figure loomed. For a moment, she could have sworn it was her aunt, and a chill ran down her spine. Then, giving herself a shake, Emily rallied.

"Yes, who is it?" she called out.

"Miss Washington, it's Odette Murat — forgive me — I should have telephoned," came a low reply.

The spell of fear and confusion broken, Emily rushed to the door and pulled it open quickly to indeed find the taller Murat sister, now dressed in trousers and accompanied by a large black dog that she held reined in firmly on a leash.

"Miss Odette, do come in," said Emily, adopting the style of address everyone seemed to use. Through the slice of open doorway, she waved at the officer in the patrol car across the street as she motioned for Odette and the dog to come in.

"Please do call me Emily. And who is this?" she added, motioning to the dog.

"This is Bonaparte, the real emperor of our house—you didn't meet him earlier today—he was banished to the back porch during Colette's baking. Are you sure it's all right for him to come in, Emily? He's used to this house—he often came with me to visit your aunt. We'll be on our way quickly, I assure you. I usually walk him around the park this time of day, and it seemed an opportune time."

"Yes, of course, it's fine," said Emily, waving a hand toward the couch. "Billy Mizell will be here in a while to spend the night, but I've got a few minutes before I tackle our supper."

Odette nodded and sat down quickly, as the dog plopped down by her feet.

"That's kind of you, Emily. Billy's a good lad," she said, as she glanced around the room. "Oh my, I'm no sentimentalist, but I have to say it is odd to be here without Elizabeth. I expect her to come out of the kitchen door any minute."

"Yes, I know what you mean," said Emily. "I'm still adjusting to that reality myself." From her perch on the edge of an armchair across from the couch, she reached down and patted the dog's back, looking up at her aunt's friend. "I know someone in New York who has a standard poodle," she continued, "but not as well behaved as this one."

"Well, his good behavior took some effort on both our parts. Lots of energy." Odette smiled and went on. "They're really working dogs, you know. I try to walk him as often as possible—it gives me a chance to get out of the house, I'll confess—" She seemed about to say more but stopped.

"How about some coffee, or tea?" It seemed only good manners to ask, but mostly Emily wanted to hear what had caused this unexpected visit by a woman who seemed anything but impetuous.

"No, thank you, I can't stay—I must get to the point." Odette paused, sighed, and went on. "I left too much unsaid when you visited earlier today, and thought it best to talk with you in private."

"Of course," said Emily, returning her gaze. "Please go on."

"Well, you asked me about Elizabeth's fish camp, and I mentioned my guilt to you—" Odette broke off, as if overcome by emotion.

The only thing she might be guilty about is not telling me about this fast enough, Emily thought, trying not to look as impatient as she felt.

"I'm sure you were a good friend to my aunt," said Emily. The older woman shook her head.

"I tried to be," said Odette. "But here's what I must tell you— you see—I was supposed to go to the fish camp with Elizabeth that day—the day she died."

"But you didn't go?"

"No." Odette paused, as if gathering strength. "Early that morning—after I was out tending to the garden—Colette came to tell me that Elizabeth had called to cancel the outing. A bad headache or something."

"I don't quite understand," said Emily.

"Colette made it all up, you see," said Odette, her voice rising with barely controlled anger. "Later she confessed that to me. She wanted me to do something that day with her, and she was jealous of Elizabeth in any case—she always has been. And today, when I tried to tell you, she—"

Ah, so that was it—the jealousy Emily had glimpsed earlier that day. She reached out to touch Odette Murat's hand, as Bonaparte looked up at them.

"I'm so sorry for your distress, Miss Odette," said Emily. "Still, there's nothing you could have done for Liz, I'm sure."

The older woman had extracted a handkerchief from her trouser pocket and blew her nose into it, as genteelly as it was possible for any human being to do.

"But if I had gone with her, if someone else had been there . . . she might still be alive," she said, quietly, starting to rise to her feet. "There would have been two of us to spot a fire—to see who might have started it."

"You think someone started it?" said Emily, also rising to her feet, as Bonaparte rose too and shook his fluffy ears, then looked intently at the front door, letting out a growl.

"Bonaparte, quiet, mon chér," said Odette, patting the dog. "Emily, it sounds like you've got more company, and I need to get home in any case. I've said enough for today."

"But do you think someone started the fire?" said Emily, now on her feet as well.

But Odette seemed not to hear her question and started toward the front door, which Emily had left open a crack, through which she heard Milton's unmistakable voice from the porch.

"Miss Emily, you home?"

My goodness, I was worried about being alone, thought Emily, and now it's like Grand Central Station. She found she always brightened at the sight of Milton, though. He would always be welcome.

"Yes, Mr. Armistead," she said, smiling. "Miss Odette's here — come in and say hello. Just give the door a push — it's unlocked."

"And why am I not happy to hear that?" said Milton, as he entered, taking his hat off and bowing slightly in their direction.

"Miss Murat, it's always an honor to see you — and that elegant pooch," he said. "Miss Elizabeth sure did take to that dog. She even bought bones to give him when he visited, Miss Emily. Hope I'm not interrupting."

"The honor is mutual, Mr. Armistead," said Odette. "It's no interruption. I was just leaving. Come, Bonaparte." Milton reached down to pat the dog's back, and Bonaparte gave his hand a lick.

"We'll talk more, Emily. You have my number," Odette said, as Emily walked her to the door. "Don't hesitate to use it. We're not far away. And I'd be happy to help you with that art show you mentioned, by the way. It was indeed important to Elizabeth."

"Thank you — that means a lot," said Emily. "I'm happy you stopped by, Miss Odette."

She waved her visitor goodbye, closed the door, and turned back to Milton.

"My goodness, Mr. Armistead — what an interesting day it's been," she said. "Come on back to the kitchen, and I'll fill you in."

"You cooking, Miss Emily?" he said, setting his hat on an end table and following her.

"Sort of. You won't be surprised to hear, I'm sure, that Billy's coming for supper—I met his father, by the way—and I need to start rattling some pots and pans, or at least heating up some leftovers."

"The boy bunked at my place last night," said Milton.

"I know, and I even know you ran into his father at the feed store," said Emily, smiling at Milton's expression of surprise. "You see, my gossip network is growing by leaps and bounds."

"My, my—I am impressed. How'd you hear that—and how'd you meet Miss Odette?"

"I'll reveal all," she said, peering into the cookie jar, where some of Mattie's handiwork remained, and soon she and Milton were seated at the yellow table, sharing the kind of before-supper snack that had always been forbidden in her youth. She filled Milton in about meeting the Murat sisters.

"What did Miss Odette want just now?" said Milton. "She looked upset—for her. The lady's usually cool as a cucumber."

"It was a little odd, but very interesting. Turns out she's been harboring guilt that she wasn't with my aunt the day of the fire. She was supposed to go along to the fish camp that day, but her sister lied to her and told her my aunt had called it off."

"You don't say. Miss Colette's wound up a little too tight, you know."

"So I'm beginning to see. She makes a mean chocolate cake, though."

"That's the truth," said Milton. "What was it that you were saying to Miss Odette just as I came to the door? Couldn't help but hear part of it."

"Yes, that's what really got my attention," said Emily. "She said something about 'whoever started the fire.' That maybe if she had been with Aunt Liz, there would have been two of them to see whoever started the fire—something like that."

"Now, that is interesting. Sounds like maybe I'm not the only one who thought that fire wasn't an accident."

"I thought that's what she was implying—but she left before she'd say more."

"I interrupted you, I expect," said Milton.

"It's fine. She was ready to go, I think. What do you make of them, by the way—the Murats?"

"Oh, I don't know," said Milton. "Guess I'm used to them—they're sort of town fixtures. Eccentric, for sure—all that French business. And different as night and day. But Miss Odette was a good friend to your aunt—Liz couldn't understand how she tolerated her dingbat sister."

"Families—there's no telling sometimes," said Emily.

"You got that right. But look here, Miss Emily—in all this talk, I almost forgot the reason I stopped by. The Western Union office downtown had a telegram for you, and I said I'd do the honors."

He pulled the paper out of his back pocket and pushed it across the table at her, as he looked up at the kitchen clock.

"Gotta get moving," he said, nodding at the telegram, which Emily had torn open and was reading. "That from your New York fella, Miss Emily?" he asked. "Not that it's any of my business."

Emily looked down at the familiar yellow paper bearing Lewis's words in all-capital letters, and sighed at the message: "DARLING. HOPE FLOWERS ARRIVED. AWAITING WEDDING DATE! CALL ME, POOH. YOURS FOREVER, LEWIS." The flowers—the gladiolas that were supposed to have been roses and now sat in a vase in the living room—had gone right out of her head with the day's events, as had her promise to herself to call Lewis. Tomorrow—she would do it then. The long-distance rates were better on Sundays.

"Mr. Armistead, my business is your business, I think. Yes, the telegram is from Lewis, in New York," she said, looking up. Milton had pushed back his chair, polished off the rest of his milk, and stood up.

"Do you want to stay for supper?" she asked. "I'm no cook, but I think Mattie left me well provided for, God bless her."

"That would be a pleasure, Miss Emily, but I told one of my drivers I'd take his shift tonight to meet the train. I'm glad Billy is staying with you. I want to hear what you thought of his daddy—and his half-uncle, I'd guess you'd call Carter. You still want to go out to the fish camp tomorrow? We can catch up then."

"I do want to go," she said. "I dread it, in one way, but it's important, I think. Odette said it was a special place for Aunt Liz—almost sacred to her."

"She did love it there—that she did," said Milton, turning to look at Emily as he made his way to the door. "Miss Emily, we're gonna do this. We're going to find out what happened."

"I believe we are, Mr. Armistead," she said. "I want to find out what and who took her from us—if it's the last thing I do."

Chapter 17

Movies in Your Pajamas

EMILY WAS STILL deep in thought about Odette and Milton's visits when she heard Billy calling to her from the back door. She had stopped for a minute to fuss with the gladiolas that had arrived from Lewis that morning, and had placed his telegram on the table next to them as a reminder to call him tomorrow. She certainly hadn't made much headway toward supper. Instead, she had passed the time rushing to the telephone and from one door to the other.

Now, here was Billy, waving a newspaper in one hand.

"Miss Emily, I got a great idea," he said as he thrust the evening paper at her.

"All right, but first, your father asked if you could bunk here tonight. To keep me company, I expect. That okay with you?"

"Swell! There's even PJ's and a toothbrush here Miss Elizabeth got for me, 'cause I stayed over so much. That fits right in with my idea—let me tell you."

"I'm all ears. And why do I imagine it involves food?"

Billy grinned and barreled ahead. "I guess it does, but it's more than that," he said. "It's a chance for a real adventure."

"Do tell." Emily raised an eyebrow, but she couldn't hide a smile. That was so much like something her aunt might have said. If she could have married John, she wondered, would they have had a boy like this—a boy so full of life that his very presence swept away her fears and sadness? And what of Lewis, who seemed so eager for her to return to New York? They hadn't really talked about children. Perhaps she had just assumed she was too old for that now—that it was an option that had passed her by—and she would probably have been a terrible mother, in any case. But there was no time for ruminating when Billy was right in front of her, practically jumping up and down, pointing to a story on the front page. "Drive-In Opens Tonight," read the headline.

"Just read this, Miss Emily! Everyone's talking about it down at the gas station—that's where I take my betting slips. This movie has a playground and a snack bar, and you just drive right in, if you got a car—and you have a beauty, Miss Emily—and you watch the movie right in your car. You can even go in your pajamas."

"Okay, just calm down and let me look," Emily said, thinking to herself that she might as well have been speaking French to the boy. "Calm" was not in his toolkit.

"Sometimes I'd go with Miss Elizabeth to the movies downtown, to the matinee," Billy rushed on. "But at the drive-in movies, well, you can get hot dogs and hamburgers—all kinds of stuff—and I figured we could eat our supper right there," he said.

"I see." Emily raised another eyebrow, but she was intrigued. She took the paper from Billy and read the article. Actually, this did sound like it might be fun—and definitely like something you couldn't do in New York City. And it might give her a chance to quiz Billy more about his Uncle Carter—why neither Billy nor his dad was keen on the man.

As she read the details in the article—bring mosquito repellent, the writer advised—she smiled at the thought of what Lewis's reaction would be to such an entertainment phenomenon. Sipping champagne at a museum or theater opening was more his idea of Saturday night pursuits. After all, if you were in your car in the dark, it would be pretty hard to mix and mingle, and the dear man did like to see and be seen. He wasn't even that keen on indoor movie theaters.

Billy grabbed the paper back from her, holding it to his chest. "Can we go, please, Miss Emily? If we go, I promise I'll do a whole bunch of chores for you—no charge."

Emily looked at Billy. Her head seemed full of voices telling her this was crazy, irresponsible nonsense. Saying a child needed a good home-cooked meal, not a greasy hamburger, for goodness sake—that voice might have been her grandmother's, while she seemed to hear her father exclaiming that surely she couldn't be serious. She could hear Lewis—an international traveler, no less!—saying the whole idea sounded dangerous—couldn't someone rob you in your car? This wasn't something for our kind of people, surely. But when she spoke, the voices faded.

"Why not, Billy? It sounds like fun. But can you play navigator again and get us there?"

"Sure thing. It's not far at all—it's just a couple of miles out on the Trail. That's the big road where lots of motels are—and nightclubs, too."

"Clubs like the Flamingo?" Emily said. She was still eager to find out more about the club where Carter Mizell had stopped them in the empty parking lot.

"Sorta, I guess," said Billy. "I can't go to any of 'em. The Flamingo is the biggest, though—the most famous. That's Mr. Charlie's place. So we can go? To the drive-in movie?"

Emily wondered how much Billy's social capital at school would rise if he could tell the kids on Monday that he'd been to the drive-in, on opening weekend, no less. The chance to go seemed like quite a big deal to the boy.

"Here's my condition," said Emily. "If it seems like a creepy place, for any reason, we'll leave. But, yes, we can try it out. I missed this in the newspaper: What movie is playing?"

"That's the really, really good part," said Billy. "It's *Abbott and Costello Meet Frankenstein.*"

For the first time that day, Emily heard herself laughing out loud. Now Lewis really would be horrified when she told him about her foray into low-brow culture.

But she could use some silly fun, and besides, seeing the movie really wasn't what appealed to her most about this adventure. She wanted to get to know Billy more, and also get out of the house, away from her memories of the night before. By the time they got home, she'd be tired out, she hoped, and sleep would come easily—both for her and for Billy.

Soon Emily and Billy found themselves in the Terraplane,

inching their way past a neon roadside sign with a blinking arrow indicating where to turn, as they waited in a long line of cars moving toward the drive-in movie ticket booth. Billy sang along with the radio, happy as a clam in pajamas from his guest-room stash.

"I hope we don't miss too much of the movie," said Emily, when a break for a commercial interrupted the music. "This line is taking forever."

"I'll bet almost everybody in town is here," Billy said. "Except for colored people. Mr. Milton took me with him once to their movie theater, though. It was fun."

"Mr. Milton's a pretty special guy," she said.

"He sure is—I make more money helping him than I do even from selling numbers. Don't you want to buy some bolita tickets, Miss Emily? Miss Elizabeth gave me bets, almost every week."

I'll bet she gave you bets, thought Emily. Her aunt would have wanted to help Billy. And her father always said Liz could take things too far, even over the edge of the law. Still, Emily had to admit she was interested, and this was the opening she'd been looking for to learn more about Billy.

"Billy, just because everybody does something, you know, that doesn't make it right. But, okay, I'd at least like to know how it works—the betting."

"You just pick three numbers and give 'em to me on a slip of paper, along with how much money you want to bet. Some folks use their dreams to pick the numbers. Say you dream about a horse—that means the number one. People got all kinds of systems. Every week they draw the numbers over in Tampa on Saturday night. If your numbers get picked, I come back with your winnings the next week."

Suddenly the boy was quiet, his attention on something ahead of them.

"Damnation," he whispered.

"Billy! What on earth? I expect Mr. Milton would box your ears at that language."

"I think Uncle Carter's in that car ahead of us," he said in a low voice. "Not the one right in front of us, but that Chevy a couple of cars up—it belongs to one of his no-good buddies. I'll bet it's full of them."

Emily looked hard but couldn't see much. Jeff Mizell had wanted Billy to stay with her to keep him out of Carter's way, and now here the sheriff was, if Billy was right—on a night off, along with half of the city, apparently. Somehow Emily had not expected such a big crowd.

She looked over at Billy and, for the second time that day, saw his brows knit with concern, his smile gone. The Chevy he had pointed out was at the ticket booth now. The driver had stopped the car too far from the window, and a tall figure got out of the back seat to retrieve the tickets. It was indeed a scowling Carter Mizell—Emily could tell from the fluorescent lights over the ticket book. He seemed unhappy with something about the transaction and was letting the woman in the booth know it, from what Emily could make out.

"Your boss is gonna hear about this, lady, and he ain't gonna like it," came one angry snippet. "I guess you don't know who you're talking to."

Emily watched Mizell get back in the car, and she turned to Billy. All the color had drained from his face. She didn't think Mizell could have seen them, but she didn't want to take any chances. She had told this boy's father she'd look out for him, and that was just what she intended to do—although she had to admit the sight of Mizell didn't exactly quiet her own jumpy nerves. He had tried to intimidate her, after all—all that business about her being alone in the house? Then again, he's only a big bully, she thought to herself. You can handle a bully. She put a hand on Billy's thin shoulder.

"Don't worry, Billy. He's so busy being angry he hasn't seen us. Here's what we'll do."

"What?" He was sliding down in his seat to avoid being seen.

"You've got sharp eyes," Emily said. "And this is a big place. We'll watch where that car goes, and head for the farthest spot away from them, near an exit."

Sure enough, in a few minutes, they had their movie tickets, and Emily and Billy watched as the Chevy headed toward the front right of the field where dozens of cars were parked in rows, their windshields pointed toward a giant screen that still displayed animated advertisements for the popcorn, sodas, hot dogs, and candy available at the concession stand in the center of the field.

"See?" said Emily. "We're far away from him."

"But what if we run into him when we go to get hot dogs?" Billy almost wailed. "That would be just my luck."

"Okay, how about this? I'll go while you stay with the car? He's only met me once, and I brought this scarf—I'll wrap it around my head. Look in the glove compartment and see if Aunt Liz had any dark glasses in there."

Sure enough, Billy produced a pair of sunglasses from the glove compartment.

"But, Miss Emily, it's dark," he said, laughing.

"Nonsense," said Emily. "It's the perfect drive-in movie disguise. Now watch—the cartoons are about to come on."

She showed Billy how to lock the car doors and headed alone to the snack bar, swathed in her scarf-and-sunglasses disguise like some poor man's Greta Garbo, and she soon returned to the car, laden with a cardboard tray filled with hot dogs, french fries, and fizzy sodas.

Thank goodness, she had seen no sign of Carter Mizell there. Just why, though, did he make her so nervous? Something about him definitely gave her the creeps, beyond Billy's concerns about him, but exactly what eluded her. It seemed to be hiding just on the outer edges of her memory.

After Emily got back in the car, she began passing Billy his food, along with a healthy handful of paper napkins. As previews of coming movies filled the big drive-in screen, she dug out some mosquito repellent from her purse.

"We'll slap some of this on as soon as we eat," she said, showing Billy the bottle. "There was no sign of anyone we know at the snack bar, by the way."

"Okay, Miss Emily," he said. "And thanks for bringing me here. This is swell. These french fries smell really good."

"They do indeed," she said, looking over at him as he dipped one into a small cup of ketchup.

"Billy, just tell me one thing, before the movie starts," she said. "What is it about your Uncle Carter that bothers you so much? Back there in the line when you saw him, you looked like you had seen the real Frankenstein monster—not that it's real, but you know what I mean. Are you afraid he'll stop you from selling these illegal betting tickets?"

Billy's eyes widened, and she could see the blue, even in the dim light. Then he burst into laughter. "Miss Emily, you got it all wrong. Uncle Carter doesn't want to stop the betting. Uncle Carter's only worry is that people don't bet enough!"

"I don't understand. What are you saying?"

"He makes a bunch of money from bolita, Miss Emily. He makes folks like Mr. DiMartini or Mr. Tiny at the gas station pay him to keep his big mouth shut about the tickets they sell—I really work for them, collecting the bets. If they don't pay Carter, he gets mean. He beat up a man at the gas station bad one time, real bad. And he wants me to pay him more, too—that's why I duck when I see him coming. One time he hit me so hard, he broke my arm."

The words themselves hit Emily like a blow. She hadn't really taken the boy's aversion to the sheriff that seriously earlier—assuming, perhaps, it was just a young boy's characteristic irreverence for authority. But breaking an arm: good grief, that was not only cruel, it was criminal. If Mizell wanted to keep the bets and the payoffs coming, what else was he capable of doing if he didn't get his way?

They sat in silence for a moment, startled by the noise coming from the metal drive-in speaker clipped to the Hudson's open window, and then looked up at the screen. Emily put her hand lightly on Billy's shoulder as they watched the opening credits, with Boris Karloff and Bela Lugosi in their monster roles looming large on the screen. No wonder Carter Mizell gave her the creeps, Emily thought. The monsters on the screen were fictional and, in this movie, objects of fun. The monster they had seen earlier was anything but.

Thankfully, the evening brought no further sightings of Carter Mizell, and the movie's antics offered diversion and fun, just as Emily had hoped. On the way home, she looked over at Billy and saw that he had dropped off into sleep, but she had a good sense of direction and was able to find her way back to Eola Lodge, where she was relieved to see a police cruiser still sitting next to the curb across the street from the house. As they pulled into the garage, Billy woke up and stumbled into the house, under Emily's guidance.

As she marched the boy upstairs, she extracted guarantees he would not only brush his teeth but also take a bath before bed. She put out clean towels and a fresh bar of Ivory soap and later even did an approximation of tucking the boy in. Billy protested that he wasn't a baby but seemed secretly pleased to have someone fussing over him.

"Miss Emily, you told me your mama died, like mine. Do you still have a pa?" the boy asked as she adjusted the fan to draw in the cooler night air. Through the open windows, she could hear the songs and chirps of unseen frogs and crickets joining in the fan's rhythmic lullaby.

"Yes, I still have a dad, Billy."

"Do you miss your ma—and Miss Elizabeth?" The blue eyes looked straight into hers.

"Sure, Billy. I miss them very much—sometimes, though, I feel like they are still with me, talking to me, helping me."

"I miss my ma, even though I'm not real sure I remember her. I have some pictures of her in my mind, though, and I feel good when I think about them."

"Yes, I have memories like that, too," Emily said, her mind filling with images of a pretty, dark-haired woman—her mother—adjusting Emily's own bed clothes long ago, turning on the nightlight shaped like a smiling moon and sitting on the edge of the bed and reading to her as her eyelids grew heavy. Then, she looked down and realized that in only a matter of seconds, the boy had fallen asleep.

She tiptoed out, leaving Billy guarded by a similar nightlight that had belonged to her aunt, a treasure kept since childhood, and by a slice of lemony light from the real moon, spilling onto the floor.

Chapter 18

Revelations in Eden

SUNDAY DAWNED bright and clear, with a hint of Florida autumn in the air that inspired Emily to wake up early. When she crept quietly down the hall to check on Billy, she found the guest room empty, with the bedclothes yanked into a ten-year-old-boy's idea of tidy.

The stairs felt cool on her bare feet as she padded downstairs to the kitchen, where the remains of a glass of milk sat among cinnamon toast crumbs on the yellow Formica table, along with a note from Billy saying he was heading off on his bike to help one of Milton's drivers meet the morning train from the North. The child was amazingly self-sufficient.

With a glance at the time, Emily hastily made some coffee, raced upstairs again, and dressed. She heard a car pull into the driveway, and a minute later, the doorbell rang—Milton, there to carry out their plan to visit Aunt Liz's fish camp, where her aunt had met her death. He had suggested they go in the morning while it was still relatively cool outside and also while most folks would be in church. Before she went to the door, she poured the coffee into a plaid thermos she'd found the night before and tucked it under her arm. She found Milton characteristically ready to greet her with advice.

"If you stay in town, at least through the winter season—and I sure hope you do, Miss Emily—you'll have to deal with church," Milton had said as he escorted her to the Cadillac. "Everybody, and I mean everybody, goes to some kinda church—except I guess the Jewish folks go on Saturday."

"Now, Mr. Armistead," she said as she slid into the back seat, "what makes you think I don't go to church?"

"Guess I figured you for a general nonconformist, like your

auntie," said Milton, grinning as he snapped his clip-on sunglasses into place.

"I think what bothers me most here is the lack of any privacy," she said. "Everybody seems to know everything about everybody."

"Tell me about it," said Milton. "Although, it's also amazing what you can hide from folks right under their noses. They see what they expect to see, and on Sunday, that's people going to church."

Even Aunt Liz had conformed to a certain extent, Milton said, when she joined the Unitarian Church a few blocks away. "Course, they're a bunch of progressive rabble-rousers like your aunt," he added. "The church was founded by some lady ministers she was right at home with—always some bee in their bonnets. Worthwhile causes, though." He smiled to himself as he started the car.

As they pulled away from the house, Emily asked Milton to stop next to the police car that still maintained a position across the street. Through the taxi's open window, she greeted the young man, an Officer Wilson, and reached out to hand him the plaid thermos of coffee. She wished she'd had some more java herself—she was finding it hard to focus.

Officer Wilson thanked her profusely, adding that his orders were to continue to watch over Eola Lodge for at least another day. The police surely couldn't keep this up, Emily thought.

"And ma'am?" added Wilson. "Detective Maxwell would like you to get in touch with him—no emergency, he said—just sometime today."

In the rearview mirror, she saw Milton shoot her a questioning look.

Maxwell—what had he been up to? She was eager to ask him more about Carter Mizell—and about Jefferson Mizell, Billy's dad, for that matter.

"Wonder what that's about," Milton said as they pulled away.

"Indeed."

Then, absorbed in thought, they rode in silence, as Milton navigated toward the road that headed east toward the river—the same road, she realized, that she and Maureen had taken the day before they turned around at the Flamingo Club. Milton seemed lost in thought as well, and she gazed dreamily at the landscape gliding by—the dairy cattle, the orange groves, the occasional building. Soon they passed the Flamingo Club, and she recalled her almost instinctive reaction to Carter Mizell the day before. What Billy had told her about the sheriff the night before—Billy's broken arm—greatly disturbed her. But even before that, something about his very presence had made her uneasy.

Now she remembered, in a flash, that Mizell had even found his way into her dreams. The night before, she had dreamt she was driving on a dark, winding road, with the black-beetle Ford following close behind her and then pulling alongside her on the right. On her left, the road fell away to a pounding ocean. As she looked over at the passenger-side window, she saw a dead-white hand reaching toward her from the Ford, its fingers laced with dark blood. But the face behind the wheel of the Ford belonged to Carter Mizell, leering at her with his teeth-baring grin. The teeth were the really scary part, in fact: they were sharpened to points, like a shark's.

Too much Count Dracula, she thought, even though the drive-in movie the night before had been humorous. With his bulging muscles and deep suntan, Carter Mizell was hardly the image of Bela Lugosi. Nor did he bear much resemblance to his half-brother Jefferson and his son Billy—how was that even possible? Her movie images drifted from Dracula to a Gary Cooper-like figure in buckskin, azure eyes ablaze.

"Miss Emily?" Startled, she realized that Milton was speaking to her above the wind from the open windows, turning his head. In her dream reverie, she had almost been dozing, with her head rolled to one side.

"You look like you could use some coffee," he said, and she roused herself and scooted forward in the big back seat so he would hear her.

"That does sound good," she said, "but I gave the coffee I made to Office Wilson—thought he probably needed it more. But I haven't seen anything like a Howard Johnson's."

"No ma'am. But I got us covered—brought a couple of thermoses and some biscuits. There's a picnic table out on your aunt's land." He held up another plaid thermos in his right hand, but a flash of something—pain? grief?—crossed his face. "Least, I expect it'll still be there."

The Boy Scouts weren't the only ones who were always prepared. Billy may have stayed with her last night, but the night before that—the night of Dead Marvin—it was Milton who had looked after the boy. He seemed to do what was needed, quietly, without effort. Once again, she was grateful to be with him.

After driving about thirty more minutes, they turned off of the main road, and the scenery began to look much more familiar, although she hadn't seen it in many years. Old oaks lined each side of the road, their branches curving skyward so they met in the center, forming what almost felt to Emily like a cathedral—a vaulted passageway that let sunlight through sparingly in dappled patterns on the hard-packed dirt. Soon Emily saw the turn to Aunt Liz's place, marked by a sign her aunt had crafted herself, Emily guessed. "Eden," it said in graceful blue letters on a piece of weathered cypress.

Her aunt had surely loved this place, and Emily wondered if she would be able to feel something other than revulsion for it now—not only because it was where her aunt had died but also because of her memories of the last time she'd been there—that long-ago day with Sam when the men had crashed through the peace of Aunt Liz's Eden and had threatened them, called them unspeakable names. She could still hear those men's voices, see their faces.

Then it hit her—why Carter Mizell had looked so familiar— and she almost jumped a foot off the Cadillac's seat. Milton had already brought the car to a stop beside a worn picnic table and was opening the car door for her when the thought came through with clarity.

"Mr. Armistead," she said, "I've just had a brainstorm! I haven't told you yet, but yesterday I met Carter Mizell. Saw him twice, in fact. I'll tell you the whole story, but here's the point . . ."

"Yes ma'am?" said Milton. He was wiping off the picnic table with a clean rag he extracted from the car's trunk.

"Do you remember that day when you and Aunt Liz brought your nephew Sam and me out here to fish, and those horrible men snuck up and yelled at us?"

" 'Course I do," said Milton, placing the thermoses on the table. "That was an awful day—but, oh my, Lizzie was something, though, wasn't she? She got her rifle and sent those Kluxers packing."

"Yes," said Emily. "She was wonderful. But here's what I just realized: Carter Mizell was one of that bunch, wasn't he? He was just a teenager then, of course—not much older than me, but I always remembered that one boy especially—he kept grinning at us, but he sure didn't look friendly. And when I met Carter yesterday, he seemed familiar to me somehow, but I couldn't put my finger on it."

"It all happened so fast that I didn't get a real good look at any of them," said Milton, "but it sure wouldn't surprise me any that Carter was one of them. Couldn't be more different than Jeff, though they share the same daddy—Carter always wanted to throw his weight around, even as a boy . . . Here, have some coffee."

He poured the dark, steaming liquid into the top of one of the thermoses, handed it to her, and began to open a paper-wrapped bundle of fresh biscuits, which Milton said had come from the kitchen at Wilson's Diner, where he knew the cook. Of course he does, thought Emily. Was there anyone in this town who Milton didn't know?

"I thought it would be good if we were fortified a little," he said. "The butter and honey are already on the biscuits, and the coffee's good and strong."

"It sure is—tastes great."

"Sort of a tradition with me, I guess. We—your aunt and I— always used to bring a picnic out here, take a minute to share some food, and breathe in the beauty."

He stopped, leaned back, and surveyed the sky, his eyes hidden behind his sunglasses. He seemed to have slipped into the past, perhaps on a similar day, with her aunt. Then, in an instant, he was back.

"Tell me about what happened yesterday—how you met Carter Mizell."

Emily quickly sketched out the sheriff's supposedly solicitous traffic stop the day before, how Billy had reacted, and then the boy's fearful behavior later at the drive-in movie, including his revelations that Carter not only took bolita payoffs but—much worse—had physically abused Billy.

"So, when you met him, Carter knew already about the dead man in the driveway at Eola Lodge?" said Milton.

"Yep, and he referred to it as a murder. Billy says he's crooked as a snake, too," Emily said as she rose and gathered up the thermoses. "Last night he told me Carter makes a lot of money—"

"Oh, I know about all that—the money. But just how did he know about that guy in the Ford being dead—how did Carter know that?"

"I don't know, but he also knew I was alone at the house. He was almost threatening about it."

"Oh, he's a bully, no doubt about it. Always has been."

"Sometimes bullies only talk big. It was the rest of what Billy said that really worried me—that Carter broke Billy's arm once."

"Damnation." Milton shook his head sadly. "I thought I knew that boy as well as anyone, Miss Emily, and he's never told me that. You've found a real fan there. He loved your aunt, too."

"I expect he needs a mother," said Emily. "I know I still miss mine. But here's more to tell you, too: I met Billy's father. Yesterday I was busier than a one-armed paper hanger—isn't that what you used to say?"

"I say a lot of things, I guess. Sometimes not enough, perhaps." He sighed and looked up at the sky again. "There's a lot to think about, for sure. So, what did you make of Mr. Jeff—Billy's dad?"

"I'm not sure, really. He wasn't what I expected at all. In his own way, he was charming. He asked for my help—with Billy."

"That's good. He sure does need it," said Milton. He paused and looked at her. "Well, you ready—ready to see the old place, what's left of it? Lots of memories."

"Yes, I think I'm ready. I'm scared, I'll admit, but I'm ready, thanks to you and the coffee. I appreciate your bringing that."

"Always good to start the day with java. Nectar of the gods, Liz would say."

"How much farther is it?"

"Not far. Just around a bend in the road. We could walk, but I'd rather move the car—keep it close to us."

"Have you been here since it happened?" she asked, as he opened the car door for her.

"Only once. I felt like I had to see it—see where she died. It was tough." He paused and took a long breath. "Then when I heard you were coming down, I thought I'd wait to go again with you."

"I'm so glad. I wouldn't want to be here alone—or with anyone else."

"It's your property now, you know, Miss Emily," said Milton. "It's a pretty sizable piece of land."

"I guess it must be," she said, "but somehow that hadn't occurred to me. There's a lot about the estate I don't yet know."

"Yes, which reminds me. One thing I'll bet you don't know is that you've still got a tenant out here—old Zeke, who lives in a little cabin on the property, through the scrub a few hundred yards from your aunt's place. He helped her out a little—knows a lot about the river, that's for sure."

"I'd love to meet him."

"I don't think that will be a problem," said Milton. "I expect he's heard the car and is already heading over from his place."

And in a few minutes, Emily found herself standing in front of what had been her aunt's Eden, or at least the painting-studio part of it. Her reaction surprised her, for the studio's ruins spoke to her not of horror but a kind of sacred beauty—even though she knew something awful had happened there—that someone she loved had died in the fire that had charred these boards.

But in this clearing of open earth, surrounded by tall oaks, what she saw reminded her in some strange way of the remains of a temple. Even in its best days, the cabin had been little more than a shack, an old fishing shack that her aunt had transformed into a retreat. Now, what was left looked a little like a crate that had exploded. Wooden slats, charred a blue-black color, pointed skyward. She could see the sky through the remains of the roof.

What struck Emily most was the stillness. No birds, or at least she couldn't hear any. They were too far from the river to hear any water sounds. It felt as though they were surrounded by a bubble — an invisible bubble over the charred cabin, keeping it safe for her so she could see it, beautiful somehow in its simplicity and terrible in its sense of loss. Her aunt had been happy here.

They stood in silence, and finally Milton spoke.

"Strange, isn't it," he said, his voice low. "Maybe it's because it's Sunday, but it feels almost like church here."

Emily nodded, and pointed to another small building that stood intact.

"Somehow I thought everything would be just ashes. Is that the old shed?"

"Yep," said Milton. "Your aunt converted it into a sort of guest bedroom — she sometimes slept there herself. She used the main cabin as her studio, and the kitchen was there, too. She even added an outhouse," he added, pointing to a small structure near the bedroom. "First-class country living."

Emily walked over to the smaller cabin and peered into the window. The furniture was still there — an old pine dresser, a single bed with a chenille spread, and even the curtains made from old drapes strewn with cabbage roses. One of her aunt's paintings hung above the dresser — a river scene that was probably painted right here, she thought. She moved toward the door and tried it, even though a substantial padlock barred the way.

"I put that lock on there, Miss Emily," said Milton. "Didn't want any vandals coming in. Zeke said he'd keep a lookout, too. I think he comes over and checks almost every day."

Just then the silence was broken by the sounds of rustling palmettos, and a cry from a voice that sounded a little like a rusty gate.

"Who goes there, who that be?"

"I told you he'd hear us," said Milton. "That's Zeke—the old coot must have known I was talking about him."

Emily looked up to see a very old Black man coming toward them, accompanied by a dog that loped at his side. He used a battered cane and carried what certainly looked like a shotgun.

"Ah, Mr. Ezekiel, my friend," said Milton. "I was just telling this lady about you—this is Miss Emily Washington—Miss Lizzie's niece. I would guess she's your landlady now," he continued, nodding at Emily.

"Hello," said Emily. "It's very nice to meet you, Mr. Ezekiel."

The old man nodded but said nothing. He looked at Emily hard and turned to Milton.

"I thought that was you, Army," the old man said. "I know that taxi of yours—big engine. But just in case, I came prepared." He shook the shotgun and turned his gaze again to Emily, who was still trying to take in the idea of Milton having a nickname, other than "General Armistead."

"Your aunt—she a good'un," he said to Emily.

She felt as if the old man's dark eyes were burning into her, and was unsure what to say. Did he mean Elizabeth was good, for a white person? She really wasn't at all clear about the racial dynamics of life here, she realized.

"He means your aunt was a good person, Miss Emily," said Milton.

"Oh, yes—she certainly was, Mr. Ezekiel," said Emily. "She certainly was good to me." As she spoke, she again felt her aunt's absence very strongly, but also her presence, too—almost as if Aunt Liz might open the cabin door any minute and wave them in.

"Mr. Armistead says you were a really good neighbor to her," she said. "Thank you for that."

She wondered if she should reach out to shake the old man's hand, but hesitated.

"We got along," said Zeke. He looked up, squinting into the sun. "We understood each other."

"Have you lived here long?" Emily asked.

"My whole life, ma'am, and my daddy and mama before me. Guess you could say the river claimed us, made us its own. The birds, the fish, even the gators—you could do worse than to live off the river."

Milton stood by silently, Emily noticed, watching the conversation unfold. He seemed far away, she thought, so when she spoke, it was again to Zeke.

"And do you need that often?" she asked, indicating the gun.

"Not often, no ma'am. Most people who come this way know me as a friend. But out in this part of the county, there are more trees than people, I reckon, and every once in a while, some no-good might turn up drunk, looking to teach a darkie a lesson." He looked quickly at Milton, who seemed to exchange his glance.

"So what brings you folks out here?" said Zeke. "Sad to see it now."

"Yes," said Emily. "I remember it from visits years ago. I guess I just had to see where my aunt died."

Zeke nodded, as he took a pipe from his back pocket.

"I hate to think of her being out here all alone that day—the day of the fire," said Emily.

Zeke had lit a match and was ready to light the old pipe, when he stopped and looked at her.

"Oh, she weren't alone," he said.

"What?" said Milton. He flipped up his sunglasses to look directly at Zeke, his eyes wide and sharp. "That's the first I've heard of it."

It was rare to see Milton genuinely shocked, Emily remembered. He clearly was now.

"Yessir, Army. I thought I told you," said Zeke. "But I guess I ain't really seen you since then."

"Please tell us now," said Emily. "Tell us anything at all you saw."

"I seen her out on the river in the boat earlier that day with someone. A man. Thought at first it might've been you, Army," he gave Milton a squinted look and Emily saw something pass between them—what, she wasn't sure.

"It wasn't," Zeke went on. "But I don't need to tell you that, Army."

"Did you see who it was?" asked Emily.

"Hard to tell. Had on a big hat."

"You tell the police about this, Zeke—that you saw somebody?" Milton asked, studying the old man. "Did you tell the police who came out?"

Zeke shook his head.

"Hell, you know who came out here, don't you? It was Sheriff Mizell hisself. I could have seen the Lord Jesus and all the angels come up outta the river for the Judgment Day, and that cracker sheriff wouldn't pay me no mind."

"Was it just him, then?" Emily asked. "The sheriff?"

"He was bossing around some folks who took the body away," Zeke said, who stopped suddenly when he saw the expressions on both Milton and Emily's faces.

"That man"—he stopped and spat on the ground—"that sorry excuse for a man has been in the Klan ever since he was a boy. He don't care about anything I have to say."

"I care very much, Mr. Ezekiel," said Emily, "I care very much about everything you have to say. And so does Mr. Armistead."

And I care about finding out what really happened out here, Emily thought. How exactly did her aunt die? Odette Murat had clearly had her own suspicions, as had Milton. Why wouldn't the old man say more? How did this fit in—this piece of the puzzle that Zeke had just revealed?

Milton reached out a long arm to put it around Zeke's shoulders.

"You're a good man. You couldn't have done anything that day, Zeke, you know—you did your best."

"The lord knows, I hope so, Army. Honest to God, someone was here with Miss Lizzie before that fire started. And when I seen the smoke later that day, I hollered so loud that some fellas who were fishing out on the river came up to try to help me. But we couldn't do anything, and we didn't find anyone else. Only her. And she was long gone. Long gone."

Chapter 19

More Funny Business

"WELL, HAVING a police car around was reassuring while it lasted," Emily told Milton when they made it back to Eola Lodge, having ridden in silence for the drive home, "but I didn't think it could last forever." The police car that had been parked outside when they'd left was gone. She just hoped her renewed focus on what happened to Liz didn't stir up more trouble—the kind that would make her wish she still had police protection, which clinched what she'd been thinking on the drive.

"I'd like to talk with Detective Maxwell right away."

"Right away? Sunday afternoon?"

"Somehow it feels urgent. What if the other night—Dead Marvin—and even the house being open when I arrived—what if it's all connected somehow to Aunt Liz's death, to the fire and the man Zeke saw her with?"

"I do think we ought to pursue what Zeke told us. Tell you what, Miss Emily," said Milton. "If you really want to see Detective Joe, I'm pretty sure I know where he is today. At the Coffee Club, over in colored town. That's our jazz club—he sits in quite a bit with the house band. Practices some Sunday afternoons by himself, when the place is closed and empty."

"Could you take me there? He did say to contact him anytime."

"Tell you what. I've got to get down to the train station—the Silver Star is due in from the North. But we could swing by later, see if Joe's at the jazz club, and I could let you off to talk with him and then come back to get you. If he agrees, of course."

"I really appreciate it," she said. "I'll see you in a little while."

Milton had pulled in the driveway and let her off in the back of the house—the more private entrance—and she rushed up the back steps, only to stop short. She thought sure she had locked up the house when she'd left, but now, behind the weathered screen door, the wooden back door stood slightly ajar. Looking at it more closely, she saw that the door had indeed been locked — something had forced the lock open. She whirled around to call to Milton, but the taxi was gone.

Inside, the old house seemed exceptionally still, except for the hum of a rotating fan she had forgotten to turn off in the dark living room. The late afternoon light crept through window blinds. Moving slowly and listening carefully, Emily became aware of another sound mixed with the fan's murmur — a faint musical tinkling. Probably an ice cream truck headed toward the nearby park. But as she approached the stairs, the sound grew louder and more distinct. And the tune seemed strangely familiar.

Her aunt's old music box!

Emily felt a surprising rush of energy and took the stairs two at a time, following the sound into her bedroom. Sure enough, there on the dresser, a tiny mechanical ballerina staggered and twirled groggily on top of the music box, careening to a halting version of Tchaikovsky's *Swan Lake* theme that was near the end of its wind-up cycle. With one swift movement, she grabbed up the box and turned the key, silencing it.

She shuddered. In the dim light seeping through the almost-closed blinds, she could see something dark on her chenille bedspread. She switched on the bedside light. The remains of one of her nightgowns lay knotted in the middle of the bed, its cotton fabric cut to ribbons and clotted with red paint, still damp but drying. A large kitchen knife had been thrust into the pile, stabbing a piece of paper. "Go home now or you die, Yankee Bitch," it read, scrawled in red.

To Emily's surprise, instead of fear, she felt roaring, red-hot anger rise in her throat.

Damnation, she thought. Whoever you are, if you imagine I'm going to curl up into a helpless mass of mush, you are sorely mistaken. You want to scare me? Well, I'm scared. But I'm as mad as hell, too.

Then another thought crossed her mind. Dead Marvin may have been creeping around her aunt's house before, but Dead Marvin could not have done this—there was someone else stalking her house.

❊ ❊ ❊

Emily was still flush with anger, her heart pounding, when Mr. Armistead pulled back into the driveway a few minutes later to take her to see Maxwell, per their plan. She had tossed the paint-stained remains of her nightgown into a paper grocery sack, along with the knife and note, and had folded the bag into as small a parcel as possible. She clutched it behind her purse as she got into the car. Billy was riding with Milton in the front seat and, on the spot, she decided to not mention her discovery in front of the boy. There would be time to talk about it later.

But Milton didn't miss much, and he turned to her with a questioning look as she slid into the Cadillac's big back seat, his brows knit in concern. She shook her head silently, mouthing the words "Tell you later." She was determined not to look upset in front of Billy, who had turned to greet her.

"How was your day, Billy?" she said to the boy, thinking what an awful actor she was at heart. But Billy seemed not to notice.

"It was pretty swell, Miss Emily. Pa's back from the ranch, so I can stay at home tonight. He took me fishing out on Lake Osceola this morning. He said he's going to ask you if it was okay for me to keep having breakfast with you, before school."

"Billy, it's more than fine," Emily said as she searched in vain for the Jesus fan.

"You're all out of breath, Miss Emily. You okay?" said Billy, reaching back to hand her the fan.

"I expect I ran down the stairs too fast." She smiled at the boy as she took the fan from him, and, surprising herself, reached across the seat to tousle his hair.

"My movie buddy," she said. "Did you tell Mr. Armistead about our adventures at the drive-in?"

"Yes ma'am," he said. "It was really swell."

"You two are regular social gadabouts," said Milton. "Next thing I know, you'll be taking in the opera." He joined in their laughter but threw her a serious look in the rearview mirror.

In a few minutes, the Cadillac pulled up in front of the building near the Carver Theater and Wilson's Diner that Emily had spotted after her visit to Wilson's—the Coffee Club. On its neon sign, not yet turned on, Emily could pick out the images of jaunty coffee cups and martini glasses that would be revealed when the sign was illuminated.

Her breathing was returning to normal, and she hoped that Milton and especially Billy hadn't gauged just how upset she had been. The note had frightened her, certainly, but now, instead of feeling shaky, her anger seemed to have settled into an almost calm resolve, a resolve to find out who was behind this threat and whether it was connected to her aunt's death—her aunt's murder, as she thought of it now.

"Wait here, Billy," said Milton. "Miss Emily's got some business inside here, and I'm just gonna make sure she finds her way inside. All right?"

"Sure," said Billy. "Can I come, though?"

"Not this time, Son—and we don't want to miss that train."

"Okay, Mr. Milton. I'll be right here." Emily noticed he was occupying himself by reading a Superman comic book.

"What gives, Miss Emily?" Milton asked in a low voice as they approached the door of the club. "When you came out of the house, you looked like you were about to explode."

"I didn't want to say anything in front of Billy," she said. "And I guess I can see the scary aspects of it now, but I was just so damn mad."

"Mad about what?" he asked, as he opened the door. The interior was dim, and from farther inside, they could hear the tinkling of piano keys.

"More funny business," she said, following him down a hallway. "But, like Dead Marvin, definitely not funny."

Milton stopped and turned toward her. "Go on."

"When the back door was open the other night, and we found those footprints—well, I still thought that might be just kids snooping. Not this—this was a knife and red paint—fake blood—smeared all over one of my nightgowns. Found it upstairs—in my bedroom. Oh, silly and theatrical, but yes, I'm still sort of shaking. Mostly mad, like I said."

"Not silly," said Milton. "You brought it to give Maxwell, I assume. That's him playing, by the way." He paused. "Damn, Miss Emily. I do not like this at all. But I'd best get on, and you can tell me more later."

He opened another door as he spoke, and as Emily followed him into a large, open room, she saw Joe Maxwell sitting alone at an upright piano on a shallow stage in the only lighted spot in the room. The rest of the space was in shadows; she could make out the shapes of tables and chairs.

"Hello?" said Maxwell, looking up. "Someone there?"

"It is two someones, indeed," Milton replied. "Hello, Detective."

"Milton?" Maxwell squinted into the darkness as they approached. "And Miss Washington? What's up? I hope something more hasn't happened over there at your place."

"Hello, Detective," said Emily, looking up at Maxwell, surprised that suddenly she felt a hint of butterflies in her stomach, just nerves over the prospect of telling him about the nightgown, she expected. Maxwell rose and walked to the edge of the stage area, in the center of the room, where she and Milton now stood. His thick brown hair was in its usual rumpled state, as was the white shirt that he wore with the sleeves turned up almost to his elbows. His tie hung unknotted around the open neck of the shirt. Emily realized she was clutching the paper bag, as well as her purse, as she looked up at him.

"Detective, apologies for intruding on your music time," said Milton, "but Miss Washington thought it best to talk with you as soon as possible. I've got to meet the Silver Star at the train station—young Billy Mizell is waiting out in the taxi for me—and if it's agreeable with you, I'll leave Miss Washington here to talk with you and then come back for her."

"Sure, that'll be fine," Maxwell said. "There are a couple of folks in the back cleaning up, but they won't bother us. And no need to come back, Milton—I know you'll have fares to the downtown hotels. I can give Miss Washington a ride home."

"Thanks for the thought, Detective, but I may check in anyway. I'd like to hear what you think after you talk with her. If I miss you, I'll catch you tomorrow." He tipped the brim of his hat to both of them and hurried back toward the door and Billy.

"Let's sit down here," Maxwell said to Emily, indicating a table at the side of the stage. He hopped down from the raised platform, pulled a chair out for her, and fumbled in his pocket, producing a match he used to light a lantern on the table. In different circumstances, Emily thought, they might have been out for the evening. In spite of her agitation, she found herself wondering what that would be like.

"Mr. Armistead said you played here sometimes," Emily said, still clutching the paper bag. Her adrenaline rush was beginning to subside.

"Yep, the place really swings," he said, turning a chair around and sitting on it backwards, with a leg on either side of the seat and resting his arms on its back. He held a cigarette up and asked, "You mind?"

"I might even join you," she said. He handed her a cigarette, lit it, inhaled from his own, and blew smoke rings into the air.

"Now, what's happened?" he said. "It has to be important. You look pretty upset."

Emily thrust the paper bag onto the table. Some of the red paint was starting to soak through the heavy brown paper.

"Someone's been in the house again," she said, nodding at the bag. "But I wanted to talk with you even before that. This was just the icing on the cake—to use an odd expression, since there's no cake involved." She let out a nervous laugh.

Maxwell opened the bag and slid the contents out onto the

table. The note and the faux blood looked even more forbidding in the flickering light from the lantern. Emily heard two men talking to each other from what she guessed was the kitchen, but they sounded a million miles away. She put her cigarette down on an ashtray that rested on the table.

"When did this happen?" he began.

"Sometime today."

"Did you hear anything? Anyone in the house?"

"No, I wasn't at home—Mr. Armistead and I drove out to my aunt's camp on the river, where she died. That's what I really wanted to talk with you about—before this happened, anyway."

Maxwell had been leaning back in his chair, still blowing smoke rings, but now he rocked forward in his seat and ground his cigarette out in an ashtray, looking at her with apparent irritation.

"What in hell were you all doing out there?" he said.

"I just wanted to see it again," said Emily. "Why—what's wrong with that? After all, it's my property now—why shouldn't I go?" She felt her face start to flush.

"No reason at all, Miss Washington, except someone was killed there, so it really should be considered a possible crime scene—even if the county idiots don't want to call it that. Which means it ought not to be disturbed."

"We didn't disturb a thing," said Emily, now feeling defensive and irritated. "And I did think, perhaps, we might find some kind of clue . . . "

"Clue?" The detective sat up even straighter, his brows knit in a frown. "You really ought to leave the investigating to me—and to the other police."

"But Detective, didn't you say you had been told to keep your nose out of anything about my aunt's death? Didn't you say it was the sheriff's jurisdiction? And now that I know a little more about who exactly the sheriff is, I'm even more troubled."

"Okay, let's deal with one thing at a time," he said, lighting another cigarette and drawing deeply as he shifted in his seat. "We'll get back to that in a minute—so when, exactly, did you find this mess?"

"Less than thirty minutes ago. We stopped by Eola Lodge for a few minutes before coming here," she said. "It was on one of the beds upstairs."

"Sweet Jesus. I just called off the watch over there early this morning. We don't have enough extra officers for me to justify it easily to my boss. Were the doors locked?"

"Absolutely. Somebody broke the lock on the back door. And I just thought of something—they must have done it very shortly before I came in the house, because whoever left this had wound up one of my aunt's music boxes, and it was still playing."

"So they could have still been around when you were in the house?" Maxwell asked.

"I guess so," said Emily, feeling a chill creep up her spine. "To tell you the truth, I was so mad, I didn't even think about that."

"Mad?"

"Yes—whoever is doing this must want to scare me, maybe scare me away from finding out what really happened to Aunt Liz."

"Maybe you should be scared." It was true, Emily thought. She should be scared, and she was. But this mess she had found seemed almost silly.

"Okay, agreed," she said. "But this is like some trick from a Hitchcock movie—*Gaslight* or something," she said. "I'm not Aunt Liz, I know. But she was strong, and I can be strong, too," said Emily. "I'll be darned if I'll be intimidated by crazy theatrics like this."

"Emily," he said, looking at her intently, and Emily registered that he had never called her by her first name before.

"Yes, your aunt was strong, very strong," Maxwell went on. "But she's also very dead. This whole business strikes me as something more than a cheap prank."

Emily felt cold again. So he is really taking this seriously, she thought. And he doesn't think Aunt Liz's death was just an accident.

"Well, one thing seems clear," she said. "Whatever Marvin Willetts was doing hanging around my aunt's place, he sure didn't do this."

"We can agree on that," said Maxwell. "So, what do you make of this mess — the note and the rest of it?"

"It's odd," she said. "I've used a lot of kinds and colors of paint, and I'd bet money that someone used artist's oil paint — probably cadmium red. Anyway, it's not cheap. The paper looks expensive, too. Someone could have even used my art supplies — I'll have to check."

She paused.

"What? What else?"

"I was just thinking that if someone hadn't done this — and hadn't been in my house, too, the day I arrived — I wouldn't have as much reason to question the accident verdict for Liz's death. If they're trying to scare me off, they'd have been better off to do nothing." Inside, she still felt chilled, but at the same time, she had never felt so alive, so ready to take action — if she only knew what the action should be.

"I get what you're saying," Maxwell said. He paused, tapping the ash from his cigarette into the glass Coffee Club ashtray on the table. "Okay, now tell me about the fish camp," he said — "what you wanted to talk with me about before this happened — if I got that right."

She sat for a few seconds, collecting her thoughts, her eyes fixed on the lantern light.

"Well, here's the essence of it — I feel really quite certain now that Aunt Liz was killed, and if it's the last thing I do, I want to find out who did it."

"What did you see out there that makes you so sure?"

"It wasn't what we saw as much as what we learned. There's an old man, Zeke — I didn't get his last name but Milton knows — he lives on the property out at the camp. He's sure that someone was with Liz that day — a man — and not Mr. Armistead."

"And that's important because . . . ?" Surely, he saw the connection, Emily thought — or maybe, after all, she was making too much of Zeke's revelation.

"Because if that person wasn't complicit in her death in some way, why didn't they come forward?"

"Did the sheriff's people talk to this man, this Zeke?"

"Apparently, but he didn't tell them anything," said Emily. "The person who interviewed Zeke was the sheriff himself, Carter Mizell—whom I've met too, since I last talked with you, and I understand now why Zeke was so hesitant." Again, Maxwell sat up a little straighter, a little more alert.

"Why?" he said. Emily studied him. Was he toying with her? Surely, if the Klan was one of his interests, he must know more about Mizell than he was letting on.

"Why?" she repeated, giving the word urgency. "For one thing, last night Billy told me that his uncle Carter—half-uncle, I guess—is not only crooked but also mean. Did you know he once hit Billy so hard that he broke his arm?"

Maxwell had been lighting yet another cigarette, but he put it down now.

"That sorry excuse for a . . . ," he began.

"Yes," Emily said, interrupting him, "it's awful. But after I met Carter Mizell, I also remembered something. Years ago, when I was a girl and was visiting my aunt, we were out at that camp with Mr. Armistead and his nephew—a boy about my age. Some men appeared out of the woods and threatened us. Aunt Liz ran them off with a shotgun."

"Good for her," said Maxwell. "But take notice, that's the kind of behavior that, with some folks, could get you killed around here. Still, good for her."

"The thing is," Emily went on, "I'm almost certain that one of them was Carter Mizell. He was a teenager himself then, but he was nasty—and scary. Later Aunt Liz told me the men were from the local Ku Klux Klan—she'd had trouble with them before."

"Do you think the Klan might have had something to do with her death, then? Perhaps she might have done something recently that got her killed."

"What do you think, Detective?" Again, she wondered if he was being straight with her, not being forthcoming about what he knew or at least suspected. "Based on what Zeke said, it's clear that Black people don't trust Mizell—at least Zeke certainly doesn't—and the sheriff doesn't seem to have done anything much to uncover the truth about her death."

"No surprise there," said Maxwell. "He would have had to actually do some work. But this Zeke—he talked with you?"

"Yes, I guess being with Mr. Armistead is some kind of credential of my trustworthiness."

Maxwell was quiet for what seemed a long time.

"Well, the truth is," he said, giving her one of his direct looks, "although I should keep telling you to stay out of it—god knows, this is a dangerous business, Miss Washington—I surely could use some unofficial help from you and Milton Armistead. I believe I really could."

Emily looked at him. She hadn't expected this change of tune. "Really?"

"Yes, as I started to say, the truth is—and please tell no one about this, except Milton—I'll tell him, but I think he already has an idea—an underground part of my job is to keep an eye on these Klan boys, and especially Mizell."

"My goodness."

"Yes, and if I can make sure you're safe—which would seem to be a big if"—he looked at the note on the table—"it might actually be helpful for you to play a kind of Miss Sam Spade . . . Say, are there any lady detectives?"

"Oh, please," she said, "you've clearly never read any Agatha Christie, Detective, although I'm no Miss Marple."

"A point well made. I'm more a Raymond Chandler kind of guy."

"Of course," Emily said. "Hard boiled, I'm sure. But, Detective, I do notice things. It goes along with being a painter—at least it does for me. I'm a good observer."

"I'm sure you are," Maxwell said, "and both you and Milton can probably talk with people who wouldn't confide in me. People who are scared of the Klan, for one thing."

"You didn't answer me a minute ago. Do you think they might have been involved in Aunt Liz's death?"

"I really don't know, Miss Washington, but their fingerprints turn up everywhere — not literally, of course."

"And . . . ?"

"And, okay, I wasn't going to tell you, but I did go out to the camp — undercover you might say — soon after the fire. At the edge of the water, I found a remnant of what sure looked to me like a Molotov cocktail, pure Klan style."

"Molotov cocktail?" she spit out.

"It's a simple firebomb — soda bottle filled with kerosene and rags. Light it and throw it. The Klan cowards love it. But other goons do, too. It's easy to make."

Emily felt a chill race up her spine — again, the fear she felt that day with Sam long ago whispered in her ear. She realized, though, Maxwell was still talking.

"Back to you playing Miss Sam Spade, can you please just do what I tell you — not go off on your own?" He stopped. "Another?" he asked, pointing to his cigarettes on the table.

Emily nodded, took one, and held up the cigarette for him to light it, but inside she was stewing more about Maxwell's instructions to do what she was told. When hell was froze over, she thought. Suddenly, she felt quite fed up with men telling her what to do — even men she liked very much. She'd do what made sense to her. But as she simmered — she hoped in secret — she smiled again and blew a smoke ring herself.

"My family — and my fiancé at home — don't even know I smoke," she said. "And I try to do so only in extreme situations."

Why had she blurted that out — about her fiancé? Was she trying to put up a barrier with Maxwell?

"Fiancé?" he said, raising an eyebrow. "Well, then, I suspect he'd understand that tracking a murderer — especially if they seem to be tracking you as well — is pretty extreme." He paused.

"You know, Emily — Miss Washington . . ."

But a noise interrupted them, and they both turned to see Milton Armistead, finding his way through the nightclub tables, into the dimly lit area where they sat.

"Miss Emily, I'm sorry about this," Milton began, an uncharacteristically pained expression on his face.

"About what, Mr. Armistead? Are you okay? Did you meet the train?"

She realized Detective Maxwell had risen from his seat.

"Yes, indeed I did," Milton continued. "And you see, the gentleman was so insistent . . ."

"Gentleman?" said both Emily and Maxwell, almost in unison.

"I told him to wait in the taxi," Milton went on.

But it appeared that the gentleman hadn't waited. Emily heard a crash and a muttered curse, as someone entered the room and apparently knocked a shin against one of the tables.

Oh no, she thought. It can't be.

But it was. There, rushing toward her, more flowers in hand and fur coat flapping around him, was Lewis.

"Darling," he cried. "Isn't this a wonderful surprise!"

Well, it's certainly that, Emily thought, as she let her cigarette fall discretely to the floor and stubbed it out with her shoe. "It certainly is a surprise."

Chapter 20

Stranger in a Strange Land

"LEWIS, OF COURSE it's wonderful to see you," Emily blurted out, as she stepped forward to take the flowers from him. "But why on earth didn't you send me a telegram, give me some warning?"

And why oh why, she thought, did you have to appear just when she had been on the verge of possibly learning more about Maxwell's Molotov-cocktail discovery, and about his mysterious "underground" role snooping around the Klan. She looked at Lewis and leaned forward to give him a peck on the cheek, suddenly very aware that Maxwell and Milton were standing nearby, witnessing her somewhat awkward reunion with her supposed fiancé. Her almost-fiancé, as she thought of him.

"Darling, it wouldn't have been a surprise if I let you know," he protested. "Mother and Father were traveling to Florida, so I joined them—decided at the last minute. The dining car was quite decent, actually, and—"

"Your parents are here, too?" Emily interrupted, realizing she was almost holding her breath.

"Oh, no, they've pressed on to Palm Beach, and a good thing, too, Emmie—Mummy's a dear, but sometimes she can get on one's nerves, you know?"

"I do know," Emily said, giving Lewis an impish grin. "You dear idiot," she went on. "You'll swelter in that fur coat. I hope you brought something lighter."

"I know, silly me," Lewis laughed, shrugging his shoulders. "I'm hopeless without you to keep me organized. I just threw things at the suitcase—just like I did in Paris, remember? We were so late for the train. 'Monsieur, vous serez en retard,' the conductor kept yelling."

Emily broke into laughter along with him, and then saw Milton, standing behind Lewis, his clip-on sunglasses raised to reveal his shrewd gaze.

"But I'm being rude," Lewis went on as he nodded at Maxwell, still in high spirits and teasing her. "I must introduce myself to this gentleman, since my surprise has obviously shaken loose your manners, Darling."

"Oh, I am sorry," said Emily, turning to Maxwell, who had a slightly amused expression, she noticed with some irritation. "Yes, I have been rude indeed. Detective Maxwell, this is Lewis Delacourt, my good friend from New York City," she said, nodding toward Maxwell, who reached forward to shake Lewis's hand, somewhat energetically. Was it her imagination, or did Lewis wince just a bit when Maxwell grabbed his hand?

"Lewis," she went on, "Detective Joe Maxwell is with the city police—he's been very helpful—and you've already met Milton Armistead, who was kind enough to bring you here."

"Police?" said Lewis. "Ah, and the cab driver, yes, it said Milton's Taxi on the car. I wondered how he knew where you would be."

"I've known him for years, Lewis. He's like part of the family," said Emily.

"You're welcome, Mr. Delacourt," said Milton.

"Milton was a close business associate of Aunt Liz's, too. He's inheriting part of her estate, actually, like me," Emily added.

"Lord have mercy, that's right," Milton said, almost to himself, as he shook his head. "I could probably stop driving cabs, one of these days."

"Well, he certainly sounds like an old friend," said Lewis, beaming, "since he knows all about me, and our plans. He told me as much on the ride here."

Now it was Emily's turn to throw Milton a look. Beneath Milton's dignified exterior lurked a bit of a provocateur, she thought.

"Yessir," Milton said with some emphasis, breaking into a smile and, Emily thought, playing his part with just a little too much schmaltz. "Miss Washington has said so much about you,

Mr. Delacourt, that I almost felt I knew you as soon as I saw you."

"But what's this about the police," said Lewis, as he nodded thanks to Milton and moved on. "Isn't this a jazz club? What are you doing in an empty jazz club on Sunday afternoon, Emily? The last thing you told me on the phone was about your aunt's will. You didn't mention the police, or jazz."

"Yes, Lewis, we have a lot of catching up to do," she said, smiling at him as her mind raced about what to do next. He couldn't stay at her house—tongues would wag, she supposed—not that she really cared, but still. A hotel? Milton would know what to do. She started to speak again, but Maxwell had beaten her to it.

"So Miss Washington hasn't filled you in on Friday night's events, Mr. Delacourt?" he said. "The body in the driveway?"

"Body in the driveway?" repeated Lewis, his voice rising.

Both Milton and Maxwell were enjoying this little scene at her expense, thought Emily, just a bit too much.

"You see," Maxwell went on, "Miss Washington is an important witness about a suspicious death. So is Mr. Armistead. They both found a car parked in the driveway at Eola Lodge on Friday night, with a dead man behind the wheel. Shot in the head."

Emily winced. Not long ago she had imagined ending her interview with Maxwell by sharing a cozy supper with the piano-playing detective and his wavy hair. Now that the shock of Lewis's arrival was subsiding, she had to figure out what to do with Lewis, and fast—and how much to tell him. She was in fact happy to see him. He was a part of her "real" life—or was he? After the last few days, she hardly knew what was real.

She looked at Lewis, who had turned white.

"Emily, what's been going on? Why didn't you call me?" he said, now sounding worried and confused.

"Calls are so expensive, aren't they?" she said, as brightly as possible. "And things have been happening so fast, Lewis."

He looked even more confused as he slipped out of the fur coat and placed it over his arm.

"The truth is," Emily rushed on, "I was going to call you just as soon as I returned home after talking with Detective Maxwell."

"Home?" said Lewis.

"My aunt's house — it's mine now, actually." She turned toward Maxwell.

"Detective, thank you so much for your time, especially on your day off. We'd better get Mr. Delacourt settled into a good hotel after his long journey. Mr. Armistead probably knows just the place."

"The San Juan," said both Milton and Maxwell in unison.

"Yes sir," Milton continued, "the San Juan will take care of a gentleman like Mr. Lewis in style. And they serve some pretty good steaks in the lounge area on Sundays, I hear."

"There you are," said Maxwell. "Proof once again that Milton Armistead is the man to ask about most anything in this town. Nice to meet you, Mr. Delacourt. You take care, Miss Washington."

Instinctively, Emily extended her hand and shook his. Again, his touch felt warm, and she held his hand for perhaps a second too long. Good grief, he wasn't the man in her life, she thought. That was Lewis, right here in front of her.

"I'll walk you all out," Maxwell continued, as he followed them down the hall to the front entrance. "It's dark in here, and the lights aren't on outside either . . . And I'll keep that package you brought, Miss Washington. Stay in touch." He turned and receded back into the Coffee Club and into the shadows.

Milton helped Emily into the big Cadillac's back seat and circled to the other side of the car to open the door for Lewis.

"Package?" Emily heard Lewis mutter as he slid into the worn leather back seat next to her. "What was he talking about? That detective fellow seems a little fresh to me," he whispered to her. "You had to notice the way he looked at you."

"Oh, Lewis, don't be silly." She was happy to see him — it was true — but she had already been taking care of Billy, gladly, yet now couldn't help but feel she had another charge to take care of, and lacked the fortitude to do it, at the moment.

"Emmie, silly?" he whispered to her. "I'm worried, is what I am. You've scarcely been gone, and I find you meeting policemen in jazz clubs and finding dead bodies. Soon I'll find out you're associating with the mafia and Al Capone."

Emily glanced up at the rearview mirror as Milton, wearing his best poker face, shot her a look. Lewis doesn't know how close he may be, she thought, if what Maxwell said about Dead Marvin was true.

"Was it awful, Darling — seeing that man?"

"I'm okay, Lewis, dear," she said, squeezing his hand. "It wasn't fun, but Mr. Armistead and another old friend, Maureen, were with me."

"That's good, at least. I remember you mentioning Maureen," he said.

"We'll get you checked into the hotel, and then we'll go to the lounge and order one of those steak dinners Mr. Armistead mentioned, and I'll tell you all about it," she said, squeezing his hand again.

"It's so good to see you, Darling," said Lewis. "Whatever is going on, you're positively glowing! Isn't she, Mr. Armistead? I say, you should treat me to dinner, Emily — since you told me you were going to be an heiress."

He smiled at her and reached over to kiss her fondly on the cheek and then spoke to Milton.

"I'm lucky I proposed to her before I found out about her aunt's bequest, aren't I, Mr. Armistead? She can't accuse me of marrying her for her money."

"There is that," said Milton.

Emily found herself wishing Milton could join them for supper. She dreaded answering Lewis's questions. Still, she leaned forward in the back seat so Milton could hear her.

"Mr. Armistead, I don't suppose you could join us for supper at the hotel," Emily asked.

"Miss Emily, you know the only way I can do that is if I was your waiter," Milton said, shaking his head. "Places like Wilson's Diner are pretty rare. Besides, you young people need to be alone.

It's a big occasion—this fine gentleman coming all the way from New York City to surprise you."

Milton, you devil, she thought. Now he was laying it on thick.

"Thank you, Mr. Armistead," said Lewis, putting his arm around Emily and giving her what she thought was one of his best warm-puppy looks. "I could tell you were a sensible fellow the moment I laid eyes on you and your superior automobile."

And here was Lewis, she thought, laying it on with a trowel right back.

"I appreciate the sign of respect, sir, but you can call me Milton. And I don't say that to all the white gentlemen. Anybody who looks at Miss Emily the way you do is all right with me."

It was true, Emily thought, Lewis was a dear. So why did she feel like kicking Milton, and Lewis, too. And Maxwell, too. Honestly, men could be so infuriating.

Chapter 21

A Cozy Dinner

MILTON WAS RIGHT about the cozy bar at the San Juan Hotel. It was a perfect place for a quiet dinner and for Emily to gather her wits after the shock of Lewis's arrival and Maxwell's invitation to be a sort of Miss Sam Spade. From their booth in the lounge area, she looked around the bar and imagined couples from years past huddling in the dark, wood-paneled room, sipping cocktails and exchanging confidences. The place reminded Emily a little of the tiny bar at the Algonquin Hotel in New York where she had met John on rare occasions—although this Florida version was larger, with booths tucked against one wall under antique prints and dim brass lanterns.

On the way to the hotel, Lewis had continued to pepper her with questions, especially about her discovery of Dead Marvin, why she hadn't called him again, and what package Maxwell had been talking about.

"Are you sure you and that police fellow weren't playing a joke on me?" Lewis had said, his arm around her in the Cadillac's big back seat. "The body in the driveway: It sounds like the title of one of your mystery books—oh yes, Pooh, I know they're your secret passion."

"Can't get much past you," Emily had joked and then turned serious. "I know it sounds sort of cheesy, but it's no joke. You know I have a habit of giving things silly names—maybe it's my way of dealing with them."

"You didn't really see someone who had been shot in the head, did you?"

"Yes, I did, Lewis. And I'm sorry I didn't call—I did plan to do that tonight. Let's get settled and order dinner and then talk about it. All of a sudden, I'm starving."

She wanted to get her wits about her — to figure out how best to report recent events to Lewis in a way that wouldn't unduly alarm him and would encourage him to go back to New York sooner rather than later. That way, she could dig into finding out more about her aunt's death, as well as more about Sheriff Carter Mizell — not to mention whoever had left her the theatrical threat scrawled in cadmium red. Lewis might cluck over her mystery books, but she doubted he would happily envision his future wife as a potential detective.

The bartender himself arrived at their booth. "I'm afraid the hotel only has limited food service on Sunday evenings," he began, "but pretty soon, when the snowbirds arrive for the winter season, we'll have the main dining room open every night, and this place will be jumping."

"Snowbirds?" Lewis asked.

"Winter visitors," said Emily. "They go back to the North in the spring."

"Dead bodies. Snowbirds. I think I've gone through the looking glass," Lewis muttered.

But the bartender just nodded amiably as he noted down Lewis's room number and took his drink order for two Rob Roys. Emily would rather have had plain Scotch. Why did she persist in letting Lewis order for her, she thought, as he went ahead and also ordered her dinner as well as his own: steaks and baked potatoes and red wine after the drinks. The food sounded good, she had to admit, even though she hadn't even been invited to look at the menu. Her father had always ordered for her when she was young. Of course, he had always paid, too. But now, she would always be able to buy her own food, thanks to Aunt Liz.

She realized the bartender had gone and Lewis was looking at her, as he reached across the table and squeezed her hand.

"Dear Emily," he said, smiling at her. "The important thing is that it is so good to see you. Judging from what they said at the hotel desk, by the way, I was lucky to get a room at the last minute. I don't usually do things so impetuously."

"No, you certainly don't," she said, absolutely meaning it. She never thought of Lewis as one to act on impulse. Had she been wrong, she wondered. "I don't know when I've been so surprised," she said, "and I've been surprised a lot lately."

"Well, I hope I was a better surprise than finding a dead body," he said, sending her an endearing grin.

"Of course you were, Silly Old Bear, and I loved the flowers you wired, too." She paused for a minute. "But Lewis, truly—why did you really come? You had just sent me flowers. Is something wrong?

"Of course not, Darling. I just had to see you—mother has been so worried about the—well, never mind about that. Just think—soon your aunt's house will be our home here. I can't wait to see it."

Emily felt herself bristling. Boy, Lewis was sure ready to play lord of the manor—lord of her manor. She still had trouble thinking of Eola Lodge as her home rather than her aunt's, but it sounded as though Lewis had no problem assuming the role of future owner. She stifled the urge to snap at him, but at the moment, she also didn't feel much like sharing her inheritance with him.

"I'm afraid you'll find the house rather old-fashioned and eccentric, Lewis," she said. "Aunt Liz was a painter, too, so there are canvases stacked everywhere. She was rather bohemian."

"Yes, the black sheep of the family, I seem to remember your father saying," said Lewis, taking a sip of his Rob Roy. Now, Emily really bristled.

"Maybe to my father, but never to me," she said, feeling a red flush of anger rise in her cheeks. "I loved her lack of convention. I wish I were more like her." She was mortified to find tears rising up.

"Oh, Emmie, I'm so sorry. I didn't mean . . . ," Lewis began, but she cut him off.

"She was quite successful, you know, both in art and in business."

"I'm sure she was, Darling. Actually, I was always rather fascinated by the stories about her—and my remark was ill-timed, for which I apologize profusely. It must be very upsetting to be here, going through her things."

"Yes, it is," she said, surprised to find herself fighting tears, and upset with herself for doing so. She took a sip of her drink and a deep breath.

Lewis smiled, took her hand again, and leaned forward.

"Why don't you come back to New York with us, as soon as Father wraps up his business in Palm Beach."

Emily said nothing, as she continued to fight for composure, dabbing at her eyes.

"Come back and plan our wedding," Lewis continued. "That's the cure for the doldrums, and you'll really want to get back in the swing, Darling. Did I tell you Patsy's taken over as head of the museum-benefit gala? I thought you wanted that job, Emily—lots of good contacts."

Emily's back stiffened again.

"Patsy? Van Rensselaer? She certainly didn't waste any time."

"Meow," said Lewis. "Put away those claws."

Emily smiled but realized that, although Patsy and her competitiveness might irritate her, she no longer had any interest in chairing that gala. She wanted time to paint. Lewis really didn't know that about her. That kind of thing, the museum gala, was much more important to him—to his mother, really—than to Emily. He was still talking full tilt, she realized.

"If you're back with us next week, Emily, I'm sure the committee would rather have you, Darling. We think Dalí is coming to the gala, you know—can you imagine Patsy hosting him? She wouldn't have a clue what to say. All that glitters, you know."

"Now who's being catty?" Emily took a sip of her drink and smiled almost in spite of herself. She was almost shocked at what a relief she felt at being away from the so-called social whirl. But she couldn't miss a chance to tease Lewis either.

"I'll bet dear Patsy hasn't let your temporarily single status pass her notice," she said with a grin.

"If I didn't know you better, I'd think you were jealous of old

Pats," said Lewis, "and I'm thrilled. You know my heart belongs to only you."

And just what does that mean, Emily thought. Lewis believed it was true, no doubt, but how much depth of feeling was really behind it?

They exchanged smiles again, and Emily shook her head, in a mix of amusement and mild exasperation with his banter and skill in always getting back to what he wanted to talk about, which right now was getting married. The bartender appeared with their steaks and baked potatoes and deftly opened the red wine, poured some in a glass, and offered it to Lewis, who sniffed the glass first and sipped the wine slowly.

"My goodness—that's an astonishingly good burgundy," he said. "Better than what I ordered—I don't believe I saw that on the wine list."

"Yes, an excellent vintage," said the bartender. "It's from a private stock, sir—only offered to special clients. We're lucky to have expert advice from Mr. Wynne, the owner of the Flamingo Club—out by the city limits. He's here tonight and asked me to send you the bottle, with his compliments."

For yet another time that day, Emily's mouth had almost dropped open. Looking up, she saw Charlie Wynne from Julian's party—the fellow Milton and Maureen had called the gentleman gangster. She could see his dimples even from across the room, as he smiled and raised his glass to her and Lewis in salute.

"Mr. Wynne, that's him—he's down at the end of the bar," their server continued, turning toward their benefactor. "He said to send his special compliments to the lady."

"My lord," said Lewis, turning his head. "He looks like the Great Gatsby." There was a touch of excitement in his voice, Emily thought.

"Lewis, you never cease to amaze me," she said with a teasing smile, her good humor restored. "I didn't know you read books."

"Ha ha, Miss Smarty Pants. I've read Mummy's copy of that one. She and Father met the Fitzgeralds more than once, you know, at parties back before he went to Hollywood and drank himself to death. Sad business."

By this time, Charlie Wynne had caught Emily's eye and was walking toward them.

"Shhh, he's coming over," Emily whispered.

"Well, there's no need to shush me — and he does indeed match my picture of you-know-who."

Looking up at Wynne as he made his way toward them, Emily could see Lewis's point. Wynne was wearing an all-white flannel suit, which set off his tanned skin and blond hair to advantage. He cut a striking figure. Arriving at Emily and Lewis's booth, he bowed as he spoke to her, extending his hand.

"Miss Washington, I hope you'll forgive my boldness. I met you the other night at Julian Sloane's, and I knew your aunt — quite well, actually. I don't think I expressed my condolences adequately at Julian's. I had to leave on business." He smiled. "Please do accept my most sincere sympathies now."

Could Wynne really be a gangster, Emily wondered — the kind of person who might have known Marvin Willetts — the very body in the driveway? Yet here he was, saying he was quite a good friend of her aunt's. Could that be true? But she smiled back.

"Thank you, Mr. Wynne," she said. "And thank you so much for the lovely wine. How kind."

"Miss Washington, with me, kindness rarely has much to do with anything, I'm afraid," said Wynne, "but I'm gratified that you find the wine suitable."

Emily could almost feel Lewis mentally giving her an elbow in the ribs to get her attention, but he didn't wait.

"It's more than suitable," he said, smiling at Wynne. "Aren't you going to introduce us, Emily?'

"I was just getting there," she said. "Mr. Charlie Wynne," she said, "this is my good friend from New York, Lewis Delacourt — he's visiting for — how long, Lewis?"

Lewis ignored the question and rose to his feet to step out of the booth and shake Wynne's hand.

"Good to meet you, Wynne," said Lewis, repeating his thanks for the wine. "Have a seat and join us?"

"Now it's you who are being kind," said Wynne, as he slid into the booth next to Emily, wafting a mysterious, elegant scent that, Emily thought, was certainly not Old Spice. Something by Guerlain? It was familiar, but nothing John or Lewis would have worn. The scent she most associated with John was Lifebuoy soap. She always kept a bar with her.

Wynne looked across the booth at Lewis. "Glad you're enjoying the wine, Old Sport," Wynne said to Lewis, and Emily felt a light kick on her leg under the table as Lewis gave her a knowing look as if to say, "See, I told you he was Gatsby." She wanted to roll her eyes. Honestly, Lewis could be so impressionable.

"I'll confess," Lewis was saying, "I didn't expect to find a wine so civilized in the South."

"Oh, there's your first mistake," said Wynne. "Florida isn't the South—at least much of it isn't. We're the escape of choice for folks from up North—we specialize in pleasure."

"You don't say," said Lewis. "You'll have to tell me more," and Emily had the strange feeling that for an instant, at least, she didn't exist for them. She had disappeared into an inconsequential femininity. Then Lewis turned to her.

"Well, Mr. Wynne, I'm here not for pleasure but on a very specific, serious mission," Lewis began, again reaching for Emily's hand across the table—"to persuade this delightful lady to come back to New York as soon as possible and marry me." Then why, old Pooh Bear, do you look suddenly uncomfortable, Emily thought. She suspected he was a little intimidated by Wynne, perhaps. Lewis was used to being the one who bought the wine, who was the center of a party.

Wynne raised an eyebrow, in good humor. "Well, well. You're a brave man indeed, Mr. Delacourt. Marriage—that is serious business. And by that I mean no disrespect to the charming Miss Washington. I wish you both the best of luck." He flashed a dimpled smile her way.

"No offense taken — and please call me Emily," she heard herself saying. She wondered what her old friend Maureen would say about all of this — about Lewis's appearance, about him sitting here with her chatting privately with someone of Wynne's apparent notoriety. And beyond Maureen, what would Milton say — or Maxwell?

She looked at Wynne, the rather fabulous figure seated next to her, as he raised his wine glass to take a sip. She noticed as the light struck his hand that he wore an elegant gold ring bearing an insignia. Lewis noticed, too.

"I say, Wynne," he said, "that's a Princeton ring, isn't it? I thought you looked slightly familiar."

Within seconds, they were trading names of college friends and acquaintances like two old fraternity brothers, which, amazingly enough, it turned out that they were — although Wynne was a few years older, and their time on campus had not overlapped by more than a semester. Both had also spent the war working in intelligence units — something Emily had known about Lewis, and which was, in his case, an assignment that had something to do with his language skills and his flat feet.

"So did you ever know Bunny Cavendish — he would have been in your class, I think," Wynne was asking Lewis.

"Oh, the Bun — what a character," said Lewis. "Oh yes, I imagine we closed down Tony's Bar more than once. The Bun was a campus legend."

"Did you ever hear about that time that he . . . ," Wynne started to say, and then looked at Emily and added, "on second thought, better not go there."

Lewis shook his head, laughing. "I say, Old Sport — what are the odds? That I'd run into someone here in Florida who knew Bunny Cavendish?"

What indeed, thought Emily, suddenly weary and feeling lost in the male camaraderie. Now Lewis was the one saying "Old Sport." And what kind of a name was Bunny for a man, anyway, she grumbled to herself.

Wynne was rising to leave, again telling Lewis what a delightful surprise it was to discover they knew people in common. She felt relieved that in her exhaustion, she didn't have to appear quite so bright and sparkling and could relax back into just coping with Lewis. Then Wynne turned to her.

"Miss Washington, I wanted to talk with you the other night but had to leave, so I was especially glad to see you here. I considered your aunt a friend, as I said, and a remarkable woman. My club is decorated with some of her Florida paintings. I'd like very much to talk with you more about her, especially since I heard you had a bit of unpleasantness on Friday night. Marvin Willetts?"

"You heard about that?" said Emily, and then to Lewis: "He's the body in the driveway."

"News travels fast in my line of work," said Wynne.

"Good lord," Lewis said to Emily, and then to Wynne, "What line of work is that?"

"Old Sport, I told you — I specialize in pleasure — in making people happy. I'd love for you to be my guests in a few days, and I'll show you exactly what I mean. The Flamingo Club — my club — is the classiest night spot this side of Miami. We're opening the season with a fabulous floor show from Havana — every bit as good as what you'd find at the Copa in New York. I hope you'll come as my guests for the opening."

Emily was about to decline — she suddenly felt protective of Lewis and his attention — when she heard Lewis speaking for her.

"It sounds wonderful," he was saying. "If I haven't whisked her away on the train by then, we certainly will."

Somehow, in New York, she had never been aware of Lewis answering invitations for her. Was this a new behavior, added on to his ordering for her, she wondered, or had she just not noticed before?

"Excellent. Adieu until then," Wynne said — and, looking at Emily, he added, "I'll give you a ring, Miss Washington — Emily — at your aunt's old number?"

She nodded, surprised that Wynne seemed determined to

speak directly to her as well. He shook Lewis's hand and then was gone.

"Amazing chap," said Lewis. "And you've met him before?"

"Yes, only briefly—Julian Sloane had a party," said Emily, as the bartender cleared their dishes and took an order for coffee and, for Lewis, apple pie. "I've mentioned him to you before, I think—before I came to Florida. He's a very old friend of Aunt Liz's, since they were young. You've heard of him, haven't you?"

"Oh, yes—and I'm looking forward to meeting him. You know, Emily, I want to go back to New York for our wedding, but I'm realizing more and more, it will be great for us to have a base here. Father says the real estate opportunities are wide open. I'll bet Sloane has some good contacts—and Wynne, too—just imagine, a Princeton man."

"Yes, imagine." She was feeling quite out of sorts, and realizing just how much strength she would need to summon to rein Lewis in and, she hoped, send him home. As she had realized in their Patsy banter earlier, she really was feeling quite relieved to be away from the gala committee and many aspects of her life in New York, which quite frankly, since John's death, had bored her silly. She felt needed here, truly—she thought of Billy—and she needed to be here right now. She needed to find out the truth about her aunt's death.

The coffee and pie arrived, and they settled into silence for a minute, with Emily thinking a bit longingly about the cigarettes she had indulged in with Maxwell. She didn't smoke often, but could have used another one now.

"So now, finally, tell me," Lewis said, bringing her back to the moment. "Tell me about this "body in the driveway" business. What happened? And, by the way, what did your aunt's lawyer say?"

"Things have happened so fast," said Emily. "Julian Sloane had the party I mentioned, Friday night, and when Milton brought me home—my old friend Maureen was with us, too—we found a car parked in the driveway with a dead man behind the wheel. Apparently, he was some sort of mobster."

"My god! And you saw him, you said?"

"Yes." She remembered the scene almost as if it were a dream. But oddly, she recalled having been more curious than afraid, more concerned with Maureen's collapse than with the blood and Willetts's poor pale face.

"I didn't actually see that much when we pulled up," she said, "only his hand—the car door was open. Then I took Maureen inside—she was quite upset."

"Good lord, I'm sure she was," he said. "What a shocking thing!"

"I did see him later, though," Emily went on, in a quiet voice.

"Later?" Lewis looked at her with wide eyes.

"Yes, there's a bit more to it," she said. "Detective Maxwell—the policeman you met earlier tonight—needed me to identify him, sort of. You see, he had been following me."

"Following you? Why would anyone follow you? Now I know I've gone through the looking glass. And you must be pulling my leg, Pooh—you have to be." Once again, he took her hand across the table, pushing aside the remains of his pie, and looked at her seriously.

"Emmie, I kidded you about Patsy, but you know she doesn't mean a thing to me. You don't need to dramatize what's happened here, you know, to get my attention."

"What?" Emily sputtered, pulling back her hand. "Lewis, you know I don't fabricate things." She felt her face begin to flush with anger.

"There must be some explanation, but it sounds to me like we've definitely got to get you out of here. Can you be packed by the morning? There's an early train, I think."

"I thought you wanted to go to Mr. Wynne's club," she said.

"Well, yes, but you come first."

"I told you on the phone, Lewis—I can't go back now and have a big fall wedding. Even before this happened, I had duties as my aunt's executor that her attorney said would take a little time, but now, well, it seems pretty clear to me—and to Milton Armistead, too—that I have important work to do here . . ."

"To Milton Armistead?" Lewis said. "That colored taxi driver? Now, he's an authority figure? I'm sure he's a nice man, but really, Emily."

"Lewis, I told you he's much more than that," she said. "And even if he were not, why should a 'colored taxi driver' be dismissed as unimportant?"

"Oh, that's right—I forgot your Marxist tendencies. Sorry, Comrade," said Lewis, half-joking but with his voice now rising from the hushed tones in which they had begun. Emily saw the bartender look up. Catching her eye, he raised a glass to inquire if they'd like another round of drinks. Reluctantly, she shook her head. More Scotch and she'd never get her points across to Lewis. He'd had most of the bottle of wine, she realized, and some of this conversation had to be the wine talking, not to mention his own fatigue.

"Let's not go down the 'Comrade' road right now, Lewis. I'll cut to the chase. The important thing is that I—not Milton, not anyone else, but I— believe my aunt was murdered, and I need to find out who did it and why."

"Murdered?" said Lewis, with a look of disbelief. "Didn't they tell you it was an accident? Are you sure finding that dead man wasn't too much for you, Darling? I can't believe you've had to deal with such things!"

"Oh really? What about the nurses during the war? What about the women in the aircraft factories?" Even without another drink, Emily now felt her cheeks aflame with anger. Hold on, old girl, she said to herself—deep breaths and no tears. You can do this.

"Emily, nursing people is not the same thing as dealing with gangsters and crime—you're a painter, for God's sake. The most dangerous thing in your world is a palette knife." He reached for her hand again, which sparked her anger even more.

"Pooh, look at me. I know you're upset, and have had a lot to deal with. But what if that wonderful imagination of yours is playing tricks on you. Maybe this man ended up in your driveway in some odd accident."

"Lewis, he had been following my aunt before she died. And

     Joy Wallace Dickinson

then he followed me. There was a connection somehow. And Mr. Charm to whom we were just talking—Lewis, he's supposed to be a gangster himself."

"A gangster—please, Emmie—he went to Princeton."

Now Emily rolled her eyes.

"But just think about it, Pooh—he's glamorous, a big fish in a small pond. He'd be a natural target for nasty gossip—you know what people can be like."

They looked at each other for a few seconds, and this time she let him take her hand again.

"I am sorry about that 'Comrade' crack. I am sure Mr. Armistead is a prince among men—I liked him very much."

"That's good, Lewis. He's very important to me."

"And that's good enough for me. But let's think about this. If it's true that there was any connection between this dead man and your aunt—and even in the unlikely event that your aunt's death was not an accident—I'm sure that detective we met earlier, that poor man's Dana Andrews, can handle it. He doesn't need your help."

"As a matter of fact, I think he does," said Emily, as they both started to rise to leave.

"Well," said Lewis, "what I mostly know right now, besides that I'm exhausted, is that I am so glad I came. Fear not—your knight in shining armor is here now. All we need to do is see that attorney and take care of whatever legal matters await, and we can get you out of here."

She felt like screaming, but, strangely, a sense of calm was settling in around the edges of her anger. She realized that she hadn't even told Lewis about the note and the knife she had just found, or about the requests in her aunt's will, or about Billy, or about Carter Mizell and what she remembered about him from years before. Perhaps, she thought, she didn't really want to tell him. Hearing about those things might just make him more determined to whisk her away. But if she played her cards right, she might even get Lewis to help with her inquiries, or at least not get in the way. If she knew him as well as she thought she did, he was probably relieved to be away from family pressures at home, at least for a few days.

"Friends again?" she heard him asking.

"Always," she said. "And we'll both feel better in the morning." She reached up and gave him a kiss on the cheek. Then, over his shoulder, through the door from the bar to the lobby, she saw Milton, talking with a bellhop as he waited to take her home. Milton would help her — of that she was sure. She would have to figure out how to deal with Lewis, but his arrival had only honed her resolve. Nothing was going to stop her from getting justice for her aunt.

Chapter 22

This Proposal Business

ON THE DRIVE HOME from Lewis's hotel, Emily did indeed pour out her thoughts to Milton, who looked at her in the rearview mirror, nodded in the right places, and did not even begin to interrupt her, for which she was exceedingly grateful.

"Honestly, Mr. Armistead, he means well," she said, feeling like a spring that had finally wound down. "In a lot of ways, he's my best friend. But his timing has never been great."

"Meaning what, Miss Emily?"

"Meaning that, even if he's decided to help—whatever that means—today was not the best time to appear out of the blue and start the 'marry me' refrain."

"Well, I'm no stranger to these New York types—no offense, Miss Emily—and Mr. Delacourt sure doesn't seem like a man who'll take 'no' for an answer—not easily, anyway."

"It's true," she sighed, "although some days he seems like he couldn't find his way out of a paper bag. But even when confused, he's as dogged as a bloodhound on the trail."

"Do you think he could help on our trail—to what happened to your aunt?"

"He thinks he can, but I'm hoping Mr. Wynne will keep him occupied instead."

"Now I am lost, Miss Emily. Take pity on an old man."

"Oh, so sorry—I forgot to tell you. Charlie Wynne was at the hotel restaurant. To make a long story short, it turns out that he and Lewis are fraternity brothers from college."

"Lord have mercy."

"I know. What are the odds? Lewis told him his mission was to get me to marry him—to marry Lewis, not Wynne." She laughed.

"And . . . do you want to marry him, Miss Emily?"

"Mr. Armistead!"

"I see," said Milton, watching her flustered expression in his rearview mirror. "None of my business?"

"No, not that," she said. "It's just that no one has ever asked me that before."

They rode in silence for a minute, as she collected her thoughts.

"Oh dear, Mr. Armistead," she finally said, "the truth is, I liked everything just the way it was before Lewis started this proposal business. In all honesty," she heard herself almost wailing, "I have no idea."

"Yes ma'am," said Milton. "I know what you're saying."

An hour or so later, as she stared at the ceiling, wide awake in spite of feeling exhausted, Emily kept playing the conversation with Lewis over in her mind. She thought, too, of Milton's concern about leaving her alone in the house and his offer to sleep in the small downstairs bedroom, originally intended for servants—no one would know he was there, he had insisted. When they had reached the house, they saw that a city police car was once again parked across the street—probably courtesy of Detective Maxwell—and she had finally persuaded Milton that she was perfectly safe and wouldn't hear of it.

Now, wondering if she had been honest, her eyes landed on the music box on the dresser—the very object that earlier that day, an intruder had taken the trouble to wind up and set playing, with the intention of scaring her silly, along with that ridiculous note—an intruder, she now realized, who had either been lucky or who had known roughly when she would return. She hadn't even told Lewis about that. She had, however, placed chairs against the front and back doors, until she remembered that Mattie would be letting herself in the back door early in the morning and had crept downstairs again to move that one.

Emily was determined to be independent—like Aunt Liz—and didn't like to admit that she was frightened, and she had very much wanted to assure Milton she was fine on her own—but the old house, with its nightly creaks and sighs, didn't help matters much. She had also found her aunt's old shotgun and placed it within easy reach of the bed. It wasn't loaded—but it made an impressive appearance.

Finally, at about 4 a.m., Emily's fatigue won the battle with her racing mind, and she fell into a restless sleep and then into dreams that she was at one of the Great Gatsby's parties, where across a crowded room she spotted Lewis dancing the Charleston with Patsy van Rensselaer. Charlie Wynne, in his white suit, was gliding toward her, about to offer her a huge platter of sizzling breakfast meat, when she awoke with a start and realized that, in fact, she did smell bacon. She opened her eyes to sunlight peeking through the blinds—it was morning. Thank goodness. Mattie must be down-stairs cooking, and that would mean Billy was probably there, too, for his before-school breakfast. Shaking off her grogginess and the dream, she suddenly felt immensely glad for both of them as she stumbled into her robe and slippers and bolted down the stairs.

The swinging door to the kitchen was shut, but Emily found herself now in high gear and gave it a powerful push, coming through the door to be greeted by surprised looks from Billy and Mattie, who were both seated at the table, reading the paper. Billy had the comics section next to his toast, while Mattie was scouring the front page. At the sight of Emily, she jumped to her feet.

"Sweet Jesus, Miss Emily," she said, clutching the paper and almost spilling her coffee. "You 'bout to scare me to death—again."

"Miss Emily! I was just telling Miss Mattie about how swell the drive-in movie was."

"I'm glad to see both of you," said Emily, "and, Mattie, you don't need to get up. It's fine to sit at the table. I am definitely not Scarlett O'Hara."

"No ma'am. For one thing, I don't see any Mr. Clark Gable right behind you. If he were, now that would have my attention for sure." And so would Lewis's visit, Emily thought. She wondered if Mattie had heard about that—how could she? But news seemed to travel in an instant in this town.

"I'm afraid my Mama never let us go to the sideshows, so—"

"I mean nothing here seems to be as it first appears. In this case, I suppose it's a good thing."

"Not sure I'm following you."

"It's Billy's dad. Before I met him, I imagined him as some kind of scruffy reprobate—but look at this lovely handwriting. I can't imagine Carter Mizell writing a note like that—how can those two men possibly be related?"

She put the note from Jefferson Mizell on the table in front of Mattie, who pulled her glasses from an apron pocket, slid them on, and peered down at it.

"My, Miss Emily, isn't that pretty writing?" she began. "Mr. Jeff's a fine man like his daddy, Mr. Frank Mizell. A cousin of mine used to work out at the ranch for Mr. Frank—and he thought that man 'bout walked on the water. He helped out when folks were sick—you still got your pay, that kind of thing. Mr. Jeff's got goodness deep in his bones—he's just had some hard times. I heard he was bad to drink after his wife died, got in some trouble."

Emily raised an eyebrow. Now there was a trail she'd like to follow, but another time.

"I see. So that's Jeff—but what happened to Carter?"

"Can't blame Mr. Frank for him. Mr. Jeff and Mr. Carter, they didn't grow up in the same house. Different mamas."

"Half-brothers, then?"

"Yep. Carter's mama was kind of a black sheep—and no friend to Black people, neither."

Mattie stirred sugar into her coffee and looked hard into the dark liquid, almost as if she were studying tea leaves.

"It is strange when you think about it, Miss Emily," she went on, now lookin0g up and into Emily's eyes. "We got these two different worlds, don't we—white and colored—where we don't go to the same schools, the same movie houses—nothin'—but because colored folks work in so many white people's houses, we tend to know plenty 'bout their business. Lot more than they think we do, I reckon."

"I wonder what people know about the sheriff—about Carter?" Emily asked.

"Well, for one thing, we know he got a big old white pointy hat in the back of his closet, Miss Emily. He's in the Klan for sure."

"So that's more than a rumor—that he's in the Klan," said Emily.

"For sure, but plenty of white folks don't want no part of rednecks like the sheriff. I guess they keep us in our place in more genteel ways. Nothing genteel 'bout Carter Mizell."

She wondered if this was information she could take to Maxwell to help prove her worth as a source of information. She leaned forward, her voice dropping.

"Mattie, one time when I was visiting Aunt Liz years ago—I was in high school—a group of men and boys scared me to death out at the fish camp, and I'm pretty sure Carter Mizell was one of them. But they didn't have any robes or anything."

Mattie shivered. "You all alone?"

"Mr. Armistead's nephew Sam was there—he was older than me, and I was pretty taken with him, to tell you the truth. I asked him to walk with me down by the river. Somehow those men saw us." Emily started to go on, but her voice faltered.

"What's wrong, Miss Emily?"

"I guess I just always felt so bad about my self-absorption—how I put that young man in such danger." Her hands were twisting the paper napkin in her lap, and she found herself staring at the sugar bowl, avoiding Mattie's gaze.

"Honey, wanting to be friends with someone you like is a good thing," said Mattie. "You just didn't know how things are here. What happened—after they scared you?"

"Aunt Liz chased them off with a shotgun—I think it's the same one I dragged out of the closet last night."

"She was something," said Mattie. "She understood what colored people face from men like that, Miss Emily—like Carter Mizell. You know, they save those long white get-ups for nighttime. Pretty silly looking, if you ask me—those big old crazy pointy hats."

"But they aren't to be taken lightly, I gather?"

"No ma'am. They're about as funny as that old electric chair up at the prison in Raiford. And like that chair, they love killing Black men."

They sat for a minute, letting Mattie's words settle in, before Emily went on.

"Mattie, here's another thing I haven't had a chance to tell you yet. Someone left me a note yesterday, basically telling me to get out of town. Is that the kind of thing the Klan would do—to scare somebody?"

To Emily's amazement, Mattie threw her head back and laughed.

"A note? I don't think so, Miss Emily. If they want to send you a message, they do something like burn a cross in your yard. Or poison your dog."

"Oh dear."

"Yes, ma'am. But wait a minute—where did you get this note? I didn't mean to sound like it was funny."

Emily paused. "Oh, someone left it on the porch." Was she trying to protect Mattie with her fib, she wondered, or herself—not really wanting to accept what had happened?

"Well, when the KKK wants to really send a message, they give you a whipping—or worse, if you're colored. They got a place outta town called the stomping grounds, with good reason."

"Did they ever try to scare my aunt, do you know? I mean recently—in the last year?"

"I expect if they did, Mr. Milton be the person to ask."

"You may know something, too, though, Mattie—something that's important without seeming like it is. You see, I think—and Milton does, too—that Aunt Liz's death wasn't an accident. I think someone wanted her dead."

Mattie took in a breath, and then looked at Emily hard. "The sheriff—same scoundrel we been talking about—said it was an accident," she said. "That never sat right with me, though."

"Any special reason?"

"Well, for one thing, the fire. The KKK, they love burning things. Scare people to death even if no one gets hurt."

"Yes, flames in the night," said Emily. "Terrifying."

"Yes ma'am. You read in the paper that some poor colored family's home goes up in flames—and then hear whispers somebody threw bottle bombs at the house. That happened just a few weeks ago to some folks in my church. But the sheriff—oh no, he don't know nothing. That's always the way."

"I can trust you, can't I, to not tell anyone—about my suspicions?"

"Sure, Miss Emily. You can trust Mattie Sayles."

"I knew I could," said Emily. "There's one more, really important thing, too. I think we're all perfectly safe here in this house, especially with the police sitting across the street and all, so I don't want you to worry—but I also want you to keep the doors locked while you're here. I promised Detective Maxwell I'd do that."

"Maxwell—the white man who eats at Wilson's Diner? Lots of wavy hair?"

"Yes, that's him; he's in charge of the investigation about the shooting here the other night."

"Usually I don't like the white police, but I believe I'd make an exception in his case," Mattie said, laughing. "Don't need Clark Gable when a handsome man like that's around."

Emily realized she was blushing. But now seemed as good a time as any to bring up the subject of Lewis.

"Well, speaking of handsome men, here's what Billy was teasing me about earlier—that 'boyfriend' thing? My friend Lewis arrived in town yesterday on the train from New York—totally unannounced."

"Really! Is he your sweetheart, Miss Emily?"

"Yes, I guess he is. He said he thought he'd surprise me. And did he ever."

"He just show up at the front door?"

"Oh no, I was talking with Detective Maxwell—at the Coffee Club. Mr. Armistead happened to pick Lewis up at the train and brought him straight there."

"In colored town? Lordy, Miss Emily, you sure be getting around to some interesting places for a white lady."

"Is there anything wrong with the Coffee Club?"

"No ma'am, it's just you won't see white ladies in there. And you were asking about the KKK? Goin' to the Coffee Club is just the kind of thing they might like to 'correct' a white lady about—as they see it."

Emily frowned and twisted a lock of her hair.

"Well, it was closed while we were there. But I do have an invitation to go to another club—and take Lewis—that sounds sort of questionable. The Flamingo Café?"

"Oooo, the Flamingo," said Mattie. "An old auntie of mine works there sometimes in the ladies' lounge—the tips are real good, and some of the secrets she hears—who been stepping out with whose wife—all the spicy stuff."

"Between you and Mr. Armistead, there must be no one, and nothing, you don't know. What does your aunt say about Charlie Wynne?"

"Oh, Mr. Charlie—he's okay. The pay's not great, but he gives a good bonus at Christmas time." Mattie was on her feet now, starting to clear the rest of the dishes.

"Is he a gangster? Is that true?"

"I don't know about that, Miss Emily. He got plenty of people out there at the Flamingo gambling—that's for sure. Your Aunt Liz really liked him, you know."

"He told me they were friends," said Emily. "Lewis is certainly taken with him. We talked with him last night in the hotel restaurant."

"Mr. Charlie, I bet he could charm the birds out the trees."

"I guess I'll see later this week. He invited us to the club's season opening."

"Opening night at the Flamingo is an event, Miss Emily. We gotta find you a special outfit to wear. You'll turn heads—and on the arm of your gentleman. This is exciting."

The mood of the conversation had certainly shifted, Emily thought—from the KKK and fear to fashion at the Flamingo.

"I don't know about a special outfit," Emily said. "But speaking of my gentleman, I'd better call him and tell him my plans. I hope to meet Maureen Davis this morning, at the newspaper office."

"Oh, yes ma'am," Mattie said, as they continued cleaning up the kitchen. "And don't you worry about what to wear to the Flamingo — I've got some ideas already."

"I'm depending on it," said Emily, giving Mattie a smile as she hung up a damp dish towel and headed into the living room to call Lewis and Maureen. She had been formulating a plan: Since Lewis would be happy sleeping until noon, she would see if she could meet Maureen at the newspaper. She was eager to look in the paper's archives to see what had been reported about her aunt's death, especially about what Carter Mizell had said — or not said — to the press.

By now, her two cups of strong coffee had kicked in, and Emily was feeling awake and alert. With Lewis in tow or not, she thought, nothing was going to slow her down — or nothing more than was absolutely necessary, she smiled to herself.

She called Maureen first, made arrangements to meet her at the newspaper, and filled her in briefly on Lewis's arrival.

"And Maureen," Emily added, "why don't you come with me to meet him for lunch? I think you'd both enjoy that. Where should I tell him to meet us — someplace close to the San Juan Hotel?"

"There's a roof garden and restaurant on the top of the department store a block away. It's not too hot today, and there are awnings."

"Perfect. I'll see you soon. And, Maureen? Thanks for this. As Billy would say, you're a peach."

Next, Emily called Lewis's hotel and left a message for him with the desk clerk to meet her for lunch. The desk clerk assured her that he would give Lewis directions.

"That's an excellent choice, Madame," the clerk said, in a rather superior English accent, Emily thought. "It's only a block away, and the gentlemen seem to enjoy it as much as the ladies."

"Wonderful," said Emily. "Thanks for the confirmation. Goodness knows, we do want to keep the gentlemen happy, don't we?"

She bathed and dressed and was just debating if the newspaper office was close enough for a brisk walk or if she should drive, when she heard voices in the kitchen and came down the stairs to see Milton standing at the back door, straw hat in hand and clip-on sunglasses in place, talking with Mattie through the screen door. Even though she had just seen him the night before, she felt immensely glad to see him now.

"Morning, Miss Emily," he said. "My, you are looking bright-eyed and bushy-tailed, if I do say so. I had business in the neighborhood and thought I'd check on you. I'm happy to see your bodyguard's still here," and at Emily's confused look he added "—the police car across the street."

"Mr. Armistead, your timing is impeccable. Come on in. I'm due to meet Maureen at the newspaper office, and I was just wondering if I should drive or walk. Or might you be able to drop me off? I think Maureen could bring me home later."

"That's a plan, Miss Emily. Happy to do it."

"You hungry, Mr. Armistead?" said Mattie. "No trouble at all to rustle you up some toast and eggs."

"You're too kind, Mrs. Sayles, but I've had my breakfast—no comparison to your cooking, though."

"You old flatterer," said Mattie with a grin.

"I mean every word," he said, turning to Emily.

"So you're headed to the newspaper, Miss Emily. Might it be to put in an engagement announcement?" He raised his eyebrows, looking as close to mischievous as it was possible for him to look.

"No, it is not," she sighed, shaking her head.

"Well, whatever your mission," said Milton. "I'm at your service. Ready when you are, C.B."

"Oh, Aunt Liz loved that line," she said.

The old punchline never failed to make Emily laugh. It capped off a joke about movie director Cecil B. DeMille filming an epic scene with thousands of extras—the parting of the Red Sea—that could only be done once. He set up three cameras, and when the action was over, he turned to Camera One, only to hear that the film had broken. Undaunted, he hailed Camera Two and learned the lens cap was still on. In desperation, DeMille called out to the last camera, on a hill high above the action. "Camera Three? Did you get it?" he hollered up. "Ready when you are, C.B.," the last hope shouted down.

"Yep," said Milton. "I learned that from Liz."

And smiling together, they bid Mattie goodbye and walked to Milton's taxi, this time with Emily smoothly entering the back seat without a murmur of complaint.

Chapter 23

Mr. Jinx's World

THE NEWSPAPER OFFICE was in an old building downtown, Milton said, not far from City Hall and also not far from the hotel where Lewis was staying. It faced one of the side streets off the town's main street, and when Emily got out of Milton's taxi at the appointed time, she saw Maureen waiting for her at the door.

"There you are," Maureen said, as they both waved goodbye to Milton. "I asked Phyllis—the editorial department secretary—to keep an eye out for you. She knows all the comings and goings—where all the bodies are buried . . . Oh, Emily, I'm so sorry—bad choice of words."

But instead of showing offense, Emily found herself smiling.

"Oh honestly, Maureen, you're a dear. Sometimes there's nothing left to do but laugh—I know you meant no disrespect to Aunt Liz, or even to Dead Marvin, for that matter."

Maureen gave her a quick hug and led her inside, where she introduced her to the watchful Phyllis, who presided over a desk near the large storefront window that faced the street.

"What an interesting building," said Emily after they exchanged pleasantries, as she took in the worn wooden floors and brick walls.

"Yes, it began as a general store," said Phyllis. "Twentieth-century journalism stuffed into a 19th-century building. The publisher swears we'll have a new headquarters by the end of 1950—imagine how modern that sounds!"

"Yes, indeed," Emily smiled. Could it be possible that in two years it would be 1950? Sometimes she could scarcely believe the war was really over; other times, she would awake from a dream about John, broken on a battlefield somewhere, and be shocked all over again to realize he'd been gone for years.

"Well, Emily, if we're going to put on our research hats and get something done before we meet your gentleman caller, we'd better get busy. Mother will be quite jealous about your Lewis, by the way. My own lack of beaux worries the poor dear, I'm afraid."

"The glamour of being a reporter doesn't impress her?"

"My dear girl, I am nowhere near being a real reporter, and believe me, there's nothing glamorous about my work—although it can be fun to whip up froth for the women's pages, or cover our artistic events."

"I'll need to cultivate you," said Emily with a grin. "You're a woman of influence."

"Hardly, but there are benefits. Sometimes, they let me cover concerts, although I hardly know Bach from Beethoven. If it's serious stuff, a professor from the college may write the review."

"Still, it's wonderful that you have a real job—with pay," said Emily. "I envy that."

"Believe me, not much pay—but I accept the compliment, Emily. I do like earning my own money."

They were walking now through a large room filled with desks bearing typewriters, and men hammering away at them.

"These are the real reporters," Maureen whispered to Emily. "On the trail of crime and corruption—supposedly."

Cigarette smoke hung over some desks. Hardly anyone looked up at Maureen and Emily as they made their way down an aisle at the edge of the room.

"The morgue's downstairs," said Maureen—and at Emily's wide eyes, she laughed and added, "Oh, no—I mean where the old copies of the paper are. I told Jinx we were coming, and he should have the issues pulled that reported on your aunt's death."

"Who's Jinx?" Emily asked. "And I hope he isn't one."

"You know, I don't even know where that nickname comes from. He's had it since the beginning of time. He's really James Oliver O'Neill IV, I think. He's been in charge of the morgue for years, and he's got a memory you wouldn't believe."

Emily followed Maureen down the stairs into a cool, dark

space, where a man sat alone behind a desk, illuminated only by a hanging fluorescent light. He was thin and pale and looked, Emily thought, like a creature who never saw the sun. But when he raised his head and saw Maureen, he broke into a wide grin that looked altogether incongruous with his sepulchral appearance.

"Ah, Mrs. Davis," he said, rising to greet them, "so this is your friend?"

He looked at Emily intently before going on.

"Miss Washington, is it? Please accept my condolences on your aunt's death, although I know they are belated. I did pull the book for that month, as Mrs. Davis suggested," he said, indicating a large gray newspaper-sized volume, lying on an empty desk behind him that was also lit from above by a fluorescent tube.

"Thank you, Mr. Jinx," Emily began.

"Oh, it's just Jinx, dear lady. And instead of thanks, you can keep mum that you've been down here."

"Of course—but why the secrecy?"

"Nothing sinister—it's just that the editor's not keen on my taking research time to help people who aren't on staff. I'm supposed to be looking up things to help the reporters who are working on stories."

"I see—well, even more thanks are in order, then." Emily made a mental note to find some way to more formally thank Jinx.

"The editor rarely darkens the door before noon," said Maureen. "He works late into the evening, so we should be fine."

"Mrs. Davis says you couldn't be here for the funeral," Jinx said to Emily, nodding at Maureen. "I'm sure you'll be happy to see the reports of the large crowd for it. She was an influential woman, your aunt."

"That is good to hear. I hope to read the reports about the fire, too—especially."

"Most upsetting, I should think," said Jinx. Emily was torn between wishing both he and Maureen would leave her in peace to pore over old issues and wanting to draw him out, with Maureen's skillful help.

"Yes, but one must seek and face the truth always, I find, even if it's painful," Emily said to Jinx. "I'm interested in seeing exactly what was reported."

"Emily has already had the dubious honor of meeting our sheriff," added Maureen.

"Oh, I see," said Jinx. "Then, I must say, I'm not surprised you wanted to find out more about the fire and the investigation."

"Why is that?"

"Because the sheriff himself was in charge of it, and, if you ask me, that's about as wise as sending a fox to guard the henhouse. I don't think there was any love lost between him and your aunt."

At that comment, Emily felt her heart beat a bit faster. She wondered just how much Jinx did know about Liz's death and, beyond the verifiable knowledge, what judgments he might make — he was clearly not above expressing opinions.

"Have a seat here, dear lady," Jinx said, indicating a seat at the work table behind him, and started to open the large volume in front of her. She looked up at Maureen, who reached over and patted her shoulder.

"Emily, I hate to abandon you, but I've got a column due to be filed before I can have lunch with you in good conscience, so I'm going back to my desk. By the way, is it okay if I put your friend Lewis's name in the column?"

"Why ever would you do that?"

"I need material, Emily — two people arriving from New York City, and one of them a bona fide artist — yes, I'm talking about you, Emily — well, it's good stuff."

"If you think so, Maureen. Goodness, I'm having trouble thinking of you as Louella Parsons. I am sure Lewis will love it — make sure you call him handsome."

"Even though I haven't met him, I'll take you at your word. And trust me, you'll like it when you read it. I'm a lot funnier than Louella."

With that she turned and sped up the stairs.

Jinx was still standing, hovering at her elbow. He cleared his throat. Emily wondered how he would look in the sunlight, outside of this underground lair that smelled of old paper and mold. He seemed almost like some kindly vampire who would crumple in the light. Very faintly, she heard the clacking of the typewriters from the newsroom upstairs.

"Miss Washington, I put paper markers at some of the pages you'll want to look at."

"Thank you, Mr. Jinx — Jinx. So you've already looked at the reports of my aunt's death."

"Oh, indeed, I read about it at the time, of course, and I've looked through it all again."

"Maureen said you had worked here a long time."

"Since before the flood," he said with a smile.

"Do you think this is a good newspaper — honest, fair?"

"Yes, for the most part, Miss Washington. I do think the people in charge here have the public's interest at heart. They are no supporters of the KKK, for one thing."

"That's a relief — the Klan seems to have a wide reach, I hear."

"Sadly, yes. True in a lot of the South, I'm afraid. Are you interested in the Klan, Miss Washington — a special concern?"

"To tell you the truth. I don't even really know what I expect to find or what I'm looking for," said Emily.

"Of course you don't — but that means you'll have your eyes and your mind open. Too many people look for what they expect to find. But enough pontificating — I'll leave you to it."

"That's excellent advice, and I wonder if I've been guilty of doing that — and missed something right in front of me."

"You're an artist, though — you must be expert at looking hard at things. I'll bet you've noticed and seen more than you're giving yourself credit for."

"You're being kind."

"No, I'll bet I'm right. Let me ask you a question: When you walked through the room upstairs, did you see anyone with a hat on?"

"I wondered about that. Yes, the man in the back corner was wearing a hat. An old-fashioned straw skimmer."

"Indeed. That would be our lead sports reporter. Anyway, I

make my case—you're no doubt a good observer—and now I'll really leave you to it."

Emily smiled. Then she sighed and lifted the front of the large volume and turned to the first marker.

She didn't know what she had expected, but it wasn't a front-page headline that declared "ARTIST DIES IN TRAGIC FIRE." Somehow it had never occurred to her that her Aunt Elizabeth had lived in this town long enough to become so well known, maybe almost an institution.

Then Emily was aware of a frantic feeling rising in her throat. Somehow the headline brought the pain and reality of her loss home to her almost as much as visiting her aunt's grave had done. She felt tears welling up and fought them back, hoping that Jinx wouldn't turn around and see her. He seemed buried in reading and making notes on a pad.

She went back to the article, which noted concisely that sheriff's deputies and then the sheriff himself had been alerted by an anonymous phone call about a fire at the fish camp, backed up by reports from people who had seen smoke from their nearby farm. Someone on a boat put in the river said they'd seen flames.

"There was nothing we could do," Sheriff Mizell had told the reporter.

"He certainly didn't have much to say about it—the sheriff," Emily muttered, partly to herself and partly to Jinx.

She heard a noise behind her and turned to see that Jinx had swiveled his chair around to face her.

"Oh, he had a lot to say that we wouldn't print."

"What do you mean?"

"I don't know if I should tell you this," Jinx went on, "because it is upsetting, but it does show what we're dealing with here when it comes to some of our supposed law officers."

"What did he say? I can take it."

She was beginning to get a sense of just how much she could take, she thought.

"One of my jobs is to fact-check for the reporters," said Jinx.

"Our guy didn't go out there—we were short that day—but he did interview the sheriff soon after they brought your aunt's body to the funeral home. By the way, there was no autopsy, which I thought was odd."

"Go on."

"Well, Mizell told the reporter he was sure what had happened—claimed there was an empty bottle of bourbon overturned near her body. I believe he told the reporter to say something like she wasn't in any condition to notice that an ember from the cook stove had caught the curtains on fire."

"Of all the nerve!" Emily cried out.

"Yes. He's got no shortage of that. The reporter came down and asked me if I'd ever heard even as much as a whisper about Elizabeth Washington, well, tippling too much. In any case, we didn't print it."

"For one thing, when she did have a drink, it was always Scotch—single malt. Or a glass of red wine. She didn't care for bourbon."

"Is it okay that I told you, dear lady? I've been told that I have a tendency to be a bit of a gossip, and I fear it's true."

"Mr. Jinx—it's more than okay. I want to know as much as I can, and I appreciate your candor."

"Good. I'm relieved—and I can see there's no point in reminding you I don't need the 'mister,' is there? That it's just 'Jinx'?"

"I'm afraid I seem to be hopelessly addicted to honorifics," said Emily.

She looked back at the newspaper page, which did include a picture of Liz, taken at an event the night before her death, according to the caption. Elizabeth Washington had been judging an art show at the Chamber of Commerce building, the caption said, and the picture showed a small group of unidentified people gathered around her as she handed a prize ribbon to a beaming artist. A figure who stood behind Liz looked familiar, but the background of the image was dim.

"Mr. Jinx, do you happen to have a magnifying glass?"

"Of course," he said, handing her a thick round disk with a handle. "What do you see?"

"I just want to get a better look at the photo that was used. It's not very clear."

She peered through the glass, feeling a little like Sherlock Holmes. Or—what was it Lewis had teased her about—Nancy Drew?

The view of the photo was much better with the glass. She didn't know any of the other people pictured, but the man behind Liz was almost certainly Julian. He wasn't looking at the camera and apparently hadn't realized that he'd be in the image. Indeed, he looked rather upset and was gazing at someone or something to Liz's left that had been cropped out of the image.

I wonder what had his knickers in a twist, Emily thought.

She was intrigued, but after all Julian's expression could have meant anything. Maybe he had been standing with his braces too long and needed to sit. She did, however, note the distinctive band around Liz's wrist—her scarab bracelet. So, she had been wearing it the night before she died.

Emily flipped quickly through the other pages Jinx had marked but didn't find anything of note, beyond the picture showing Julian. She had learned one big thing, though, from this visit, if not from the pages of the paper directly; Carter Mizell had tried to smear her aunt's good name as he reported her death—at least if what Jinx said was true. But was Jinx a fount of information or, as he himself had suggested, devoted to gossip? Perhaps she could speak to the reporter who'd written the article—who'd heard the words from Sheriff Mizell himself. Thoughts raced through her mind about what Jinx had told her, and about the photo and Julian's odd expression. What in the world was going on there, she wondered.

Chapter 24

Ladies Who Lunch

"DID YOU FIND anything?" Maureen asked her as they walked toward the restaurant, crossing to the shady side of the street. The calendar was moving into autumn, and the nights had felt cooler, Emily thought, but at noon the sun blazed and the heat sizzled. The light cotton dress she wore felt damp and sticky.

"I sure found out something from talking to Mr. Jinx. Maureen, he joked about being a gossip. Do you think he's trustworthy—I mean if he tells you something, is it likely to be true?"

"Oh, he's definitely trustworthy. He keeps his eyes and ears open. And, remember, I told you—he has an incredible memory."

"Well, get this. He said Carter Mizell was spreading the story that Aunt Liz must have been drunk—passed-out drunk—and that's why she didn't see the fire in time."

"Oh dear. I confess, Emily—I knew Mizell was peddling that story. Our reporter asked me about it too, and I told him it just was not possible. But I didn't want to dignify it by repeating it at all, least of all to you."

"Why not?" Emily stopped walking, reaching out to touch Maureen's arm lightly so that her friend stopped to look at her. "I mean, really, why didn't you tell me, Maureen?"

"You're upset."

"I'm surprised. I'm not a China doll, you know."

"Honey, relax. I figured it was just Carter being Carter—so set on his habit of bad-mouthing people he considered carpetbaggers that he didn't care the poor woman was dead, and this wasn't the time to continue his propaganda campaign."

"Did he have it in especially for Aunt Liz, do you think?" The two women started walking again.

"Oh, he did," said Maureen. "She had crossed him several times, and instead of being glad for her closeness to his half-brother Jeff and to Billy, he seemed to resent her for that, too."

"Yes," said Emily. "I noticed that when he stopped us the other day. He didn't seem genuinely fond of Billy—and since then, Billy's told me Carter has been downright abusive to him."

"That may all go back to who got the ranch and the property in that family, which was Jeff. And, I don't know, Emily, maybe it was just partly because Liz was a woman. There are some men who can't stand a woman who speaks her mind."

"Don't I know it," said Emily. "I hate to say it but my dear Papa is one of them. He just couldn't understand Liz, even though she was his sister."

They had arrived at the department store with the roof-garden restaurant, and Emily followed Maureen's lead into the building.

The redhead moved like a bullet toward the back of the large first floor, exchanging greetings with both saleswomen and customers as she and Emily passed large glass cases filled with scarves, handbags, and in the rear of the store, cosmetics. It all looked very up to date, Emily thought, remembering the fashionable ads she had seen in the newspaper soon after arriving.

Maureen guided Emily toward one elevator that stood apart from the others.

"That's the one we want," said Maureen, guiding Emily by the elbow. "We're right on time, and it's a good thing. The maître d' can get quite snippy."

Emily hoped Lewis hadn't had any trouble finding the place. He probably expected something quite different, she thought, but the meal last night should have shown him that restaurants here weren't back in the dark ages, or whatever he might have imagined.

The elevator opened to reveal a uniformed operator, an elegant Black man who Emily thought looked a little like a younger version of Milton.

"Hello, James," said Maureen. "How's your mother doing?"

"Much better, Mrs. Davis. I'll tell her you asked about her."

"Please do—my father will be happy to hear that, too."

Emily wondered if Maureen's doctor father treated Black people. Everything seemed so divided here. She was about to ask when the doors opened onto a surprising vista—tables of diners under striped tents lined with greenery. There was a nice breeze, and the heat was actually manageable, Emily thought.

As if by magic, the maître d' appeared in front of them, holding large menus. He exchanged greetings with Maureen, who introduced him to Emily.

"Ladies, the gentlemen in your party have preceded you," he said, bowing slightly in greeting. "Please follow me."

"Gentlemen?" Maureen asked. "I thought we were just meeting Mr. Delacourt."

"I understand, Mrs. Davis," said the maître d'. "But Mr. Delacourt arrived with a companion, and fortunately we were able to accommodate the extra gentleman."

Emily and Maureen exchanged raised eyebrows.

"He just arrived in town," Maureen whispered to Emily. "Who could he possibly bring?"

"No idea," said Emily. "Unless his father arrived early from south Florida."

They followed the maître d' through a maze of greenery but couldn't yet make out the table to which he was guiding them.

Then, suddenly, Emily knew the answer—of course, it had to be—and as they rounded a corner and two men rose to greet them, she saw that she was right.

"Hello, isn't this festive?" said Lewis, moving to kiss Emily on the cheek as he clasped her hand. "I can't wait to meet your old friend." He nodded and smiled at Maureen, stepping forward to kiss her hand. Emily remembered how charming he could be, and from good motives. He genuinely liked people.

"And look who I encountered this morning, just on a stroll outside the hotel. Naturally, I had to ask him to join us."

"Naturally," said Emily, reaching out to shake the hand of the golden-haired man in the white suit.

"How enchanting you both look," said Charlie Wynne. "How could any chap in his right mind stay away?"

"Always good to see you, Mr. Wynne," said Maureen. "You wouldn't happen to have some tasty tidbits for my column, would you? Off the record, of course?"

Then Maureen looked at Lewis, turning on the full warmth of what Emily was beginning to realize was Maureen's Southern Belle persona—Emily half expected her to say "fiddle-dee-dee."

"And this is your Lewis, Emily," Maureen cooed. "Oh my, aren't you the lucky girl."

She extended her hand and grasped Lewis's, who looked as though he might actually blush right there.

"I just want you to know—she has done nothing since she arrived except talk about you," Maureen said to Lewis, while Emily stopped herself from staring at her incredulously.

Oh, Maureen, you do love a good joke, don't you? Emily thought, producing what she hoped was a suitably demure smile. "Be careful, Maureen, he'll have absolutely no humility left if you don't lay off," she said. "Let's all sit down and order, shall we? I know I'm famished."

"I'm afraid I joined you under false pretenses, Old Sport," Charlie said to Lewis. "I can't stay for lunch—too much going on—but I wanted to see you all and invite you to come to the preview VIP opening at the club tonight. You, too, Mrs. Davis. I had planned to make it later in the week—when we have all the possible kinks ironed out. But why wait? I very much want you three to come as my guests. It'll be a night you won't forget—and the drinks are on me."

"That sounds capital, Wynne—I'm sure the ladies would welcome a chance to show off a new frock, and as Emily can tell you, I do enjoy a whirl around the dance floor now and then."

"Excellent," said Charlie, looking at Maureen and Emily.

"Ladies? Is it unanimous? I can send a car for you—it would be my pleasure. My driver could take you home too. And, Mrs. Davis, I'm sure that if you come, there'll be no shortage of column items—and I promise, I'll slip you a couple of confidential tidbits myself."

With that, he stood and made his goodbyes.

"Well, that's an exciting prospect," said Lewis. "Maureen, I do hope you will indeed join us. We love to step out in New York every once in a while, even to the jazz clubs up in Harlem. Great music."

"Well, Mr. Wynne certainly made it difficult to say no, dangling the prospect of juicy column items, I'll say that. And it's true that on special nights, you're likely to see anyone and everyone who matters in this town out at that club."

The waiter appeared quietly and slipped a basket on the table that, based on its smell, contained fresh baked goods. Now Emily really did feel famished. They placed their orders: the chicken salad plate for Emily and Maureen and the seafood platter for Lewis.

"I glanced at the paper and saw that there's quite a robust nightlife here, based on the ads," said Lewis. "That surprised me. What makes the Flamingo stand out?"

"Well, there's no sense being coy about it," Maureen responded. "You'll find out soon enough, Lewis—it's all right to call you Lewis?"

"Of course! I feel like we're old friends already." He flashed her one of his best Lewis smiles, Emily noted, and she smiled, too. She was happy Maureen and Lewis seemed to be taking to each other. She had few enough people she cared about, now that Aunt Liz and John were gone, and it was important to her that they got along.

"Good, and I'm Maureen, of course, although I will ask you not to call me 'Red' or 'Scarlett' or any of those other nicknames. Having hair this color can be a bit of a trial. I've read that long ago, some people in the old Pilgrim colony thought it was a sign of being a witch—although, on second thought, I might plead guilty to that."

"Maureen, you know your hair is absolutely beautiful," said Emily. "You're shameless when you want a compliment."

"And why not—she deserves them," chimed in Lewis, and they all laughed.

"But, you were about to spill the secret of Wynne's club," he continued.

"Yes—it's the worst-kept secret in town. It's gambling, Lewis. The food is excellent and the shows are first-rate, but the big attraction is the casino at the back, which operates as a private club—although anyone can join."

"Surely that must be illegal," said Lewis. "Isn't Nevada the only state where gambling's legal?"

"Yes, but Lewis, don't you play cards and make wagers and so on at your men's club back home?" Emily said.

"Certainly, Emily—but that's just friendly wagers between the chaps in the club—there's no roulette wheel or anything."

"There certainly is at the Flamingo," said Maureen, "and you can see plenty of pillars of the community around it on Saturday nights—it's closed on Sundays, of course. But Monday, oddly enough, is a big night."

"Well, I'll be," said Lewis. "I admit I just met the man, but I would never have guessed. Did you know, Emily—when we talked with him last night?"

"I met him briefly on Friday night, at the party at Julian Sloane's I was telling you about—and Maureen mentioned something about it." Emily looked at Maureen, who nodded.

"And how does it stay open?" Lewis asked.

"I think it's partly that it's a beloved remnant of Prohibition days, for one thing—it's an institution," said Maureen. "No one here paid much attention to Prohibition—it would have been bad for business, for one thing. People come to Florida to get away from their real lives up North, and if they wanted a drink, we were happy to oblige—and I guess Charlie's father just added on the gambling as an extension. It only meant a bit more payoff money to the sheriff."

Interesting, Emily thought. Apparently it was well known that Carter Mizell took payoffs. She tucked that fact away but returned to the subject of Wynne's family heritage.

"So the nightclub has been in the family?" she asked. "Wynne inherited it?"

"Oh sure. Charlie's father was much less polished than our Mr. Dimples, but he knew how to keep people happy and to keep the right eyes turned the other way. He did so well that he was able to send his son to an Ivy League school."

Lewis looked up. "Mr. Dimples?"

"Lewis, you must have noticed," Emily said. "He's very good looking."

Lewis's cheeks colored, just slightly, but he said, "Men don't notice that kind of thing about other men, Darling."

But for some reason, Emily was sure—in this case, anyway—that was not indeed true.

The conversation shifted to practical matters related to the evening ahead at the Flamingo, and over coffee and dessert, the three of them agreed that Emily and Lewis would accept Wynne's offer of a ride while Maureen would meet Emily and Lewis at the club, so she would have the option of leaving early because of deadlines she faced the next day. With that settled, Maureen excused herself after a glance at her watch.

"Wonderful to meet you," Maureen said to Lewis. "You sure know how to sweep a girl off her feet with a surprise visit. Hope you both can get a beauty nap to look your best tonight. No such luck for me—newspaper duties beckon."

"That's right—the newspaper," Lewis said to Emily as Maureen waved goodbye and headed toward the elevator. He was attacking a slice of lemon icebox pie the waiter had just delivered. "You mentioned it in your message—how did it go there, Darling? Learn anything new, Nancy Drew?"

"It was fine, thanks," she replied briskly. She had thought about telling him all about Jinx and about Carter Mizell's outrageous attempt to smear Aunt Liz's reputation, but now his teasing tone somehow got under her skin.

"Not much to report," she added. "It wouldn't have been worth your time."

Later, Emily thought about the exchange as she got ready for the evening. Lewis had wanted to help but, truly, the best way he could do that was to go back to New York. A whole day had gone by without her checking in with Detective Maxwell to find out if he knew anything more about Marvin's murder Friday night. A police officer still sat in a car across the street, watching the house, which eased her mind a bit—but who or what was she being protected against, really?

Mattie had offered to stay and help her dress, but Emily sent her downstairs to await Billy's arrival, glad to have some time alone, especially since she was expecting Billy to stay the night. Fortunately, Mattie had also agreed to stay the night so the boy would have supervision while Emily was out.

Just as the housekeeper had said she would do, Mattie had indeed found an excellent ensemble for Emily to wear, culled from her Aunt Liz's clothes—a simple black jersey gown, dressed up with long Mexican silver earrings and a bracelet, though not her aunt's signature scarab bracelet, which had still not turned up.

Emily rejected wearing stockings and a girdle—if bare legs were a scandal, she thought, so be it. But she was concerned that her high-heeled pumps might hurt. *Ready as I'll ever be,* she thought, as she stuffed some money, a lipstick, and a handkerchief into an evening bag and hovered near the door. She had to admit she was excited at the prospect of exploring the scene at Charlie Wynne's notorious nightclub and finding out more about her aunt's association with its glamorous owner.

Her plan was to go by the hotel and get Lewis when Wynne's driver came for them. But when the appointed time came, she was shocked to see that Wynne himself appeared at the door, looking almost ghostly in his white suit as he appeared on the front porch in the twilight.

"How charming you look, Miss Washington," he greeted her. "I'm so glad you agreed to come tonight. I think you'll find it an interesting adventure. I decided to slip away and come chauffeur you myself."

"You don't need to greet your guests?"

"No guest is more important than you," he said with that

dimpled grin of his. "And my staff have everything under control."

As she locked the front door and went down the steps on Wynne's arm, she waved to the police car across the street, which was beginning to feel like a permanent fixture.

"You have friends in high places," Wynne said, nodding to the car. "Always a good thing."

Emily started to say something but stopped short as she saw Wynne's vehicle. Somehow she had expected a limousine, but here was a rather spectacular British sports car, with the top down.

"I'm afraid I did make one mistake, though," said Wynne, "and you've noticed it—I grabbed the wrong car. I love to drive this thing, but I know it isn't the best mode of transportation for a lady's hair style. Maybe this will help," he added as he opened the door for her and handed her a lightweight chiffon scarf, printed in tropical floral against a black background. It looked rather smashing with her dress, Emily thought. How could he have known that?

"But what about Lewis?" she said.

"The rumble seat is really more comfortable than it looks," said Wynne, nodding to the back of the car, which truly was a beauty. "Delacourt's a good sport—he can handle it—and the sooner he realizes he's not in New York, the better, I'd say. I must confess, though, I wish I had you all to myself—I need to talk with you on a private matter."

Emily's eyes widened. "What kind of private matter?"

"We'll manage that later—I need to show you something of Liz's that's at the club. Trust me, all will be revealed. Now, we'd better get over to the hotel, or your beau will be pacing."

Which was exactly what Lewis was doing, on the sidewalk in front of his hotel, as Wynne pulled up with a mild screech. Lewis let out a whistle at his first sight of the car, but he did indeed show his good sportsmanship by fitting himself in the rumble seat at the back of the vehicle, after he gave Emily a kiss on the cheek.

"We'll call a taxi to get home, or ride with Maureen," Emily whispered to him as he bent to kiss her.

Then they were off, skimming along the city's brick streets

and turning heads as Wynne's British sports car sped by. As she had in the Hudson, Emily loved riding in the open air. Streaks of coral-colored clouds stretched across tones of lavender blue in the twilight sky, and sweet scents laced the air. In only a few moments, they were pulling up in front of the fabled Flamingo Café.

Chapter 25

The Fabulous Flamingo

CHARLIE WYNNE'S NIGHTCLUB looked considerably more dazzling after dark than it had when Emily visited its dusty parking lot a couple of days before. A colorful neon sign by the highway spelled "Flamingo" in coral-pink script, below the image of a glowing bird that appeared to be flying above chartreuse palm trees. More neon birds and palm trees blinked brightly on the building itself, their colors reflected in Emily's silver bracelets.

After Wynne pulled his sporty convertible into a spot near the door that bore a "reserved" sign, he opened the door for Emily and then helped Lewis extract himself from the rumble seat at the back of the car.

"Old Sport," he said to Lewis, who was running a comb through his hair," I hope you'll do me the honor of allowing me to escort your lovely lady into my club. Her aunt was a special friend of mine, you know. Besides," he turned and grinned at Emily, "she looks absolutely smashing!"

"You, Mr. Wynne, are an absolutely shameless flatterer," said Emily, laughing as she shook her head. "Isn't he, Lewis?"

"Incorrigible," said Lewis, with equal good humor. "Not to diminish his compliment to you, Darling—may I say, too, how lovely you look—we'll humor the poor old thing because he has no date, right?"

"Yes, we'll take pity," she joked, taking Wynne's arm. Lewis fell in behind them amiably as they headed toward the striped portico awning over the club's entrance, also topped by the name "Flamingo" in swooping neon letters. After all, making a good entrance at a nightclub was something Lewis knew how to do well, Emily smiled to herself, as she watched him nod and smile at a news photographer.

As they neared the entryway, tall carved doors swung open for them as if by magic, and Emily was amused to note she felt a little like Moses with the Red Sea parting. Once inside, she could see that the doors had actually been pulled open by two darkly handsome young men wearing white dinner jackets.

"Good evening, Mr. Wynne," the young men said, as they bowed in unison. "Good evening, ma'am. Good evening, sir. Welcome to the Flamingo."

"My goodness, Wynne," Lewis said from behind them, "this place is the nuts—old Billy Rose has nothing on you."

"Just wait, Old Sport," Wynne said to Lewis over his shoulder as he swiftly guided his guests toward a tall, tuxedo-clad man.

"Roberto, we'll be using my private table," Wynne greeted him. Lewis was right, thought Emily—he does sound like the Great Gatsby. What was this going to be like?

"Of course, Mr. Wynne," said Roberto, who greeted Emily and Lewis with a bow and appeared almost to click his heels. He might have been played by the actor Cesar Romero, Emily thought, suddenly feeling as if she had tumbled into a world that was more cinematic than real. After following Manuel and Wynne down a hallway to a curtained area, they were seated in a soft leather banquette illuminated by a petite lamp on the table, which also bore a small vase of roses. The curtains that separated the booth from the restaurant's main dining room were open enough to give them an unobstructed view of the bandstand and the front of the dance floor.

Before Roberto left, Wynne gave him their orders for drinks and asked him to keep an eye out for Maureen Davis and bring her to the table as soon as she arrived. Then he turned his attention back to Emily and Lewis.

"I can't thank you enough for doing me the honor of letting me show off my pride and joy to you both," said Wynne. "By the way, I value my privacy, but we won't be holed up in here all night. Our show tonight is excellent, with a first-rate dance band right from the Copa in Havana. You both mentioned that you enjoyed dancing, I recall."

"I'm no Ginger Rogers," said Emily, "but, yes, I do like to dance, if the music is right."

"You're too modest, Darling! Remember at the Lido when you . . . ," Lewis jumped in somewhat giddily, then stopped suddenly in response to the gentle kick Emily gave him under the table. Good grief, they had just met Charlie Wynne, and she wasn't about to pour out her secrets to a stranger, dimples or no dimples. Sometimes Lewis could be maddening.

"Oh, the music will be better than right," beamed Wynne. "You'll put Ginger to shame."

When hell freezes over, thought Emily, but she smiled as she reached up to fix a stray curl that had fallen across her face. In spite of the scarf she'd worn, the ride in Wynne's convertible had played havoc with her hair—unruly under even the best conditions. Clearly, a trip to the Ladies' Room for some repairs was in order. With any luck, the aunt Mattie had mentioned would be working there, and Emily might pick up some backstage tidbits. She excused herself from her companions—already deep in Princeton gossip—and asked for directions from one of the waiters who hovered near their table.

Making her way down a dark hall lined with photographs— she thought she spotted Frank Sinatra in one—she heard a familiar low vocal rumble.

"Miss Emily, over here!"

She turned to see Milton Armistead, standing in a dim alcove lit only by a cigarette machine. He motioned to her as he put his finger to his lips to indicate quiet.

"Miss Emily," he whispered. "What in heck are you doing here with Charlie Wynne?"

Emily bristled a little. "I could ask you the same thing, Mr. Armistead. What are you doing lurking there?"

He smiled at her. "Just like your auntie—tossing it right back," he said, and Emily felt pangs of both love and grief for the woman she'd never see again. "I dropped off a fare in the front and saw you and Mr. Lewis getting out of that car," Milton continued. "I told you, Miss Emily, be careful, now. Mr. Charlie—well, he's got a reputation."

"You said Aunt Liz liked him."

"Yes. And I do, too, when it comes right down to it. But he does keep some interesting company, let's just say. And your daddy's not going to be happy if you show up in some scandal sheet back home."

Damn it, she was a grown woman. And Milton knew perfectly well that her father's stupid, stuffy ideas had caused her enough grief already—and hurt her late aunt, too—his sister.

"How possibly—" she began. She loved Milton dearly, but he was testing her patience. "Mr. Armistead, I appreciate your concern, but I can take care of myself—I live alone in one of the toughest cities in the world."

"I know, this seems like a little town," he went on, "but this club attracts a big clientele—just look at those pictures." He nodded to the photos Emily had noticed.

"Look," she said, "the main reason I came was because Wynne said he needed to speak to me about something privately. Something about Aunt Liz. You wouldn't have any idea what that might be, would you?"

"No, I don't—but—"

"Besides," she rushed on, "I can't really believe he's a gangster—he went to Princeton."

Milton rolled his eyes. Just then, a patron crossed the hallway a few feet down and turned to look Emily's way, and though he could not have seen Milton from there, she realized it probably wasn't a great idea for her to be seen having a private conversation with a Black man, even here, where the Jim Crow laws seemed to hold a looser grip than, say, at the Country Club. The last thing she wanted was to get Milton in trouble—especially when he was looking out for her.

"Okay, but you be careful, Miss Emily," Milton said. "You know my number if you need me; the phone booths are right here. You all right for a way home?"

"Maureen is meeting us, and she has a car—that's an option."

"I tell you what—seeing as how I haven't booked any more fares for tonight, I think I'll renew my acquaintance with the boys in the kitchen—always a fine source of scuttlebutt."

"Maybe they'll know something about Dead Marvin—or even gossip about Aunt Liz's death," Emily said, eager to get to the Ladies' Room and do her own sleuthing.

"Yes, indeed. There might indeed be some loose talk about Willetts. And whether Wynne might be up to anything suspicious—Princeton or not." Emily couldn't help but smile. "You'll most probably see a young colored fellow near Wynne's table," Milton went on. "Good-looking, wavy hair, little mustache. His name's Ray. Looks like a host, but he's security. If you need anything, you tell Ray to come and get me. He's never going to get into Princeton, but he knows what's going on."

As Emily shook her head and smiled, he turned to walk away, then spun back to her.

"Oh, and in the Ladies' Room, you'll see an older lady—an attendant. She may look and generally act like Aunt Jemima, but don't let that fool you. She doesn't miss a trick. It wouldn't hurt for you to get to know her."

"Is that Mattie's aunt?"

"That's the one," said Milton. "Her name's Queen Esther, and believe me, she's the queen of lots of secrets. Liz adored her."

And sure enough, as Emily entered what proved to be an imposing Ladies' Room, an elderly Black woman jumped to her feet.

"Hello, ma'am," the woman said. "Don't you look pretty. I don't think I've ever seen you before. Welcome to the Flamingo. You need anything, just ask—I got it all. Alka Seltzer, aspirin, anything a lady might need to feel or look her best. You just come and see me. I'm Queen Esther."

"Thank you so much," Emily said. "My name's Emily Washington. I know your niece, I believe—Mattie Sayles? She mentioned you, and so did Milton Armistead."

"Oh, now I know who you are," said Esther. "You're Miss Elizabeth's girl—the one from up North." What did Esther mean by Elizabeth's girl? Surely she didn't think Liz had a daughter?

"Yes, she was my aunt," said Emily. "I wondered . . . " But the older woman interrupted her thought as she looked at Emily intently.

"That was a sad business, Sugar. Miss Elizabeth didn't deserve all that trouble she got from the KKK . . ." She was about to say more when the door flung open and two young women burst through, giggling loudly.

"Oh, Esther, I'm in a pickle," said one. "I've split a seam—I know you can fix it, with your magic needle and thread. Otherwise, I'll have to hide in here all night, and I'm supposed to be my date's lucky charm!" She and her friend dissolved into more giggles, no doubt fueled by champagne, as Esther clucked over them and searched for her sewing supplies, her attention diverted from what she had been about to say, much to Emily's chagrin.

More sleek, well-dressed women appeared in the lounge area of the Ladies' Room, greeting Queen Esther as they peered into oversize gilt mirrors, applying lipstick and powder. Emily longed to quiz the older woman about why she had mentioned Aunt Liz and the KKK, but she had already been gone a good while; Lewis and Wynne were probably wondering if she'd been kidnapped, she thought. Besides, the tipsy girl with the split seam was still monopolizing Esther. Watching the drama in a vanity mirror, Emily made her hair repairs in haste and left a generous tip in the dish that was discretely left on the counter. As she left, Esther caught her eye and shrugged her shoulders slightly, as if to say she'd like to talk more. Emily raised her hand in a tentative wave.

But she needn't have flattered herself about being missed too much, she thought with some amusement when she returned to the table. Instead of looking at her with concern, Wynne and Lewis appeared to be deep in discussion, heads together as they traded names of old classmates and stories from their undergraduate days. Maureen had arrived and seemed to be providing the men with an appreciative audience. Looking up as she approached, Lewis rallied and jumped from his seat.

"Darling, you look lovelier than ever," he said, helping her to her seat. "I hope you don't mind, but Charlie took the liberty of ordering for you."

Emily did mind but managed to look gracious—or at least, hoped she had.

"You see, our chef is introducing a new paella tonight," said Wynne, seeming to sense her reaction, "and I expect it to be quite special. Otherwise, I would never have presumed. And while we're waiting, try some of this Cuban bread; we make it right here in our kitchens."

With the fresh butter on the table, the bread was delicious, and Emily vowed to not eat too much of it before the meal. Wynne had also ordered a dry white wine that tasted wonderful. As she took another sip, Emily noticed that the young man standing a few feet from the curtained entrance to the booth area matched Milton's description of Ray. Hands clasped before him, he scanned the room and, Emily thought, almost imperceptibly shot a glance her way. Milton must have talked with him, she thought. Except for the mustache, he reminded her a little of Milton's nephew Sam.

After dinner—the paella was excellent indeed, filled with plump shrimp—Emily found herself on the dance floor with Lewis, moving smoothly to a foxtrot with a subtle Latin beat. As they danced, a young woman appeared on the bandstand and began to sing "Begin the Beguine" softly, standing in a gauzy spotlight.

Feeling Lewis's hand in the flat of her back and following his lead, Emily was suddenly overcome with a wave of memory that transported her back to nights when the arms around her belonged to John. How could she feel this way when Lewis was right here with her—when he had come all this way to see her? And yet all she could think about in that moment was what she would give to have one more dance, one more night, with John.

Wynne and Maureen were dancing together on the other side of the floor but moved their way when the music paused, and when they got close enough, Wynne said, "Hey, Old Sport, let's switch—I need to ask Emily about something." Lewis raised his eyebrows at Emily, but when she nodded, he went agreeably to take up Maureen's arm. As Wynne guided Emily to the center of the dance floor, she wondered if perhaps now he would bring up whatever it was he'd wanted to discuss. The lights were quite low in the room, but she thought she saw some of her fellow dancers glance their way. One tall man with sleek gray hair nodded to Wynne.

"Shall I say a penny for your thoughts?" Wynne said. "You've become very quiet. I hope you're not upset that I ordered dinner for you. It's the kind of thing your Aunt Liz would have boxed my ears for doing."

"Oh goodness, are you still thinking about that?" said Emily. "No, the paella was delicious. It's just . . . "

"What?" He looked at her intently.

She shook her head, but found herself answering anyway, somehow relieved to be confessing. "That song the band played while I was dancing with Lewis — 'Begin the Beguine' — the music just grabbed me up and took me long ago and far away."

"To someone you loved, I'll bet," said Wynne. Was it so obvious, Emily wondered, and yanked herself back to the present, as Charlie guided her into a turn.

"Mr. Wynne, you show disconcerting signs of having psychic abilities — I think that's what they call it," said Emily. "If you're as kind as you seem, you won't bring that up to Lewis."

"Understood," said Wynne. "And speaking of psychic abilities, it doesn't take those to see that a significant someone we both know is trying to get our attention — your attention, at any rate."

Chapter 26

Foxtrotting and Table Hopping

CHARLIE WYNNE gestured to a table across the dance floor, where Julian Sloane sat surrounded by several exquisitely dressed older women who seemed to hang on his every word. Tendrils of smoke wafted from the long cigarette holder he waved and then punched in the air, as if to punctuate his conversation. His companions were laughing and nodding.

"Julian?" said Emily. "Somehow it hadn't occurred to me that he might be here."

"My dear lady," said Charlie. "Didn't I tell you everyone who's anyone in our little burg would be here tonight? Perhaps Sloane didn't realize you might be here—though you, Miss Emily, are the It Girl of the moment."

Emily felt her face flush a little. She wasn't sure if she was flattered or irritated. Just when she felt like confiding in Charlie as a genuine new friend, she had to wonder how much he could be trusted—or whether he was, well, what John would have called a bullshit artist. Right now, though, she needed to focus on Sloane.

"I'd love for Lewis to meet him," she said. More important, she wanted to talk to Sloane herself. Just how close had he really been to her aunt? Was he really the only other person besides Odette Murat whom Aunt Liz had invited to the fish camp? She thought of the photo of them on the beach, so young, with the man who looked like Picasso, and the newspaper photo from years later, the night before Liz's death, when a camera had accidentally captured Julian in a secret scowl.

"Let's think—how shall we do this?" Charlie said, to himself as much as to her. "I'm not keen on getting embroiled with some of those ladies at Julian's table. Let's hope he's up for a visit to ours."

"How could he turn you down? I do get the impression he likes to be the center of attention, and what better place than with the evening's host?"

"Where indeed?"

The music was ending, and she joined Charlie in applauding the band as he nodded toward Sloane's table, where Juan Blanco started to rise from his seat and looked in Emily and Charlie's direction.

"Look out. I'll bet good old Juan's headed our way right now, with an invitation from Julian," Wynne whispered as he leaned toward her.

"I have a feeling I'd lose that bet," she said, but even as she watched, Blanco disappeared in the crowd of dancers lingering on the floor.

"Where the hell did he go?" muttered Charlie, as they both scanned the room. Then, sensing a movement right behind her, Emily whirled around to see Sloane's assistant at her elbow. Sneaky, like a spy, she thought.

"Good evening, Mr. Wynne, Miss Washington," Blanco said, in silky tones. "Mr. Sloane is so pleased to see you, Miss Washington. He hopes you'll both join him at his table, if that's possible."

"Juan, please give him our thanks," said Charlie. "I need to be at my own table shortly to conduct a bit of business, and then we'll be moving to the Havana Room. Do you think he could be persuaded to join us, instead? You too, of course, Old Sport—I know I can depend on you to arrange this." He slipped something into Blanco's palm, as deftly as Emily had ever seen that done—and she had seen Lewis do it very well indeed, to secure a good table at a Manhattan supper club.

"Certainly, Mr. Wynne," said Blanco, smiling conspiratorially as he glided away.

"I'm sure Julian will come over shortly," Charlie said to Emily, as they started to dance again—a smart foxtrot. "He looked a little bored."

"Bored? He looked like he was holding court," Emily said with a grin. "Happy as a clam."

"Trust me. He'll want to see you, and he'll want the early entry to the Havana Room that only I can provide. Soon, quite a few of these good gentlemen will politely excuse themselves from their female companions and slip behind the scenes."

"I know—your gambling lair," said Emily. "Maureen told us all about it." Now Wynne broke into a wide smile.

"Speak of the devil," he said, nodding at Maureen and Lewis, who sent them a mock salute as he guided Maureen across the floor so they were just a few yards away.

"Did she now?" Charlie continued, saluting Lewis in return. "She probably told you that it exists, but not 'all' about it. Not too many people know that." He turned her in a quick spin, as if to remind her of just how in control he was in this place.

"And probably for their own good," Emily kept on in a teasing tone, once she was face-to-face with him again. "But it sounds like Julian knows plenty—he's a good customer?"

"You could be a reporter like Maureen Davis, Emily. You've got me talking about things I shouldn't—my customers' privacy is vital to my success. But when we visit the Havana Room—yes, no doubt Julian will join us there."

The foxtrot had stopped, and they stood side by side, applauding again, as Wynne smiled and nodded to people, a bit like a genial king with his subjects.

"So, women are allowed in the hallowed lair?" said Emily, raising an eyebrow.

"That depends on the woman," he said. "Your aunt was certainly welcome, although she didn't visit often." He looked over her shoulder and paused. "Well, well—here comes the esteemed Mr. Sloane," he said, nodding in the direction behind Emily.

She looked up to see that Julian was indeed headed their way, with Juan Blanco pushing his wheelchair across the dance floor while the band took a break. Maybe it was her imagination, but her aunt's old friend seemed to be looking at her strangely, almost as if he had seen a ghost. Then his expression turned to exuberance, as if nothing in the world could have made him happier in that moment than to see her. She hurried forward to greet him, with Wynne following suit, and bent over to clasp Sloane's hands in greeting.

"Julian, what a wonderful surprise," she said, a bit too loudly, in an effort to be heard over the music. "Mr. Wynne said that anyone and everyone would be here tonight, but I had no idea that might include your illustrious self." She reached down to give him a polite peck on the cheek.

"My dear Emily, how wonderful to see you." Sloane paused and shook his head. "You know, you gave me quite a start. When I looked up and saw you across the room, at first I again thought your aunt had come back to me—in her younger guise, of course. A beautiful ghost."

He extracted a silk handkerchief from a pocket and dabbed at his eyes.

"My goodness, Julian, I'm so sorry I gave you a turn. I'll confess, this is her dress."

"And it's very becoming on you," he nodded emphatically. "How are you, Emily? I've been worried sick since I heard about what happened at Eola Lodge the other night."

"Oh my, yes, that seems a long time ago now," said Emily. "But, it was rather dramatic—and after we had such a lovely time at your party."

"I tried to call you several times," said Julian, "but got no answer. I'm relieved to see you here, and looking so ravishing. And I do want very much to talk with you privately. Perhaps we can arrange that later?"

"Of course," she said, smiling down at him. But why did Julian's apparent tears and his compliments seem just a little off? She seemed to be surrounded by men—Milton excepted, of course—who flattered her extravagantly, and perhaps not always sincerely. Or was it just that she had trouble trusting any man who wasn't John, she asked herself. Was she holding them all, including Lewis, up to an impossible standard, modeled on how she wanted to remember John? She thought of the photo her aunt had kept on her dresser for so many years—the one of Julian and Liz at the beach. Perhaps they had been lovers, and if he had truly loved her aunt, he might indeed be upset to be caught unawares by the sight of her dressed in her aunt's clothes. Emily hadn't even considered that possibility.

She was pulled from her short reverie by Charlie's voice behind her, where he had been hovering while she greeted Julian.

"Our distinguished Mr. Sloane," he began, "please do me the honor of being my guest at my table. You too, of course, Juan," he added, nodding to Blanco.

"Yes, Julian," said Emily. "There's someone I'd very much like you to meet—my friend Lewis Delacourt, from New York, who surprised me yesterday by appearing for a visit."

"Delacourt's no fool," Charlie said to Sloane. "He wants to make sure Emily doesn't marry anyone else," said Wynne. "And he's a wise man with bachelors like me on the loose here in Florida."

"Emily, my dear," said Julian. "How charming. I'm just so sorry that your aunt isn't here to meet the young man."

"So am I, believe me," said Emily, "but Mr. Wynne's exaggerating. There's no wedding in the offing, believe me."

"You'd better tell that to Lewis," Wynne said with a wink at Sloane. "He told me the date was already set."

"Oh, for Pete's sake!" Emily exclaimed before she could stop herself. "We're hardly even engaged!"

They were almost to Charlie's table, where Emily saw that Maureen and Lewis had returned and were deep in conversation and laughter. With a nod from Charlie, Milton's friend Ray stepped forward and took over the wheelchair duties from Blanco, who whispered something to Sloane and politely excused himself, disappearing into the crowd.

"Please forgive Juan, Mr. Wynne," Sloane said to Charlie, as Ray smoothly maneuvered his chair into a spot at the table. "I've asked him to take care of some business for me." He greeted Maureen warmly and, before Emily had a chance to speak, turned the full force of his charm on Lewis.

"And this must be your young man, Emily. The gallant visitor from New York."

"Mr. Sloane—what an honor," said Lewis, rising from his seat and leaning over to shake Sloane's elegantly proffered hand. "I've wanted to meet you ever since your show at the Downtown Gallery. My mother bought one of your sketches—a scene at Antibes."

"You must have a wonderful memory, young man—surely you were only a schoolboy then."

Lewis smiled his trademark boyish grin, one of the things that endeared him to Emily. What she didn't find endearing was all this pressure about marriage plans. As if on cue, Sloane asked, "But what's this I hear about a wedding on the horizon?"

"It isn't really—" Emily began, but Lewis cut her off.

"Of course, I'm absolutely thrilled," Lewis said. "That's why I decided to surprise my Emily with a visit—to sweep her off her feet. We're just about to set a date, aren't we, darling?"

Emily heard herself making sputtering sounds. Her mind didn't seem to be in gear. How dare Lewis blindside her like this, in public! As if his unannounced visit weren't enough already.

"Well, I have an idea," said Julian, with a mischievous gleam in his eye. "I'll throw you an engagement party to end all parties, out at the Studio—how's that? And we'll announce the date then. Let's do it soon," he urged, his expression turning more serious—"it's the least I can do in memory of dear Liz. She'd want me to do this, I know."

Emily felt almost like she was drowning. What was the rush? Why couldn't her friendship with Lewis stay exactly like it was? And why in heck was Julian so keen on promoting their engagement? True, he had been Liz's friend, but he'd only just met Emily.

"Well, you two are the most charming pair of steamrollers I've ever known," was all she could manage. That, and the smile she pasted to her lips. Inside, though, she felt frozen, as if she had moved beyond anger to a place of absolute stillness. What was she going to do?

Chapter 27

Happy Days Are Here Again

FOR THE MOMENT at least, Emily couldn't do much except stay glued to her seat, because a bevy of waiters had suddenly appeared, filling the whole club with a glittering array of trays and sparkling glasses. The curtains that screened Wynne's private table from the Flamingo's main dining room were suddenly pulled back, and Emily had an unfettered view of what was surely the largest assemblage of handsome young men she had seen in a long time. Moving quickly about the room, they offered tall flutes of champagne to every guest, while the band swung into a cheery tune.

Julian had been seated next to her, and as they took their champagne, he leaned forward in the midst of the hubbub and spoke to her in a low voice, their heads together like cozy conspirators.

"My dear, about that private matter. We might not have another chance tonight . . . You know, your aunt was probably closer to me than anyone else in my life."

A lock of silver hair had slipped down over his forehead, and Emily caught a glimpse of how he must have looked in his youth — in the beach photo. Perhaps her aunt had been in love with him. If so, he must have been deeply devastated by her death.

"You two traveled together, didn't you," she said, "in your art school days?" Just like she and Lewis had traveled, Emily thought as the hubbub around them continued, with some of the waiters calling for more champagne.

"Yes, indeed," Julian went on, "and I know that with all you have to attend to, this is such a minor thing, a silly thing, but it's about something dear to me — a little painting, you see, of Elizabeth, made long ago during those traveling days. I wondered if you've come across it in her bequest. I doubt it would mean a great deal to anyone but me, and to me it means the world."

"Julian, of course I understand," said Emily. "No, I haven't come across anything at all about a portrait of her. But I've only met with her attorney once. I'm supposed to see him again this week, and I'll know more then."

Sloane looked down, shaking his head, and suddenly Emily felt her heart go out to him. How much she would value another keepsake to remind her of John, she thought.

"I hoped you might at least have found a note in her things—in the house—that mentioned it. You see, she knew it meant a great deal to me—I was there when the portrait was created—and we used to joke that we were like parents sharing custody of it. It would mean so much to me . . . " His voice trailed off.

With the waiters and excitement swirling about them, it seemed like an odd time to bring up something that seemed so important to Julian, and also so private, Emily thought—although all the activity did provide a kind of privacy. Emily's mind raced—had she forgotten anything? Her aunt's studio was full of paintings, but she had assumed they were all her aunt's work. She hadn't looked through everything in detail, though. Remembering the last few days, she envisioned the charred ruins at the fish camp and almost winced.

"What's the matter?" Sloane asked. "Did you remember something—anything at all?"

"No, no," Emily assured him. "I was just thinking of the ruins out at the fish camp. I hope she didn't have it out there . . . which reminds me. There is something you can maybe help me with," Emily said, feeling bold. "You see, I've been trying to find something of my aunt's, too. You don't perhaps know where her scarab bracelet went?"

"No. Why would I? Wasn't she"—a pained look crossed Julian's face, and for a moment he was unable to speak. "Wasn't she buried with it? She never took it off." He pulled a handkerchief from his pocket, as if overcome with emotion, and Emily regretted bringing it up in company.

But before Emily could apologize, or tell him that no, in fact, Liz had not been buried with her bracelet, Julian's gaze slipped away. He was looking past her, across the table at Charlie, who had risen and was preparing to speak. The older man's face wore a shaky smile as he looked up from his wheelchair, but she noticed that the color had drained from his cheeks.

"We'll talk more later," he said, patting her hand. "Our good host is about to take the floor."

"Try not to worry about the painting," she whispered. "I'll bet the Judge just didn't want to overwhelm me with everything all at once. And I'm sure the bracelet will turn up."

"I'm so glad you're here to sort it all out." He blinked at her through eyes that seemed misty again.

"Me, too, Julian. So glad. And so glad to be with you."

Then Emily looked up to see Charlie signal to the young man named Ray, who had moved from Sloane's side to a large gong by the bandstand that he now struck with an elegant gesture. As the echoes of merriment subsided, Wynne raised his glass and spoke in a hearty voice. Impressively, he was able to project without a microphone so that the whole crowd heard him.

Lewis, on Emily's other side, whispered to her, "Princeton Drama Club," with a humorously knowing look, and she almost giggled in spite of herself. She might be irritated at his rush to marriage, but he was a darling, too—he could always make her laugh. Now they both turned toward Charlie.

"My friends," their host began," I'm so happy you could all be here tonight and indulge me in showing off my pride and joy—the fabulous Flamingo Club, renovated and even better than ever—as we celebrate the twenty-fifth anniversary of this fine establishment."

"We wouldn't miss it, Charlie," someone shouted. "We're indebted to you—in every possible way!"

A ripple of laughter went around the room, and Emily shot Lewis an amused look, to which he shrugged his shoulders.

"And I to you, my friends," Wynne continued. "This community has been extraordinarily good to my family, now Mama and me"—he paused and nodded to the next table, where Emily realized that Wynne's mother was seated with the tall, silver-haired man Charlie had acknowledged earlier.

"Indeed, you and your families have been good to us," Charlie continued, "since my father opened the Flamingo a quarter century ago during the dark days of Prohibition."

More murmurs and laughter came from around the room.

"We've been through a lot together," Charlie went on. "We made it through the Depression and a terrible war against the darkest evil humankind has faced. Now, we can see only good times and good business ahead here in the land of sunshine and orange blossoms."

"Here's to that," someone shouted, followed by cries of "hear, hear, Charlie."

"So please join me, dear friends," Charlie almost shouted, "in drinking a toast to another twenty-five years of good food, good times, and good fun at the Flamingo!"

The sounds of more cheers mixed with the laughter and filled the air as the hundreds of people in the large dining room raised their glasses in a toast and the band broke into a spirited version of "Happy Days Are Here Again."

Charlie had moved around the table and now spoke to Lewis, who stood up to shake Charlie's hand. Emily could hear Charlie, too, through the cheery mayhem that continued all around them.

"Old Sport, would you be so kind as to allow me one more dance with your beautiful lady to finish off the public part of my performance here? Then I'd like to show you all the Havana Room—it looks grand, and we've added a few new wrinkles."

Lewis clapped Wynne on the back, grinned, and swept another champagne glass from a nearby tray, nodding an enthusiastic yes as he joked and made conversation with the waiter. Honestly, Emily thought—as her recent delight at Lewis's humor ricocheted back to mild exasperation—give that man a glass of champagne and he never met a stranger. Sometimes, he could and would talk with anyone, everyone—except her.

And she had to admit—her irritation growing—she was beginning to feel like some kind of prize livestock. She was surrounded by men who decided what she would eat, who she would dance with, and when—even, it seemed, whom—she would marry. And she had forgotten about Lewis and champagne—it was his Achilles heel when it came to drinking. If he kept draining flutes of the stuff from Wynne's seemingly bottomless source, she'd have to pour him into Milton's taxi. And really, John would never have been so eager for her to dance with other men.

Nevertheless, when she once again found herself on the dance floor with Charlie, this time gliding to the "Anniversary Waltz" as a young crooner did a passable impersonation of Bing Crosby, her fit of exasperation simmered down and she found herself smiling. After all, Charlie truly was a fun dance partner. And she had to admit she was curious about the Havana Room.

"Thanks for indulging me again, Miss Washington," he said, looking at her directly as they glided to the waltz, other couples now crowding onto the dance floor around them. "It's just that I couldn't help but overhear Sloane's conversation with you, and—I need to speak with you alone, at least briefly. Tell me, do you trust Mrs. Davis—I mean, would you trust her with your deepest secrets?"

"What a question," said Emily. "I suppose I would, actually. We were friends as girls, and those bonds tend to last—at least they have in our case. But why?"

"Because I want to show you something, and after we go to the Havana Room, it might be easier to draw the two of you—you and Maureen—away from the gentlemen rather than you alone. I don't want to irritate your beau, you know—he's a good fellow."

"He is indeed," she said. "And I love him dearly, but—" Emily stopped herself from the admission that was on her tongue, an admission she realized she had only just made herself—that she wasn't sure the love she and Lewis shared was a wedding-bells kind of love.

"But what?" Wynne said.

"I guess I'm feeling rather panicked about the whole thing—the wedding."

"Ah, of course. Deep waters, Emily. Someone as bright as you should have questions, I'd wager. But, you know, the world is full of people who married successfully for all kinds of reasons but were hardly Romeo and Juliet. I'd like to talk more about that, much more, but right now, let's go back and gather up our friend Maureen."

"All right," Emily said, relieved. She didn't have the heart — or the stomach — to wade further into those deep waters tonight — to delve into meditations on true love. She had already thought too much about John and the past instead of being in the present, and she wanted to use what wits and energy she could command to find out more about her aunt's life and death.

As Charlie took her arm and they began to make their way around the dance floor to his table, he leaned closer to Emily as they walked, interrupted a couple of times by jovial guests who stopped to shake Wynne's hand.

"Once we get to the Havana Room and get Julian and Lewis settled at the blackjack table, I'll make some excuse and spirit you and Maureen away to my office — actually to the safe." Emily's jaw almost dropped.

"The safe — whatever for?" And what was the need for such secrecy?

"Because I helped your aunt hide something there, and now that she's gone, I'm assuming it's yours," said Charlie. "And frankly, it makes me very nervous."

Chapter 28

The Infamous Inner Sanctum

"WHAT ON EARTH are you talking about?" said Emily. "You're hiding something for my aunt? She was the least secretive person I've ever known." Or was she? Mysteries about Elizabeth Washington seemed to be multiplying, including the painting that seemed to mean so much to Julian Sloane.

They were almost back at Charlie's table, but he stopped and looked at her.

"Honestly, didn't your aunt tell you that she had asked me to keep something for her?"

"Absolutely not. I don't know anything about it—nothing," Emily gulped.

When they reached the table, they found both Maureen and Lewis deep in conversation with Julian, who seemed to be in his element.

"Tell me, Julian, what artists have you admired the most—been your inspiration?" Maureen was asking, leaning forward toward the older man. Emily noticed that her friend's notebook was on the linen tablecloth, near her champagne glass and mostly hidden by a napkin.

"So many, my dear—but I can tell you who definitely wasn't. Picasso—what a poseur! I think someone else painted a great deal of what he claimed was his—the Blue Period especially."

Emily opened her mouth to challenge him, but Charlie caught her eye and gave the smallest shake of his head.

"My friends, I'd love to show off the Havana Room," he said. "If we go now, before my other guests descend, we'll have the best views of the décor. Julian, you'll be impressed, I hope. We've added some excellent artwork."

"I'll be impressed that I'm even seeing the place," quipped Maureen. "I thought women weren't welcome."

"Certain fabulous ladies, such as present company, are always welcome," said Wynne, giving Maureen a mock bow. "Shall we retire there, then?" He swept a hand toward the doorway, and Emily thought again of Jay Gatsby. "Just follow me. We can enjoy a digestif—we keep an excellent stock of liqueurs—I've even got a stash of absinthe."

"I thought that was banned," said Emily.

Wynne flashed her his best dimpled smile. "Nothing to fear from it, like most things," he said, "as long as you don't overdo."

Was that really true, Emily thought. Or weren't there some things that could do you harm, even in small amounts? Charlie seemed so charming, but she had no idea what kind of person he really was, or what he could possibly be storing for Liz in a safe.

As they readied to move, Julian's assistant, Juan Blanco, appeared to check on the older man. "I'm fine, Juan"— Julian told him with a wave of his hand—"go enjoy yourself. I know you've got your eye on a special someone. Come to the Havana Room in a couple of hours."

"Very well, Señor Sloane," said Blanco, turning away without a hint of a smile.

The group followed as Charlie led them down a long hallway, with Maureen and Emily following him and Lewis bringing up the rear, pushing Julian's wheelchair and leaning forward to hear what the older man, now in a jovial mood, was telling him.

When they reached an imposing door at the end of the hall, Wynne knocked three times and said, "Colonel, it's Mr. Wynne."

The door was opened by a tall, white-haired man with an imposing beard, dressed in a tuxedo. In a different costume, it occurred to Emily, he might have made an imposing Santa Claus.

"Colonel, welcome my esteemed guests this evening," Wynne said to him, introducing them each in turn. "Please give them the best of your always excellent attention. Make sure they have beverages, on the house of course."

The Colonel-Claus leaned over to shake Julian's hand, after he had greeted the two women and Lewis. "Mr. Sloane—if I may say so, you are looking in fine form," he said, clasping Julian's hand. "It's good to have you back to the Havana Room. It's better than ever, and I think you'll find the roulette tables are even better, too." He bent further, and Emily could barely hear him murmur to Julian, "I believe Mr. Wynne has made sure the odds are favorable tonight, for our special guests."

Taking it all in, Emily was wondering how she could gracefully leave Lewis to visit the safe, when Julian unwittingly solved the problem for her, as he turned to Lewis. "Young man, would you be kind enough to join me at the roulette table? I'd be honored to show you just how it's done. Mr. Wynne will look after the ladies, I'm sure. It's one of his specialties."

Lewis looked at Emily. "You don't mind, do you, Darling? You ladies seem to be in a decided minority," he said as he looked around the room, where early arrivals were already beginning to fill up some of the tables.

"Of course not," said Emily, as Wynne gave her a nod and a smile from behind Lewis. "You two go enjoy yourselves." She made a jaunty wave as the two of them receded toward a far corner of the room, even though she felt slightly annoyed that Lewis was pawning her off and Charlie was ordering her about yet again. Still, she couldn't deny she was dying to see what was in the safe.

Wynne added a jovial wave as well, before nodding to the Colonel, who had picked up a telephone receiver and was speaking into it. When Charlie noticed Emily's gaze, he said conspiratorially, "The Colonel likes to make sure the roulette tables are well attended."

"So this is the Flamingo Club's infamous inner sanctum," said Maureen, casting her gaze around the room. "My father has told me about it—actually, my mother has told me what my father told her about it, in confidence."

"I hope it lives up to your expectations," said Wynne. "The officers at the Air Base were good to us during the war—that's one reason I was able to spruce the place up."

As she listened, Emily surveyed the large room. An imposing bar took up most of one side of the room, the wall above it adorned with a large mural depicting flamingos and other water birds against an expansive Florida landscape of palmettos under towering clouds. It was breathtaking and looked both exotic and strangely familiar.

"What a beautiful mural," she said, to herself as much as anyone.

"Who painted it?" Maureen asked, as Charlie guided both of them toward a curtain at the back of the room, tucked into a corner next to the bar.

"I especially wanted you to see that, Miss Washington," Charlie said.

"I thought we'd agreed you would call me Emily. No need to be so formal."

"Ah, but in my case, there is a need, dear lady. I have to hold myself a little apart, you see — at least in public. It comes from the role I play with my clientele — some of whom end up being quite in debt to me. I can't afford to have many real friends, but your aunt, I'm honored to say, was one of them. Which is why I asked for her help with this mural."

"My aunt?"

"I'm surprised you don't recognize the style, although I dare say, you've never seen it displayed in something so large. But your aunt's appreciation for the beauty of Florida — and her ability to put it on canvas — had few peers."

"Aunt Liz painted this?"

"Indeed. It was quite our secret — one of them, at any rate."

They had arrived at the curtains he had been directing them toward, and he drew them back and opened a door.

"Welcome to my office, ladies, and thank you both for joining me in this little subterfuge," he said.

"What subterfuge?" said Maureen. "Will you two tell me what's going on?"

"Absolutely," said Wynne, as he held the door and gestured for them to pass through. "As I told Miss Washington—Emily—earlier, Mrs. Davis, I need her to see something that's in my office, and we agreed you could keep a confidence."

"Now you've really got me curious. Lead on, Macduff."

They entered an elegantly appointed room with a desk and large desk chair, several paintings of colorful Florida scenes on the walls, and a set of golf clubs slung into one corner. One wall of the room was covered with another curtain, which Wynne pulled back to reveal a tall metal door.

"What in the world—" said Maureen.

"It's our safe—more a vault, really. It actually is an old bank vault our builder found for me. It's not that I have piles of money—but sometimes clients leave me things as collateral on their debts and so on that are large—antiques, for example—and I needed a place to store them."

Emily and Maureen waited while Wynne worked a large combination lock on the door and swung it open. He stepped inside and turned on a light.

"Don't be shy, ladies—do come in—time is of the essence. I expect your Lewis will soon wonder where I've taken you for so long," he said to Emily. "Just step over here and you can see it," he said, as he pointed to what seemed to be a large painting leaning against one wall of the room they had entered. It was enveloped in a velvet drape that Charlie pulled aside, revealing a striking portrait of a woman with long dark hair.

"How funny," Maureen murmured. "It looks like something from Picasso's Blue Period. Julian was just talking about that! But I've never seen it—at least I don't think I have—in my books about him. It must be a good copy."

Emily didn't say anything. All she could do was stare at the large canvas, until she realized she needed a handkerchief to blot the tears that had filled her eyes.

"Very good, Mrs. Davis," said Wynne. "But it's not like Picasso's Blue Period—it is Picasso's Blue Period. He painted it."

"He painted it of my aunt," whispered Emily.

"Yes, and he gave it to her," said Wynne. "Though why she held it as such a secret, I'm not sure — although I have my ideas."

Emily's head was spinning. So it was Picasso in the picture she had found in her aunt's bedroom — the man she thought looked like him. And Julian had asked her about a painting, a painting of her aunt — but surely he must mean something else. He had only just been deriding Picasso's Blue Period paintings as all being fakes.

"And why did she ask you to keep it?" she asked Charlie.

"Besides her wish for secrecy, I think there's a pragmatic answer to that," said Wynne. "Not only do I have a very large safe, but it's also in an air-conditioned part of the building, and air-conditioning itself is pretty rare here."

"So I gather," said Emily.

"It's expensive, but I couldn't keep the club open without it," Wynne went on. "Anyway, she said she was worried about our swampy climate harming the painting — so she asked me to keep it. Actually, she paid me to keep it — a small amount each month. If you'd be inclined to pick up her tab from the estate, by the way, I won't turn you down," he added with a grin.

"I thought you said it was a small amount."

"Every little bit counts, Miss Washington — Emily. This old place eats money. There's always something to replace — and of course, the sheriff constantly has his hand out."

"Carter Mizell?"

"Yes, of course — It's a time-honored tradition in our supposedly honorable county. Some things that are illegal but good for business are just fine, if you pay the sheriff and his boys to look the other way. Although few sheriffs seem to have liked that system as much as Mizell. He's raised the payoff amount considerably."

"And what if you don't pay?" Emily asked, thinking of what Billy had said about Carter skimming money from the bolita game, and how scared he seemed of his uncle.

"They'll shut you down — which they do, anyway, for a few days every once in a while, just to stay in practice — and also to show the Bible-thumpers and the governor and other concerned citizens that they're doing their job."

Emily wanted to ask another question, when one of several phones on Wynne's desk began to ring. He stepped quickly back into the office and answered it, leaving Emily and Maureen to stare at the portrait of her aunt's younger self. Her reverie was almost immediately interrupted, though.

"Yes," Charlie said into the phone, his manner suddenly tense. "All right, I'm coming right now." Then he turned to them.

"Ladies, speak of the devil, quite literally. I'm afraid we have some excitement on our hands. Someone will escort you back to the dining room right away. We just received word from a friendly deputy that the sheriff himself has decided to pay us a visit. And I definitely don't want him near this safe."

Chapter 29

A Visit from the Sheriff

CHARLIE USHERED Maureen and Emily through the metal door of the huge vault and back into his office, where he quickly closed the door, spun the handle to secure it, and pulled the curtain that concealed the vault into place. They followed him into the main gambling area, where he scanned the room and motioned to Ray, the young Black man Emily knew was Milton's friend—although neither she nor Ray had acknowledged that.

"Ray, please escort these ladies back to the main dining room," Charlie said. "Better yet, get them a taxi—there's no time to lose. I'll alert Mr. Delacourt, who came with them."

As Ray rushed away, Charlie leaned toward Emily. "We'll talk soon," he said. "I apologize for abandoning you, but I've got to move fast. If my source is right—and he usually is—Mizell's making another stop before this one, so we've got about 20 minutes—that's enough time, but there's not a moment to waste."

"But what about Lewis?"

"Don't worry, Emily—I'll take care of him. I'll make sure he gets back to his hotel. There's probably not much hope of you two enjoying a romantic night now."

"That was the last thing on my mind—I just don't want him to have a nervous breakdown," Emily said.

"I know," said Wynne, reaching out and giving her hand a squeeze. "But I need to get you out of here."

While they were talking, Charlie had grabbed and yanked a long velvet cord that Emily saw was attached to a bell that rang clearly throughout the room. At the chime of the bell, the room sprang into motion. At the poker tables, players shrugged, stood up, and aided the tuxedo-clad Flamingo hosts and dealers as cards and chips were removed and the tables were covered with damask cloths. A waiter moved quickly throughout the room placing small centerpieces on the tables and lighting the candle in each.

Charlie moved fast, too, going from table to table and talking with patrons. "Nothing to worry about," Emily overheard him tell several prosperous-looking older men nearby. One lit a cigar as another nodded and shook his head.

"Wow, this is better than the floor show," said Maureen as she took in the flurry, pulling her notepad from her purse.

"I would feel better if we could see Lewis," said Emily.

Then Charlie caught her eye. "I said, don't worry," he called. "Just go. Now! Ray will have your cab out front."

But to Emily's own amazement, she didn't want to go. What was there to be afraid of? Carter Mizell wouldn't put her in jail — she hadn't done anything other than look at paintings — her aunt's mural and her portrait. Lewis might be mortified to be swept up in a raid, but as long as the news didn't reach the New York papers, even that probably wouldn't matter to him as much as the adventure of it all. More than anything, she felt stunned by the news of the Picasso's existence. She did have Billy to think about, she suddenly remembered. He would surely be at Eola Lodge by now. But Mattie had agreed to stay overnight and expected her to be home late so there was no rush. And the police car was still outside Eola Lodge — they were fine at home without her, she thought.

Besides, watching the scene unfold was fascinating, as the Havana Room was transformed as if by magic into just another room in an elegant supper club. The Colonel-Claus joined Charlie in talking with patrons. Emily turned to Maureen, who was jotting on her small notepad with furious speed.

"Grist for your column?" Emily said, nodding at Maureen's pad and the small silver pencil she was now wielding furiously. "Walter Winchell would be impressed."

"Hardly," the redhead replied. "For one thing, I won't use any real names — but shrewd readers won't need them."

"What should we do?" said Emily. "I'll confess, I'm reluctant to turn tail and leave—especially after what I learned about Mizell today—how he was trying to smear Aunt Liz. I'd love to give him a swift kick."

"I feel like that every time I see him," said Maureen, "just on general principles. Milton doesn't have much use for him—I can tell you that."

"Oh good lord—what a ninny I am," said Emily. "Milton! Milton's here. I forgot to tell you. I ran into him earlier on the way to the Ladies' Room. I got so caught up in this painting business that it went right out of my head. I'm surprised he hasn't found us."

But when she looked up, it was not Milton but Lewis whom she saw rushing toward them.

"Darling! Are you all right?" he said, out of breath and flushed.

"Fine, Dear Lewis. Actually, I'm rather guiltily enjoying all this mayhem. By the looks of it, you are, too."

She had rarely seen Lewis look so animated—only a few times on their travels, like the day in Egypt when they had scrambled up one of the Great Pyramids, evading their guide. Most of the time lately he seemed so bound by his parents' expectations, but occasionally it was as though he escaped and the real Lewis slipped out. That was the man she loved—maybe not in the way she had loved John, but she did care for Lewis nevertheless, she thought, as she looked at his face, filled with excitement. But was she really ready to marry him? She couldn't believe she'd allowed Julian to press her into agreeing to an engagement party in a matter of days.

"I am glad to see you, Pooh," she said. "I was afraid Julian had permanently appropriated you."

"Pooh?" Maureen snorted, looking at them both in mock horror. "You two take the cake in the adorable department. Sophisticated New Yorkers? My Aunt Fanny."

"Look, Hedda Hopper—that's not for your notebook," Emily began, but Lewis was already in mid-sentence on another subject entirely.

"Oh Emmie, what a fascinating old bird Sloane is, but I'm afraid he's had a bit too many Cuba Libres. He kept asking me if

I knew anything about some painting—something to do with your aunt."

Maureen looked up from her notes and caught Emily's eye.

"How odd," said Emily, exchanging glances with Maureen.

"Yes, some painting he's sure she wanted him to have," Lewis rushed on. "He can't believe it wasn't in her will."

"Where is he now?" asked Maureen.

"That fellow Blanco came to retrieve him," said Lewis. "I think they were going to make a speedy exit. And you both should, too. Charlie asked me if I'd give him a hand with a couple of things—I hope you don't mind, Emily. Can't let an old Princeton man down."

He grinned a smile almost as dazzling as Charlie's.

"Especially when he's being raided by the police," said Emily. "Safe to say, it's a good thing your parents are still in south Florida."

"Don't you know it," he said, reaching forward to give her a light kiss. Then he made a comic salute to Maureen, turned, hailed Charlie across the room, and was off.

Right after Charlie had rung the bell, a quartet of musicians had taken their places on a small stage at one end of the Havana Room, obscuring the entrance to the roulette area, and now a crooner took the stage in front of several couples dancing to the music. Some of the women were much younger than their partners and were dressed in dazzling style.

"Those girls are from the show," said Maureen, following Emily's gaze. "Most of the men here wouldn't let their wives near the place. The dancing is part of Charlie's set dressing."

Above the music, Emily thought she heard police sirens, now distant but drawing closer.

"There they are," she said, "or it certainly sounds so."

She looked up to see that Ray was headed back their way.

"Ladies, Mr. Armistead wanted me to collect you. He's got the taxi ready to go and is at your service. Just follow me."

"Thank you, Ray," said Emily. "That's right, isn't it?"

"Yes ma'am," he said with a smile.

Emily looked at Maureen. "I expect it would not be good for

Billy's dad to find out he had left his son with a jailbird. Maybe we'd better skedaddle."

"At least let's head toward the exit and confer with Milton," said Maureen.

They followed Ray from the Havana Room through the main dining room, which remained crowded and festive. A woman dressed like Carmen Miranda was in the middle of an exuberant performance on the stage, snapping her fingers and swinging her hips to a samba beat. Ray reached the imposing front doors of the club before the two women and pulled one of the doors open for them.

Emily looked through the door and saw Milton's taxi, sitting rather grandly at the end of the canopied stairs that led into the Flamingo. Milton was at the wheel, clip-on sunglasses in place in spite of the dark skies overhead. She was looking at him so intently that she didn't realize Carter Mizell had slipped around the corner of the building, gun in hand and flanked by two deputies. As Emily and Maureen rushed down the stairs, they ran smack dab into him.

Mizell almost knocked them over, but Maureen slipped an arm around Emily to steady her. Emily did the same for her taller friend, and they stood, locked together momentarily.

"What the hell?" said Mizell. "You two turn up like bad pennies. Outta my way. I'm here for bigger fish."

"That would be me, Sheriff?" they heard a voice behind them.

Emily turned her head and saw Charlie standing behind them in his white suit, arms akimbo and flanked by two very large Black men.

"What's the matter, Wynne—can't take care of yourself? I see you still have your jungle protection. No self-respecting deputy would work for you off-duty, that's for sure."

By now, Milton had gotten out of his taxi and was standing by it, watching intently.

"To what do I owe this honor, Sheriff?" said Charlie, looking down at Mizell from the steps. "I'd invite you in, but the Flamingo has a dress code, I'm afraid. Do join us some other time."

"You know why I'm here, Wynne. You've got illegal gambling going on. And I also hear you've got a colored girl singing in the band, even dancing with some of the patrons. That alone is grounds to arrest you."

Emily's face turned hot. Suddenly she had a mental picture of a young Mizell, menacing her and Milton's nephew Sam twenty years ago. Her anger rose. She and Maureen remained rooted on their step, between Mizell below them and Charlie and his men behind them.

"I thought we had an arrangement, Mizell," Emily heard Charlie say in a low voice. "No funny business on opening night. It certainly cost me enough."

Mizell started forward but to her own amazement, Emily reached out and placed a hand on his chest as if to stop him.

"Have you been calling my aunt a drunk?" she heard herself say. "How dare you pretend to enforce the law when you obviously care nothing for the laws of decency."

Mizell stopped short, his face a twisted combination of shock and anger at the audacity that anyone, especially a woman, would challenge him.

"Lady, if you know what's good for you, and if you don't want to end up like your nigger-loving aunt, you'll get your Yankee ass out of my way."

"Don't you threaten me, you liar!" Emily began, swinging an arm back to strike out, but Milton came between them then, with a grim determination that scared Emily, when another voice called from a long black limousine that had pulled up on the other side of Milton's taxi.

"Gentlemen!" At the sound of the voice, everything seemed to stop.

Two men got out of the limo, dressed in black, and stood by the taxi. One was the tall silver-haired man Emily had seen Charlie talking with earlier, and even before that, talking to Charlie's mother at Julian's party. When he spoke to them, his voice was soft and smooth but also laced with a sense of menace.

"Gentlemen, gentlemen, surely enough has been said here," the smooth Silver Man said. "Sheriff, you've clearly been misinformed. You can look inside, but all you'll find is fine food, drink, and entertainment. We drove all the way from Tampa to enjoy it, didn't we, Joey?'

The other man simply nodded.

"No place like the Flamingo," the Silver Man said. "And I have great respect for Mr. Wynne—a fine businessman."

Emily thought she could hear Charlie breathing behind her.

Mizell began to raise a hand, but he used it only to take off his Stetson hat. He turned and stalked away from the cluster that was Emily, Maureen, and Milton, only to slam his hat down on the hood of Milton's taxi. Then, to her shock, he turned, motioned to his deputies, and walked the few yards to his patrol car, but not before giving her a look that chilled her heart. Just as he was about to get into the car, he looked up at Charlie.

"You'll regret this Wynne," he said. "You whole sorry lot— this isn't over." Then he put the car in gear, turned on the siren, and sped onto the highway.

The tall, slick Silver Man raised a hand in salute.

"Lovely evening," he called to Wynne, and with the man he had called Joey, he got into the limousine still parked next to Milton's taxi, and it also sped away.

From beside her, Milton spoke. "Ladies, I do believe your taxicab is here." He tipped his hat to Charlie, who was still standing on the step behind them, looking after the departing vehicles.

"What just happened?" Emily said.

Inexplicably, Charlie began to laugh.

"You know, I'm sure, Miss Emily, that people call me a gangster. I don't even come close. Not even close."

Chapter 30

Plenty of Questions

MAUREEN AND EMILY rode in quiet in the back seat, and Milton, too, said nothing as he guided the old Cadillac taxi under a moonlit sky.

"Well, that was something," he said finally. "How you ladies doing?"

"I don't know about you, Emily, but that was about as much excitement as I can handle for one night," said Maureen.

"Enough for a year, I think," said Emily, who then turned to Milton. "Mr. Armistead, who were those men in the limousine—that tall man Mizell seemed afraid of?"

"From what Mr. Charlie said, I'd guess they're pretty serious bad guys. Mob men from Tampa, I reckon. The times are changing."

"What do you mean?" asked Maureen.

"I mean these outsiders—the Tampa tough guys. Before they started nosing around, things were the same at the Flamingo for a long, long time. Mr. Charlie inherited that club from his daddy, who started it way back during Prohibition, when most folks here pretty much ignored the law."

"But Charlie's dad kept right on ignoring it," Maureen said to Emily.

"Yes ma'am," Milton went on. "After Prohibition, folks here just kept on ignoring some laws about things they enjoyed, like where to have a drink or placing a few bets—but it was always a local operation—everyone was in on the deal."

"Even the sheriff and his men, who could collect a pretty penny just to look the other way," Maureen added.

"But now, especially since the war, these mob guys from New York and New Jersey been moving in, operating out of Tampa and taking over a big slice of the action. And I bet our Sheriff Mizell isn't just taking the payoffs these days—I bet he's paying, too—to guys like that."

"If Mizell takes payoffs from Charlie and from the people who sell bolita tickets—why would he pay these men?" asked Emily.

"He's paying them to stay out of his territory," said Milton. "To stay out of the bolita game here and all. But those mob guys are sniffing around, and I hear they've been gambling out at the Flamingo. And I tell you, owing money to those guys is a whole different thing than a poker debt to the Wynnes used to be in this town."

Emily's thoughts turned to some of what Charlie had said about her aunt, and had a vision of Liz in the Havana Room, maybe at a poker table—the only woman.

"Milton, I know Aunt Liz could, let's say, flout convention," she said.

"Uh-huh. You can say that again, Miss Emily."

"Charlie said she had played cards in the Havana Room. Could she have ever played cards with men like that? Could she have owed them money? Is that why Marvin Willetts was following her around? Do you think he could have killed her? Oh God."

She pulled her wrap more tightly around her and shrank back in her seat.

"Miss Emily, calm down," said Milton. "If a man like that wants you dead, you end up like Willetts did—with a bullet in your brain. Guys like that don't start fires to kill people. They're more direct."

"Okay, but did she ever owe them money? Did she gamble there?"

"It wasn't exactly that she gambled, Emily," Maureen chimed in. "It's just that every once in a while, she'd had enough of some of the old fools who think they run this town and take them down a peg or two in the high-stakes poker games out at the Flamingo."

"Yep," said Milton. "She had the kind of mind that could remember all the cards—she won some big hands. Cleaned their clocks when she put her mind to it."

"I'm sure that made her some enemies," said Emily.

"Sure, but being good at cards made her some fine friends, too. The old Judge—her lawyer—he used to play bridge with her at the Flamingo. They'd be partners, mostly for fun, but sometimes they'd bet. He really liked her, honestly."

"I didn't think she'd choose him as a lawyer unless she really trusted him," said Emily. "But, I don't know—I'll confess, I had my doubts about him."

"Oh, I know he comes across like a breath of the Old South," said Milton, "but he's okay. I used to play nickel poker with him and your aunt, as a matter of fact—at that same yellow kitchen table, Miss Emily."

Emily looked out the window and sighed.

"I've played cards with some men who really don't like to lose to a woman," she said, suddenly far away.

Milton paused and looked at her in the rearview mirror.

"It was never like that with Lizzie—Miss Elizabeth," he said. "Man, she could bluff like nobody's business. A game with her was just a good time—a battle of wits. And let's be clear: she didn't win all the time. The Judge and I could hold our own, fair and square, too."

"Looking back, I kind of resent being told as a girl to always let the boys win at games," Maureen said, more to herself than her companions. "Liz had no fear of winning—I loved that."

"I'm no stranger to strong women," said Milton. "Wish you ladies had known my mama—nobody messed with her. But getting back to what you were asking, Miss Emily—if your aunt owed money to men like those Tampa guys? She didn't."

"That's what I would guess," Emily started to say, but Milton wasn't finished.

"She wasn't one to rack up card-playing debts, for one thing, but if she ever did owe anybody for anything, she had the money to pay them. Now, some folks were always coming to her to bail them out, truth be told. She held the notes on some big pieces of property—maybe some of that belongs to you now. She was pretty secretive about some of her business dealings."

Her aunt had indeed kept secrets, Emily thought, including that she had known Picasso, and that he had painted her. She couldn't understand why Elizabeth Washington had gone to such pains to keep that particular secret. Maybe Milton, who seemed to know her aunt so well, had some idea about the painting that was stashed in Charlie Wynne's safe. If not, why not? Might Milton know whether it was "the little painting" Julian had asked her about at the Flamingo?

But they were almost at Maureen's house, and Emily wanted to delay any more questions for Milton until she was alone with him. It just felt better. Maureen was an old friend, but she had no idea, really, how deep Maureen's friendship had been with Liz. Soon they pulled into Maureen's driveway, and as her old friend squeezed Emily's hand as she slid out of the big taxi, the two women vowed to talk soon. After Milton walked Maureen to the door, Emily waited a minute and then plunged ahead. What was she willing to ask him, she wondered? What did she really want to know? Rather than asking about the painting directly, she tried a different tack.

"Mr. Armistead, you were talking about your mother," Emily said, once they were back on the road. "I'm guessing you, too, never kowtowed to anyone, but when Aunt Liz's estate is settled, you'll really be able to call the shots, won't you? You won't have to drive a taxi anymore."

"I really don't have to drive now, Miss Emily—I could just be the boss to the other drivers, but it keeps me busy—you know? Keeps my mind off things I don't like thinking about."

Like her aunt's death, Emily thought. Was there any way he could possibly blame himself?

"I know what you're saying, though, Miss Emily," Milton continued. "It's easier to have backbone when you have money than when you're poor. To some of these jerks like Carter Mizell, the only thing worse than a poor colored man is a rich one. He'd use more colorful language, though."

How did Milton stand it—all the limits, all the danger, really.

Could Emily live here, even for part of the year, she wondered. Did she want to? It was a far different world than New York.

"I'm surprised Liz stayed here, in a lot of ways," she said.

"All in all, she loved it," said Milton. "She loved the light, she said, and the night breezes, and she loved the people. Not the jerks, of course, but so many good people, she said. She believed things were gonna change, and they are, Miss Emily—they are—although many days it seems like the change is mighty slow in coming."

Emily listened, nodding, taking in his words. She remembered Milton sitting by Elizabeth's grave—how he called her Lizzie in unguarded moments. Julian might have talked about how close he was to Elizabeth Washington, but Milton might have been the one person who was truly close to her aunt—closer even than Emily had ever realized.

"Did you know she owned a secret painting—a very valuable painting by another artist?"

Milton didn't respond for what seemed a long time. Had she crossed a line, Emily wondered. Once again, she felt like she was at sea, without a compass.

"So you know about that," he said, letting each word fall into the dark hush. "Yes, I knew about it. I only saw it once. Her insurance policy—that's what she called it. I reckon it's yours and your problem now."

"Why do you say it's a problem?"

"I guess, Miss Emily, because she seemed to fret over it, but she never really told me why. In a lot of ways, you know, she was a very private person."

"Why did she call it an insurance policy?"

"I assume, because it must be worth a bunch of money," he said. He looked at her in the rearview mirror, although she couldn't really see his eyes in the dark. "She never loved him, you know," he said in a low voice.

What to say to that? They were nearly at Eola Lodge now, and it was very late and Emily suddenly felt very tired. Another day was ending with more questions in her mind than answers. Milton pulled into the driveway, got out, and opened the door for her.

"Since you're so full of questions, I have one for you, Miss Emily," he said. "What you gonna do about Mr. Lewis? You gonna marry him? Didn't I hear some talk about Mr. Sloane gonna have a party to announce the happy news?"

"Mr. Armistead!" Emily snapped as she got out — "or should I say 'general'? Did anyone ever tell you that you could be a bit of a nag? A very nice nag, but still . . ."

"All right," he said. "None of my business. Just thinking about what your aunt would say. Sometimes, you know, you have to make a decision. Sometimes, you can't please everyone and yourself, too."

Chapter 31

A Detective Calls

EMILY HAD EXPECTED the house to be dark, with no lights on and
Mattie and Billy sound asleep, but when she unlocked the front
door and slipped inside after waving goodbye to Milton, she found
both of them hovering just inside the door, as if ready to pounce
on her.

To her surprise, Billy even flung his arms around her, hugging
her waist.

"My goodness, what's the matter, you two? I thought you'd be
asleep long ago," she said.

"I tried, honest to God, Miss Emily, but the boy was all wound
up like a spring, and to tell you the truth, I was too," said Mattie,
her hands clutched at the neck of her bathrobe.

"What happened? I thought you were going to listen to Jack
Benny and go to bed."

"Jack Benny's on Sunday night, Miss Emily," said Billy. "Not
Monday."

"Never mind, Billy," Mattie began. "I was getting him ready
for bed, Miss Emily—"

"And then HE came by," Billy interrupted.

"Who?"

"My least favorite person in the whole entire universe, that's
who," said Billy. "Uncle Carter—but I'm going to stop calling him
that. I don't care if he is sorta my daddy's brother."

"What on earth did he want?"

"Sounded to me like somebody told him you wouldn't be here,"
said Mattie—"that you were going to the Flamingo."

"Really?" Emily felt a tide of anger start to rise.

"Yes, really," said Mattie, "and then he pushed his big ol' self in here and said he needed to see Miss Liz's painting studio—where she kept her paintings. It was official business, he said."

"How could that even begin to be possible?" said Emily. Mizell had wanted to see paintings, Mattie said—surely he couldn't have been looking for the Picasso. That would be too crazy.

"Beats me, Miss Emily," said Mattie. "He said something about how Miss Elizabeth had debts to be settled, and he could seize things that belonged to her to pay them, if he needed to. He sure had me scared."

Debts? From what Milton had said—and from what she knew of her aunt's finances—that seemed most unlikely. Surely the sheriff was lying, and Emily wanted to know why.

"I wouldn't ever let him hurt you, Miss Mattie," said Billy, looking at the housekeeper with wide eyes and then turning his gaze to Emily. "He bragged he was going out to the Flamingo, Miss Emily—said he was gonna arrest everyone there—show all the fancy folks a lesson."

"We were afraid you might be in jail," said Mattie.

"Just relax, everything's fine, just fine," said Emily, not feeling so fine at all. "I'm so glad to see you both—although I'm sorry you've lost sleep."

She turned and pulled back the front-window curtain to reveal a slice of streetlight. "I see a police car is still parked outside."

"Yes, and I think that's the only reason the sheriff didn't stay longer, to tell you the truth," said Mattie.

"And whatever he was looking for, he didn't find it," Billy said. "I kept an eye on him, Miss Emily—he didn't take anything with him."

Emily placed a hand on his shoulder. "That was excellent work, young man. Now, it's time for all of us to start counting sheep—and you especially, or you'll be asleep tomorrow at school. Let's go—upstairs, pronto."

"Aw, Miss Emily, do I have to go to school tomorrow? We're not doing anything special."

"I think the appropriate answer is that every day of school is special."

"Ummm-hmmm," said Mattie, walking up the stairs behind them.

They were almost at the top when Emily heard the doorbell ring. Now what?

"I'll go, Miss Emily," said Mattie.

"I think we'll all go," said Emily, as she picked up a tennis racket in the press that she'd found in the back of a closet and carried it with her.

"What good would that do," whispered Billy. "We need a baseball bat."

"I'll put it on the shopping list, "said Mattie.

When they got to the front door, Emily peeked through curtains and saw the young policeman who had been pulling guard duty nervously standing on the porch, cap in hand. She opened the door a crack.

"Officer Wilson, isn't it? Are you okay? You startled us."

"I'm real sorry, ma'am. I wouldn't have, but I could see a couple of lights on in the living room, and just heard voices, so I figured you were still up." He looked over Emily's shoulder to Mattie. "By the way, ma'am—thank you for the sandwich you brought me earlier—and the thermos of coffee. You were a lifesaver."

"Happy to do it," said Mattie, who turned quietly and headed for the kitchen, pulling Billy along with her.

"What can we do for you, officer?" said Emily.

"The dispatcher just sent me a message, ma'am, from Detective Maxwell. He wanted me to check on you all in person—see that you were okay—and asked me to see if you might still be up. He's on his way over to talk with you."

Just a few minutes ago, Emily had been almost asleep in Milton's back seat, but now she was so awake that she felt almost electrified. Her heart was racing. And as if on cue, a dark car pulled up and parked in front of the house. Maxwell emerged and trotted up the front walkway to the house, his tie askew. He looked serious, almost anxious. His hair was even more unruly than usual, and Emily was shocked to find how pleased she was to see him.

"Good man, Wilson," Maxwell said, giving the young officer a slap on the shoulder. "Thanks for being my advance guard. It's good you were here tonight."

"Happy to help, Detective. I'll get back to my post."

"Just a minute, young man," said Mattie from behind Emily. "This is for you."

She reached past Emily and handed Officer Wilson a small package, wrapped in wax paper, that she had retrieved from the kitchen.

"Oatmeal raisin," Mattie said to him. "Hope you still got some coffee."

"I do, ma'am. Much obliged. Good night, now."

"Mrs. Sayles," said Maxwell, turning to Mattie. "All I have to say is, I hope you saved some of those cookies."

Then he looked at Emily. "I wouldn't ask if it wasn't important, but I need to talk with you, Miss Washington. May I come in?"

As she nodded yes, she felt like shaking herself. If she was supposed to be engaged to Lewis, this was hardly the time to feel her heart go pitter-pat at the sight of another man. Deep breaths, old girl, she thought, and in a few minutes, she felt a bit more under control as she and Maxwell sat down in front of steaming cups of coffee and a plate of cookies provided by Mattie with Billy's help.

"Okay, young Mister Mizell, it's time for bed, for real this time," Emily heard Mattie say to Billy, when Maxwell intervened.

"Mrs. Sayles, if you don't mind, I'd like to talk with both you and Billy, too. Come over and sit down for just a second," he said, gesturing to chairs on the other side of the coffee table.

"And dear boy," said Emily, "please don't kick the legs of that chair —it's a lot older than all of us put together."

"Yes ma'am," said Billy, who looked suddenly sober —not because of her admonition, but presumably at the gravity of being questioned by a police detective.

"Office Wilson said the sheriff was here tonight," Maxwell began, pulling a small notepad from his pocket. "What happened? Tell me about it."

"He was in a state," Mattie began.

"We were afraid Miss Emily would be in jail!" Billy blurted out. "He said he was going to raid the Flamingo and give Mr. Charlie what for."

"So you were there—at the Flamingo?" Maxwell asked, nodding to Emily.

"Yes, the owner—Mr. Wynne—asked Lewis and me to come to the season opening; it turns out he and Lewis are brothers in the bonds of Princeton—and their fraternity."

"Lewis?" said Maxwell. "I presume that's the fellow I met the other night at the Coffee Club—the one who arrived on the train?"

"Yes," said Emily, looking down at her hands, and feeling a blush rise in her cheeks, to her great chagrin. Maybe in the dim light no one would notice, she thought as she rushed on, rather breathlessly.

"The sheriff did come out there, although Wynne said he had paid him to stay away—Mizell went back on his word."

"What happened? Did he bust the place up?"

"He sure seemed ready to, but the oddest thing happened," Emily said. "Two men in a big black limousine pulled up—I had seen one of them earlier, inside the club—and at scarcely a word from him, the sheriff got in his car and drove away."

Maxwell looked up from his notepad and frowned. "Did you see this happen—this confrontation?"

"Oh, yes—somehow Maureen and I ended up right in the thick of it. We were running down the front steps to Milton's taxi when we almost collided with the sheriff on his way in."

"Golly," said Billy. "I hope you slugged him, Miss Emily."

"Actually, I almost did," she said. "I don't know what got into me." Mattie shook her head, as Billy looked up at Emily with a wide grin.

"I wish you had, Miss Emily!" said the boy, bouncing up and down on this chair.

"I almost wish she had, too," said Maxwell, turning back to Emily and studying her for what felt a little too long.

"What did the man look like," he asked, "the one who did the talking?"

"Tall, with gray hair—it looked like silver. Very smooth. Just after they left, Charlie Wynne made a kind of joke about them—something about how the local folks who call Charlie a gangster had absolutely no idea what they were talking about."

"Meaning that these men were the real thing?"

"Yes. That's what Milton said, too, on the way home. Whoever they were, Sheriff Mizell didn't argue with them—he just left."

"And he stopped here on his way to the Flamingo?" Maxwell asked, turning again to Mattie and Billy, who was fidgeting in his chair until Mattie gave him one of her most penetrating looks. "About what time was that? What did he do here?"

"I think it must have been about 10 o'clock," said Mattie. "He wanted to see Miss Elizabeth's painting studio, of all things. Claimed she owed him—or somebody—a bunch of money when she died, and he knew just how to get it back."

"He was acting crazy," said Billy. His lower lip was beginning to tremble a bit, Emily thought, as if he might cry.

Mattie reached over and patted his hand. "I know, son, it was all sorta crazy—but I wouldn't let that big bully hurt you either, you know that," Mattie added.

"Yes ma'am," said Billy.

"And that young officer—Mr. Wilson—helped a lot," Mattie said to Maxwell. "He came to the door—which was when Bully Boy made his exit out the back."

"Now, Detective, I think it really is bedtime for my young guest here—well past it," Emily said to Maxwell as she looked at Billy, still determined not to cry. "Let's let these two get some rest, and if you need to know any more about what happened at the Flamingo, I can tell you that, surely."

She and Maxwell said good night to Mattie and Billy. Despite the coffee that Mattie had supplied, the adrenaline that had been fueling Emily seemed to be letting go of its grip on her, and she could feel herself wilting as well. She looked at Maxwell.

"It's always good to see you, Detective, but it is late, and I need to get some sleep, too. Can we talk about this tomorrow? I'll confess, I'm not sure why you found it necessary to talk with us tonight."

"Okay, I'll get out of your hair," Maxwell said, rising to his feet and pausing for a second. "And I'll come clean," he added. "I mostly wanted to see that you were all right—"

"I'm fine," she said, now suddenly defensive. Did he think she couldn't take care of herself?

"And I wanted to make sure those men who turned up at the Flamingo were who I think they are," Maxwell went on. "I figured talking with you would settle any doubts." Again, he looked at her for what felt like a second too long. "You see, I'm almost certain Marvin Willetts had been working for those guys."

"Do you think they killed him?" she asked, looking up at him and changing her mind about her urge to say good night. In spite of her fatigue, her mind was starting to make connections—or at least possible connections.

"I know I was about to kick you out, Detective, but sit down for just a minute more." She motioned toward a chair, and he sat back down.

"The man who talked," Emily began—"like I said, he was very smooth. He bore no resemblance to Al Capone, or the gangsters in the movies."

"Oh, no—smooth as silk, I'm sure, and he'd have not an ounce of compunction about smoothly and quickly ending someone's life who crossed him, I can assure you."

A chill ran through Emily, despite the warm night. Milton had said those men wouldn't bother with starting a fire if they wanted to kill someone—they'd just use bullets—but had he been wrong about that? Was it possible the gangsters had killed her aunt? Did they aim to kill her, too? She felt shaky, but she smiled at Maxwell, determined to keep her composure.

"Never thought I'd feel a chill in this humidity," she said with a smile, rubbing her bare arms.

"It's chilling stuff. And you've been through a good deal since you arrived."

"Well, that tall man at the Flamingo — the Silver Man, that's how I think of him — sure cooled Mizell right down."

"I wonder what he has on the sheriff," said Maxwell. "And what the sheriff was looking for here?"

Emily opened her mouth to speak but then stopped, unsure whether to tell Maxwell about the Picasso. For whatever reason, it was a secret her aunt had guarded with intensity. But her instinct was to trust him.

"Billy said the sheriff was going on about some painting when he was here. Tonight I learned about something that just might be connected."

"Go on," he encouraged her

"It turns out my aunt did own an extremely valuable painting, which for reasons I don't yet understand, she hid from almost everyone. I certainly knew nothing about it. She asked Charlie Wynne to store it for her, and tonight he showed it to Maureen Davis and me. It appears to be a portrait of my aunt — as a young woman — by Pablo Picasso, of all things."

"Good lord." Maxwell almost dropped his notepad. "Seriously?"

"Yes, and there's more. At the Flamingo tonight, Julian Sloane asked me about a mysterious painting — a painting he said was actually his. It seems fantastic, but maybe it's just all too coincidental not to be the same painting, don't you think?"

"Why would she keep it so secret?" Maxwell asked.

"I'm sure some people would see it as scandalous. It's not quite a nude but not Whistler's Mother either. Maybe Aunt Liz thought it would add to her mystique a bit too much — I just don't know."

"Did anyone know about it besides Wynne?"

"Milton knew it existed, he told me tonight on the way home. He said Aunt Liz called it her 'insurance policy' — but for what? I can tell you it was quite a shock to see it. We got word that the sheriff was coming to the Flamingo just as Charlie was showing the painting to us."

"It's Charlie now, I see," said Maxwell.

"Oh, he's not so bad. I like him, once you get past the glamour and the dimples—and the fact that he runs a gambling den—I know. Lewis seems almost like he's found a long-lost brother."

"You don't say?" said Maxwell. A hint of a smile appeared on his lips and vanished.

Emily let out a yawn in spite of herself.

"Well, I think that's enough for tonight. I'll let you get to sleep," said Maxwell. "We've got a lot to think about, don't we? Maybe things will be more clear in the morning."

"They usually are," Emily said.

"Since you've confided to me, I guess I should tell you that the FBI task force I've been working with has found that Mizell is up to his neck in payoffs, and they're building a corruption case against him."

"That's good to hear. I'd like to see him far away from Billy."

"Indeed," said Maxwell. "What isn't good is that he's been acting more and more reckless. I think these mob guys are making him sweat, trying to get more money out of him. Willetts's death has something to do with it, but I can't quite tie it all together yet. But somehow your aunt—and you—are in Mizell's crosshairs. I keep telling you to be careful, I know, but it's even more important now."

He got up to leave.

"I'll walk you out," said Emily. "I need some fresh air."

They went out onto the big porch where they had sat a few nights before, and as tired as she was, Emily felt the spell of the Florida night air wrap around her like a caress. She remembered Milton saying Aunt Liz had loved the night breezes, and she understood exactly what he meant.

Maxwell turned and looked at her.

"So this Lewis—Mr. Delacourt, I think you said his name was. Is it true you're going to marry him?"

"Did I tell you that?" Emily couldn't believe she was being so coy. Hadn't she as much as agreed to be the guest of honor at an engagement party?

"No, but Maureen Davis sure hinted at it in her latest column."

"That devil!"

"Don't be too hard on her. After all, men don't take the train from New York just to visit a pal. Are you?"

"What?"

"Going to marry him?"

Emily let out a huge sigh. "I think so," she said. "It seems to be what everyone wants me to do." Except Milton, she thought.

"Maybe, but not me," Maxwell whispered, and before Emily knew it, he had bent over and kissed her quickly on the lips just before he turned and leapt lightly down the front steps like that dancer Gene Kelly.

Emily tried to muster a sliver of outrage, but she was too shocked and too tired, and if she were honest with herself, too pleased. Later, as she drifted off to sleep, she thought of little else.

Chapter 32

Time to Stop Shilly-Shallying

AFTER A SOMEWHAT restless night—and despite her thrill at Maxwell's kiss, or perhaps because of it—Emily awoke in the morning with fresh resolve to make a decision about Lewis. She owed it to him. It was time to stop shilly-shallying around, she told herself. After breakfast, she decided to talk it all over with her father, via long distance—a rare extravagance in their family. She would not, of course, tell him about Maxwell, she thought as she dialed the phone. She'd never confided that kind of thing to him—or to anyone, really—but still, she and her father shared a bond.

"Haven't you said many times that Lewis is your best friend?" her father had asked. "That kind of friendship is a wonderful foundation for a marriage. Your mother was my best friend, you know."

She wondered, though, if he had ever felt about her mother the way she had felt about John. Surely, there would never be another John in her life. It was true that Maxwell's kiss the night before had rekindled some old feelings, but that's all it was—a kind of shadow memory of John. Maxwell even looked a little like him. If the passion she had shared with John seemed absent with Lewis, surely she and Lewis could have a good life together. And thanks to Aunt Liz, they would have the means to live pretty much as they wanted, at least financially.

"You don't want to end up like your Aunt Liz—dying alone—an old maid," her father had added, echoing an old theme song. Even when Emily was a small child, her mother had always stressed how important it was for a woman to find the right husband—and by a much younger age than Emily was now.

"Daddy, that's no way to talk about your sister," she had told him. "She was not 'an old maid.' She had a rich life."

"I know you admired her," her father replied. "But she never had good sense, Emily. I don't have to remind you how close to danger she let you come in Florida . . ."

"Yes, well, we don't need to talk about that," Emily said, as the memory of the day with Sam and the Klan men sent the same kind of chill around her heart that she'd felt the night before. She hated her father's words, his harsh judgment of his sister. Yet he was right about one thing: She had admired her aunt, had always wanted to be exactly like Elizabeth Washington—always. But even though she might wear her aunt's clothes and her jewelry, the resemblance was only superficial, she feared; she didn't have her aunt's talent or her strength of character.

But a small, nagging voice in the back of her mind kept underlining her father's criticisms. Maybe she was more like her aunt than she had realized—if her father was right about her aunt, and Emily had deluded herself. After all, she had recklessly pursued her affair with John even after she had learned that he was married. Didn't Emily have terrible judgment, as shown by her heedlessness, her delay in agreeing to marry Lewis—an eminently sensible match for her?

In the end, it had come down to the realization that it just made sense to marry Lewis. Hadn't she long expected she would eventually do just that, as her father had pointed out? Why had she been so resistant? She just wanted it settled, more than anything. So, soon after talking with her father, Emily called Lewis at the hotel and told him her decision to marry him.

"Pooh, I knew you'd see this is the best thing for both of us!" he exclaimed—not exactly the most romantic response, Emily thought. But later that day, another enormous bouquet, this one actually of red roses, appeared by delivery at Eola Lodge, with an effusive note, pledging Lewis's undying love and suggesting a round-the-world cruise, just as soon as Lewis's father had made him a partner.

That evening Charlie Wynne joined them to celebrate over steaks at the hotel restaurant, and the three of them jotted down answers about invitees, food, and other questions that Sloane had asked Charlie to give Lewis and Emily to prepare for the engagement party. They laughed and toasted one another and the Flamingo, and a life devoted to Art. Now, maybe she could also devote more time to pursuing the mysteries surrounding her aunt's death, she thought, assuming Lewis wouldn't object too strenuously.

In the next couple of days, Emily was so busy with arrangements for the party that she barely had time to pursue thoughts of her aunt—of thoughts of the Silver Man, Sheriff Mizell, and the Picasso. She was almost glad for a respite from it all, because she couldn't seem to quite put the pieces together, and she thought a break might help. Fleeting thoughts about Maxwell's kiss snuck into the corners of her consciousness, though, like ants at a picnic, despite her efforts to sweep them away. She couldn't get that out of her mind. When it came time for Milton to drive them to Julian Sloane's party to announce her engagement to Lewis, the resolution she had felt after talking with her father was elusive. As the Cadillac rolled along toward Sloane's through the orange trees, Emily felt distinctly anxious, if not downright queasy. Maybe it was just the excitement, she told herself.

Billy's voice yanked her from her reverie, calling back to her from the front seat. She knew bringing him along was unconventional—but what wasn't in this town? And when Billy heard about the engagement party, he had begged to go. Jeff Mizell had come back from his ranch the day before, and Emily had asked Julian to please include both Mizells, father and son, as a favor to her. Milton had promised to take the boy with him during the festivities; they'd go to the kitchen area, where Billy could visit with the chef's young son.

So now Billy sat in the front seat next to Milton, with his father Jeff riding shotgun, as Billy called it, next to the window, while Maureen, Lewis, and Emily occupied the Cadillac's big back seat. The expanse of worn red leather was so large that they weren't cramped—although it certainly was cozy. Emily had dressed for the Florida weather again, in a halter top and wide palazzo pants, her right arm full once more of silver bracelets—a mix of her aunt's and her own. Lewis had his arm around her shoulders, which felt good, she thought. She had made the right decision.

"Miss Emily, now I remember," said Billy. "I've been out this way before—haven't I, Pa?"

"If you say so, Son," Jeff Mizell said softly. "Not sure I remember."

"We did, Pa. We went to pay a visit to an old man. I think he was some kind of cousin, Pa. Remember? The old man with the big alligator? He's a monster!"

"The man or the alligator?" Maureen teased.

"Ah, yes," said Jeff Mizell. "Billy's right—he was with me one day when I stopped to call on old Aaron. He lives real near Mr. Sloane. He's never been quite right. Has this huge alligator he treats like a pet. Used to have a sorry little zoo and charged people to see it. I will say, it's the biggest gator I've ever seen."

Emily looked at Lewis and saw that his eyes had grown quite wide. She wondered what he made of Jeff Mizell, in his boots and pressed denim shirt. When Lewis had learned that Billy's father owned a large ranch, he was impressed by that, at least. But Jeff certainly wasn't the sort of society Lewis was used to mingling in. His arm tightened around her shoulders.

The breeze pouring through the open car windows made it difficult to hear, and Milton had turned on the radio, so they rode on companionably without further conversation. Emily's mind drifted to her aunt and her father's words earlier in the week, his charge that Aunt Liz had terrible judgment. Had Emily idolized her so much that she'd been blind to the truth, she wondered? Had Liz gambled unwisely and made enemies, as Julian intimated? She had certainly kept the Picasso a secret. Perhaps Emily had never really known her at all, and would never learn the truth about her death. Here she was, on what should be a happy day, but mostly she felt confused and unsettled. Well, she'd better pull herself together, she thought; the big Cadillac was again arriving at Sloane's Studio, where she had been only a week before. It felt like a century.

Milton pulled up to the entrance, and Lewis and Jeff helped Maureen exit on the passenger side, while Milton got out and opened the car door rather grandly for Emily on the driver's side, which brought a genuine grin to her worried face.

"No lack of theatrical ability in the Armistead family," she whispered to him.

"You don't have to get married, you know, Miss Emily," Milton whispered back, leaning down to help her. "You do what's right for you." He nodded at her and turned to Billy, who had clambered out of the front seat clutching the things he'd brought with him—a model airplane kit his dad had given him to keep him busy during the party and a braided cattle whip like the one he'd shown Emily. He wanted to show it to the boys in the kitchen, he had said.

"You stay with me, Billy," he said. "Miss Emily, just send someone for us in the kitchen when you're ready to go—or if you should need me."

Julian met them at the door himself, seated in his wheelchair with Juan Blanco behind him. He greeted them all warmly, especially Lewis, and also made quite a fuss over Jeff Mizell.

""Mr. Mizell, or should I say—Captain Mizell? You had quite a war record, as I remember. How nice that you could join us. Dear Elizabeth spoke so highly of you, and your young son. And what a happy occasion for her Emily," he said, beaming at her. "You're a lucky man, Mr. Delacourt."

"Don't I know it," said Lewis, "and doesn't she look smashing tonight? I can't wait to see her walking down the aisle."

The moment Lewis uttered that nerve-wracking phrase, Charlie Wynne appeared, gave Lewis a warm handshake and clap on the back, kissed Emily's cheeks in the French manner, and swept Lewis away to the drinks table, leaving Emily feeling an odd mixture of irritation and relief. She and Lewis were being fêted as a couple, but she felt more comfortable on her own, in many ways. Sloane gave her an avuncular wave and moved to welcome a group of new arrivals. A man and woman descended on Jeff, who was behind Emily, greeted him warmly, and guided him to a group of several people.

"Those are some old high school friends of Jeff's," Maureen whispered to Emily. "I'm proud of him for coming. He was injured during the war—had to come home early—and then his wife died, and he just disappeared, for years. And of course, tongues wagged. Some people always think the worst."

Emily recalled the sight of Jeff Mizell, a few days before, raising a pocket flask to his lips as he disappeared into the twilight. She regretted seeing that, and had pushed the image from her thoughts. She wanted to believe Jeff was a good father to Billy—the father Billy deserved. But it did seem that he had his problems. Still, for now, the flask wasn't something she wanted to report to Maureen.

"I remember you told me that—about him disappearing," Emily said.

"I'll fill you in more sometime," said Maureen, pulling a small notebook out of her bag. "But right now, I'd better circulate." And notebook in hand, Maureen was gone, but Lewis reappeared at Emily's elbow and handed her a Cuba Libre.

"Hello, Pooh," said Lewis, "or should I say soon-to-be wife of mine. Quite sporting of old Sloane to throw us this party." He grinned and reached down to kiss her cheek.

"It is indeed," she said, smiling back. "And speaking of old sports, I see Charlie's here—"I'll bet you two even know some kind of secret Princeton handshake."

"Of course we do!" said Lewis, laughing but looking a bit uncomfortable, Emily thought. A waiter appeared with a tray of hors d'oeuvres, and they each took an empanada. Suddenly she felt quite empty, and realized it had been a long time since breakfast. She scooped up another.

"Did he mention any aftermath of our adventure the other night at the Flamingo?" she said, as she took a bite. "Anything about the sheriff or the Silver Man?"

"Nope, not a word. No chance—someone interrupted us." Suddenly he looked quite serious. "Emily, I want to tell you something. After just a few days, I understand the appeal of this town. You've got friends here, like old Julian—he adores you."

"Lewis, this is a big change. I'm delighted—you really mean it?"

"Of course, and even though I kidded you—called you Nancy Drew—I support you all the way in wanting to find out about your aunt—what happened to her. Wynne says you're quite good at sleuthing."

"Really?" What was Charlie basing that opinion on, she wondered, feeling a bit irritated at the thought of Lewis discussing her with their new friend.

"Absolutely," Lewis burbled, on a roll now. "I'm actually looking forward to having our winter home here, and we could even get married here, if you like. Old Armistead could drive us in that big Cadillac."

Old Armistead? Oh dear, Emily thought, as she downed a healthy gulp of her Cuba Libre. Milton would love that characterization.

"Yes, I'm ready to let go of the New York wedding," Lewis chatted on. "We could even have a garden wedding here, and go back home just in time for the Beaux Arts Ball. Then we could come back here for the winter. I've talked with Dad about managing his Florida properties, for one thing."

Maybe it was the slug of Cuba Libre she had just gulped down, but Emily suddenly felt like the creation of another Lewis—Lewis Carroll. Like his Alice, she seemed to be shrinking and tumbling down a hole into another realm. In one minute, her Lewis seemed to truly understand her wishes, her point of view. And then, in an instant, he whiplashed back to his old priorities: New York society functions, his father's influence. All of a sudden she felt quite woozy.

"Look, Lewis dear, I'll be right back," Emily said. "I've got to powder my nose pretty badly, if you know what I mean. Let's talk about this later."

Before Lewis could say anything, she rushed to the guest bathroom off the hall, only to see a line of women waiting, and seized on the idea of using the private bathroom Maureen had mentioned on her first visit. With every second, she could feel the

Cuba Libre and the empanada she had tossed down with it wanting to free themselves from her jittery stomach. Swallowing hard, she rushed down a long hallway and opened a door, only to find not the bathroom but a workroom stocked with artists' supplies.

But the next door she tried did lead to what surely must be Sloane's private suite, lit only by candlelight like the rest of the Studio, and Emily slipped into the adjoining bathroom in near darkness, just in time to bend over what her aunt had always called the porcelain throne.

Damnation, I hate throwing up, she thought—had hated it since she was a little girl—and wouldn't everyone be surprised she was doing just that instead of toasting her pending engagement. Maybe it was just the idea of being the center of attention that had her stomach doing backflips, she thought.

She dampened a face cloth and was cleaning her face with cool water, still in near darkness, when she heard voices in Julian's room. She felt like a kid with her hand in the cookie jar, for some reason. She knew from her aunt's stories that Julian was very private, and she had ventured into his quarters without asking— although she surely had an urgent reason. Thank goodness the voices subsided, and Emily was alone again in the near darkness of the bathroom.

She wanted to adjust her makeup and spotted one of the candles that seemed to be everywhere in the Studio on the vanity counter, unlit, along with matches. She struck a match and lit the candle easily, and began to search in her purse for her lipstick.

Hell's bells, she thought. Why am I always scrambling through a purse? Can't I ever be the least bit organized?

She found the lipstick, but in her fumbling, she dropped it on the floor. As she bent down to look for it, she spotted it and then noticed something near it on the tile floor, hidden by one of the ubiquitous sculptures that filled Julian's world—even in the bathrooms, she thought. Art everywhere.

Whatever was behind the sculpture reflected the candlelight and glimmered in the darkness. It looked like a piece of jewelry.

Instinctively, Emily reached to pick it up. Sure enough, it was a bracelet. One of Julian's guests must have dropped it. She turned it over, looking more carefully. Then she froze.

The object was jewelry indeed, but it didn't belong to Julian. Or one of his guests. At least, not a recent one.

What she held in her hand was her aunt's beloved scarab bracelet—the bracelet Emily had been looking for ever since she heard about her aunt's death. Emily had asked Milton and Judge Stimpson, her aunt's lawyer, about it. She had even called the funeral home about it, to double-check. She had asked Mattie Sayles and the Murat sisters—everyone she could think of. Her aunt was almost never without it. She had asked Julian about it, too. He had no idea, he had said.

Looking at the bracelet in the dim light, she saw that the clasp was broken. She remembered the photo of her aunt from the newspapers Jinx had pulled for her, taken just hours before the fire that had extinguished her life. Liz was wearing the bracelet in the photo. Why was it here, then, in Julian's house? She held it up to the candlelight and saw that it indeed bore the initials EW on the back of the clasp.

Emily had stopped feeling woozy. Her imaginary Alice pill had reversed its mental effects, and she now felt like she was growing, becoming an enormous Emily, her sadness exploded by anger that she tried to contain, to reason with. Surely there had to be some explanation. Surely, Julian—kindly, elegant, artistic Julian—had no connection to her aunt's death. But why was the bracelet in his house, and why had he lied about it? Maybe there was some simple explanation. A tiny voice inside reminded her, though, that somehow, something about Julian had never rung quite true with her. But she hadn't trusted herself.

Chapter 33

Ember-Red Eyes in the Night

EMILY STOOD in shock and silence. She had to find Lewis. Even more importantly, she had to find Milton. He'd know what to do. But before she got very far, Milton found her. As she slipped out of Julian's private quarters, she saw him barreling down a back hallway toward her.

"Trouble, Miss Emily," he said, almost gasping.

"Milton, are you okay?"

"No ma'am, I am not. Billy's gone—Billy's disappeared." He paused. "And I'm to blame."

It was unnerving to see the always unflappable Milton looking so shaken.

"I'm not sure of too much right now," she said, "but I'm sure that's not true—that you're to blame."

"I took my friend who works in the kitchen—I took him out to the taxi to get some tools and left Billy alone in the kitchen—he was working on that model airplane kit his dad had brought for him—the other boys came outside, too, to see the Cadillac—and when we came back, Billy was gone, and . . ."

"What's happened?" Another voice asked. To her shock, Carter Mizell was standing behind Milton.

"Sheriff Mizell? Why on earth are you here," said Emily. "Surely, you didn't want to pick up where we left off the other night at the Flamingo."

"Relax, Miss Washington," said Mizell. "Let's move into the kitchen, shall we—don't want to disturb the party."

Since when did he start being Mr. Manners? Emily thought. Still, she and Milton moved with Mizell into the now-empty kitchen. A model airplane kit sat on the table, its pieces spread on a newspaper.

"Like I said, Billy was working on that," Milton said to Emily, nodding at it, his hands clasped tightly in front of him.

"I'm here because Mr. Sloane asked me to come by, ma'am," said Mizell, in reply to her question. "Some of the colored grove workers down the road were raising a ruckus earlier today," he said, looking at Milton as if he were somehow responsible. "He wanted to make sure everything was calm while he was having his party."

"Does everyone get the sheriff's personal attention?" Emily asked, wondering what any of this had to do with Billy's disappearance.

"Mr. Sloane's been real generous to the deputies' retirement fund, ma'am. Just trying to be neighborly. Now, what's happened here? You say Billy's disappeared? I told you the boy was trouble, Miss Washington."

Emily turned to Milton. "Where's his father?"

"I looked for him," said Milton. "Nobody's seen him in quite a little while, according to Mrs. Davis. She's looking for him now."

"Jeff's probably drunk," said Carter Mizell. "That's one thing you can always count on."

Emily shot him a look. Where was Jeff Mizell? Then she turned to Milton.

"On the way here in the car, Billy was talking about the big alligator—remember, Mr. Armistead? The one the old man used to have in a zoo? Could he have . . ."

Mizell jumped in before she could finish. "Crazy old Aaron and his gators. That might be just where he is. The boy's always had too much curiosity, and you know what that does to cats," he said, laughing without sounding at all funny. "I'm sure he's okay, Miss Washington," he added.

Now, in contrast to his taunts at the Flamingo raid, the sheriff sounded almost helpful, but somehow that made Emily trust him even less. It seemed she could no longer be sure which Carter Mizell she was going to be talking to next.

"Look here, folks," the sheriff went on. "I think we can handle this without disrupting Mr. Sloane's party."

Down the hallway from the kitchen, Emily could hear the murmur of conversation growing with the swell of the music. The party was going full tilt, and she had hardly even been a part of it yet. She stuck her head back into the hallway and saw Lewis from a distance, talking and laughing with Charlie. He seemed somehow very far away.

"Perhaps I should get Lewis," she said. She realized she was still clutching her aunt's bracelet and slipped it into the pocket of her palazzo pants. She felt torn between her need to tell Milton about the bracelet and her fears about Billy.

"No need, ma'am," said Mizell. "A Yankee gentleman like that'll just get his nice suit dirty. I think what might work better—and I hate to ask this, Miss Washington, but the boy likes you—why don't you come with me—when we find him, he won't give you a hard time, like he will me."

"Whatever it takes to find him," she said. She could stomach cooperating with Mizell if it would help find the boy.

"It's not far," said Mizell—"I know the way." Then he looked at Milton, who was standing with his arms folded, eyes hidden behind his clip-on sunglasses.

"All right," she said, though every nerve in her body was jangling with alarm, "let's go."

"Armistead, if you see the boy's dad, tell him we'll be back with Billy in a flash. No need to bother Mr. Sloane. No one will even have to miss a sip of his fancy cocktails."

"I joked about him, but I'm worried about Billy, truly," Mizell went on to Emily. "I know he don't like me—his Pa set him against me, see? But he's my kin—I'm his uncle, after all. We'll find him." He began to guide Emily by the elbow toward the back door of the kitchen.

He actually sounded concerned about Billy. Was that possible? This corrupt bully she nearly struck a couple of nights before? How did he fit in with Julian? And with her aunt?

"Yes, that's what matters—Billy," she said. But she felt hyper-alert, every muscle tense as she pulled her elbow away from Mizell in a subtle gesture.

"I'll follow you," she said to him.

"Miss Emily . . . ," Milton began, his forehead furrowed with worry. "I'll go."

"Armistead, why don't you try to find the boy's father, like I said," Mizell answered, an edge to his voice, Emily thought. "Miss Washington and I can handle this."

"It's okay, Mr. Armistead. I'm sure we'll be back in just a minute." As she passed him, she quickly reached into her pocket, took Milton's hand, and placed the bracelet in his palm, folding his fingers over it.

"Keep this for me," she whispered to Milton as she followed Mizell out the door, fighting the fear rising in her throat.

Remember, this was Carter Mizell, she thought to herself—the man who may have had something to do with Liz's death—who certainly had something to do with besmirching Liz's name. But the main thing was to find Billy. And it wasn't as though no one knew where she was going. She could depend on Milton.

She looked out the path that led toward the big lake that lay next to Sloane's property. Deep purple twilight filled the sky above the lake, with only a few streaks of coral where the sun was dipping below the horizon.

"Step carefully, Miss Washington," said Mizell, now all Southern gentleman: courtesy and consideration. "I know a shortcut. Aaron—the old man who owns that big beast—lives on the land right next to Mr. Sloane."

The sandals Emily had chosen to wear slipped on her feet on the sandy path, and as she stumbled, Mizell gripped her arm again. His touch made her skin crawl, but the support did steady her and she didn't pull her arm away this time. At least she hadn't worn heels, she thought.

As they continued on the path, Emily turned around to see Milton looking after them intently, his brows knit in concern, but as soon as they rounded a bend in the path, she could no longer see Milton or Sloane's Studio compound. The music from the party floated down the path on the warm air, as if from another world.

Billy was her first concern, but this was a rare chance to talk with Mizell about her aunt, and she aimed to use it.

"Sheriff," she began. "I just have to ask. In a newspaper interview, you suggested my aunt was drunk the day she died." Her voice was rising. "How could you know? Were you there?"

Before he could answer, though, she heard muffled sounds nearby. They sounded like a voice, but she couldn't make out words.

"Well, yes, ma'am," said Mizell, "we can certainly talk all about that." His voice had changed, and now sounded as if he heard something incredibly amusing. When she looked at him, he bared his teeth in a grin that looked anything but friendly. It made her blood run cold.

"I told you it wouldn't take long," he said, as he nodded toward a clearing in front of them, and Emily gasped as she saw where the muffled noise was coming from.

A pond lay in the center of the clearing into which they had stepped, and about six feet above the dark mirror of the water, a shape was suspended in a kind of rope harness—not a shape, she now saw, but Billy—blindfolded and gagged with rags in his mouth. The harness was connected to a length of rope that was looped over a branch of a small tree and tied to the tree's spindly trunk. The limb groaned and swayed under the weight of the boy, whose hands were bound behind him. Emily took in the scene in horror—her blood turned to ice.

"Billy, I'm here," she yelled out. Muffled sounds came in response.

"My god, who did this?" she said to Mizell. But she was already beginning to grasp the answer.

"Who do you think, pretty lady?" Mizell's voice had changed totally. The soothing sounds of Southern courtesy had vanished, and he smiled that horrid grin again. "And you come right along just like a lamb to the slaughter."

Now he held both of Emily's arms so tightly that she couldn't raise her hands, so tightly that she started to scream, but Mizell silenced her the instant her mouth opened, roughly stuffing a rag into her mouth and dragging her toward the water.

"See," Mizell growled, "both of you—you and the brat—are about to have a terrible accident. Just have a look-see in that water—we're not alone. We got company."

For a split second, Emily thought maybe Milton might have followed them—that he was the "company." Then, in the dark water of the pool, two red eyes reflected the dying light, just above the surface.

"There's our friend," said Mizell. "That ain't Bone, actually—he's up in that cage on the other side of the pool. I guess you could say our friend there is his missus. Bone's so old he hardly moves, but the lady—she's a terror when she's got young'uns to protect—and she's hungry. Real hungry."

Emily struggled and tried to kick him, but his grip was too strong, as he pushed her toward the dark water.

"See, you just know too damn much, lady, and so does the kid—although you two know about different things."

Emily tried to scream again, but only ended up making guttural sounds. What in hell did Mizell mean—she knew too much? She knew so little—except for finding her aunt's bracelet, and she wasn't even sure what that meant.

"Don't waste any energy trying to scream," Mizell hissed. "They won't hear you up there because of the music—but I'm gonna shut you up real good, like the kid, just in case. Nobody will believe Armistead's word over mine—nobody who matters in this town, anyway."

She kicked a leg out again and connected a sandal with Mizell's shin, but it did little good.

"Feisty, just like your aunt," he said. "The main thing is, with you outta the way, it clears the way for me to get hold of a big pile of money—but you don't need to know how—we better get this over with before that Black bastard Armistead gets down here. There's no one else coming—I knocked out the boy's dad and stashed him in a shed—he's out cold."

Billy thrashed on the rope, causing a part of the branch to fall into the water.

"Keep doin' that, you little vermin, and you'll be in the soup before you know it." Mizell's awful laugh came again.

Not if I have an ounce of strength in my body, Emily vowed. Still in Mizell's grip, she looked around for anything she could use. A coil of braided leather lay on the ground a few feet away—the cattle whip Billy had brought with him to the party and had planned to show off to the other boys.

Summoning all her strength, she drove a knee, hard, right where she knew it would hurt Mizell the most. As he buckled over, Emily grabbed the whip. Though she was long out of practice, she still knew what to do. Milton had taught her well, all those years ago. She stepped back and lashed out with it, striking Mizell in the face.

He yelled like a wounded bear. "You fucking bitch!"

Emily freed herself from the makeshift gag and now she yelled with all her strength, her voice tearing out of her, ragged and raw. "Milton! Help!"

Mizell was grabbing for his holster. Giving it all she had, she flicked the whip again, striking Mizell's hand and knocking the gun to the dirt. She felt just as amazed as Mizell had looked.

She pulled her arm back, raising the whip again—when a crashing sound filled the clearing, and Milton flung himself on Mizell, hitting him so hard that the sheriff slipped to the ground like a wet noodle.

Emily stared at them in shock and then saw Jeff Mizell bolting down the path that led from the Studio into the scrub, followed by Detective Maxwell—where had he come from?—and another man, who shouted "FBI" at the out-cold sheriff. Then came Charlie and Lewis, who rushed up to her. Much to her chagrin, she bent over and got sick all over again.

As soon as she'd straightened, Milton just looked at her for a moment before she was engulfed in his arms.

"Lordy, Miss Emily, and I thought Lizzie was a wildcat. Lordy."

And then he was whisking her back up the path towards the Studio. She protested at first but found her surge of strength had vanished. As she looked back, she saw Jeff working to free his son, calling "Billy," as he was aided by Lewis, Charlie, and even Maureen, while Maxwell and the FBI man wrestled Carter Mizell into handcuffs. Soon, she found herself seated in Sloane's kitchen, while the chef, Manuel, and Milton fussed over her. Milton poured some Scotch in a glass and put it down in front of her.

"The party?" she managed to mutter, looking up at Milton. "Where is everyone?"

"The party, Miss Emily, is most decidedly over," said Milton—"and in more ways than one. Sloane was pretty slick about it—I'll give him that."

"What happened?"

"No sooner were you out the door than he announced that there had been a terrible accident and that the sheriff wanted everyone to leave at once. And boy, did they."

"It was all so crazy—I didn't even know most of the people here."

"That was just the start of the craziness," said Milton. "You're shivering, Miss Emily. You gotta be in shock."

He took her hands in his and rubbed them, while Manuel disappeared quickly and came back with a soft shawl that he put around her shoulders. She took a sip of Scotch and looked around.

"So where is Julian?"

"That's the most interesting development, other than you bringing down that crazy man outside with a cow whip—and the bracelet. Lordy, Miss Emily, where did you find Elizabeth's bracelet? But about Mr. Sloane—there's no sign of him. Manuel says the car was all loaded—Julian had told him something about a trip to Cassadaga—and it seems Sloane and that flunky of his—Blanco—have flown the coop."

"Really? Honest to God—he's gone? Milton, this is so hard for me to believe, but I found the bracelet—the one we've been asking everyone about—on the floor in his bathroom. I don't think he realized it was there."

"How did it get there? How on earth did it get there?" Milton held up the bracelet to the light, his voice breaking a little now. "She was never without it, you know. It's so strange to see it without her. Without her." He repeated the last phrase almost in a whisper.

"Dear Mr. Armistead—Milton," she said, taking his hand. "I think it was there because he dropped it somehow and then couldn't see it in the shadows. And, as hard as it is for me to believe, I think he had it because he was with her the day she died. I think he's the man old Zeke saw with Liz out on the water."

The pieces Emily had been struggling with for days were fitting together now, forming a picture. "I think Julian was behind all this somehow," she went on—"along with the sheriff."

"Mr. Sloane? Damn, he claimed to be her best friend. I could never quite figure that out, but she'd always help him out—bailed him out again and again."

"You know that note I got—the one we told Detective Maxwell about? I'm pretty sure Julian made it, too—or got Juan Blanco to make it."

"Good lord, Miss Emily. Let me have a swig of that Scotch."

"Oh for goodness sake," Emily said, shaking her head. "Pour yourself some. If Julian's really taken off, looks to me like we're in charge here now." She looked up to see Manuel again, hurrying breathlessly down the hall toward them.

"What now, Manuel?" said Milton.

"For the señorita," Manuel said, thrusting an envelope across the table. "I just found this on the mantle." He handed her an envelope addressed to her in Julian's elegant hand. Still shaking a little, she opened it slowly.

"Here," said Emily. "We'll read it together."

Emily looked down at the page.

"My dear, if Mizell fails in his bloody mission, and I pray he will fail, and you are reading this, I want you to know that I never meant it all to go this way. I never meant any harm to come to you, and I surely never meant for Elizabeth to die.

The fire was only meant to scare her. I loved her. She could have stopped it all, you see. She only needed to give me the painting. She owed it to me. She would never have met that scoundrel Picasso if it hadn't been for me.

Tell that pesky detective not to try to find me. I have contacts, too. Before long, I'll be far away, and if you do survive, and Liz's will goes the way I think it will, the Studio will probably be yours before long, too.

I hope you'll find some way to forgive me.

Au revoir,

Julian"

Her hands fell into her lap and she felt tears start to come.

"Miss Emily?" Milton asked.

"Carter did the dirty work, I think, Mr. Armistead, but Julian was behind it—what happened to Liz. He says he loved her, but I don't think he's ever really loved anyone but himself."

Before she could say more, the kitchen door banged open, and Lewis and Maureen burst in, full of news that Maxwell and his FBI companion had taken Carter Mizell away in handcuffs, and Jeff and Billy had left with Charlie, who had promised to give the boy and his dad a ride home.

"Darling," said Lewis. "What on earth happened down there?"

"I'll tell you all about it," she said, but even as she did, a sudden, terrible clarity broke over her. It must be the result of a near-death experience, she thought. She'd solved Aunt Liz's murder, and come out of it alive, but if only she'd trusted herself sooner, maybe she wouldn't have gotten so many things so very wrong.

Chapter 34

A Heart-to-Heart Talk

EMILY DID INDEED have a great deal to tell Lewis, she thought as she slid into Milton's back seat, but only part of it was about what had happened earlier between her and Carter Mizell. She was still trying to take in what had happened—Milton had said she had to be in shock—but after shilly-shallying for so long about Lewis's marriage proposals—and then finally accepting them—suddenly a heart-to-heart talk with him felt urgent.

Milton and his three passengers rode home in near silence, broken early in the drive by another "Will somebody please tell me what happened?" from Lewis, but when Emily turned to respond, she felt his head on her shoulder and saw he was sleeping soundly. From the front seat next to Milton, Maureen turned to Emily and nodded toward Lewis as she pantomimed raising an invisible glass to her lips. Then, she promptly dozed off herself. How could they possibly be sleeping after all that had happened? Emily looked at the rearview mirror to see Milton smiling at her in its reflection.

"You did real good, Miss Emily," he said in a low voice. "Real good."

"I guess I did, didn't I?" she murmured. What would John think, she wondered? Surely her father would have a hard time believing she had taken down a burly man with a flick of a cattle whip. Aunt Liz would have believed it, though.

She watched out the windows at the landscape passing by, the gray moss hanging from the trees ghostly in the moonlight. Soon they were at Maureen's house, and Milton pulled into the driveway and got out to rouse Maureen and walk her to her front door.

"We'll talk tomorrow," Emily whisper-called to her red-headed friend, as Maureen turned and blew her a kiss from her front walkway.

"Mr. Armistead," Emily said when Milton returned to the taxi and started it again, "when we get to Eola Lodge, would you help me get Lewis into the house? He can stay there tonight. I know I can trust your discretion," she said, and smiled.

"Good idea," said Milton. "I didn't want to leave you alone. The sheriff's got friends, for one thing. Mr. Lewis can look after you."

Emily smiled to herself. When it came to Lewis and her, she was usually the one doing the looking after—especially if spiders were involved. But she didn't want to denigrate Lewis, either. He had been a dear friend for a long time. He deserved her care—and her honesty.

When they arrived at Eola Lodge, Milton pulled down the driveway to the back of the house—the same spot where only a few days ago she had identified Marvin Willetts's pale, dead face. Lewis woke up, barely, and Emily and Milton guided him into the house and deposited him onto the sofa, removing his shoes.

"Out like a light," Milton said. "He'll sleep good. He and Mr. Charlie were hitting the bar at the party pretty hard while you were looking for Billy."

That would have been during her adventure by the dark pond, Emily thought. She hoped Charlie had been okay to drive—hoped he had delivered Billy and Jeff home safely.

"Don't worry about Mr. Charlie driving, Miss Emily," said Milton, as if reading her mind. "He can handle those Cuba Libres better than Mr. Lewis." Emily liked thinking of Billy and Jeff, safe in the log house at the end of the sandy path through the woods. She hoped Billy had gotten his whip back—it certainly had served her well in those terrifying moments by the dark pond. Maybe Jeff Mizell could help her find a whip of her own. It felt like years instead of a few hours since she had used Billy's.

"I'll be going, now, Miss Emily," said Milton, speaking almost in a whisper to not disturb Lewis. "You need rest to get some rest."

"How about staying here, too—I've got room, and I don't like the idea of you going home alone. You took down the sheriff as much as I did—held him down. He may have cronies who are out to get you."

"That's kind of you, Miss Emily—but I'll be all right. I'm so keyed up that I don't think I could sleep anyway. I may go down to the Coffee Club and see if I can help any folks who need rides home after they've had a few too many."

He paused and clasped his hands together, touching them to his lips almost in a gesture of prayer.

"Miss Emily, I thought somehow I'd feel better if I knew the truth about what happened to Liz, you know? I never believed it was an accident. But I don't feel any better tonight, I can tell you. It's like losing her all over again—and feeling that I might have been able to stop it somehow—warn her about Sloane, that he was a snake—which I always thought he was, deep down."

"I know," said Emily, her throat tightening. "And it's just sinking in that he maybe just sashayed away, without any kind of justice for her—that feels awful."

"God knows I never liked that pretentious S.O.B., but I still can't quite believe he'd hurt Liz. And I can't believe he worked with Carter Mizell—I can't wrap my head around it. And how about that dead gangster—Willetts—how does he fit in?"

"I think Willetts was working for those men we saw at the Flamingo—the ones Charlie called the real gangsters. Julian owed them a fortune—that's what Detective Maxwell hinted. Julian told them he'd pay them as soon as he got the fortune Aunt Liz owed him—she had something really valuable of his," said Emily. "I think they figured they'd just go get it themselves."

"I guess we'll get it figured out in time, but what good will it do? Liz is dead, and Sloane's in the wind."

"Don't give up," said Emily, reaching out and touching his arm. "Don't give up on justice. It's possible they'll find Julian—then we'd know more. Good grief, they've got the FBI out after him."

"Didn't stop Al Capone for a long time," Milton said. He paused for a minute, and looked at her. "I'm grateful for a lot about tonight. You and Billy are both okay. That's plenty. It's too bad your party got spoiled, though, Miss Emily."

"Don't worry about that," she said, nodding at Lewis, gently snoring on the couch. "We won't be getting married. I'm guessing that doesn't surprise you, Mr. Wise Person." She smiled.

"No, it doesn't surprise me, I'll confess. Are you sorry about that, Miss Emily?"

"Oh, Milton," she said, instinctively calling him by his first name, "I'm sad, I'll confess, but also so relieved. I don't know why I didn't see it sooner. Let's talk more tomorrow," she added. "And I do hope you can get some sleep. You're always welcome here — come back after your Coffee Club fares."

"I appreciate it, Miss Emily," said Milton. "Oh, I almost forgot," he added, reaching in a pocket and pulling out Elizabeth Washington's scarab bracelet, wrapped in one of his pressed cotton handkerchiefs. "You asked me to keep this safe, but it needs to come home to you." he said, taking Emily's hand and tenderly placing the bracelet in her palm. "Liz would want that."

She reached up and hugged him and walked him to the back door, taking care to double-lock it behind him as she switched off the kitchen light. Then she went back to the couch, covered Lewis with a light afghan, and switched off the lamp next on the side table, leaving the house in darkness except for the night light at the foot of the stairs.

As Emily took off her shoes and slipped up the stairs quietly, she felt as though she had been carrying a heavy weight for a very long time and somehow it had just dropped away. At the same time, she didn't think she had ever felt so tired. She placed her aunt's bracelet carefully in the jewelry case on the dresser before slipping into bed and, almost immediately, to sleep. As she drifted off into a sort of half-dream, she saw a pair of ember-red eyes that looked at her long and hard before they slipped slowly into black water and disappeared.

She awoke in the morning to the smell of coffee and a sense of confusion, because Mattie had the day off. Who was making coffee? She had a brief vision of Julian Sloane, hiding in her kitchen surreptitiously getting out the percolator while Juan Blanco slit her throat in her sleep, before the two of them ransacked the house.

Get a grip, old girl, she told herself as she stretched and took some deep breaths to wake up more fully.

Then she remembered Lewis. If he was the source of the coffee aroma, clearly he was more self-sufficient than she imagined. Sometimes she didn't give him enough credit. Despite his boyish charm, and although his family was well off, it wasn't like he had servants bowing and scraping at his beck and call. He was a grown man, capable of understanding what she had to tell him—what she had wanted to tell him for a long time, she realized. Had she pushed those thoughts aside because she hadn't wanted to hurt him—or had she been selfish, she wondered—had she wanted to hold onto him because she was afraid to be on her own?

She lay still for a few more minutes, stretching her arms and legs and gathering her thoughts, and then arose. She brushed her teeth, combed her hair, put on one of her aunt's robes, and then padded down the stairs, opening the swinging door to the kitchen just a crack and peeking in. She didn't want to startle him.

Lewis was sitting at the yellow table, dressed in the pants and shirt he had worn to the party but in his stocking feet. She turned around to see his shoes by the couch and the afghan carefully folded on one of the couch cushions, with his necktie folded on top of it. He was far more neat in his habits than she was, she thought. He hadn't heard her yet—the radio that Mattie kept on the kitchen counter was on, with the volume low, the voices indistinguishable. He was hunched over the table, looking intently at the morning paper—specifically, the comics page. Besides making coffee, he had also produced one of their shared favorites from childhood—cinnamon toast, which stood in a tidy stack on a plate before him.

Almost as if he were sensing her presence, Lewis looked up, a grin creasing his features.

"Good morning, Morning Glory," he said. "Glad you got some sleep."

"Was the couch all right?" she asked, moving to pour herself a cup of coffee and open the fridge to get out some milk.

"To tell you the truth, Pooh, I probably could have slept on a bed of nails," he said. "I was surprised to wake up here instead of at the hotel, though."

"It was my idea," said Emily, "and Mr. Armistead made it happen. I hope you don't mind."

"Not at all. We've even been bunkmates before—remember Egypt?" He rolled his eyes and chuckled, and she smiled at the memory of the two of them huddled in Lewis's tent after he had been menaced by an especially formidable scorpion.

"But I thought you were determined not to feed even a morsel of kindling to the pernicious flames of neighborhood gossips," Lewis went on.

"Good lord, Lewis, even when you're looking a little green around the gills, and I suspect fighting a monster hangover, you've still got the gift of gab."

"Looking that bad, am I? I thought the toast might help. I'll admit last night is a bit of a blur, Pooh. I hit the drinks table a bit hard before the, err, stuff hit the fan."

"Maybe feeling a little anxious, like me," she said.

"Charlie just kept them coming, and before I knew it, I was gone. I do remember running out of the house and down the hill—it's coming back to me now. What the hell happened?"

"It was pretty ghastly. You were in the thick of it at one point, on the side of good—you and Charlie. I'm sort of glad you didn't really take it all in. It was awful."

"Go on—tell me, how awful?"

"In a nutshell, Sheriff Mizell threatened Billy and me with our lives—and in the most creepy way, involving an alligator—to find out where something of my aunt's was hidden—something very valuable—and Julian, who it appears was in some kind of unholy plot with Mizell—the brains behind it—took off and fled in secret, and . . ."

She had been methodically cutting slices of toast into quarters as she talked, and now she looked up at Lewis, to see his eyes, and mouth, wide open. She couldn't believe it, but at the moment, it all seemed almost funny—almost like she was telling him about some far-fetched movie or play she had seen. Except, she remembered, that it also involved her aunt's death—and that Mizell's threats to her and Billy had been very real and very scary.

"Emily," he sputtered. "Say you're kidding me. This didn't really happen, did it?"

"Oh, it happened." She started to say more, when she heard a knock at the back door. "Miss Emily, you up?" she heard Milton's voice. She jumped up to open the door and usher him in.

"Morning, Miss Emily, Mr. Delacourt," he said, taking off his snap-brim hat. His sunglasses stayed over his eyes, and Emily wondered whether, behind them, his eyes were as tired as she thought they might be. Maybe he hadn't slept at all.

"Here, sit down, Mr. Armistead, have some coffee," said Emily, pointing to a chair.

"Thank you, but I'll pass, Miss Emily—I've already had too much—went by Wilson's before they opened even, and Earlene took pity on me—gave me some in a cardboard cup."

He leaned against the countertop by the sink, holding his hat in front of him.

"Did you get any sleep? Have some toast?" Emily asked.

"You and that cinnamon toast." He shook his head. "Just like your aunt."

"I love it too," Lewis blurted, to no one in particular.

"No sleep, Miss Emily," said Milton—"just like I suspected. I was too wound up, as Liz—Miss Elizabeth—used to say. This morning I showered and changed into a fresh shirt. Got an early start. I wanted to check on you all and on Jeff and Billy, too.

"Emily was just filling me in," said Lewis. "Thank you for your help last night, Armistead."

Milton nodded, looking at Lewis for the first time.

"Happy to oblige, Mr. Delacourt. She tell you about her and that whip?"

Lewis's eyes again grew wide.

"I see," said Milton. "She didn't yet. Well, we've got a real heroine here, Mr. Delacourt. Couldn't have been more proud of her if she was my own daughter." Then he looked down.

"No offense meant, Miss Emily."

"My goodness, I'd be proud to be your daughter — I hope you know that," she added.

"Well, one thing I do know is that thanks to you, Carter Mizell is in a cell downtown — Mr. Jeff says he may have to go down there, because he's Carter's only kin — but I guess what's stuck in my craw is that Sloane may just get away with murder — with our Elizabeth's murder — just like I was saying last night."

He looked down again, at his hands, holding his hat tightly. Behind the glasses, Emily thought he was struggling to retain his composure. The depth of his feeling seemed to have stripped away his ability or desire to play the role of the faithful retainer in front of Lewis. Or perhaps on some level he had assigned Lewis a new role as family insider — someone for whom he didn't have to play a role. Even if Lewis wasn't going to be Emily's husband, he was surely her special confidante.

"Let's have faith they'll catch him, like I said last night," said Emily, reaching out and placing a hand on Milton's arm.

"Easier to have that faith in the law when you're white, I'm afraid," said Milton. "But maybe we'll know something soon enough," he said. "I did talk with Mr. Jeff a few minutes ago, like I was saying — stopped by there to make sure they were okay. He said to tell you he hopes to come by and thank you in person for saving Billy. The boy was still asleep when I stopped by."

"You sure you won't have breakfast?" said Lewis.

"No sir, but thank you. And Miss Emily, if you hear anything from Detective Maxwell — anything they've learned — give me a call. I check with my answering service for messages. Now, I'd better get going. It's about time for the Silver Meteor to come in down at the station. I'll stop by again later — be happy to get Mr. Delacourt back to his hotel."

"Thank you, Armistead," said Lewis, looking up at the older man. "You've been very decent to me, much more so than I deserve."

"You're okay, Mr. Lewis," Milton said, tipping his hat as he exited through the back door.

When Milton was gone, Lewis got up, rinsed out the coffee pot and filled it again with grounds to make a fresh batch.

"That was very decent of you, Pooh," Emily said. "Speaking to him like that."

"It just hit me, I think, that I hadn't really seen him as a person, much less a friend — and he is like a member of your family, isn't he?"

"To me, he is."

"Yes, and when he talked about being proud of you, I realized that you are almost like a daughter to him, and the way he looks when he talks about your aunt . . ."

"The way he looks? How?"

"I mean, think about it, Pooh. It's not the look of a faithful employee. When he talks about your aunt, it reminds me of the way you looked a few years ago when you told me about your friend John — the one who died in the war? He was more than a friend to you, Emily. You loved him, I know, and maybe Mr. Armistead loved your aunt."

Emily started to protest, but instead sat silent. She reached for Lewis's hand, and they both sat in silence, broken only by the thrum of the coffee percolator.

"Lewis, you don't mind that I told you about, John?"

"Of course not. It was pretty soon after you learned of his death. Pooh, you know you can tell me anything — always could. And I'm right about Armistead, aren't I?"

"That he loved her, you mean?"

He nodded.

"Now that I think about it, I must have known it at some level," Emily said. The day at the cemetery flashed through her memory. Milton, with the single red rose. "He certainly hasn't tried to hide it from me, and I would guess she loved him, too. But I just accepted the picture they presented to me as a girl. The iron-willed lady boss and her right-hand man — General Armistead — who executed her wishes. Even coming back here, I think I still saw them with a child's eyes. But now some things are clicking into place for me more clearly."

"Like what?" said Lewis, leaning forward and giving her hand a little squeeze.

"Like my father's enmity for his sister, for Liz. His insistence that she had bad judgment, and that I shouldn't come back to visit her. I never thought it made any sense."

"You mean your father realized what they meant to each other?"

"I think so, looking back," Emily said. "He just couldn't accept that, and I guess he thought he was protecting me. He knew I had met Mr. Armistead's nephew Sam, too, and really liked him. Did I ever tell you about that?"

"About the time the KKK men scared you out of your wits?"

"Yes! Goodness, Lewis, you've remembered much more than I would have guessed."

"I do care about you, Pooh." She smiled and placed her hand on his.

"I'll bet my father was convinced I would follow my aunt into some kind of forbidden love—it sounds so tawdry to say it like that. But my father has never been the most forward-looking soul. He has dreadful attitudes about people whose skin isn't white. Not that he really knows any."

"Remember that old movie *Imitation of Life*?" Lewis said. "The daughter in that was part Negro, and she looked white, and she turned her back on her mother. I cried my eyes out—that poor mother. Maybe you're like that girl—not the turning-your-back part, of course."

He stopped cold, his eyes wide. "Good grief, Emily, it just occurred to me—you could be like that girl, except instead of a secret mother, Armistead could be your father."

She was shocked to find herself bent over in laughter. Here they were, talking about death—murder even—and racism, and she was inching her way toward a truthful revelation that on one level she worried might hurt Lewis deeply, and she was giggling. *I am hopeless*, she thought.

"You and your movies, Lewis. First, don't you think if Milton Armistead were my father, I'd have a different complexion? And

Aunt Liz would be my mother. Believe me, she would have told me if that were the case. And basically, he is sort of like a father to me—even if he's not my biological father—do you know what I mean, Pooh?"

Lewis nodded. "You can see it in the way he looks at you."

"And now I see even more why Carter Mizell must have deeply hated my aunt, if she had defied his crazy taboos and loved a man of another race—and also why Julian must have hated Milton, and maybe Liz, too."

"You're getting ahead of me. Why did Sloane hate Milton?"

"He wanted to be the man in Liz's life—and they had been close in their youth, although I'm not sure it was ever truly a romance. I think he was really in love with her money and talent. And I'm not sure what she might've felt for him—"

"But he was jealous of Armistead?"

"Oh yes, I think so. I found a news photo in the paper's archives—the newspaper Maureen works for—and Julian's in it—he didn't realize he was being photographed. He's staring with a look of utter hatred at someone who's not in the picture—someone just out of the frame. I think it was Milton."

She paused and took both his hands in hers.

"But with all this talk about love, forbidden or otherwise, Lewis—I need to get back to our love." She paused in an effort to gain control of her voice, which had started to quaver a bit, and then went on.

"You see, Lewis, the shock of what happened last night somehow made me realize that I have not been fair to you at all. All my shilly-shallying around about the wedding."

"Go on," he said. "I think . . . I wonder if we've been thinking along the same lines, Pooh. We often do, you know. You say it first."

"Oh, dear Pooh," she said, tears starting to come now. "I love you dearly, but really like a brother. I can't marry you. I don't know why I couldn't see it."

He reached over and kissed her cheek, almost spilling his coffee.

"I know, dear Emily. I see it now, too."

"You do?" she said, dabbing at her eyes. "It's just that I don't want to lose what we do have," she went on. "You are my best friend, and I was on the verge of losing that by becoming a wife that I didn't really want to be."

"Yes, I do see," said Lewis. "This trip has made me see a lot of things."

"But what will you do about your father's demand?" Emily asked. "You know—the ultimatum that you marry? The deadline?"

"I've decided to follow your example and stand up for myself," said Lewis. "Charlie has been talking with me about it all. He's so brave about these things. He helped me to see that I can't let Father dictate my life. I'm seriously thinking about staying in Florida and going into business with Charlie, Emily—I don't really want to be in Father's firm, down deep."

Emily's eyes widened. "Really? That's wonderful! I'm amazed, Lewis—I never imagined you'd consider leaving New York, ever." Just when she thought she had Lewis all figured out, he could still surprise her, she thought.

"We can get up to all kinds of Florida adventures," he said, with a wink.

"We can! I've been thinking about staying here too—well, most of the year," Emily said. "I could live without the big bugs, but the nights sure are nice. And I hear the beaches are wonderful—and not that far a drive."

"Yes, Charlie says you can get over to the east coast in no time," said Lewis, "especially if you drive like he does."

"Especially if you drive like he does," Emily said with a laugh. "I don't know if I can stand that kind of excitement." Then she paused and fixed him again with a direct gaze.

"Then are you okay about us calling off the engagement, truly?" she asked.

"You mean the engagement that never quite was?" He paused for a minute. "Honestly, I think I'm relieved, Pooh—truth be told. Maybe one reason I got quite so drunk last night is I didn't want to let you down. The big wedding and all that."

"You know I never wanted some kind of spectacle. The blushing bride? Good lord."

"All right, I'll let you have that one—even though I still suspect, deep down, that every woman wants a big wedding. But tell me one other thing, Pooh—you were just a tiny bit jealous of old Patsy van Rensselaer, weren't you—when I told you she'd been hanging around?"

"Well . . . ," said Emily, "let's just say that, back in New York, if I felt a sharp pain in my back, I might wonder if I'd find a knife buried between my shoulder blades with dear Patsy's name on it." First Lewis started to laugh, and she joined him. She literally laughed until she cried, bending over and holding her midriff as she grabbed a paper breakfast napkin to wipe her eyes.

"Careful, Dear Emily," said Lewis. "You don't want crumbs in the eyes. Crumbs can be painful. Remember that night in Paris?"

"I do indeed," she said, wiping her eyes, calmer now. Lewis took her hands in his.

"I look forward to all kinds of adventures, both crumby and crumb-less," Emily said. "I confess, Dear Lewis, to feeling inordinately happy—for the first time in a long time."

"I'm glad, but good lord, how? It's been a dark few days. You nearly got eaten by an alligator, remember?"

"I don't think she would have ever done that," Emily said, her shoulders still shaking a little. "It was a lady alligator, you know. We women stick together." She smiled back at him and paused.

"But I know what you mean," Emily went on. "That was all pretty awful. . . . I think I'm happy because we've got our friendship back."

Lewis nodded and gave her his most dazzling smile.

"And also because, for the first time in a long time," Emily said, "I feel like I'm looking ahead rather than behind me—to the future. After yesterday, I feel like whatever big boulders or bolts of lightning the gods hurl down at me, I can handle them."

"One tough cookie," said Lewis.

"I'll accept that," she said, "crumbs and all."

Epilogue

On a crisp-for-Florida sunny afternoon a few weeks later, Emily stood next to Mattie, grappling with a large roll of brown wrapping paper, when she heard a familiar crunch on the gravel in the driveway next to Eola Lodge.

"There's Milton and his taxi," said Mattie. "You going to take this load out to the Studio now?"

"I'd like to," said Emily. For a couple of weeks, the two women had been going through the stacks of Elizabeth Washington's canvases—dusting, cleaning, and making selections for the women's art show Liz had envisioned. After all, the show had mattered so much to Elizabeth Washington that she had made a special request in her will for Emily to complete it in the event of death. Looking back, Emily understood why Aunt Liz had experienced that sense of foreboding—felt she was in danger. With the brave choices Liz had made in her life—the cages she had rattled, the people she had chosen to love—perhaps she had always known danger on some level.

And now Emily was following her wishes, making selections for the show from Liz's work and that of other Florida women artists such as Odette and Colette Murat. With Milton's help, she had begun moving the chosen paintings to what had been Julian Sloane's Studio, where Manuel Rojas—Sloane's former cook—was using his considerable carpentry skills to make frames for the paintings. Manuel and his family were staying on as caretakers, working for Emily. Judge Stimpson had assured her that she was now the rightful owner of the place, which Sloane had never actually owned, it turned out; Liz had held the mortgage.

"Right now it's an absolute mess at both places, here and the Studio," Emily said. "But Mr. Armistead and I are planning to go out there after we take Lewis and Charlie to the train station."

"You think there will be room? Mr. Lewis might have plenty of luggage," said Mattie.

"He swore to me they would travel light," said Emily, "and the taxi's trunk is so huge that we should be able to take a few canvases."

Traveling light had never been one of Emily's strong suits. She also needed room in Milton's trunk for the carpet bag of odds and ends she had packed to take to the Studio—everything from a couple packs of playing cards to boxes of kitchen matches for lighting candles during storms.

"So Mr. Lewis is going back to New York?" said Mattie.

"Just for a visit. They're going up to soak up some culture— opera, Broadway, that kind of thing. Lewis is leaving some of his things here—he's paid for a room at the San Juan for the season."

"You happy about that, Miss Emily? It's not everyone who can stay friends with a fiancé they turned down."

"I know," said Emily. "I'm happy—and grateful. We were always better friends than potential husband and wife, to tell you the truth."

Mattie nodded as the two women worked together to secure the wrapping around one canvas with a sturdy cord. They looked up at a familiar sound at the front door.

"Miss Emily, Mr. Milton says it's time to go!" Billy hollered.

"Lord, that child's voice can cut like a knife through butter," said Mattie.

"Hurry up," Billy went on, "or Mr. Lewis and Mr. Charlie will miss the train!"

"That's not exactly what I said, young man," Emily heard Milton chime in.

"Come in, you two—it's unlocked," she called out. Milton and Billy came toward them, Milton touching the brim of his hat in greeting.

"You got some more paintings ready to load up to take out to Sloane's?" he asked.

"We're not calling it that, remember, Mr. Milton?" said Billy, in a serious voice. "We're not saying that name."

"I remember," said Milton, with a grimace. "Not to mention that the place belongs to Miss Emily now."

"Indeed, and time will tell if that's a blessing or a curse," said Emily.

"Property, that's a good thing, Miss Emily," said Mattie. "Just ask folks who can't afford any."

"What you going to call it, Miss Emily?" Billy said. "You got a special name?"

"I have a new idea every day," said Emily. "Today, I'm thinking about Casa Elizabeth. What do you think?"

"I like that," said Milton. "Little hard to say, though, maybe? How about Casa Liz?"

"Yes! That's better. One thing's for sure," said Emily. "It'll be a perfect place for the art show that meant so much to her. Now, we'd better get going."

They bustled out the door toward the taxi. Milton carried the canvases, and Billy opened the door of the back seat for Emily before clambering into the front seat himself. As Milton steered the taxi out of the driveway, she waved toward the window of Mrs. Jackson's across the street and thought she saw a hand waving back in response. Mrs. Jackson was still serving as a one-woman sentinel, keeping watch over the street almost around the clock. It's true, she was a bit of a nosy parker, but she's also my friend, Emily thought.

"How's your daddy, Billy?" asked Emily.

"Pa's good—he said to tell you hello, Miss Emily. He's looking for that special cattle whip for you, too—so you can keep in practice. And he's driving down to Arcadia today to look at a new horse."

"That's good," she said. "You tell him hello, too." She had scarcely seen Jeff Mizell since the confrontation with his half-brother Carter. It was almost as if he were avoiding her. But that was silly. Why should he avoid her? He was probably just busy—the way he'd been from the moment she'd learned of his existence. And he did seem to have his demons, some in that flask she'd seen him take out of his pocket. It was true that he was not at all like Huck Finn's Pa—the role in which she had first cast him—but he was a mystery.

They rode on in silence for the few minutes it took to reach the San Juan Hotel downtown, where Lewis was staying. Charlie Wynne had arranged to meet them there. Emily wondered what Lewis's parents would make of Wynne—but, after all, Charlie could charm the birds out of trees. He and Lewis had a lot in common in that regard, as well as their Princeton memories.

"Hello, Darling," Lewis greeted her, almost as if to prove her thoughts, as Milton pulled the taxi into the loading area in front of the hotel. Even with their engagement broken, he still called her Darling. She hoped his parents would take the news well and not give him a hard time.

"I'll help you, Mr. Lewis," said Billy, as he burst from the taxi and headed toward Lewis's bags.

"And it's a good thing, William," Lewis said solemnly, nodding a greeting to Milton, too. "We need your help, indeed. I think I've done something to my back, and Old Sport Charlie might get a spot of dust on his suit." She saw that he slipped the boy two dollars.

"Where is Mr. Wynne?" said Milton. "We'd better get a move on."

"He'll be right out," said Lewis. "He's in at the hotel office, wheeling and dealing as usual—trying to sell the hotel managers on some kind of deal to promote the Flamingo. The man never rests."

"I heard that, Old Sport," said Charlie, who had just hurried out of the hotel's large front door, and now doubled back to hold it open for an older woman who was entering, bestowing on her his most dimpled smile.

"I'm certainly looking forward to a break from business on this trip, I can tell you that. Mr. Armistead, most grateful for this send-off. Hi ho, Silver, away—let's go."

They all piled into the taxi and in minutes—thanks to Milton's expeditious driving—they arrived at the graceful Spanish-style train station where Milton had first greeted Emily. As Milton had warned, they had no time to spare. The engine of the Silver Meteor, the train north from Miami to New York, sat by the platform, steam hissing around its wheels. Passengers clambered up the steps into its sleek, streamlined cars.

"Tickets? Do you have the tickets?" Emily shouted at them over the general din, as Milton and Billy got out their bags.

"I have them," said Charlie, pulling an envelope from his jacket pocket as he reached down to give Emily a peck on the cheek. "Wish me luck, dear Emily," he whispered. She nodded and then hugged Lewis, who kissed her other cheek.

"I'll send you a telegram about when we'll be back," Lewis said. "Please, you three, promise you'll behave. No more discovering dead bodies. No more encounters with rogue sheriffs, gangsters, and giant reptiles."

"Mr. Lewis, you make me laugh," said Billy. "Even though it was not funny then. At all."

"Lewis is speaking for himself," said Charlie. "Get in all the hot water you want, Billy—just make sure you keep up your bolita tickets! I need the money."

Emily just shook her head. "I'll pretend I didn't hear that," she said. "You both are impossible."

As Lewis and Charlie scrambled up into one of the cars, clutching their train cases and turning to wave goodbye, Emily heard the call of "All aboard!" and the train began to move slowly forward. For just a few seconds, Emily felt a pang that she wasn't going with them—off for an adventure, or an expedition, as her Aunt Liz would have said. But that was all right, she thought, as she joined Milton and Billy for the short walk to the taxi. Sometimes staying home could be an adventure, too—certainly her time at Eola Lodge had already been more exciting than she could have ever imagined when she'd arrived. And riding in Milton's taxi was always special in its own way, she thought as she slid into the big back seat. Billy had restaked his claim to the front seat next to Milton and then had gone inside to the concession stand, in search of a grape soda.

"You still want to take a run out to Casa Liz? That's what I'll call it for now, anyway," Milton said.

"Yes," said Emily. "I'd like to see what kind of progress Manuel's making with the frames. And I expect the Murat sisters may be there—they've volunteered to help today. I thought we'd take Billy along, too."

"Good," said Milton. "I figured as much—I took the liberty of calling Manuel and asking if he had anything he could whip up for an early supper for us—I hope that's okay, Miss Emily. He's doing arroz con pollo—good stuff."

"It's a great plan," she said. "I'm glad you called him."

Looking out the window for Billy—could it take this long to get a soda?—she was startled by a tap on the side of the car and looked up to see Detective Joe Maxwell hailing them. To her irritation, Emily felt her heart race just a little faster.

"Detective, what brings you here?" she said through the open car window. He wore no suit coat, and his white shirt sleeves were rolled up above his elbows, exposing his tanned forearms. He might not have Lewis's charm, but he had something.

"I gave our FBI friend Roberts a lift to the train," said Maxwell, leaning over to talk with her through the window. "You remember? He's the fellow who was after Carter Mizell."

"I remember his entrance well," said Emily. "Here," she said, as she opened the back door and slid over to make room. "We're waiting for Billy—he's getting a soda. Can you sit down for a minute?"

"Happy to see you all," said Maxwell, as he slid in beside Emily and greeted Milton.

"Haven't had a chance to tell you," he began. "I don't know how happy I am about this, but Roberts is thrilled. Carter Mizell is singing like a canary, as they say in the movies. He's giving the feds a lot of information they can use to build racketeering cases against the mob types who have been moving into Central Florida."

"But what about Carter's role in my aunt's death—and kidnapping Billy? When Billy gets back to the car, by the way, we may not want to talk about Evil Carter in front of him."

"Agreed," said Maxwell. "Especially if Carter's plea deal with the FBI is as good for him as I think it's going to be. He refuses to admit any involvement at all in your aunt's death, Emily."

"Oh dear," she said, looking at Milton, whose eyes were inscrutable behind his clip-on sunglasses.

"I see Billy coming," said Milton. "Better save any more talk about his no-good uncle until later."

"Good idea," said Maxwell. "That boy's been through plenty." As he spoke, Emily had a sudden inspiration: why not ask him to join them for Manuel's arroz con pollo. When Billy was out of earshot, she and Milton might learn some more from the detective.

"Detective," she started to say, when she looked up and saw Maureen, wearing a spiffy new dress and a broad grin, just as Billy got back and climbed into the front seat.

"Hi Mrs. Davis," Billy said. "And Detective Maxwell—this is swell!"

"That it is, Billy," said Maureen—"some of my favorite people, huddled here in the classiest taxicab south of Atlanta. Are you all planning a cabal?"

"Maureen, I thought you were busy," Emily said out the window, talking past Maxwell, who began opening the door to get out. "We just waved Lewis and Charlie off on the Silver Meteor."

"I know—Princeton men take on New York!" said Maureen. "I wanted to be here, too—but I had that darn meeting with my editor I told you about, Emily—couldn't get here in time."

"So why did you come?" said Emily. "Not that it isn't great to see you."

"I have a date to meet a detective," Maureen said brightly. "This good gentleman right here, in fact."

Emily looked up at Maxwell, now standing by the car. He had put on his hat, which cast a shadow over his face, so it was hard to see his expression. Perhaps she imagined it, Emily thought, but his face looked like it might be turning pink.

"It's for a story," Maxwell said—"that's right, isn't it, Maureen?"

From the front seat, Billy slurped his grape soda through a straw and turned a page of his comic book. Milton appeared to be absorbed in fiddling with the radio.

"Yes, Em—it's the greatest thing," said Maureen. "That's what my meeting was about. My editor is letting me try my hand at a bit of feature writing that's not strictly women's page stuff. At least once in a while. Detective Maxwell has agreed to tell me some juicy tidbits about organized crime—off the record."

Emily distinctly remembered Maureen telling her that Maxwell was a "dreamboat."

"Wonderful!" she said, sounding perhaps just a tad too chipper. Oh, come on, she thought to herself. Maureen's friendship meant a lot to her, and Maureen deserved some happiness after losing her husband.

"I'm happy for you, Maureen—about the chance to spread your wings at the paper," Emily said. "And don't forget, we need to talk about the art show—we must have some of your pieces in it. Aunt Liz's notes were very clear about that."

She heard Milton clearing his throat.

"We'd better get going out there, Miss Emily," he said. "You wanted to catch the Murat sisters while they were still there."

"Yes, better get going," said Emily. "Well, great to see you both," she added to Maureen and Joe Maxwell. "Have a good interview."

"Thanks," said Maxwell. "She promised to buy me a steak dinner at the San Juan in return for my help. But remember—and especially you, Billy—I'm talking off the record."

"Our lips are sealed," Emily laughed, making a zipping motion across her face. Boy, Maureen didn't waste any time, she thought to herself, as her mind strayed back to that night on the porch at Eola Lodge—Maxwell's sudden kiss. It had obviously meant less than she'd thought. She pulled her mind back to the present.

"It would be good indeed to get out there," she said to Milton. "I'd like to talk with Odette Murat before they go home."

As they headed toward the orange-tree-lined path to the lakeside artists' complex, the place where her engagement to Lewis was supposed to have been announced, Emily pushed away thoughts of the dangers she and Billy had faced that night, as well as thoughts of her newly single status.

"Penny for 'em, Miss Emily," Milton said finally, looking at her in the rearview mirror. "I thought maybe Detective Maxwell might come along with us."

"So did I, Milton, so did I," she said in a small voice, gazing out the window.

Billy had fallen asleep, his hand curled about his empty grape-soda bottle, and as they neared heir destination, Emily woke him, shaking his shoulder very gently from behind.

"There's Miss Odette's car," he shouted as they pulled up, any trace of slumber vanished in an instant.

While Milton and Billy unloaded the canvases, Emily went on ahead inside, hoping to catch up with her aunt's old friend without interference from Odette's problematic sister, Colette—who had been jealous of Odette's friendship with Elizabeth Washington.

"Manuel," Emily called out, "we're here!"

She heard an indistinct greeting in return from the direction of the kitchen.

Emily headed into the main gallery space, where she found Odette gathering her things together, her large black poodle, Bonaparte, curled on the rug at her feet.

"Ah Emily, how good to see you," Odette said, as Emily went forward to greet her, kissing her lightly on both cheeks.

"And you, Miss Odette. Is Miss Colette not with you?"

"Not today," said Odette. "A bad headache—or maybe she really wanted to stay in bed and listen to her radio soap operas. I've been relishing the quiet time, and I think I've come up with some good ideas about what pieces to put in this room. I've been working on label copy for some of them too," she said, pointing at a legal pad full of neat writing.

"And Manuel—he's a godsend," Odette went on. "Just look at the frames he's making. They are works of art in themselves. He has a beautiful touch, a sense of how to enhance a painting."

"He did that for Julian, too," said Emily. "Julian may have been a first-rate scoundrel, but he had good taste."

"Has, you mean," said Odette, a frown creasing her forehead.

"It's true," said Emily. "I think of him as dead—but he isn't. Dead to me, I guess."

Milton and Billy had gone on into the kitchen, and she could hear their voices mixing with Manuel's and drifting down the hall.

"Would you like to stay and eat with us?" Emily asked Odette. "I'm sure there's plenty."

"That's very kind of you, but I'd better get home to Colette—and I thought I heard thunder a few minutes ago." Still, she didn't move, and looked at Emily. Finally she said, "Speaking of Mr. Sloane, Emily, I should tell you about something that happened today—although I'll confess I'm loath to do so.

"What is it, Miss Odette? You look worried."

"Perhaps I am," said Odette. "All right. Here it is. Mr. Foster came by today—he's the horticulturist who is really responsible for the gardens here—he was a friend of your aunt's and of Sloane's. He's just come back from a trip to Belize to gather specimens, and he stopped by today to drop off some bromeliads he aims to plant around the driveway—with your permission. I talked with him briefly, and . . ." She looked down.

"Go on."

"He thinks he saw Julian Sloane in Belize. It was in a busy marketplace—but he knows Sloane well, and was pretty sure it was him. Mr. Foster headed toward him, but when he got to the other side of the square, where he'd seen the man—at an outdoor bar, I gather—he was gone."

"My goodness," said Emily, feeling shaky inside.

"Mr. Foster could have imagined it," said Odette.

"That's easy to do," said Emily. "It's happened to me in a crowd." But it could just as easily be true, Emily thought. Julian was out there somewhere, and why not Belize? And yet the thought of Julian Sloane—even so far away—made her uneasy. She hated that he had escaped justice. But now, she wondered, could he somehow pose a threat to her? Would he be upset that she'd ended up not only with a painting by Picasso but with the land Julian had so wanted to protect?

Odette looked out to see dark skies over the lake.

"I'd best be going, Emily," she said. "I can outrun that storm, I think," she said, as she put a leash on her elegant dog. "We'll talk soon," she said as she headed for the car.

Trying to take in what Odette had said, Emily went to the kitchen, where she found Manuel and Milton sipping what she guessed might be sangria as they sat at the large rustic kitchen table that dominated the room. Billy perched on a chair next to them, reading his comic book again and sipping more grape soda. Too much sugar, Emily thought. The boy consumes too much sugar.

She was aware of Milton and Manuel talking—Manuel's wife and children had gone to visit her mother, Manuel told them; the boys would miss seeing Billy, he said—but she couldn't seem to keep her focus on the conversation, her attention instead drifting out the window.

So far the rain had held off, but Emily pointed out at the darkening sky over the large lake the artists' retreat bordered.

"It looks like it did the first afternoon I was here," she said to Milton. "Remember?"

"Oh yes," said Milton. "It sure looks like one of our barn-shakers is coming. Hear that?" he added, as thunder rumbled in the distance.

"Would you rather head home, Miss Emily?" he asked.

"No indeed. We've ridden out other storms together, haven't we? Let's hunker down here. Manuel, there must be candles, aren't there—in case we lose power?"

"Most definitely, Miss Emily," he said, and went to the pantry to get them.

"Whatever that is you're fortifying yourself with there, General Armistead, I wouldn't mind having a glass, too," Emily said.

"By all means," said Milton, finding a glass and pouring some ruby-red liquid from a pitcher.

"Manuel says the food is all cooked too, whenever we're hungry," he said.

Another rumble sounded, and a jagged web of lightning filled the sky across the lake.

The raindrops started to come, pounding the roof.

"Well, gentlemen," said Emily, to Billy and Milton. "There's no one else I'd rather ride out a storm with than you two." She meant it. Sloane be damned, wherever he was. She was glad to be right here, right now.

"How about some cards, what do you say?" she added.

Manuel was back with the candles, which he placed on the table, lighting a couple that cast flickering light on the walls.

"Join us, Manuel, please," she said, indicating a chair.

"I don't know where any playing cards are, Señorita Emily," he said.

"That, gentlemen, is not a problem," she said.

She pulled a couple of decks of cards out of her large carpet bag and started to shuffle them.

"Miss Emily, you never cease to amaze me," said Milton.

"What'll it be?" she said with a sly grin. "Gin rummy?"

"Oh no, Miss Emily," said Billy. "Five-card draw! We only bet a penny."

"All right, young man," she said, shuffling the cards, pushing thoughts of maybe-Julian out of her mind and instead taking in Milton's warm, familiar face and Billy's eager smile — "but I should warn you all, I'm feeling lucky — very lucky indeed."

ACKNOWLEDGMENTS

Because I've written for many years about the history of Central Florida, especially Orlando, it's perhaps worth stressing that this book is something new: a work of fiction. The characters, businesses, places, and incidents are the product of my imagination or used in a fictitious manner and not to be construed as real. Although a Flamingo Café or Flamingo Club was once a center of nightlife just outside the eastern Orlando city limits, for example, the version presented here is entirely a work of make-believe. Long before I had thought about writing mysteries, I had a chance to interview Patrick Smith, the author of *A Land Remembered*, perhaps the most beloved book of historical fiction about Florida. I remember him saying that after he gave his characters a name, they seemed to have a life of their own and, in some cases, dictated the course of their own fictional lives.

While I had the greatest respect for Smith, I recall registering a certain amount of disbelief. And yet, much to my surprise, years later, when I began the path to Emily and Milton's story, darned if I didn't find the same thing to be true. So, as I offer deep thanks to the many folks who have helped me on this journey, my first debt of gratitude is to them — those characters — for showing up and sticking with me. I'm so glad you've joined us, and hope you enjoy getting to know them and their world.

My road to this book has been as long and winding as Emily's cattle whip, and I owe deep thanks to a great many people.

That includes teachers and mentors at Florida State University, especially the late Jerome Stern and David Ammerman, and *Orlando Sentinel* editors including Jim Robison and Nancy Pate. Christine Blackwell believed I was a writer well before I did, when she included an essay of mine in the book *The Orlando Group and Friends* (2000), published by her Arbiter Press.

I'm grateful to other friends and family who have encouraged me over the years, including Annie Amendola, Pat Birkhead, Midge Bowman, Christopher De Arcangelis, Margaret De Arcangelis, Bill Dickinson, Rachel Dickinson Weigel, Lelia Elliston, Joan Erwin, Jean Esther, David Girshoff, Christy Grieger, Jennifer Greenhill-Taylor, Joseph Reed Hayes, Jeremy Hileman, Polly Howells, Nancy Kiger, Mary Anne O'Boyle Leary, Glenn J. Link, Clare Novak, Judy Olson, Susan Omoto, Betsy Owens, Ann Patton, Tana Porter, Janice Stieber Rous, Pam Schwartz, Judith Starnes, Pat Street, Fredrika J. Teute, and Katherine Vaccaro.

Special thanks to Asher Yesowitch, Nora Yesowitch, and Ruby Nova Link, who knew from a young age the value of a good story, whether in books, movies, or musicals. Martha Link Yesowitch ,read early drafts and offered encouragement and advice, and Pam Link's reading and notes also proved invaluable.

Early on the path, I found good advice and kindness from members of Florida chapter of the Mystery Writers of America, Thanks especially to Sharon Potts and Deborah Sharp, and to Shelby Isaacson, who helped me take my work seriously.

I am indebted to wise and gracious writing teachers and mentors. I've never met the incomparable Anne Lamott, but I remain a devoted fan, including of her classic advice in *Bird by Bird* to let yourself write terrible first drafts and to take it one small step at a time.

G. Miki Hayden, who knows mysteries like few others, got me started in an online class and kept me going. The brave and wise Laraine Herring welcomed me to her tribe, as did Peggy Tabor Millin, whose workshops at Great Tree Zen Women's Temple in North Carolina meant the world to me. (Thanks, too, to Rev. Teijo Munnich at Great Tree.) Both Laraine and Peggy brought me in touch with spiritual aspects of writing and practical guidance as well.

It's fun to look back and see how one step led to another. Through Laraine, I learned about Jennie Nash's Author Accelerator program, which was tremendously helpful, and it was Peggy who told me that a great writing teacher, John Dufresne, resided in Florida, and I should look him up. Boy, was she right.

As a professor at Florida International University, John has informed and inspired countless writers. I was fortunate to join workshops with him organized by the fine writer and teacher Kim Bradley of Flagler College.

Over years and even a Bloomsday trip to Dublin, these workshops created a community of generous, kindred spirits that have kept me going. Huge thanks to Jim Herod, Scott Archer Jones, Stephanie Josey, Lisa Mahoney, Charlyn Rainville, Helena Rho, Lauren Rivera, Anne Baldridge Salafia, and especially to longtime workshop compatriots Jean Dowdy, Maureen Welch, and Sherry Dickerson.

Rick Kilby not only supplied a perfect cover design for Emily and Milton's adventures but also optimism, encouragement, and wise counsel during our many collaborations over the years in pursuit of Florida's history and culture. In the home stretch to the book, Dave Girshoff and Marty Haddad kept me going with the best proofreading ever.

My greatest debt and thanks go to my writing coach, Erin Lindsay McCabe, who shares with me ties to California and a love of historical fiction, of which she's a master. When it comes to storytelling and endless patience, she's a Jedi master. In phone conferences over the years, I loved hearing her family's rooster expressing himself in the background. Believe me, these birds don't just crow at dawn. Somehow the rooster's call became a rallying cry to finish the work, take it to the finish line, one step at a time, bird-by-bird style. There must be a rooster in Emily's future somewhere.

Erin, I cannot thank you enough, and that goes for my other teachers and comrades, too. I'm crowing with thanks to have finished the journey to this book and to be planning others to come.

About the Author

Joy Wallace Dickinson grew up in Orlando, Florida, where she remembers seeing at least one alligator in the lake across from her childhood home near the city's busy downtown. She has edited historical books at the Institute of Early American History in Williamsburg, Virginia, and Stanford University Press in California. For more than two decades, she wrote the *Orlando Sentinel*'s "Florida Flashback" feature about Central Florida's fascinating past, receiving honors from groups including AIA Orlando, the Florida Historical Society, the Historical Society of Central Florida, and the Winter Park History Museum. She's also the author of three nonfiction books: *Orlando: City of Dreams, Remembering Orlando: Tales from Elvis to Disney,* and *Historic Photos of Orlando. Secrets of the Flamingo Café* is her first foray into writing fiction. To learn more about her work, visit FindingJoyinFlorida.com.

A Note on the Type

"Cochin types are no spiritless imitations of forerunners and have none of the affectations to which many copies of eighteenth-century elegance have degenerated," J.L. Frazier wrote in 1925 in his book *Type Lore: Popular Fonts of Today, Their Origin and Use.* "The Monotype Cochin, designed by Sol Hess, is wide and round," Frazier wrote; "the capitals are large in relation to the lower-case, the ascenders being longer than the descenders; the serifs are pronouncedly sharp."

The prolific British type designer Matthew Carter revised and expanded Cochin for Linotype in 1977. Carter's Cochin has been adapted for use as a system font on Apple's Mac OS, and that version has been used in *Secrets of the Flamingo Café.*